By the Billabong

Annie Seaton

Daughters of the Darling: 3

By the Billabong

Annie Seaton

Annie Seaton lives near the beach on the mid-north coast of New South Wales. Her career and studies spanned the education sector, including working as an academic research librarian, a high school principal, and a university tutor until she took early retirement and fulfilled her lifelong dream of a full-time writing career.

Each winter, Annie and her husband leave the beach to roam the remote areas of Australia for story ideas and research. She is passionate about preserving the beauty of the Australian landscape and respecting the traditional ownership of the land. For those readers who cannot experience this journey personally, Annie seeks to portray the natural beauty of the Australian environment—its spiritual locations, stunning landscapes and unique wildlife.

Readers can contact Annie through her website, annieseaton.net, or find her on Facebook and Instagram. To stay up to date with her new releases, subscribe to her newsletter on the home page of her website:

http://annieseaton.net

Also by Annie Seaton

Daughters of the Darling
From Across the Sea
Over the River
By the Billabong (2025)
Beneath Still Waters (2025)

A Bec Whitfield Mystery
Bowen River
Shadows on the Shore
(June 2025)

Duckinwilla Days
Coming Home
Secrets and Surprises
Wishes and Whispers
New Beginnings
Chasing Dreams
Together at Last

Pentecost Island Series
Pippa
Eliza
Nell
Tamsin
Evie
Cherry
Odessa
Sienna
Tess
Isla
Anthologies
Pentecost Island 1-3

The House on the Hill series
Beach House
Beach Music
Beach Walk
Beach Dreams
The House on the Hill Boxed Set

Sunshine Coast Series
Waiting for Ana
The Trouble with Jack
Healing His Heart
Sunshine Coast Boxed Set

Porter Sisters Series
Kakadu Sunset
Daintree
Diamond Sky
Hidden Valley
Larapinta
Kakadu Dawn

Second Chance Bay Series
Her Outback Playboy
Her Outback Protector
Her Outback Haven
Her Outback Paradise
The McDougalls of Second Chance Bay ***Boxed Set***

Pentecost Island 4-6
Pentecost Island 7-10
The Richards Brothers
The Trouble with Paradise
Marry in Haste
Outback Sunrise
Richards Brothers Boxed Set
Love Across Time Series
Come Back to Me
Follow Me
Finding Home
The Threads that Bind
Love Across Time 1-4 Boxed Set
Bindarra Creek
Worth the Wait
Full Circle
Secrets of River Cottage
A Clever Christmas
A Place to Belong
Hearts in Harmony

Others
Whitsunday Dawn
Undara
Osprey Reef
East of Alice
An Aussie Christmas Duo
Four Seasons Short- Sweet
Deadly Secrets
Adventures in Time
Silver Valley Witch
The Emerald Necklace

The Augathella Books
The Augathella Girls Series
Outback Roads
Outback Sky
Outback Escape
Outback Wind
Outback Dawn
Outback Moonlight
Outback Dust
Outback Hope
Augathella Girls Anthologies
Augathella Girls 1-4
Augathella Girls 5-8
Augathella Short and Sweet
An Augathella Baby
An Augathella Spring
An Augathella Christmas
An Augathella Wedding
An Augathella Easter
An Augathella Masquerade Ball
<u>Boxed Set</u>
Augathella Short and Sweet 1-3
Augathella Short and Sweet 1-4

Dedication

Always to Ian, the love of my life.
This year, we celebrate our 50th wedding anniversary.

What candles may be held to speed them all? Not in the hands of boys, but in their eyes Shall shine the holy glimmers of goodbyes.

Wilfred Owen - *Anthem for Doomed Youth*

Wilfred Owen wrote *Anthem for Doomed Youth* in 1917 while he was recovering at Craiglockhart War Hospital in Edinburgh, Scotland. He had been sent there after being diagnosed with shell shock following his traumatic experiences fighting in the trenches on the Western Front.

The poem was revised with the help of Siegfried Sassoon, another noted war poet who was also recuperating at Craiglockhart at the same time. It was published posthumously in 1920, after Owen's death in battle in November 1918, just one week before the Armistice that ended World War I.

Prologue

Ceann Mara - 1907.

'Race you to the big tree!' Gilbert O'Byrne shouted, already taking off along the riverbank, his bare feet kicking up puffs of dusty earth. His sandy hair flopped with each stride, too long as usual, because he'd squirmed too much at his last haircut.

'That's not fair! You got a head start!' Matilda from *Wambool*, the station that bordered the northern side of *Ceann Mara*, called after him, but she was already running too, her dark plaits bouncing against her shoulders. At ten, she was a year younger than Gilbert, but what she lacked in age, she made up for in determination.

Gilbert's six-year-old sister, Olive, trailed behind them, clutching Millie, the rag doll she took everywhere. 'Wait for me!' Her voice was small against the rush of the wind in the trees above them.

The Darling River stretched wide and lazy beside them, its muddy waters the colour of strong tea. Ancient river gums leaned over the water, their twisted roots clinging to the banks like gnarled fingers, some exposed where the water had eaten away the soil. The summer heat shimmered above the surface, making the far bank waver like a mirage. In the shallows, tiny fish darted between sunken logs while dragonflies hovered over lily pads near the edge.

Matilda slowed, glancing back. 'Come on, Olive. We'll wait for you.'

Gilbert reached the ancient river gum first, slapping its rough trunk with triumph. 'I win!'

The tree stood sentinel over a small, sandy beach where the river curved, creating a gentle eddy. Years of floods had sculpted this natural playground, depositing soft sand and smooth river stones perfect for skipping across the water. Behind them, the land rose in a gentle slope towards the paddocks—dry, brown paddocks dotted with sheep.

'Only because you cheated,' Matilda said, hands on her hips. But she was smiling, her eyes bright with the joy of the perfect summer day—and she was with Gilbert, whom she worshipped.

They settled in the dappled shade, Gilbert pulling out three slightly squashed jam sandwiches from his pocket. 'Mum made these,' he said, passing them around. 'Though Olive sat on them, I reckon.'

'Did not!' his sister protested, accepting her sandwich with a scowl. The river flowed lazily past them, its surface glittering in the midday sun. Dragonflies skimmed across the water, and somewhere in the distance, a kookaburra laughed. The air smelled of warm earth, eucalyptus, and the sweet tang of the river itself.

'When we get married,' Matilda said matter-of-factly, licking jam from her fingers, 'we're going to live right here by the river.'

Gilbert rolled his eyes, but there was no meanness in his expression. 'You always say that.'

'Because it's true.' She nodded with the absolute certainty only an eleven-year-old could possess. 'We'll have a homestead as big as *Ceann Mara* with four children.'

'Four!' he exclaimed. 'That's too many.'

'Three, then,' she conceded. 'But I get to name them all.'

Olive, who had been arranging a bed of leaves around Millie, suddenly pointed downriver. 'Look! A big boat!'

The drawn-out mournful echo of a steam whistle lingered in the afternoon quiet. Around the wide bend in the river, a paddle steamer appeared, its giant wheel churning the muddy water into froth. The vessel was an impressive sight—two stories tall with an ornate wheelhouse perched on top like a crown. Its red and cream paintwork stood out vividly against the muted greens and browns of the riverscape. Black smoke billowed from its tall stack, rising into the cloudless sky.

'The *Catherine Anne*,' Gilbert said with authority. 'She comes up from Echuca to collect wool from all the stations along the river.'

They watched, transfixed, as the paddle steamer approached the wharf a couple of hundred yards from their beach. Men moved purposefully about the deck, preparing to dock. Great bales of wool were already stacked there, secured under canvas tarps. The captain called orders from the wheelhouse, his voice carrying across the water.

'Look, I can see Father and Cecil there with our wool.' Matilda jumped up and down, waving, but they were too far away to be seen.

'That's our wharf,' Gilbert said, sitting up straighter as the steamer angled towards a sturdy wooden jetty that jutted into the river. 'My great-great-uncle Samuel built it back when they used to ship everything by river. Dad says they'll load our wool and take it all the way to the ocean, and then it goes on bigger ships to England.'

Matilda frowned. 'What does great-great mean?'

'It means my grandfather's uncle,' Gilbert explained. 'Really old family. Dad says the O'Byrnes have been on this land since before federation.'

'What's federation?'

'When Australia became a country, silly,' he said without malice, his tone the same one he used when explaining homework or cricket rules to her. 'Don't they teach you anything in school?'

Matilda tossed a twig at him. 'They do so. I just wasn't listening that day.' She watched the steamer dock, crewmen tying thick ropes to the old wooden posts. On the bank above the wharf, men were already gathering with horse-drawn wagons loaded with wool bales. 'I don't know anything about my old family. My mother and father moved here just before I was born. My grandparents live in Melbourne.'

'The city?' Gilbert sounded impressed and horrified at the same time. 'Have you been there?'

'I did once. It's a long way. I'm not going back again; I told Mother that.'

'What's it like?'

'Noisy and smelly.' Matilda wrinkled her nose. 'Mother hated it at first when she moved from Ireland with her parents. She said the buildings were so tall they blocked out the sun, and people never said hello on the street. She cried every night for a month. Then she met my father, and they got married.'

'Why'd they stay in Melbourne then?'

'Grandad was sick. He needed looking after, but he died before I was born.' Matilda picked at the grass. 'Father said as soon as he saw the river, he knew they were home. And Mother said that Grandad was rich. We came here when I was a baby and Cecil was seven.'

'I remember when you went to Melbourne last Christmas,'

Gilbert said. 'I'll go there one day.'

Matilda's eyes widened. 'You've never been to the city?'

'Course I have,' he said defensively. 'I've been to Wilcannia.'

'Wilcannia's not a real city. It's a river port,' she scoffed.

'There's big sandstone buildings there,' Gilbert justified.

Not to be outdone, Matilda folded her arms. 'Melbourne has trams and buildings taller than twenty trees stacked on top of each other. And shops with more sweets than you've ever seen.' She leaned closer, lowering her voice. 'But I do like it better here. Don't tell Mother.'

'Your secret's safe with me,' Gilbert promised solemnly. It was their ritual—the sharing of secrets by the river.

Olive had wandered closer to the water where the wind was whipping up tiny waves that lapped at the muddy bank. 'Can we go see the boat?' she asked, looking back at them hopefully.

The paddle steamer had docked completely now. Men were rolling wool bales down planks from the wharf onto the deck, muscles straining as they manoeuvred the heavy cargo. The captain stood on the wharf, clipboard in hand, checking off each bale as it was loaded. 'Careful with that one!' he called as a particularly large bale teetered precariously on the plank. 'That's prime merino from the O'Byrne station!' The great paddle wheel had stopped, but steam still escaped in puffs from the stack, and they could hear the crewmen calling to each other as they secured the growing load of wool on the deck, preparing for the journey downriver to the markets in Adelaide. Gilbert glanced at the sun's position. 'We've got time before dinner. Race you there?'

This time, they all started running together, their laughter mingling with the rustle of the river red gums and the hiss of the steam from the paddleboat.

Chapter 1

Wagga Wagga - January.

Erin O'Byrne-Hayes struggled with the awning leg of the motorhome, her fingers slick with sweat and trembling against the metal. As the leg suddenly slipped free of her grasp, her throat constricted with the familiar knot of anxiety that had been there since Jack had signed the contract with *Terra Lens* before they'd gone to *Ceann Mara* for Christmas. They hadn't mentioned it to the family, in case anything went wrong. As they travelled back to Wagga, the call from the magazine came advising him that his flight to Sydney had been booked for the eleventh of January. As his departure date drew closer, her tension grew, and the slightest things upset her. The stepladder wobbled beneath her as she scrambled to steady herself.

'Careful.' Jack grabbed the hanging track and passed it back up. 'It's the third one along from the top, sweetie.' His voice was patient. Erin stood precariously on the top of the stepladder and looked down at her husband of two years.

'I was sure I counted four holes on the other side,' she said.

'No, it was definitely three.' His green eyes crinkled in a smile, and her heart filled with a surge of love, immediately followed by the worry that wouldn't leave her.

'Okay, one, two, three,' she said, slotting the mechanism into the awning with a satisfying click. She looked over to the other side and then up to where she was positioning the awning of their motorhome. 'No, you're right; it's even now. Now help me down from here.'

Jack had insisted that he go through every aspect of their motorhome with her so he could be confident that Erin could manage everything while he was away. She planned on spending most of that time in the caravan park at Wagga Wagga before heading home to *Ceann Mara* for a visit.

He held her hand, and she gripped it tightly as she stepped off the ladder, his arms around her.

'Another skill you've learned,' he said. 'My job's going to be easy when I get back. You'll be able to set us up.'

'I'll be handing it straight back to you.' Erin forced a smile, resting her head on his shoulder. 'I am going to miss you, Jack. Three months is a long time to be apart.'

'I know, sweetheart, but it's going to give us a head start. We can put a deposit on a house somewhere later this year.'

'Somewhere?'

Jack nodded. 'When we decide where we want to live.' As they'd travelled around Australia, they'd found many places that they would both like to settle when they finished their travels. Since they'd been back in New South Wales, the closer they got to the Darling, the more Erin tried to ignore the call of home. 'What's your favourite so far?' he asked.

'Well, I do love North Queensland, but I've been looking at the rain up there lately, so that's been crossed off the list. What about you? What's yours?'

'I love Exmouth in Western Australia,' Jack said.

'A bit too far from home.'

'I know you very well,' he said, putting his arms around her, his embrace tightening as he gently kissed her neck. 'I think you'd like to get a bit of land on the Darling, wouldn't you?'

'Maybe not land, but we could live in one of the small towns around there, not more than a few hours from *Ceann Mara*. But that's a decision we have to make together, and both agree on. The first thing we have to do is get these three months over and done with, get you home safely, and then we'll sit down and have a good talk about it. It all depends on how this assignment of yours works out. They might want you to go again.'

'I can only hope. I'd love to get a permanent job with the magazine. That would be a dream come true.'

Erin's smile faded, and Jack frowned again.

'Do you ever regret not marrying a country boy, love? One who would jump at the chance to go on the land and live by the Darling with you?'

'Don't be silly. I fell in love with you the day I met you in Broken Hill, and I've never regretted a single minute of our time together.'

'And then *you* ran away from your family and eloped.' Jack ran a hand through his shaggy blond hair. 'I still feel as though I'm not completely accepted by them yet, although at least Cat calls me Jack now.'

'Calls you Jack?' Erin frowned. 'What do you mean?'

'She called me Joe for the first few months.'

Erin pulled away and met Jack's eyes. 'I married the man *I* fell in love with. And my family accepts that.'

But even as she spoke the words with conviction, a familiar doubt flickered in the back of her mind. She'd chosen Jack without hesitation, but sometimes she caught the careful way her family navigated conversations around him as if walking on eggshells. They were wary of him at first; Erin's self-esteem had suffered when her first boyfriend left her with no explanation a few months before she met Jack. She had been depressed, and Mum had insisted she see a clinical psychologist in Broken Hill.

Meeting Jack had changed her life, but her family had been

slow to warm to him. Dad's tight-lipped nods when Jack talked about his photography, Mum's overly bright questions about their travels that never quite reached her eyes. Her relationship with Jack had created a wall between her and her sisters, too—unspoken tension that made their lifelong closeness feel strained. Cat tried her hardest, but even she sometimes slipped, showing flashes of the worry they all seemed to share—that Erin had chosen a life too uncertain, too nomadic, too different from the generations of O'Byrnes before her. Taking a different path from her sisters—embracing freedom and exploring the country with Jack in her early twenties had brought her genuine joy. As the second sister, she'd always felt as though she didn't quite fit in, but with Jack, she'd found where she belonged.

'What about settling here?' Jack's voice broke into her thoughts as he gestured over to the Murrumbidgee River. 'Around Wagga?'

Erin's thoughts drifted to their first trip away together when Jack was working at his father's pub at Tilpa. They'd camped here at Wagga Beach, the sandy riverbank along the Murrumbidgee. Jack had photographed her among the large river red gums. She remembered how the soft, golden sand had felt between her toes as they'd walked, how the afternoon light had filtered through the eucalyptus leaves, creating patterns on the calm water. They'd settled in one of the picnic areas, spreading a blanket while families barbecued nearby and children splashed in the shallows. It was there, surrounded by the peaceful, natural setting of her childhood, that she'd first realised she'd fallen for him—this man who saw beauty in places that no one else seemed to notice.

She turned her attention to her husband, who was looking

at her with a frown etched on his brow. 'Not a bad idea. I do have a job if we decide to settle here.'

Jack chuckled. 'But I don't think you want to be a checkout chick for the rest of your life, do you, love?'

'It gives me a lot of time to write,' she said.

'Hopefully, you'll get a lot done while I'm away. That way you won't be too lonely.'

'We'll get through this.' As soon as she spoke the words, Erin regretted them. It was taking the gloss off Jack's achievement: an all-expenses-paid three-month contract with a world-renowned magazine and a fabulous payment was pretty special. 'I didn't mean that how it came out. I know it's an amazing opportunity and such an achievement for you. I'm proud of you.'

'I just wish you'd go back home to *Ceann Mara* while I'm away.' Jack held her tightly. 'I'll worry about you. I worry about you coping by yourself.'

So did Erin, but there was no way she was going to put that burden on Jack.

'No, I couldn't handle being back home for three months, but I will go home for a week or so. And then we'll be back there for Cat and Logan's wedding in May. You will be back by then, won't you?'

'Of course I will. As soon as I know the date I'm coming back, I'll let you know. Are you sure you'll be alright staying here in Wagga?'

'I've got Jill and Aaron, and their kids to visit here. It's not as if I don't know anyone.'

'Yes, that makes me feel better about going away.'

'That reminds me. Jill asked us if we could come for dinner on Saturday. Aaron's home from the mine this weekend, and they want to catch up with us before you go.'

'Sounds good. I don't leave until Monday morning, so that will give us Sunday together to get the last of everything organised here.'

'I'm organised,' Erin said. 'You worry too much. I can do it.'

'I still have to show you how to fill the water tanks and check the power on the solar meter.'

'If I'm staying here in the park, I can just plug into the power and tap into the water. But I suppose I'll need to know how to do that at *Ceann Mara*.'

'But aren't you going to stay in the homestead with your parents when you visit?'

'I don't know yet. Maybe not.'

'I'd rather you did. It'll be safer.'

'Says the man who's going to be sleeping out in the wild with lions and elephants!' Erin shook her head and giggled. 'The worst I can expect is a hairy wombat.'

'And snakes.' Jack frowned.

'I grew up with them, city boy.'

'Right. Come and we'll look at the control panel inside, and I'll show you the power and water tank monitors.'

'Okay, you'd better show me everything in case I do stay in the motorhome. I wouldn't mind camping by my favourite billabong.'

'We can camp there when we go to the wedding.' Jack kissed her neck, his voice low and teasing. After two years of marriage, their connection had only deepened, the spark between them as electric as the day they'd met at a music festival. His touch still sent shivers down her spine, familiar yet thrilling every time.

Erin leaned into his kiss, her body responding instantly before she reluctantly pulled away. 'Three months apart is going to feel like forever,' she whispered, running her fingers through his hair. 'When you get back, I don't intend to let you out of my sight for at least a month.' She pushed his shoulder gently. 'Come on, show me this power meter thing, and then we can go for a swim.'

Chapter 2

Wagga Wagga - Saturday night.

On Saturday night, Erin stood at the window of her friend Jill's kitchen and looked out at Jack and Aaron, who were manning the barbecue. Jill's two little boys had finally gone to bed, and they were preparing the last salad.

'Top up?' Jill asked, holding up the bottle of white wine.

'Why not?' Erin said. 'We walked here.'

'I noticed that,' Jill said, holding the bottle and tilting her head to the side. 'Are you sure you'll be okay with Jack going away for three months? I know what it's like when Aaron goes away, and that's only ten days at a time.'

'I'll be fine. It's just me to look after. You've got the kids to handle by yourself.' Erin drizzled a splash of balsamic vinegar over the green salad.

'It's the nights and the quiet after the boys go to bed that I find the worst,' Jill said. 'And sleeping in the bed by myself.'

'I know, I am worried about being lonely, but there's no way on God's earth I'll tell Jack that. It's such an incredible opportunity for him. For us.'

'Tell me again what he's doing,' Jill said, topping up Erin's wine glass.

'Have you ever seen those spectacular portraits of the local indigenous workers that he posted on Facebook? The ones from the Eastern Kimberley? I shared a few of them on my profile. It turns out that the photo editor from *Terra Lens* magazine saw them. One thing led to another, and he got offered the paid assignment in Africa. In Eswatini.'

'I've never heard of it. Where is it?'

'It's the new name for Swaziland. Apparently, it has a huge game reserve, home to lions, elephants, rhinos, giraffes, and antelopes.'

'Sounds fantastic.'

'Yeah, it's a brilliant opportunity for Jack. It could mean more travel in the future, too, and hopefully, if there's a next time, I'll be able to go with him. This trip, the magazine's paying for everything for him. It might put his name on the international stage.' Erin shrugged. 'We can only hope.'

'And you're going to stay here in Wagga while he's away?'

'Yes, I'll take on the permanent job they've offered me at IGA. It'll make the time go fast, and then just after Jack gets back, we'll be heading home for Cat and Logan's wedding.'

'Exciting,' Jill replied. 'Have you got something to wear to the wedding yet?'

'I don't have to.' Erin pulled a face. 'I'm a bridesmaid. You know how I feel about weddings—all that fuss and stuff.'

'Yeah. I was really cross that I didn't get an invitation to your wedding.'

Erin smiled cheekily. 'You're cross? You should have heard Mum and Dad when they found out we got married in Darwin.'

Jill passed her wine glass to Erin and picked up the salad. 'You take my glass, and I'll take the salad and wine out. You know, Erin, if you have any worries while Jack's away, you know where to find us.'

Erin and Jill had met at boarding school, and their strong friendship had endured through email and Facebook while Erin and Jack travelled around Australia over the past three years. When they met Aaron, Jill's husband, a couple of months ago, he and Jack had hit it off, sharing common interests.

'I do appreciate that,' Erin said. 'It's good to know that you're here. The only thing I'm worried about is holding myself together at the airport next week. Jack's so excited about going, but at the same time, he's worried about leaving me. We haven't spent a single night apart since we set off on our travels.'

'We'll discuss some things we can do while we're outside. We can go to the cinema when Aaron's home, and when I've got a day off, you can come here for dinner.'

Erin linked her arm through Jill's. 'You're a sweetheart.'

Chapter 3

Wagga Wagga Airport - 11th January.

The terminal buzzed with the energy of a busy regional airport. The fluorescent lights cast a glow over the floor, but Jack's excitement seemed to illuminate the entire space. His camera bag was slung over his shoulder, and his khaki backpack rested on the floor at his feet. Erin gripped his hands, trying to memorise every detail of her husband's face: the way his eyes lit up when he smiled, the small scar above his left eyebrow from a surfing accident he had in Noosa. She smiled, trying to absorb his excitement; his face was alive with anticipation.

'I still can't believe it,' he said, his voice filled with happiness. 'It's real now that I'm about to go, sweetie.'

'You deserve it. Those photos you took when we were in the west were amazing. It's just lucky you posted them on Facebook and that photo editor from *Terra Lens* saw them. Now you're going to meet them.'

'I nearly fell off my chair when his email arrived,' he replied. 'He said he was very impressed by my ability to capture animal behaviour. I think it's because I've got such a good lens.'

'I think it has more to do with your talent than any lens.' Erin held Jack's hand tightly; touching him settled her nerves a little.

'You know how much I appreciate you being happy for me to spend so much on my photographic gear.'

'It's your job, Jack. You're my own David Attenborough,' she teased him, her finger tracing the strap of his camera bag on the side of his chest.

'I'm looking forward to meeting Lars, the photo editor. He'll be at the Sydney office to meet me tomorrow before we fly out on Wednesday. And Natalie. She's been an incredible help in polishing my portfolio and has been quick in organising the trip.' His eyes brightened. 'At last, I'll have someone with me on assignment. It's all new to me.'

'You're the creative. It's great that they've given you a PA.' Erin hadn't let on that it had surprised—and unsettled—her when the email arrived saying Natalie would be travelling to Africa with Jack.

'And you're right. Natalie said that the magazine wants a comprehensive spread focused on wildlife conservation, and my job is to take the photos without worrying about the details.'

Erin's smile felt brittle. 'I do wish I was coming with you.'

Jack's expression softened. 'Next time, you will. Right now, we can't afford the extra ticket. This is the beginning of my career, of our future.' He kissed her forehead. 'I've got faith in you too, sweetheart. With your writing and my photography— we're going to make this work.'

'We're going to have a creative life no matter where we settle, but the motorhome stays our security blanket for the time being,' she told him. 'Just in case.'

'Absolutely,' he nodded. Their shared understanding was palpable; two years of travelling and chasing dreams on a shoestring budget had taught them both caution. 'Promise me something.' Jack's voice softened as he pulled her close. 'You keep yourself safe while I'm gone. Look after yourself. When you feel lonely or down, email me. I'll call you every couple of days.'

'You call me.' Erin held his eyes. 'I don't want to ring at a bad time. You could be staring down an elephant or a lion.'

'Okay. The time will fly, and I'll be back. We'll be celebrating Cat and Logan's wedding before we know it.'

'I'm fine. I've got Jill for company, and then I'll go home to Mum and Dad for a few days. You keep safe, work hard, and come home to me.'

'Always.' Jack's hands cupped her face, his touch gentle yet firm. Despite Erin's determination not to cry, a tear traced a delicate path down her cheek. She blinked, but with infinite tenderness, Jack wiped it away, his eyes meeting hers with a depth of love that made her heart clench. 'I love you so much, Erin,' he whispered. 'Absolutely and completely.' His voice caught slightly, and she knew he was nervous about going away without her.

'To the moon and back?' Her voice strengthened as she basked in the warmth of his love.

'No, to infinity.' He rested his forehead against hers, and they stood together quietly.

They both knew this was so much more than a work trip; this was their future, with the promise of much more to come.

'You keep safe on the roads. Promise me you'll be careful driving the motorhome alone.'

Erin managed a smile. 'I've been driving those dirt roads since I was sixteen, Jack. I know every dirt track between here and *Ceann Mara* with my eyes closed.'

'Still,' he pressed, pulling her close again. The scent of Jack—a mixture of sunscreen, leather, and something uniquely his—filled her senses. 'Promise me.'

'I promise,' she whispered back, her arms tightening around him. 'You keep safe. You come home to me.'

'Always,' Jack murmured into her hair. 'Always.'

Chapter 4

Wagga Wagga - two days later.

Erin curled up on the motorhome's foldout couch, her laptop balanced on her knees as she edited the last chapter she'd written. After her shifts at IGA, she'd come home and immerse herself in her story; it made the night less lonely. Even after two days, she'd noticed an increase in her word output. Two days and nights had passed since she'd watched Jack disappear through the security gate at the regional airport, his camera bag slung over one shoulder like a badge of honour. He'd called each night since he'd left—long, sweet, loving conversations that had eased her anxiety.

When her phone rang again early on Wednesday morning, she answered with a smile in her voice. 'Hey, you.'

'Hey.' Jack's voice was higher-pitched and charged with excitement. 'Sorry, it's earlier than usual. I'm at the office. We're about to head for the airport.'

'Everything okay?' She shifted, setting the laptop aside for a long chat.

'Better than okay. It's incredible, Erin. The offices here are amazing—all glass and steel, overlooking the harbour. Lars has been through the final itinerary with me and Natalie.' Erin's fingers tightened around the phone as he continued. 'She's fantastic, Erin. An experienced photographer, she knows exactly what equipment I'll need for each location. I've already got some new lenses from here.'

Erin's throat tightened as she swallowed the unease that had settled in at the mention of Natalie's name. Something in

Jack's voice changed when he said her name—his usual laid-back tone held a different tone.

'What time is your flight?'

'Noon.' There was a slight pause. 'That's actually why I'm calling. There's been a bit of a change to the assignment. I wanted to run it by you before we leave.'

'Oh? Run what by me?' She fought to keep her tone calm, despite the tightness in her chest.

'It's bigger than I was first told. Lars wants a comprehensive series, not just the conservation angle but the whole ecosystem. Multiple locations across Eswatini.'

'And?' Erin prompted, hearing the hesitation in his voice.

'It's going to be a little bit longer trip away now.'

The words hit Erin like a physical blow. Longer? She'd prepared herself for three months—had figured out how to manage the motorhome payments and lined up enough shifts at IGA to cover their expenses. Now it was going to be longer?

'Erin? Are you there?'

'I'm here.' She took a deep breath. 'How much longer?' She wanted to say no, but held the words back.

'A couple more weeks, but I'll let you know when I can, love. We've been given access to a restricted area, and Lars doesn't want to pass up the opportunity. It's weather dependent, so we're not sure yet.' His voice softened, but an undercurrent of excitement remained. 'But the money—Erin, with the extra weeks, they're increasing the original payment. This will set us up properly when I get back. You can write full-time. No need for any more IGA shifts.'

She forced a smile into her voice. 'Maybe we can finally afford to buy some land and build?'

'Exactly!' He laughed; relief evident in his tone. 'Start

looking—that's my suggestion. Maybe some land near *Ceann Mara*? You've always loved the Darling River area, and I can base myself anywhere.'

'I have,' she agreed quietly, even as she wondered why this felt like Jack was planning *her* future rather than their future. Basing himself there had sounded like an addendum. 'What about Cat and Logan's wedding?'

'But I'll be back by then. That's not until May.' There was a rustling of papers on his end. 'Listen, I've got to run. The taxi to the airport is waiting downstairs.'

'Already?' Erin glanced at the clock. They'd been talking for less than five minutes. 'But—'

'Natalie's got all our boarding passes sorted. She's amazing with the logistics.'

Erin's heart squeezed. 'Okay. Well, have a safe flight. Let me know when you land?'

'I will.'

'Jack,' she started, then hesitated. 'I love you.'

There was talking in the background, and then he said quickly, 'Got to run! Taxi's waiting. Bye!'

The call ended, leaving Erin staring at her phone. No, "I love you too." No lingering farewell. Jack had just hung up on her.

The motorhome suddenly felt claustrophobic. Erin hugged her knees to her chest, trying to ignore the hollow feeling expanding beneath her ribs. It was just excitement for his career, she told herself—the assignment of a lifetime. Of course, he'd be distracted.

But as she stared at the silent phone, remembering the way his tone had changed each time he mentioned Natalie, a small, insistent voice whispered warnings she wasn't ready to hear.

Jack had agreed to the longer trip too readily. He should have talked it over with her first, before he'd accepted.

Erin pushed herself off the couch, restlessness driving her to movement. She'd promised Jack she'd go to *Ceann Mara* for a visit while he was gone. Maybe that wasn't such a bad idea after all. The familiar comfort of home, the distraction of family—it might be exactly what she needed to quiet her silly imagination. The first opportunity she got, she'd go home.

Her eyes fell on Jack's worn sweater, thrown carelessly over a chair before he left. She picked it up, burying her face in the fabric that still held his scent.

Chapter 5

Ceann Mara - February 1915.

The sun hung low in the western sky, casting long shadows across the billabong on the Darling River. Gilbert O'Byrne sat motionless on the bank, his fishing line disappearing into the depths. The water glistened like molten gold in the late afternoon light, carrying thoughts of places far beyond *Ceann Mara*, the sheep station his grandfather had established nearly fifty years before.

At nineteen, Gilbert felt restless. His shoulders had broadened over the past year, and a day's work no longer left him bone-weary as it once had. His father had begun to consult him on matters of the property, and the station hands now looked to him for direction when Thomas O'Byrne was away.

'You've been awfully quiet,' said Matilda Ellis, breaking the comfortable silence between them. She sat beside him on the old blanket they'd spread across the red earth, her own fishing rod propped against a nearby eucalyptus tree. 'Penny for your thoughts?'

Gilbert turned to look at her, taking in the sight of her as though for the first time. Matilda had been a fixture in his life for as long as he could remember, the daughter from *Wambool* Station next door. But something had shifted in recent months. The gangly girl with dark plaits who had once challenged him to climbing contests and races on horseback had transformed. At eighteen, she carried herself with a quiet grace that both intrigued and intimidated him. She had grown up quickly after her mother had passed two years back.

'Just thinking about the war,' he replied, picking up a smooth stone and skipping it across the water's surface. 'Father brought the newspaper back from Bourke yesterday. They're calling for volunteers.'

Matilda's expression clouded. 'And you're keen to go, aren't you? I can see it in your face.'

Gilbert looked down at his hands, calloused from years of working the land. 'Wouldn't any man want to do his duty? They say we'll be home by Christmas.'

'And what does your mother think of that plan?' Matilda asked, her voice gentle but pointed.

Gilbert's jaw tightened. 'She's not well, Tilly. You know that. Father says I'm needed here, at least until she's stronger.'

Matilda nodded, her gaze drifting to the river. A pair of black swans glided past; their elegant necks curved in perfect symmetry. The breeze carried the sweet scent of the eucalypts and the earthy smell of the river.

'The world feels so far away from here, doesn't it?' she said after a moment. 'All this talk of Europe and Germany and war . . . it seems like a story that we read in a book.'

Gilbert pulled his line from the water, checking the bait. 'That's just it, though. I've never been anywhere, Tilly. Never seen anything beyond Wilcannia and Bourke. Sometimes I wonder if I ever will.'

'Is that so terrible?' Matilda asked, turning to face him fully. The late afternoon sun caught the highlights in her hair, creating a halo effect that made Gilbert's breath catch. 'This land has everything a person could need.'

Gilbert smiled despite himself. 'Your father let you manage the southern paddocks on your own last month. You've got purpose, Tilly. Everyone knows *Wambool* will be yours someday, war or no war.'

'As *Ceann Mara* will be yours,' she countered. 'And Cecil will manage *Wambool*.'

'Yes, but your father trusts you with real responsibility. You've earned it.' He cast his line again, watching the ripples spread across the water's surface. 'Meanwhile, Father still checks my work as though I'm twelve years old.'

Matilda laughed, the sound carrying across the water. 'Thomas O'Byrne would check God's own handiwork if given the chance. It's not about you, Gil.'

A flock of galahs passed overhead, their raucous calls filling the air as they settled into the river red gums for the evening. In the distance, a mob of kangaroos grazed cautiously at the river's edge.

'Father asked after your mother yesterday,' Matilda said, changing the subject. 'After I brought over the preserves.'

Gilbert nodded, his expression solemn. 'The doctor from Broken Hill is coming next week. Father's worried, though he tries not to show it.'

'She's strong, your mother. Irish stock, as she likes to remind everyone.'

'She is that.' Gilbert smiled fondly, thinking of his mother's fierce determination despite her frail health. 'Caught her mending shirts yesterday when she was supposed to be resting. Claimed she'd "go mad from all this lying about".'

Their conversation lulled as Gilbert felt a tug on his line. He tensed, waiting for the right moment before giving a sharp pull. The struggle was brief but satisfying as he reeled in a decent-sized cod.

'Well done!' Matilda exclaimed, moving closer to examine

the fish. 'That'll make a fine dinner.'

A flush of pride warmed Gilbert as he removed the hook and placed the fish in the bucket of water they'd brought. Her approval shouldn't matter so much, he knew, but it did nonetheless.

'We should head back soon,' he said, noting the deepening dusk. 'Your father will have my hide if I don't get you home before dark.'

Matilda rolled her eyes. 'I'm perfectly capable of finding my way home in the dark, Gilbert O'Byrne. I've been walking along this river since before you could ride a horse properly.'

'Nevertheless,' he replied with a grin, 'I value my skin too much to test Robert Ellis's patience.'

They began packing up their things, working in the comfortable rhythm that years of fishing together had instilled. Gilbert found himself watching Matilda's movements—the precise way she wound her fishing line, the gentle handling of the day's catch, the absent-minded tucking of a loose strand of hair behind her ear.

As she bent to fold the blanket, a pendant slipped from the collar of her blouse—a small silver disc that caught the fading light.

'What's that?' Gilbert asked, curiosity getting the better of him.

Matilda's hand flew to the necklace, as though she'd forgotten she was wearing it. 'Oh, this? It was my grandmother's. An old Celtic knot. Mother gave it to me when she was ill.' She hesitated, then added, 'For protection.'

Gilbert stepped closer, examining the intricate pattern. 'It's beautiful.'

They stood mere inches apart now, closer than propriety

strictly allowed. Gilbert became acutely aware of her breathing, of the faint scent of lavender that clung to her hair, of how her eyes seemed to shift between green and grey in the fading light.

'Tilly,' he began, uncertain of what he meant to say.

Her eyes met his, wide and expectant. 'Yes?'

The moment stretched between them, and Gilbert felt something new and terrifying unfurling in his chest—an acceptance that the girl he'd known all his life had somehow become essential to him in ways he was only beginning to understand.

A kookaburra's raucous laugh shattered the moment, startling them both. Gilbert stepped back, clearing his throat.

'We should go,' he said, reaching for the bucket of fish. 'It'll be dark soon.'

Matilda nodded, a flicker of disappointment crossing her features before she turned away to gather her things.

They walked in silence to where they'd left their horses, the sounds of the bush enveloping them as day turned to dusk. Cicadas thrummed their evening chorus, and somewhere in the distance, a dingo howled.

As they reached the horses, Matilda turned to him suddenly. 'Promise me something, Gil?'

'What's that?'

'If you do go—to the war, I mean—promise you'll write to me.' Her voice was steady, but Gilbert could see the concern in her eyes.

'Of course I will,' he replied, surprised by the request. 'Though Father says it'll likely be over before I even have a chance to enlist.'

Matilda didn't respond immediately, her gaze drifting to

where the evening star had appeared in the sky.

'The world feels different now, doesn't it?' she finally said. 'Like something's ending, though we don't know what yet.'

Gilbert helped her mount her horse, his hands lingering perhaps a moment longer than necessary at her waist. 'Or beginning,' he suggested.

Their eyes met once more, and in that moment, Gilbert felt something was indeed beginning between them; more than the lifelong childhood friendship they shared.

'Race you to the gate,' Matilda suddenly challenged, her sombre mood dissolving into a familiar mischievous grin.

Before he could respond, she was off, her horse kicking up dust as she galloped along the riverbank, her laughter trailing behind her like a banner.

Gilbert laughed despite himself and swung onto his mount, spurring the horse forward. The war, his mother's illness, the uncertain future—all of it receded as he chased Matilda through the gathering darkness.

Chapter 6

Ezulwini Valley, Eswatini, Africa - mid-January.

The Ezulwini Valley in Eswatini was nothing like anything Jack had experienced in their travels around Australia. He had spent his first three nights in a daze, his senses overwhelmed by so many new experiences. The small town was a jarring mix of the traditional and modern—thatched-roof shops sitting alongside concrete government buildings, luxury safari lodges bordering streets where goats wandered freely amid pedestrians.

Mornings brought sounds unlike anything he'd known: the distant calls of unfamiliar birds, the chatter of market vendors setting up their stalls, the constant bleating of livestock being herded through side streets. By midday, the air grew thick with the scents of dust and diesel fumes from ancient buses, mingling with the aromas of street food. Spices he couldn't name, meats grilled over open flames, something sweet and fruity that reminded him vaguely of mangoes but sharper, more intense.

The Grand Ezulwini Safari Lodge, where they were staying, stood in stark contrast to the dusty landscape surrounding it; a colonial-era building that had been renovated into a five-star retreat for wealthy tourists and many photographers. He'd encountered a group of American photographers in the bar last night and had felt out of his depth. For the first time, he wondered what the hell he was doing here.

His suite featured a four-poster bed draped with mosquito netting that looked more decorative than functional, a claw-foot bathtub big enough for two, and a private balcony overlooking the savannah. Each morning, a breakfast spread appeared as if by magic: fresh tropical fruits, pastries still warm from the oven, and coffee that made him groan with appreciation after months of drinking instant coffee, which Erin and he had survived on in their motorhome.

'You should have seen your face when we pulled up,' Natalie laughed as they settled at their usual table on the hotel's veranda for dinner. Tonight, she wore a simple white linen dress that somehow managed to look both practical and elegant. 'Like you'd stumbled into the wrong movie set.'

'Not exactly what I was expecting,' Jack admitted, still uncomfortable with the luxury accommodation *Terra Lens* had arranged. 'I've spent the last two years in a motorhome, with occasional stops at country pubs. This feels . . .'

'Civilised?' Natalie offered, signalling the waiter for another round of drinks.

'Excessive,' Jack corrected, thinking of Erin and their careful budgeting, how they'd celebrate finding good, free camps on Wiki Camps or scoring discount groceries. What would she make of this?

Natalie tilted her head, studying him over the rim of her gin and tonic. 'You should enjoy it while it lasts. Tomorrow, we head into the conservation area. Tented accommodation for three nights; you might feel more at home, although still with proper beds and en-suite facilities.' A smile played at the corners of her mouth. '*I* don't do roughing it unnecessarily.'

'I think the best photography happens when you're willing to get uncomfortable,' Jack countered, thinking of pre-dawn hikes with Erin to catch first light on high mountains, or hours spent motionless in swamps waiting for the perfect bird shot.

'I've helped some of the greatest wildlife photographers in the business,' Natalie said, her tone casual but with an undercurrent of pride. 'I think my trip with Hagen Heinrich in Tanzania was probably the best. Six weeks tracking the great migration.'

Jack nearly choked on his beer. 'Hagen Heinrich? *The* Hagen Heinrich? You've assisted him?'

'Yeah, I've been with a few of the internationally known ones.' She shrugged, as if assisting photography legends was a minor detail. 'I picked up a lot about being a good assistant.'

She held his gaze a little too long, and Jack found it hard to look away. Her eyes were the most intense blue he'd ever seen, made more striking by the flickering lantern light. He'd noticed her beauty immediately, of course—the kind of classically perfect features that seemed designed for magazine covers rather than trudging through wildlife reserves. However, it was Natalie's competence that had impressed him most over these first few days: her effortless navigation of permits and local officials, her extensive knowledge of equipment, and her seemingly endless contacts.

'Well, you've got a lot to teach me,' he said finally.

'I can handle the mechanical aspects, Jack, and that's what I do for all my photographers. But you're the one with the creativity; you take the shots. I'm just here to pass things to you.'

Jack looked away and smiled, thinking of Erin and the nights she had spent in a paddock with him in the early hours as he tried to capture wild shots under a full moon—sometimes in the freezing cold, sometimes in the drizzling rain. She'd always been so enthusiastic: no complaints, just quiet support and occasional suggestions that often led to his best work. She'd developed an intuitive understanding of what he needed before he asked, and a rhythm had developed between them that didn't need words.

The realisation of how much he missed Erin hit with unexpected force. Three days without contact already felt like forever.

'You're sure there's no way we can get messages out?' he asked Natalie again, pulling himself back to the present.

'Not yet. Apparently, the phone lines have been down for about three weeks, so we've got no email or internet either. There's no satellite working, and we'll just have to wait until we arrive in Mbabane to send messages home.'

'What alternatives are there?' Jack frowned.

'None. This happens quite frequently on our trips here. Will your wife be worried about you?' Natalie asked, tilting her head to the side with a curious expression that didn't quite reach her eyes.

Jack frowned, images of Erin checking her phone, waiting for his call, filling his mind. 'Knowing Erin, she will be worried about not hearing from me. Well, at least she'll know by reading newspapers and looking at the internet that there have been no accidents, plane crashes, or photographer deaths in Africa.'

Natalie's laugh was like glass—beautiful but with a hard edge. 'She'll be fine. Wives of photographers learn to cope with the absences, or they don't last.'

The wives or the photographers, Jack wondered. He was taken aback by Natalie's clinical approach. There was something cold about it; the casual dismissal of Erin's concern made him uncomfortable. It took away the gloss of Natalie's beauty. He'd always been the same; it was the person beneath that he looked for, and Natalie was starting to show that she was a little hard-edged.

He shook himself out of his thoughts. 'It's no matter. I'm

here to do a job, and the time should pass quickly as we move around, experiencing new things and taking advantage of incredible opportunities to capture some great shots. I won't let anything take away from my focus; it's important that I put one hundred percent of myself into this assignment.'

'You're learning, Jack. When we get to Mbabane, you can message her. Now, let's look at this itinerary again.' Natalie pulled out her phone, and his eyebrows raised when it dinged with the sound of an incoming message.

'You've got service?' he asked hopefully.

'No, just an alarm I set,' she said. 'Okay, now we start off tomorrow morning before sunrise.'

He sat back and listened, holding a local beer as she went through the plans for the next ten days. But part of his mind remained with Erin, wondering what she was doing, hoping she wasn't too worried, and already counting the days until he could share his experiences.

The night sounds of Africa drifted through the open windows: crickets, frogs, and distant calls that belonged to animals he'd only seen in zoos or documentaries. Tomorrow would bring new experiences for him. But tonight, despite the exotic location and the comfortable luxury, Jack felt the first pangs of homesickness for a small motorhome and the woman who had chosen to share his wandering life.

Chapter 7

Wagga Wagga - mid-January.

Jill had invited Erin to see a new romantic comedy at the cinema, and she had gone along willingly, knowing she had to pull herself out of the low mood that she found it hard to shake.

The lack of communication from Jack since he'd arrived—hopefully—had her worried.

At least it meant no bad news, and she assumed that if anything had happened, the magazine would contact her.

Jack had been explicit in his instructions. He had left all her details with the magazine, including her phone number and where she was staying in Wagga.

'Is it that dangerous over there?' she'd asked worriedly.

'No, I could trip over and break my leg, and I'll need to contact you to come and get me.' He chuckled. 'It's okay, sweetie. It's just protocol. They just wanted the next of kin details on all the forms.'

As she and Jill walked out of the cinema together mid-afternoon, all Erin could think of was that phrase, "next of kin". What if something happened to Jack? What would she do without him?

'Penny for your thoughts?' Jill asked.

Erin sighed. 'I'm just worrying about Jack. I haven't heard from him since he arrived. He's been there three days. I'm guessing there are communication problems.'

'Could you ring the magazine?'

'Oh gosh, no! Not this soon. Jack would kill me. He told me it was going to be like this, but I thought at least I'd have something from him to say he'd arrived safely.'

'You know what they say,' Jill said, linking her arm through Erin's. 'No news is good news. Now come and have a coffee. I need cake. The kids wore me out this morning.'

'Have you got time for coffee before you pick them up from daycare?'

'Yes, we've got an hour and a half. Let's go and make the most of it.'

Fifteen minutes later, they were sitting in Jill's favourite coffee shop, a place Erin hadn't been to before. They both demolished a huge slice of Victoria sponge and then ordered a second coffee each.

'You look a bit more settled now,' Jill commented as she reached for her cup.

'Yes, there's no point worrying. Mum tells me I've always been the worrier of her five daughters. I think it's my imagination.'

'No point worrying. I've learned that with the kids, no matter how much you worry, it doesn't change anything, and all it does is fill you with negative energy. Are you sleeping well?'

Erin pulled a face. 'Fairly well. I slept a little bit better last night because I had a late shift at IGA, but most nights I've been getting up and writing through the night.'

'Writing?'

Heat ran into her cheeks. 'I just scribble. I'm writing some stories.'

'That's great! You were always fabulous in English at high school. What sort of stories?'

'Just silly little romances.'

'I read that romance is the biggest-selling genre in the

world. You could make a fortune. You could be the next Liane Moriarty,' Jill said with a grin.

'I can only hope. I need to make the most of these months while Jack's away and get something done. Who knows? I could even have something sent off to a publisher before he gets home. Wouldn't it be nice if I told him I had a contract too?'

'You go for it, girl. Where are you guys going to head to when he gets home? Travelling around again?' Jill asked.

'After the wedding? I don't know. We really haven't talked about it. We'll probably spend some time at Mum and Dad's station, have a bit of a rest, and then we'll head off on another adventure. I suppose a lot of it depends on what happens with how this assignment works out, and whether he gets more work with them.'

'You'd go next time though?'

'Absolutely,' Erin said. 'Even if I've got to sneak into his luggage. That's why I'm taking as many shifts as I can at IGA while Jack's away. I'm putting it all aside, and if there is another assignment, I'll have my airfare. Accommodation won't cost more because I can share a room with him wherever he is,' she chuckled. 'Or, depending on where it is, it could be a tent.'

'Or an igloo,' Jill said with a giggle. 'You're both so clever; you make me feel a bit boring. Aaron flying off to the mine, and me working at the high school office a couple of days a week.'

'Boring?' Erin said. 'Look at those two beautiful boys of yours.'

Jill's eyes softened. 'Yes, you're right. I shouldn't complain; they are just at a very tiring age. Are you and Jack planning on having kids one day?' she asked.

'Of course we are. We want a whole brood between us, but that's a way off yet. We have to decide where we're going to live and have something behind us. I can't imagine having a newborn in a motorhome.'

'No, that would be difficult. When Rohan was born, he just about took over the whole house. I'll never forget it—nappy buckets in the laundry.'

'I thought disposable nappies had put paid to cloth nappies.'

'I'm still an old-fashioned girl. My mum drilled it into me: cloth nappies. You know they're really hard to buy these days.'

'Things have changed; that's for sure.' Erin's thoughts went to Africa, and she wondered what cultural changes Jack was experiencing there. She couldn't wait to hear about it.

When he called.

Jill put her cup down. 'I'd better go and collect the boys. Why don't you come over for dinner on Friday night? Aaron flies out on Friday. Bring your PJs with you. We can have a sleepover if you want; drink wine and watch movies.'

Erin smiled. 'That sounds good.'

##

Later that week, Erin sat outside under the awning. The laptop screen glowed softly in the darkness, the newly fixed lights casting a warm circle around her camp chair. She took a sip of tea, pulled her fluffy cardigan around her shoulders, and began to type:

Dearest Jack,

It's hard to believe you've been gone a week. You would have loved the light over the Murrumbidgee just before sunset, that golden hour you're always chasing. I got some decent shots with that new lens you gave me for my phone (though I'm sure my amateur photos are nothing compared to what you're getting in Africa!).

The water's so still tonight it looks like glass—you'd be setting up your tripod right now, muttering about ISO settings and perfect reflections.

Had dinner at Jill's—Aaron's away—and then called home. Dad's still being Dad; he commented on "proper" jobs, but he's excited about some new documents from the National Library for his research. He's chasing an ancestor from the early 1900s, someone called Gilbert. I chatted with Cat, too. They're so happy, Jack. The wedding's really coming together. And I'm so looking forward to being there with you, even if I have to be a bridesmaid.

The motorhome's working well, though I had a bit of trouble with the Anderson plug for the outside lights. And guess what! I fixed it myself! It was good to get it sorted without having to ask anyone for help. I felt very capable. I could just hear you saying "check the contact points, love," and it turned out that was exactly the problem!

The stars are incredible tonight—makes me think of that time you taught me astrophotography at Uluru. Remember how many shooting stars we saw? The Milky Way's so bright here, it really does look like a river in the sky. Though I bet the African night sky is giving you some amazing shots.

One week down, how many to go? I know this assignment is huge for you (and us), but I miss you so much. I miss watching you work, miss your random photography facts, miss the way you see beauty in everything. But don't worry, I'm keeping busy.

Stay safe, my love. Try not to get eaten by lions (though what a photo that would make!).

All my love, Erin

P.S. Give my love to the elephants—get some good shots of

the babies.

She read it over once, smiling at the memories, then hit send. Writing to Jack made her feel closer to him, even with half a world between them.

After two weeks of being alone, the motorhome felt huge in Jack's absence, and the bed seemed extra big without him next to her. Erin had been staring at her phone for hours every day, waiting for it to ping with a message and checking her email hourly. She understood about poor connectivity in remote locations, and she knew that photography assignments could be challenging and time-consuming, but not a single word in the first week—not even a message saying that he arrived safely. His last message had come from Sydney Airport as they'd been about to board the flight to Africa.

'Love, Natalie is fantastic. She'll be a great PA and will make such a difference to my photography.'

Strangely, that had depressed Erin. For the past three years, she'd been standing there holding lenses, changing lens caps, passing him the filters, and providing support for Jack's photos.

Then again, she told herself she was being stupid. This woman obviously had all of the photographic skills—worse, Erin was an amateur.

Her mind drifted back to their conversation a few nights before Jack had left. Her fears about Africa had been a constant undercurrent despite trying to appear supportive. One night, curled up in the motorhome, she asked, 'Are you really going to get close to lions, Jack?' He had shown her some of his preliminary research.

'Not just lions, love. Africa's got amazing wildlife: leopards and elephants in the conservation areas. They're incredible.'

Her vivid imagination began conjuring endless scenarios: Jack inching too close to a pride of lions, a charging elephant, a venomous snake hidden in the tall grass. She realised she'd seen too many wildlife documentaries and nature shows where things had gone spectacularly wrong. She warned him repeatedly, 'Be careful. These animals aren't like our general wildlife in Australia. These are predators.'

He kissed her forehead. 'I know what I'm doing, love. I've studied their behaviours. I'm not some rookie tourist with a camera.' But now, with days of silence stretching between them, her fears flared up again. What if something had happened? What if one of those magnificent, dangerous creatures had—? No, she pushed that thought away. Erin turned her phone off and picked up her bag. Her shift at IGA was starting in half an hour, and she'd walk down; at least there should be someone to talk to.

The motorhome felt both confining and too empty at once. The caravan park wasn't far from Wagga Beach on the river where she and Jack had spent their first trip away together. The irony wasn't lost on her. Here she was, surrounded by memories of beginnings while everything else was starting to make her feel insecure.

Her phone rang, startling her from her dark thoughts. Róisín's name flashed on the screen. Erin considered letting it go to voicemail—she wasn't in the mood for her sister's relentless optimism—but guilt won out.

'Hello?' Even to her own ears, her voice sounded flat.

'Erin? It's me.' Róisín's usual brisk tone had an

undercurrent of something Erin couldn't quite place. 'I need to tell you something.'

Erin closed her eyes, leaning back against the motorhome's small couch. 'What's up?'

'It's Dad.' Róisín paused. 'He's had a heart attack.'

The words floated somewhere outside Erin's comprehension, like they belonged to someone else's story. 'What?'

'He collapsed yesterday at the farm. They airlifted him to Sydney from Dubbo.' Róisín's voice wavered slightly. 'Mum's flying down, Cat and Logan are driving.'

'Is he . . . will he . . .?' Erin couldn't seem to form complete sentences.

'They're hopeful. The doctors say he's strong, and Cat and Logan got the defibrillator onto him quickly. Luckily, they were there.' Róisín paused again. 'Erin, are you still there?'

'I'm here.' She felt strangely detached, as if she were floating somewhere near the ceiling, watching herself have this conversation.

'Look, we're fairly certain Dad is going to be fine, and I promise to keep in touch. We're going to put his room number on the family chat group.'

'I'll call you in a few days,' Erin said mechanically.

'Are you okay? Is Jack there? I don't want you to be worried there by yourself. Where are you now?'

'In Wagga, so I haven't got far to come home. Where will you be? How long are you staying at *Ceann Mara*?'

'I'm not sure. I have to go to Wilcannia sometime this week. I'm about to make a call to my new boss to find out when they want me to start now that I'm back in the district.'

Erin said nothing, her mind unable to process this new crisis on top of everything else. The phone slipped slightly in her grasp.

'Erin, are you there?'

'I'm here.' She was staring at the photo of her and Jack taped to the motorhome wall, wondering if she should try and call him. But he'd only been there a couple of weeks; there was nothing he could do at home.

'What are you doing? Are you sure you're alright?' Concern filled Róisín's voice.

'Not really,' Erin said, 'but that's not something I'm going to go into now. It doesn't matter now, with Dad being so sick.'

'Are you well?' Róisín jumped in quickly.

'Oh yes, physically, I'm fine,' she said, though the constant knot in her stomach and sleepless nights suggested otherwise. 'Don't worry about me. I'm coming home.'

'What's happened? Is Jack there?'

'No,' Erin said, fighting back the tears that had become her constant companion. 'When I come home, we'll grab a bottle of wine and go sit down by the billabong.'

'Sounds good to me.' Róisín's voice was gentler now, probing but careful. 'I'll text you Mum's motel details.'

After hanging up, Erin sat motionless, staring at nothing. Her father—the man who'd taught her to fish in the billabong, who'd held her hand at her mother's hospital bed when Bridget was born, who'd never quite approved of her choices but loved her fiercely anyway—was fighting for his life. And Jack was gone. Not physically, not yet, but sliding away from her with his enthusiastic message about Natalie and no "I love you."

The tears came then, hot and fast, streaming down her face as she curled into herself.

Too much. It was all too much.

Later, when the emotional storm had passed, leaving her hollow-eyed and empty, Erin made a decision. She texted Róisín: **Need time to process. Will stay in Wagga until we know more about Dad. Keep me posted. Love you.**

And then she sent a brief email to Jack, telling him what had happened. Maybe he'd come home? Maybe she'd get a reply?

Her heart lifted when the phone rang immediately after she sent the text.

But it wasn't the call she was hoping for.

'Hey, Erin, it's Jill. Want to catch another movie tonight after work? I'm going with a couple of girls from daycare. Aaron's home, and he's happy to be with the boys. Nothing heavy, just that new comedy.'

Disappointment flooded through her, and Erin's first instinct was to refuse. The thought of putting on a social face, making conversation, and pretending everything was normal when nothing would ever be normal again was too exhausting to contemplate.

'Thanks, but I don't think I'm up for it tonight,' she said quietly.

'No pressure. The offer stands if you change your mind. Seven o'clock at the Riverside cinema.'

After hanging up, Erin sat in the silence of the motorhome. The walls seemed to be closing in, saturated with memories of Jack. His favourite mug on the counter. The dent in the pillow where he slept. The jumper, which she still couldn't bring herself to wash, smelled like him.

The hours crawled by at IGA. When she came back to the

motorhome, Erin moved slowly, mechanically making tea she didn't drink and checking her phone for messages that didn't come. By early evening, the thought of another night alone with her spiralling thoughts became unbearable.

Her mind drifted back to their conversations before he left. Her fears about Africa had been fears of danger to him physically.

But now, with almost three weeks of silence stretching between them, those fears bubbled up again. What if something had happened? What if one of those magnificent, dangerous creatures had—

No. She pushed the thought away.

She called Jill back. 'Is that movie offer still open?'

'Absolutely. Meet you at the entrance?'

'I'll be there.'

The cinema was mercifully dark, allowing Erin to hide the worst of her red-rimmed eyes. Jill, to her credit, didn't press for details. She simply squeezed Erin's shoulder in greeting and bought her popcorn, which she couldn't taste.

'You doing okay?' she finally asked as they found their seats.

No, she wanted to say. My dad might be dying, and the man I love might be falling for someone else on another continent. I'm drowning in fears I can't even voice because saying them out loud might make them real.

'I'm fine,' she said instead. 'Just tired.'

Jill didn't look convinced, but she nodded. 'Remember, I'm here if you need me.'

As the lights dimmed and the screen flickered to life, Erin stared unseeing at the images before her. In her mind, she was with her father in that hospital room and simultaneously in

Africa, watching Jack photograph wildlife with Natalie at his side. Both scenarios filled her with a helplessness that settled in her chest like a stone.

Somewhere in the darkness, surrounded by laughter at jokes she couldn't hear, Erin wondered if this was what drowning felt like—this slow, inexorable sinking, unable to call for help because your lungs were already too full of water.

Chapter 8

Ceann Mara - August 1915.

Thomas O'Byrne's office smelled of leather, pipe tobacco, and worry. Gilbert stood by the window, watching shearers move across the yard—fewer men than there should have been, older faces where young ones used to be. Behind him, his father's chair creaked as Thomas leaned forward, fingers drumming a restless rhythm on the worn ledger before him.

'I don't like what I'm seeing here, Gilbert.' Thomas's voice was gravel-rough from years of shouting over shearing shed noise. 'Third month running we're behind on our quota.'

Gilbert turned from the window. His father looked older somehow, the lines around his eyes deeper than they'd been even six months ago. The worry of his mother being ill had taken its toll, but she had turned a corner and was getting stronger each day. The morning sun picked out the silver threading through his once-sandy hair—the same colour Gilbert had inherited.

'How bad is it?' Gilbert asked, moving to take the chair opposite the massive oak desk that had been his grandfather's before his father's.

Thomas rubbed his eyes. 'Bad enough. We're down to half our usual shearing team. Collins joined up last week, and both the Mitchell boys left yesterday.' He gestured towards the yard. 'Most of the men we have left are either too old or too vital to the station to enlist.'

The ledger lay open between them, columns of figures telling the story more eloquently than words could. Gilbert had grown up in this office, learning the business of wool alongside his schoolwork, understanding from an early age that their livelihood depended on those neat rows of numbers making sense.

'The young men are all gone to fight,' Thomas continued, his voice softening. 'Can't blame them. King and country calling and all that.'

'What about the wool prices?' Gilbert asked. 'You said last month they were rising.'

Thomas nodded, sitting back in his chair. 'Aye, they rose at first. Military needs wool for uniforms—good, strong Australian merino is what they want.' He sighed heavily. 'But getting it to market? That's another matter. German U-boats are making shipping a gamble. Some stations have wool sitting in warehouses that can't be moved.'

Gilbert watched his father's weathered hands close the ledger with a finality that spoke volumes. 'There's more, isn't there?'

'The government's stepped in.' Thomas stood, moving to the cabinet where he kept a bottle of whiskey for difficult conversations. 'New scheme as of last month. All wool now sold at a fixed price to the British government.' He poured two fingers into a glass, offering it to Gilbert. For the first time, he'd treated him as a man, not a boy. 'It keeps us afloat, but just barely. No chance to negotiate better prices when the market shifts.'

Gilbert accepted the glass but didn't drink. 'What can we do?'

Thomas gave a short, humourless laugh. 'Do? We keep going. What choice do we have? The O'Byrnes have weathered worse than this. My grandfather made it through droughts that would make this war look like a Sunday picnic.' He took a long sip from his own glass. 'We'll manage. Might have to sell off some of the north paddock if things get tighter, but we'll survive.'

Gilbert stared into the amber liquid in his glass. 'What about bringing in some of the Aboriginal workers from the mission? Or hiring women? I know the Wilsons have their daughters working the sheds now.'

'Already ahead of you,' Thomas nodded approvingly. 'Got some of the *Ngarrindjeri* men coming next week. And your mother's talking to the women in town.' He studied his son's face, a question forming in his eyes. 'Why the sudden interest in the station?'

Gilbert set his untouched glass on the desk. He'd rehearsed this conversation a dozen times, but now that the moment was here, the words stuck in his throat. 'Dad, I'm going to enlist.'

The silence that followed seemed to stretch for years. Thomas's face didn't change, but something shifted in his eyes—pride and pain warring for dominance.

'When?' Just one word, but it carried the weight of everything unsaid.

'I'll go down to Broken Hill when the shearing is finished.' Gilbert stood straighter, chin up the way his father had taught him when facing difficult things. 'As much as I'd like to stay and help here, I can't sit by while others fight. Not when I'm young and able. Matilda's brother, Cecil, is going to enlist too.'

Thomas moved from behind the desk, and for a moment, Gilbert thought his father might try to stop him. Instead, Thomas placed a hand on his shoulder, grip firm enough to anchor him to this moment, this place.

'Your grandfather would be proud,' he said finally. 'As am I.'

The weight of his father's hand on his shoulder, the unspoken worry in his eyes, the ledger of figures that wouldn't balance—Gilbert knew he would carry these images with him across oceans.

Chapter 9

Lobamba, Eswatini - late January.

The lowering African sun painted the savannah in shades of gold that made Jack's fingers reach for his camera. After two weeks, this landscape still overwhelmed him—the vastness of it, the raw wildness that made Australia's outback seem tame by comparison. Today's shoot had been particularly spectacular: a family of elephants at a watering hole, the matriarch standing guard while the calves played in the mud.

Jack had spent hours setting up the perfect shot, belly-down in the dirt, sweat trickling down his spine as he adjusted his lens millimetre by millimetre. The results had been worth it—the backlit spray of water as a young elephant tested its trunk, the texture of ancient wrinkled skin against the mirrored surface of the water, and the protective formation of the adults. Lars would be impressed.

But now, trudging back to the hotel with dust coating his boots and equipment, a hollow feeling settled in his chest. These were the moments he'd always shared with Erin   the triumph of capturing something extraordinary. Instead, he'd turned to Natalie, who'd nodded professionally and said, 'Good work, Jack. Lars will be pleased. There's a good market for shots like those.'

The small hotel lobby was mercifully cool after the day's heat. Jack headed straight for the antique desk where the manager had promised working internet tonight, a rare luxury in this remote corner of Eswatini.

'Any luck with the connection, Joseph?' he called to the

desk clerk.

Joseph gave him a thumbs up. 'Working now, Mr Hayes. For how long, who can say?'

Jack didn't waste time. He pulled out his laptop and connected, watching anxiously as his emails slowly downloaded. Two weeks had passed with barely any communication with Erin. The so-called satellite phone that Natalie had promised would keep them connected had never materialised, and the hotel's internet was sporadic at best.

The emails finally appeared, mostly work correspondence from Lars with additional location requests. But there, nestled between updates from the magazine, was Erin's name. His heart jumped, then plummeted as he read the brief message that had been sent a over a week ago:

Jack, Dad had a heart attack yesterday. They've taken him to Sydney for surgery. Doctors say the outlook is positive but serious. Will update when I can. Missing you. Love, Erin

'No, no, no,' Jack muttered, immediately hitting reply. His fingers flew across the keyboard:

Erin - just saw your message. I've had no service, phone or internet for two weeks. I'm so sorry about Tom. Let me know how he's doing as soon as you can. Communication here is terrible - nothing like what they promised. The satellite phone Natalie was supposed to bring isn't available. I've been trying to reach you. Missing you desperately. Give Tom my love when you see him. I love you. Jack

He hit send, watching anxiously as the progress bar inched across the screen. Just as it reached the end, the connection dropped.

'Damn it!' Jack slammed his hand against the desk.

'Connection gone?' Joseph asked sympathetically.

'Would my email have gone, do you think?'

Joseph looked sympathetic. 'No, Mr Hayes. I don't think it would have. Is it still in your outbox?'

'Yes.' Jack ran a hand through his dust-caked hair, frustration gnawing at him. Tom had a heart attack? Jack respected his father-in-law despite his disapproval. He was a good man. And Erin, dealing with the situation alone, waiting for him to call. Hopefully, she'd gone home to *Ceann Mara*. But then, there was probably no one there.

Damn it, he couldn't even call because there was no satellite phone.

'Problem with the internet again?' Natalie's cool voice cut through his thoughts as she descended the hotel stairs. As always, she looked immaculate despite the day in the field—not a blonde hair out of place, her safari outfit somehow managing to look stylish rather than functional.

'My father-in-law had a heart attack over a week ago,' Jack said bluntly. 'And I'm just finding out now because the communication here is shit.'

Something flickered across Natalie's perfect features— was it irritation? Or calculation? It was gone so quickly that Jack couldn't be sure.

'Oh, how awful,' she said, her voice softening as she placed a manicured hand on his arm. 'Is there anything I can do?'

'That satellite phone you said *Terra Lens* was providing would be helpful,' Jack couldn't keep the edge from his voice. 'The one you assured me would keep me connected no matter where we were.'

Natalie's expression turned apologetic, but her eyes remained cool. 'I told you, there was a mix-up with the equipment. Lars is still trying to sort it out with head office.'

Jack shook off her hand, frustration mounting. 'It's been two weeks, Natalie. If I'd known communication would be this bad, I never would have taken the assignment.'

'Don't be dramatic, Jack.' Her tone shifted, becoming brisk and professional again. 'This is *Terra Lens*. Photographers would kill for this opportunity.'

'Maybe,' Jack conceded, 'but I should have done my homework better. Asked more questions.' He picked up his camera bag, suddenly needing to be away from her. 'I'm going to try to call Erin from the radio in the office. Joseph said I might get through from there.'

'You don't have time. We have the sunset shoot at the ridge in an hour,' Natalie reminded him. 'Lars wants those silhouette shots for the conservation spread.'

'My father-in-law is in hospital,' Jack repeated slowly. 'I need to talk to my wife.'

'Of course.' Natalie's smile returned, warm and understanding, though it didn't reach her eyes. 'Family first. I'll push the shoot back an hour. The light might actually be better then, anyway.'

As she walked away, Jack realised he quite disliked Natalie. She was undeniably brilliant at her job, but beneath her efficiency lay a coldness, tempered by a calculated warmth that made him uncomfortable.

In their first week, he'd caught her watching him with an expression that reminded him of a series he'd once photographed: crocodiles—patient, assessing, waiting. When she noticed his attention, she immediately smiled and asked a technical question about his camera settings, all with professional interest and admiration.

Jack picked up his laptop and headed for the office. Two more weeks in the field, then back to the hotel for data editing, then another expedition to the mountain regions. The schedule stretched endlessly before him, and for the first time since arriving, the thrill of the assignment was overshadowed by what he'd left behind.

He missed Erin desperately—her laugh, and the way she genuinely cared about the stories behind his photographs rather than just their commercial potential. And now Tom was in the hospital; he was on another continent, unable to even offer the support a husband should.

'If you'd known, would you really have stayed behind?' he asked himself honestly. After leaving the office with no luck reaching home, Jack trudged back to his suite, his worry increasing. Tom could have died, and there'd be no way for Erin to reach him. He swiped his keycard and pushed open the door, immediately greeted by the blast of air conditioning against his sun-scorched skin.

He tossed his camera bag onto the plush armchair and stepped out onto the balcony, the contrast between luxury and wilderness still jarring. Erin would have loved this: the ornate ceiling fans, the local artwork adorning the walls, and the infinity pool that seemed to merge with the horizon at sunset. She would have snapped photos of the colourful birds sipping nectar from the flowering trees outside their window or sketched the patterns in the handwoven rugs covering the polished hardwood floors.

The extravagance made Jack uncomfortable, as it wasn't the adventure they'd planned together, roughing it in remote locations with their meagre savings. This was another world entirely, one that *Terra Lens* had arranged, and the luxury felt hollow without Erin's wonder-filled eyes seeing it too.

He checked his watch. Forty-five minutes until the sunset shoot. Just enough time to shower away the day's dust and try the hotel phone one more time, though he held little hope it would connect any better than his previous attempts.

As the water washed over him, Jack couldn't stop thinking about Tom in a hospital bed, and Erin facing it alone. What was he doing here, chasing elephants and perfect light, when the people who mattered to him were a world away?

Chapter 10

Wagga Wagga - mid-March.

February had flown by. Mum had been in contact every day, and worrying about Dad had left Erin less energy to worry about the lack of contact from Jack. Still no emails or messages. She'd tried to call, but the connection wouldn't go through. She'd Googled the country code and how to place a call, but in the end, she had to accept he was either out of range or had his phone turned off.

Finally, some good news arrived when Mum called to say Dad was coming home. Sydney to Broken Hill on a commercial flight, and then Róisín was flying the Cessna to Broken Hill to bring them home.

Jil had insisted that she borrow a car to make the quick visit to *Ceann Mara* to be there with the rest of her sisters when Mum and Dad arrived home.

'Take them, please, Erin. Seriously,' Jill urged, holding out her car keys. 'The motorhome will be fine in the park while you're gone.'

Erin stared at the keys in her friend's outstretched hand. 'It's dirt roads for the last hundred kilometres, Jill. Your Mazda doesn't deserve that.'

'I've seen how worried you are, sweetie. Just take it and go for as long as you need.' Jill pressed the keys into Erin's palm, closing her fingers around them. 'I can use our family car while Aaron's away. I don't need two cars.'

Erin opened her mouth to protest again, but Jill's expression stopped her. There was something about accepting help that felt like admitting weakness these days. As if needing anything from anyone was one more failure.

'Thank you,' she said finally, the words thick in her throat. 'I'll be careful with it.'

'I know you will.' Jill pulled her into a quick hug. 'Call me when you get there, okay? And if you need anything—'

'I'll be fine,' Erin said automatically.

Jill stepped back, her eyes searching Erin's face. 'Did Jack get back to you yet?'

His name sent a familiar pang through Erin's chest—not quite pain anymore, more like the ghost of it. 'Last week, finally,' she said, her voice flat. 'A text arrived.'

It had been the worst two months of Erin's life. Dad's heart attack, and total silence from Jack. The text had finally arrived, with no mention of her email about Dad's heart attack, no mention of when he would be home and worst of all, nothing personal in it.

The single text had sent her spirits plummeting. **We're here. Great shots today. Heading deeper into the wildlife reserve tomorrow. Might be out of range for a few days.**

No, "How's Tom?" Or no "I love you." No "I miss you." Just . . . information.

'Well, that's something, you got a text,' Jill said, clearly hoping for more details. When none came, she squeezed Erin's arm. 'Drive safe, okay?'

But reading it had been like watching a film with the sound turned down—Erin recognised the shapes of the words and understood their meaning but felt nothing, as if she were reading it through glass.

She'd read his text twice, waiting for the relief, the comfort, anything. When nothing came, she'd turned her phone off and gone to work, Jack's words echoing in the hollow space where her heart used to be.

***

Mkhaya Game Reserve

Jack sat on the veranda of their rented cottage, scrolling through the day's photographs as stars emerged in the African sky. The cottage—a sparse but comfortable structure on the edge of the Mkhaya Game Reserve, where he was much more at home—was their base for the week. The jagged silhouettes of acacia trees stood dark against the indigo horizon, and somewhere in the distance, a lion roared.

His fingers hesitated over a particular image—a mother elephant guiding her calf through golden grass at sunset, their elongated shadows stretching across the savannah. The composition was perfect, the light exactly what he'd hoped for when they'd set up the shoot. Lars would love it.

But as he studied it, an unexpected heaviness pressed on his chest. What would Erin say about it? She'd always had a way of seeing beyond the technical aspects of his work, finding stories in his photographs that even he hadn't recognised.

'That's a beauty,' Natalie's voice startled him as she appeared with two glasses of wine. She handed one to him before sitting in the adjacent chair. 'Lars will feature that prominently, I'm sure.'

'Thanks,' Jack said, accepting the wine but setting it aside untouched. He continued scrolling through images while Natalie sipped her drink, the silence between them growing awkward.

'You're quiet tonight,' she observed finally. 'Unhappy with the shoot?'

Jack shook his head. 'The shoot was fine. Great, actually.'

He paused, then admitted, 'I was just thinking how Erin would say these elephants remind her of the way the old matriarch elephants at Western Plains Zoo would walk with the calves between them for protection. She noticed that pattern the first time we went there.'

Natalie's expression tightened almost imperceptibly. 'Your wife has quite the eye.'

'She does.' Jack smiled faintly, remembering. 'We were at a zoo in Queensland once, and she spotted this interaction between two monkeys that I completely missed. I got the shot because of her, and it ended up winning a state competition.'

He scrolled to another image—a cheetah perched on a termite mound, scanning the horizon. 'She would have loved watching this one. When we travelled through the Kimberley, she'd sit for hours just observing. Said she needed to understand a place before she could write about it.'

The memory hit him with unexpected force—Erin's rapt expression as she watched a family of dingoes near a waterhole, the way she'd clutched his arm in excitement but stayed perfectly silent to avoid startling them. They'd sat there for two hours, neither of them speaking, just sharing the moment.

'I'm sure there will be many more assignments where she can join you,' Natalie said, her tone professionally sympathetic. 'Once you've established yourself properly with the magazine.'

Jack glanced at her, suddenly irritated by her responses. Everything about Natalie was calculated—her sympathy, her enthusiasm, even her casual touches that had become more frequent in recent weeks.

'I need to try calling her again,' he said abruptly, closing his laptop.

Natalie checked her watch. 'The office will be closed now. And you know the satellite connection is unreliable here anyway.'

'It's ridiculous that *Terra Lens* hasn't sorted out the communications issue,' Jack said, frustration edging his voice. 'Every time I ask about the satellite phone you mentioned before we left, there's a new excuse.'

'These things happen in remote locations,' Natalie replied smoothly. 'I've told Lars about it repeatedly.'

Jack stood, unable to sit still any longer. 'I'm going to try the hotel's main office. Maybe their landline is working.'

'Jack,' Natalie's voice stopped him at the door. 'We have the dawn shoot tomorrow. Rhinos at the watering hole. You should rest.'

He hesitated, torn between his professional obligations and the growing knot of anxiety in his chest. The rhino shoot was a rare opportunity—the local guide had promised perfect light and an almost guaranteed sighting.

'The rhinos will still be there if I get an hour's less sleep,' he decided. 'I need to at least to try to reach Erin.'

Walking down the dirt path towards the main lodge, Jack felt a strange sense of displacement. The African night was alive with unfamiliar sounds—insects he couldn't identify, birds calling in patterns he'd never heard before, the rustle of creatures moving through the underbrush. Under different circumstances, he would have enjoyed the new landscape, the adventure. Now, it only emphasised how far he was from home.

Home. The word caught him by surprise. When had he started thinking of anywhere as home? He and Erin had spent the past three years deliberately rootless, drifting from one beautiful location to another in their motorhome. Yet somehow, without his noticing, home had become wherever she was.

The lodge was quiet when he arrived, only the night manager on duty behind the reception desk.

'Excuse me,' Jack began, 'I need to make an international call. To Australia.'

The man looked up apologetically. 'I'm sorry, sir. The phones are down again. The lines were damaged in yesterday's storm.'

'But I was told they'd been repaired,' Jack protested.

'They were working earlier,' the manager explained, 'but they're out again now. Perhaps tomorrow?'

Tomorrow. Always tomorrow. Jack thanked him and stepped back outside, frustration churning inside him.

He pulled out his phone, checking again for service—nothing. On impulse, he opened his photo gallery, scrolling past the professional shots to his personal album. There was Erin beside their motorhome at Uluru, sunrise painting her skin gold. Erin laughing as she tried to surf at Byron Bay. Erin asleep with an open book on her chest, the evening light through the motorhome window creating a halo around her hair.

As he stared at the images, Jack realized with startling clarity that he couldn't remember the last time he'd felt truly excited about a photograph that didn't have her in it. His best work had always been when she was nearby, her presence somehow sharpening his eye, her enthusiasm fuelling his own.

What was he doing here, chasing recognition from strangers, when the person whose opinion he valued most couldn't even see his work?

A message alert suddenly chimed through the window of the bar—someone's phone connecting briefly to a service tower.

Jack looked up hopefully, but his own phone remained obstinately disconnected. Across the compound, he glimpsed Natalie through the window of her cottage, her face illuminated by her phone screen as she typed rapidly.

A cold suspicion began to form. Before he could examine it further, a staff member approached, flashlight bobbing.

'Sir, you shouldn't be out alone after dark. There are predators about. Let me escort you back to your cottage.'

Jack allowed himself to be guided back, his thoughts churning. Something wasn't right with this assignment. The isolation, the communication problems, Natalie's constant presence—it all felt increasingly manufactured, though he couldn't yet see the pattern clearly or a reason for it. His imagination was working overtime.

As he prepared for bed, Jack made a decision. After the rhino shoot tomorrow, he would insist they return to the main city. From there, he would find a way to contact Erin, with or without *Terra Lens'* assistance. This lack of communication had gone on long enough.

In the darkness of his room, Jack picked up his wallet from the nightstand and removed a small photograph—Erin at the billabong on *Ceann Mara*, the place she loved most in the world. He'd kept it with him throughout their travels, a private talisman.

'I miss you,' he whispered to the image. 'More than I thought possible.'

For the first time since arriving in Africa, Jack acknowledged the truth he'd been avoiding: no photograph, no assignment, no professional recognition was worth the growing distance between them.

Chapter 11

Ceann Mara - mid-March.

The journey from Wagga to *Ceann Mara* spanned over six hundred kilometres, cutting through the heart of western New South Wales. In the past, Erin had loved this drive—the gradual transformation of the landscape from the lush Riverina to the stark beauty of the outback, the isolated towns that appeared like mirages on the horizon, the vast blue sky pressing down on the red earth.

Today, she barely noticed any of it.

The distance disappeared quickly as she drove Jill's car, kilometre after kilometre of asphalt giving way to gravel, then dirt. Erin drove mechanically, stopping only when the fuel gauge indicated it was getting close to empty. Near Cobar, she pulled over at a roadhouse, automatically ordering a coffee she didn't finish and a sandwich she couldn't taste.

An elderly couple at the next table were huddled over a map, planning their journey with the kind of excited anticipation that comes with retirement adventures. The woman's laugh carried across the nearly empty café—a free, happy sound that made Erin flinch. She'd laughed like that once, planning routes with Jack, both of them giddy with the freedom of the open road and each other.

'You okay, love?' The waitress appeared with her coffee; concern etched in the lines around her eyes. 'You look a bit peaky.'

'Fine,' Erin managed. 'Just a long drive.'

'Where you headed?'

'*Ceann Mara*. Family property.'

'Going home then,' the waitress nodded. 'That's good. Nothing like family when you're feeling rough.'

Erin didn't correct her. What would be the point? How could she explain that home no longer felt like somewhere she belonged, but rather a place she was returning to because there was nowhere else to go?

Back on the road, the landscape grew increasingly arid. Dry brown grass plains stretched to the horizon, broken only by the occasional stand of scraggly gum trees. Dust devils danced across the flats, whirling columns of red dirt that appeared and disappeared quickly. Dozens of goats, many with twins and triplets, ran off the road as she approached, and in the distance, a wedge-tailed eagle soared on thermal currents, a solitary hunter against the endless sky.

The beauty of it all—the harsh, uncompromising splendour of the outback—registered somewhere in Erin's mind but couldn't penetrate the numbness that had settled over her like a shroud.

By the time she turned onto the familiar red dust road leading to *Ceann Mara*, the sun was low in the sky, painting the landscape in shades of gold and purple. The homestead appeared as it always had—a solid presence against the darkening sky, welcoming lights glowing in the windows like beacons.

Róisín was the first to spot her, rushing down the veranda steps as Erin pulled up. 'You made it!' she called, her smile wide and genuine. 'How was the drive?'

'Long,' Erin said, accepting her sister's hug with arms that felt like they belonged to someone else. 'How's Dad?'

'Getting stronger every day. They'll be back tomorrow.' Róisín stepped back, her gaze sharpening as she took in Erin's appearance. 'You look exhausted. And you've lost weight too.'

'I have,' Erin admitted. It was the most honest thing she'd said in days.

Cat appeared in the doorway, her smile faltering slightly as she saw Erin. 'Where's Jack?'

The question hit Erin like a physical blow. She hadn't prepared herself for it, hadn't thought about what she would say when her family inevitably asked about her husband's absence.

'Not back yet,' she said, her voice hollow.

Cat's eyes narrowed. 'Back from where?'

'He's in Africa.' Her words hung in the still evening air.

'Africa?' Cat exclaimed, eyes widening. 'Why?'

'A contract with a magazine,' Erin explained mechanically, as if reciting a script.

'Why didn't you go too?' Róisín asked gently, her voice carefully neutral.

'We can't afford it,' Erin replied with a tired smile that felt like a grimace. 'My job at IGA in Wagga goes towards paying off the motorhome.'

She could see the questions forming in her sisters' eyes— why hadn't she mentioned he was away for so long? Why was she alone? Why did she look like she hadn't slept properly in weeks?

'Can we do this later?' Erin asked, suddenly feeling as if her legs might give out. 'I'd really like to lie down.'

'Of course,' Róisín said quickly. 'Your bed's made up. Mum's been in Sydney with Dad, but she'll be so glad you're here.'

Erin nodded, gathering what little energy she had left to climb the steps and navigate the familiar hallway to her childhood bedroom. The room was exactly as she'd left it years ago—the same faded blue curtains, the same quilt, the same bookshelves lined with the adventure novels of her youth.

She sank onto the bed, not bothering to undress or draw back the covers. Sleep claimed her immediately, a black, dreamless void that was the closest thing to peace she'd found in weeks.

##

'Want to talk about it now?' Cat's voice was firm.

Erin looked up from the campfire they'd built near the billabong. Night had fallen, the Southern Cross bright against the velvet darkness. She'd slept for four hours straight, waking disoriented in the dark to find her sisters had left her to rest. Shea and Bridget had gone to bed; Cat had left a note on her door telling her to come to the billabong when she woke up.

'Not really,' she said, prodding the embers with a stick.

Róisín exchanged a glance with Cat. 'You know we're worried about you, right? This isn't like you, Erin.'

'What isn't?'

'This . . .' Cat gestured vaguely at Erin. 'Whatever's going on with you and Jack. Why didn't you tell us he was in Africa? And why do you look like you haven't eaten in weeks?'

Erin stared into the fire. The truth hovered on her tongue— *I think he's falling for someone else*—but she couldn't bring herself to speak it aloud. Saying it would make it real, and she wasn't ready for that yet.

'It's nothing,' she said instead. 'Just stress about Dad, and work, and Jack still being away.'

'For how long?' Róisín asked.

'I'm not sure. At least until the end of next month.' The words tasted bitter.

'That's a long time,' Cat said carefully. 'When did he leave?'

'January. It was organised very quickly. When he signed the contract.'

The fire crackled in the silence that followed. Above them, a shooting star traced a brief, brilliant arc across the sky—the kind of sight Jack would have tried to capture with his camera—the kind of moment they would have shared.

'I'm fine, really,' Erin said, unable to bear the concern in her sisters' eyes. 'Tell me about you two. What's been happening here?'

It was a transparent attempt to change the subject, but her sisters allowed it. Cat discussed the wedding plans, her voice growing soft as she mentioned Logan. Róisín was quieter, sharing less, until Cat nudged her.

'Tell her about Seth,' Cat urged. 'And everything else that happened.'

Róisín hesitated, then began speaking in a low voice about the past weeks—her kidnapping, the terror, the uncertainty, finding her way back to herself and, eventually, to Seth.

As Erin listened, her problems receded slightly, replaced by horror at what her sister had endured. Yet even as she reached out to hold Róisín's hand, part of her couldn't help but notice the way Róisín's eyes lit up when she spoke of Seth, the quiet confidence in her voice when she talked about their future.

The same way Cat glowed when mentioning Logan. The same connection Erin had once felt with Jack—a certainty, a belonging, a rightness that made everything else fall into place.

Now, watching her sisters, seeing the love they'd found, Erin felt like an intruder. Their happiness reflected her emptiness, and she couldn't bear it a second longer.

'I should go back,' she said abruptly, standing. 'To Wagga, I mean. I have shifts on the weekend.'

'What?' Cat looked up, startled. 'You just got here this afternoon.'

'I know, but I can't afford to lose the hours.' The lie came easily. 'Now that I know Dad's okay and Mum's fine, I should get back.'

'Hang on, just one moment, Erin.' Róisín reached out and took her hand again. Erin looked down at her sister's hand, and emotion welled up and stuck in her throat. She couldn't move.

'We're going to ask you outright because we've been skirting around the issue,' Cat said, staring at her. 'Have you and Jack split up?'

Erin gasped. 'What? No. Why would you think—'

'Because you've been acting weird since you arrived. You look like someone's repeatedly punched you in the heart. You barely speak, and half the time you don't listen when we do.' Cat folded her arms. 'Something's wrong, and you're not talking about it.'

Erin stared at her sisters, feeling the careful walls she'd built begin to crumble. 'It's . . . complicated.'

'We've got time,' Róisín said, pointing to the camp chair that Erin had vacated. 'Sit and talk.'

And somehow, by the billabong in front of the crackling fire, Erin found herself telling her sisters everything—Jack's sudden assignment, the almost total lack of communication, and her spiralling doubts and fears about Natalie.

'I keep telling myself it's nothing,' she finished, her voice hoarse. 'That I'm overreacting. But something is wrong. Different. Like he's slipping away from me across all those kilometres. If we could just talk.'

Cat and Róisín listened without interrupting, and then Cat snorted. 'Oh, come on, Erin. It's Africa, for God's sake. Communication is the issue. Do you think you're overreacting? Jack adores you.'

'You don't understand—'

'No, I think I do.' Róisín leaned forward. 'You're scared. This is the first time you've been apart since you met. And you never got over Jacob Williams dropping you like he did. He did a huge number on your self-esteem. Of course this feels weird and awful. And maybe this Natalie person is a supermodel photographer who's throwing herself at him, or maybe it's your vivid imagination, I don't know. But I do know Jack. I've seen how he looks at you, how he's built his entire life around making you happy. And he took this opportunity to make some money, so you two could settle. Do you really think he'd abandon you?'

Cat looked at her and shook her head. 'Jeez, Erin. Get a grip.'

Embarrassment, doubt, hope, and confusion all churned through Erin. Tears filled her eyes. 'Then why am I doubting him? Maybe I don't have what it takes for a marriage to work when I crash at the first hurdle? The same weakness I had when Jacob dumped me.'

Róisín's expression softened. 'Because love is terrifying? Because trusting someone means giving them the power to break your heart?' She leaned forward closer to the fire and threw another small log onto it. 'But you don't throw away a good thing because you're scared it might end. That's like . . . I don't know, burning down your house because you're afraid of fires.'

Despite everything, Erin felt a laugh bubble up inside.

'That's the worst analogy I've ever heard.'

'Maybe,' Róisín grinned. 'But am I wrong?'

Erin thought about Jack—his gentle patience when teaching her photography, his unwavering support of her writing, the way his face lit up when she entered a room. She thought about their dreams together, the life they'd planned.

'I don't know,' she admitted. 'I just . . . I need to hear his voice. I need to see him. To know that we're still . . . us. I need to know he's coming home to me.'

'Then call him,' Cat said simply. 'Have you tried recently?'

'I've tried heaps of times with no success. I don't know if it's the phone service or if he's switched his phone off.'

Róisín shook her head in disbelief. 'Or maybe there's no service, or no electricity out in the wild to charge a phone?'

'Have you called the magazine office?' Cat asked.

'No, I haven't.'

'Do you have the number? '

'I do.'

'I can't believe you haven't called them, Erin. When did he leave?'

'January.'

Her sister rolled her eyes.

'Do it. You'll get reassurance, I'm sure. Just explain you can't get in touch with him. They must have a way of contacting them.'

'Jack said they would have a satellite phone.'

'Well, call and they might put you through.'

'I will!'

'Trust him.'

'Please don't leave. Stay until tomorrow,' Róisín urged. 'Dad would be devastated if you left without seeing him.'

'I promised Jill I'd have her car back quickly, but okay, one more day,' Erin said, the lie sitting heavy in her stomach. Her sisters had given her a lot to think about. She'd call the magazine as soon as she got back to Wagga.

##

The next day, Róisín flew the Cessna to Broken Hill to collect Mum and Dad. As Erin helped her sisters prepare for the welcome-home barbecue in the camp kitchen, she found herself going through the motions mechanically.

She busied herself with tasks, trying to ignore the significant glances her sisters exchanged when they thought she wasn't looking. She knew they were concerned, but she couldn't bear their questions, their well-meaning worry.

The truth was, there had been no contact from Jack since she'd emailed him about Dad's heart attack.

'Erin? You with us?' Bridget's voice pulled her from her thoughts.

'Sorry,' she said, forcing a smile. 'Just thinking about Dad. It'll be good to see him home.'

Shea caught her eye, and Erin knew her sister wasn't fooled. Of all of them, Shea had always been the most perceptive, the sister who could see beneath the surface.

She turned her attention to the welcome banner that Shea and Bridget had put up, making sure it hung straight. She would smile and celebrate her father's recovery. She would deflect questions about Jack with practised ease. She would pretend everything was fine because admitting otherwise meant that the wandering life she'd built with Jack, the dreams they'd shared, might be ending before they'd truly begun.

When the Cessna flew over, Cat and Logan drove to the

airstrip to meet them. The sound of the Landcruiser approaching from the airstrip brought her back to the present, and Erin stood beside Bridget and Shea as Logan helped a visibly thinner, yet smiling, Tom from the passenger seat.

Erin swallowed hard at the sight of him—her strong, stubborn father, suddenly looking older, more fragile. He caught sight of her, and his face lit up, making her heart twist with guilt at her plans to leave so soon.

'There's my wanderer,' he said after he'd hugged Bridget and Shea, amidst many tears. 'Come here, love.'

Erin stepped into his arms, and his hug was weaker than she remembered, but the familiar scent of him—leather, Old Spice, and the indefinable smell of *Ceann Mara* that seemed to permeate everything here—brought tears to her eyes.

'Dad,' she whispered against his shoulder. 'I was so worried about you. We all were.'

'Takes more than a ticker hiccup to keep me down,' he said gruffly, though she felt him lean on her slightly as they walked inside. 'Now, when's Jack coming to visit? It's been too long since I gave him a hard time about his city ways.'

Erin forced a smile. 'He's actually away. In Africa. Wildlife photography for a magazine.'

Tom's eyebrows rose. 'Africa? When's he back?'

'A while yet,' Erin said vaguely. 'Work's keeping me busy in Wagga in the meantime.'

Dinner passed in a blur of conversation Erin barely followed, her mind already on the drive back, the emptiness waiting for her in Wagga, the uncertainty beyond that. She helped clean up and went to her room. She was up at dawn, packed her small bag, and found Dad on the veranda, watching the sun rise over the river with the contentment of a man returned home observing his land.

'Heading off, then?' he asked as she approached.

'Work,' she said, the excuse sounding thin even to her own ears.

Tom studied her face. 'Everything okay with you, love? You don't seem yourself. And you've lost weight.'

For a moment, Erin considered telling him everything, but the concern in Dad's eyes stopped her. Her father was recovering from a heart attack. The last thing he needed was to worry about her.

'Just tired,' she said instead. 'And worried about you. But now that I've seen you're on the mend, I'll sleep better.'

He reached for her hand, his grip stronger than she expected. 'You know you can always come home, Erin. For any reason. Or no reason at all.'

The simple kindness in his voice nearly broke her. 'I know, Dad. I'll be back for the wedding in a few short weeks.'

'*You* will? If that husband of yours has taken off—' There was a warning in his tone that told Erin he sensed more than she was letting on.

'I'm fine,' she interrupted. 'And Jack's fine. I meant *we* will. We're just adjusting to being apart . . . with the difficulty of poor communication. It's great, and it's going to set us up financially.' Even to her ears, her voice sounded hollow.

Tom nodded, clearly unconvinced but unwilling to push. 'Drive safe. Call when you get there.'

Erin kissed his weathered cheek, breathing in the scent of home one more time. 'I will. Take care of yourself, okay? Listen to the doctors. And Mum.'

'No promises.' He grinned, looking more like himself. 'But

I'll try.'

As she drove away, watching *Ceann Mara* recede in the rear-view mirror, Erin felt the numbness creeping back, settling around her like a protective skin. Ahead lay Wagga, and beyond that—nothing she could see clearly—just an emptiness where her future with Jack had once been.

The outback stretched around her, indifferent to her pain. Somewhere in Africa, Jack was photographing wildlife, building his career, perhaps building a life that no longer included her.

Chapter 12

Wagga Wagga -March.

Erin stopped to drop Jill's car off as soon as she got back to Wagga, but there was no one at home. She sent a quick text to Jill, who replied immediately, asking her to put the keys inside the back screen door.

Erin did as she asked and then walked to the caravan park. It was good to open the door of the motorhome and sink onto the sofa; it had been a long drive home, and her excitement at calling the magazine had grown with every kilometre she drove. Pulling out her phone, she dialled the number of the magazine's Sydney office.

'*Terra Lens*, how may I direct your call?' The receptionist's voice was cheerful and polished.

'Hi, I'm trying to reach Jack Hayes. He's one of your photographers on assignment.' Erin kept her voice steady, professional.

'One moment please, I'll transfer you to the photography department.'

Classical music played for almost a minute before another voice answered. 'Photography, this is Melissa.'

'Hello, I'm trying to reach Jack Hayes. This is his wife, Erin. He's currently on assignment and I need to get in touch with him.' Erin stood, pacing back and forth along the river path, one eye on her phone's signal bars.

'Jack Hayes? Let me check our schedule.' The sound of typing filled the line. 'Yes, he's part of the team in the field this week. I'll transfer you to Editorial Projects. They'll have more information.'

This week!

Before Erin could object, she was listening to the same instrumental music again. Her resolve was beginning to falter, but she forced herself to stay calm. This was about getting answers, not letting her emotions take over.

'Editorial Projects, this is Dev.'

'Hi Dev, I've been transferred twice already. I'm trying to locate Jack Hayes. He's a photographer with your magazine, and I need to know exactly where he is and if he's alright.' The edge in her voice was becoming harder to conceal.

'Jack Hayes . . .' More typing. 'He's in Africa. You'll want to speak with Assignments. Let me put you through.'

I know he's in bloody Africa.

'Wait—' But music was already playing on the line again.

Erin checked the time—she'd been on the phone for nearly ten minutes and was no closer to an answer. She considered hanging up, but the thought of another night wondering was worse than this frustrating runaround.

'Assignments, Kate speaking.'

'Kate, hi. I'm trying to locate Jack Hayes. He's a photographer with your magazine, currently in Africa, and I need to know where he is and if he's alright. I've been transferred three times now.' Erin couldn't keep the frustration from her voice any longer.

'I'm sorry, who am I speaking with?'

'Erin O'Byrne-Hayes, his wife—' She hesitated. 'I'm having trouble contacting him.'

There was a pause, and Erin could hear muffled voices as if Kate had covered the receiver with her hand. When she returned, her tone was more formal.

'Erin, I can only tell you what's in our system. The team is currently in the Lobamba Conservation Area doing a feature on endangered species.'

'But are they alright? Is Jack alright?'

'We've been receiving photographs by email.' Kate replied, her voice neutral.

'Can you get a message to him? It's important.'

'I'm sorry, he's not taking calls this week. He's in meetings with the conservation team and local officials.'

'Jack is? I think you have the wrong person. Meetings? In a conservation area?' Erin questioned, finding the explanation increasingly suspicious. 'What about a satellite phone?'

'Yes, they have a satellite phone. That's all the information I have, Mrs Hayes.' Kate's tone made it clear the conversation was concluding. 'Would you like to leave a message?'

Defeated, Erin simply asked Kate to tell Jack to pass on a message for Jack to call her as soon as possible. As she ended the call, the knot in her stomach had only tightened. That was the most unsatisfactory and evasive conversation she could have imagined. They had a satellite phone over there. And photos were being sent to the office in Sydney. Was Jack purposely avoiding contact? She took a deep breath. It was clear that her sisters had been wrong, and her instincts were right.

Despite her doubts, she forced herself to send a brief chatty email, telling him she'd been home and Dad was recovering.

When she pressed send, Erin closed her laptop and put her hands over her face.

Chapter 13

Lobamba, Eswatini - late March.

Fireflies danced outside the lodge window, their intermittent glow punctuating the African darkness. Inside, Jack sat on the edge of his bed, scrolling through the images from the day's shoot. His finger paused over a photo of a child from the village—a boy of about seven, his face alight with joy as he played with a homemade toy fashioned from wire and bottle caps.

Something about the image transported Jack back three years, to a moment he hadn't thought about in months.

Broken Hill, January 2022

The mid-summer heat was oppressive, the kind that seemed to press down from above and radiate up from the baked earth simultaneously. Their motorhome's air conditioning had given up the ghost two days earlier, and they'd pulled into the caravan park outside Broken Hill in desperate need of shade and a cold shower.

Jack sat at the small folding table, staring at his laptop screen with growing dismay. The email from the Brisbane photography exhibition was polite but final: his submission had not been selected. Third rejection this month.

He closed the laptop with more force than necessary, prompting Erin to look up from her book.

'Bad news?' she asked, already knowing the answer from his expression.

'Brisbane said no. Apparently, my work lacks distinctive

perspective.' The bitterness in his voice surprised even him.

Erin set her book aside and moved to sit across from him. 'I'm sorry, Jack. Their loss.'

He shook his head, frustration overwhelming him. 'Maybe everyone's right. My dad, your dad—maybe photography really is just a hobby I'm taking too seriously.'

'Hey.' Erin's voice was firm. 'Look at me.'

When he met her eyes, the absolute certainty he saw there caught him off guard.

'Your work isn't just good, Jack. It's extraordinary. Those judges, they're looking at technical skill and composition, but they're missing what makes your photographs special.' She reached for his camera, scrolling through recent images. 'You see things other people don't notice—not just beauty, but meaning.'

She stopped on a photo he'd taken yesterday—an elderly Aboriginal man sitting outside the local store, his weathered face in profile, eyes focused on something distant.

'This,' she said softly. 'Do you know why this image works? Because you waited. I watched you. Most people would have taken the shot when he was facing the camera, but you waited until he looked away, until you captured what he was seeing, not just what he looked like.'

Jack stared at the image, seeing it through her eyes.

'You don't just photograph subjects, Jack. You photograph moments, connections, and stories. That's rare.' She reached across the table, taking his hand. 'The right people will recognise that eventually. Until then, I'm not going anywhere.'

That night, they'd spread a blanket on the hood of the motorhome and lay beneath the vast outback sky, counting shooting stars until dawn broke. Jack had taken a single photograph with his phone—Erin asleep against his shoulder, starlight in her hair. It remained one of his favourite images, though he'd never submitted it to any competition. Some photographs weren't meant to be shared.

The memory faded as Jack returned to the present, to the African lodge and the day's images. Erin had been right—six months later, *Terra Lens* had contacted him.

She had believed in him when he couldn't believe in himself. And how had he repaid that faith? By leaving her behind, by prioritising this assignment over their relationship, by allowing himself to be manipulated into isolation.

The past three months had passed in locations where there was no opportunity to email or phone home. He'd been naïve in accepting this contract; he should have looked into it more than he had. Jack had emailed Erin every week, but was unsure if any had reached her. He hadn't had a reply from her for weeks. He still didn't even know how Tom was or where she was. At times, he felt like pulling the pin, but the one time he'd mentioned that to Natalie, her response had been chilling.

'You break the contract; you don't get paid.'

The promised satellite phone had never arrived, and they had spent most of the time in isolated locations with no Wi-Fi.

A knock at his door interrupted these thoughts. He opened it to find Natalie standing there, a bottle of wine in one hand and two glasses in the other. She'd changed since dinner, her practical field clothes replaced by a loose sundress that dipped low in front.

'Thought you might want to celebrate,' she said, moving past him into the room without waiting for an invitation. An overpowering scent of musky perfume surrounded him. 'Lars loved the waterhole sequence we sent yesterday. Said it's exactly what they wanted for the opening spread.'

'*You* sent. So, tell me, Natalie. How are you managing to talk to Lars?'

Her eyes widened. 'There was a brief window of service on my laptop while you were shooting today. I managed to download a couple of emails. You of all people know how bad the service is.'

'I do.' Jack remained by the open door, his posture deliberately unwelcoming and his tone cold. 'That's good news, but it's late, Natalie. Can we discuss this tomorrow?'

She set the glasses on the small table and began opening the wine. 'Come on, Jack. We've earned a little relaxation. The schedule's been brutal.' She glanced up, her smile perfect, but contrived. 'Besides, I thought you might want some company tonight.'

The invitation in her tone was unmistakable. Anger surged through Jack—not at her advances, which had been building for weeks, but at his own blindness. How had he not seen this coming?

'I'm married,' he said, his voice even but firm.

Natalie laughed lightly. 'To a woman half a world away, who you haven't spoken to in what—weeks?' She poured the wine, her movements fluid and confident. 'Long-distance relationships rarely survive these assignments, Jack. You wouldn't be the first.'

Another memory surfaced, sharp and clear.

Townsville, September 2022

The hospital corridor was too bright, the fluorescent lights harsh against the institutional beige walls. Jack paced outside the emergency department, his heart hammering against his ribs as he waited for news.

Three hours earlier, Erin had fallen while climbing to photograph a waterfall. The sound of her cry, the sight of her crumpled at the base of the rocks—those memories wouldn't leave him.

'Mr. Hayes?' A doctor emerged from the swinging doors. 'Your wife is asking for you.'

Erin lay on the hospital bed, her face pale but her eyes clear. A bandage wrapped around her forearm, and a nasty bruise was forming along her jawline.

'Hey, you,' she said, attempting a smile that turned into a wince.

Jack took her uninjured hand, squeezing gently. 'Don't you ever scare me like that again.'

'It's just a sprained wrist and some bruises,' she assured him. 'Though I think my pride took the worst beating.'

'I don't care about the waterfall shot,' Jack said fiercely. 'I care about you. We'll find another waterfall—a shorter one. Or we'll skip waterfalls entirely. No photograph is worth risking you.'

Erin's eyes softened. 'It wasn't your fault, Jack. I was the one who insisted on climbing higher.'

'I should have stopped you.'

'Since when have you been able to stop me doing anything?' she teased gently.

That night, Jack slept in the uncomfortable hospital chair beside her bed, unwilling to leave her side even after the nurses assured him she was fine. When he woke with a stiff neck at dawn, he found Erin watching him, her eyes filled with something he couldn't quite name.

'What?' he asked, self-conscious under her gaze.

'I was just thinking,' she said softly, 'that I've never felt safer than when I'm with you. Even here.' She gestured to the sterile hospital room.

Jack understood then what he was seeing in her eyes— absolute trust. It humbled him, made him vow silently to always be worthy of that trust.

'I'm not interested, Natalie,' Jack said, moving to the door and holding it open pointedly. 'Please leave.'

Her expression hardened, the practiced warmth vanishing. 'Don't be silly, Jack. We're both adults here. What happens in Africa can stay in Africa.'

'That's not who I am,' Jack replied, his voice steady. 'And if that's what you think of me, you don't know me at all.'

Natalie studied him for a moment, calculation evident in her gaze. When she spoke, her tone had shifted to something colder, more professional. 'You're making a mistake. This assignment is just the beginning of what *Terra Lens* can offer you. Lars values photographers who understand how things work in this industry.'

The implied threat was clear, but Jack found he didn't care. 'I value my marriage more than any assignment. Now, please leave.'

For a brief moment, something like genuine surprise flickered across Natalie's features. Then her professional mask returned as she gathered the wine bottle, leaving the untouched glasses behind.

'We'll discuss the schedule for tomorrow at breakfast,' she said briskly, as if the previous conversation hadn't happened. 'Six a.m. sharp.'

After she left, Jack closed the door and leaned against it, a strange sense of clarity washing over him. He'd been drifting for weeks, caught between professional ambition and personal loyalty, but in this moment, the path forward seemed suddenly obvious.

He moved to the desk, retrieving a worn leather wallet from his backpack. Inside was a photograph he kept separate from his professional work—Erin on their wedding day. Not the formal portrait, but a candid moment he'd captured with his phone after the ceremony: Erin laughing, her face tilted towards the sun, a wildflower tucked behind her ear.

Another memory surfaced, perhaps the most important of all.

Darwin, November 2022

They stood in the park overlooking the harbour near Government House, the afternoon sun turning the usually brown water to liquid gold. Darwin wasn't where either of them had imagined getting married—they'd only been passing through on their way to Kakadu National Park—but something about the wildness of the place, the sense of standing at the edge of something vast and untamed, felt right.

No family, no friends, just two people who had found each other and decided that was enough.

The celebrant, a local woman with kind eyes and an easy smile, asked them to exchange vows. They hadn't prepared anything formal, preferring to speak from the heart.

Erin went first, her voice steady despite the tears

shimmering in her eyes. 'Jack, I promise to be your partner in all things—to support your dreams as fiercely as my own, to stand beside you through whatever life brings, and to always find my way back to you, no matter how far we roam.'

When Jack's turn came, the words he'd planned seemed suddenly inadequate. Instead, what emerged was simpler, truer:

'Erin, before I met you, I was always searching for the perfect shot, the right light, the next destination. I thought happiness was somewhere out there, waiting to be discovered.' He gestured towards the horizon. 'But you showed me that home isn't a place. It's a person. You're my home, Erin. And I promise I will never forget that, no matter where life takes us.'

Later, as they watched the sunset from the small balcony of their rented room, Erin had asked him, 'Do you think we're crazy? Doing this without our families, without a plan for what comes next?'

Jack had pulled her close, breathing in the scent of her hair. 'Maybe. But it's our kind of crazy. And whatever comes next, we'll face it together.'

Chapter 14

Wagga Wagga - late April.

The weeks passed. March's warm mornings gave way to the chill of April. The willows and poplars along the river turned golden, carpeting the riverbank with fallen leaves that reminded Erin of confetti. Wedding confetti. Cat and Logan's wedding was fast approaching, and with it, the worry that maybe Jack mightn't be there. She had no idea how many extra weeks he was going to be away.

The rhythms of her daily life gradually filled the empty spaces in her days, bringing a semblance of normality to her life. Morning shifts at IGA, afternoon writing sessions at the library, evenings with Jill and her new friends from work—the routine became a lifeline, something to cling to when thoughts of Jack threatened to pull her under.

Never any contact. No emails, no texts, no calls. Her thoughts varied from the logical: there was no way for him to call me, to the terrifying: he doesn't want to call me because he knows I would pick up his feelings from his voice. She began to believe the latter; she hadn't sent a text or an email to Jack for a month.

What was the point?

During a talk with Jill one afternoon over coffee, Erin finally admitted she was depressed. She could feel herself spiralling down to the terrible place she'd been in before she met Jack. She made an appointment and went to a local GP, but after a long discussion, had refused his suggestions of medication and visiting a psychologist, determined to fight her way to health again.

I'm an O'Byrne. We're strong women, and I will heal myself, was her new daily affirmation.

Think about what Róisín and Cat have been through in the last year.

Her bank account grew steadily, each deposit satisfying her. Often, alone and awake in the motorhome at night, she would check the savings app, finding a measure of comfort in the increasing balance. Financial independence had never been her goal—she and Jack had always pooled their resources, dreams, and struggles—but now it felt like an insurance policy against a future she couldn't quite imagine.

'You're our fastest scanner,' Jeff, her manager, remarked one busy Friday afternoon in late May, when the checkout lines stretched to the back of the store. 'I could use two more like you.'

Erin offered a small smile, her hands continuing the practised movements across the barcode reader.

Beep, bag, repeat. There was something comforting about the monotony, tasks that required just enough focus to quiet her mind but not so much that she couldn't function through the fog of her emotions.

'Are you taking anyone to your sister's fancy wedding?' Jeff asked one night after their shift, as a group of them gathered at the local pub.

'Just myself,' Erin replied, stirring her lemonade with practised nonchalance.

'Where's that husband of yours again? Kazakhstan? Timbuktu?' He'd taken to joking about Jack's absence, unaware of how each comment landed like a blade between her ribs.

'Africa,' she said, the word still strange on her tongue after all this time. 'Still on assignment.'

Jill shot Jeff a warning look, changing the subject with the concern of true friendship. Later, walking Erin back to the caravan park, she linked their arms together.

'Ignore Jeff,' she said quietly. 'He doesn't understand what you're going through.'

'Sometimes I don't either,' Erin admitted.

In the quiet hours between work and sleep, Erin wrote. The novel she'd started two years ago—a Scottish historical romance inspired by Dad's research—had been little more than an idea and a few scattered scenes. Now, it became her sanctuary. The problems of her fictional MacNeil family were simpler, and their paths to happiness were clearer. In this logical world, love conquered distance, misunderstandings were resolved with heartfelt conversations, and happy endings were guaranteed. In a way, it helped her examine her feelings.

'This is really good,' Jill said one Sunday afternoon, returning the printed chapters Erin had hesitantly shared. 'I want to know what happens to Andrew and Flora's family.'

'So do I,' Erin admitted with her first genuine smile in weeks.

Her calls home became more frequent. Dad's enthusiastic updates about his family history research became a strange comfort, his voice strengthening with each conversation as his recovery progressed.

'We're still looking for Gilbert's war records,' he announced one evening, his disappointment palpable even across the distance. 'But no luck.'

'Tell me more,' Erin encouraged, curling up on the motorhome's small couch, the familiar sound of her father's historical detective work washing over her like a balm.

These small connections—to her family, to Jill, and to her characters—began to rebuild her confidence. Not whole, not yet, but no longer in chaos.

'Now, I sometimes forget to check if Jack's emailed when I wake up,' she confessed to Jill one evening as they shared a bottle of wine at Jill's kitchen table.

'Is that good or bad?' Jill asked, refilling their glasses.

'I don't know,' Erin replied honestly. 'Both, maybe. The three months is almost up, and hopefully he'll soon email to tell me when he's on the way home. Cat's wedding is only a couple of weeks away.'

Chapter 15

African Wilderness - mid-April.

The African night pressed close around their camp, alive with chirping crickets and the distant howls of hyenas. Jack sat by the fire, watching the flames dance against the vast darkness of the savannah. Behind their camp, the acacia trees stood like sentinels against the star-strewn sky, their twisted shapes black against the light of the full moon. The air was thick with the scent of smoke and wild sage, mingling with the remnants of their dinner and the ever-present dust of the Serengeti. A few weeks ago, his camera would have been out to preserve the image, but now his enthusiasm was waning.

Their small crew—Mohammed the driver, two porters named Robert and Daniel, and their guide Jabari—had retired to their tents, leaving Jack alone with Natalie. The safari camp was simple yet efficient: five tents were arranged in a semicircle around the fire pit, with their vehicles parked nearby, always positioned for a quick departure if needed.

Jack couldn't quite believe what he was seeing. Natalie sat cross-legged on her camp chair, meticulously applying bright red nail polish as if she were in a Sydney salon rather than the middle of the African wilderness. The firelight caught the glossy surface of each nail as she worked, her face a study in concentration.

'For God's sake,' he muttered, 'you're painting your nails? Here?'

She looked up and flashed that practised smile that irritated him. 'A girl's got to maintain her standards, Jack. Just because we're in Africa doesn't mean I have to let myself go.'

He shook his head, trying to suppress his irritation. She was an excellent help; he had to give her that. Her technical knowledge was impressive, and she handled the equipment with practised ease. Well, except for that heart-stopping moment when she'd dropped his most expensive lens. The memory still made his jaw clench. Her reaction had been equally infuriating; she'd been more annoyed at his anger than apologetic about the near-disaster.

Later that night, she'd sought him out, wrapping her arms around his waist in what he supposed was meant to be a comforting gesture. 'I'm so sorry, Jack,' she'd whispered, resting her head on his shoulder. 'I didn't mean to be careless. I just had some things on my mind.'

He'd stood stiffly, keeping his hands at his sides, uncomfortable with her closeness and the overwhelming scent of her perfume—completely out of place in the bush. Just like those nails she was painting now.

He thought of Erin. How she'd looked the last time he saw her, hair wild from the wind off the Murrumbidgee, not a trace of makeup on her face. His chest ached with missing her. The months in Africa had produced some incredible shots, but they sat untouched on his SD cards. The thought of editing seemed impossible out here, where every rustle in the grass could be a predator and the ceaseless insect chorus did his head in.

A distinctive ping cut through his thoughts. Natalie's hand flew to her pocket.

'Is that your phone?' he asked sharply.

'No, no, just an alarm.' Her voice was too casual.

'Sounded like a message to me. Do we have service out here?'

'No, of course not.' She wouldn't meet his eyes. 'It's just an alarm.'

'What for?'

'Just . . . to remember to stretch. You know, after sitting all day.'

'First time I've heard it.' His eyes narrowed. 'Are you sure you haven't got service? Can I check?'

'No!' She placed a flat hand on her pocket protectively. 'My phone's private. Besides, my nails are wet.' A sly smile played across her face. 'Unless you'd like to reach in and get it yourself?'

'No, thank you.' Jack's patience evaporated. 'Have you heard from Lars yet about going to Hlane Royal National Park for the white rhinos? Does he still want us to go there? And more to the point, do we have a return date?'

Natalie shrugged casually. 'Don't tell me you've had enough of my company.'

Jack stared at her, and her mouth tightened.

'No, Jack. I haven't heard anything. You know that the communication is less than satisfactory.'

He stood abruptly. 'I'm going to clean my camera.'

In his tent, surrounded by the familiar smell of camera equipment and the mosquito netting, Jack let out a long breath. The laptop screen showed his last five emails to Erin, still unsent. If he'd known how isolated they'd be, how much he'd miss her . . . but no. This assignment was the opportunity of a lifetime. If these shots were good enough, their future would be set. He told himself that every night, but he felt completely helpless.

As a lion roared in the distance and the African night pressed in, all he could think about was home and the woman he'd left behind.

He would stick it out. He would be home with Erin soon.

Chapter 16

Ceann Mara - September 1915.

The dining room was awash with golden light from the kerosene lamps that hung above the long cedar table. Outside, the spring heat had finally relented with nightfall, though the air remained dry. Through the open windows came the rhythmic chorus of cicadas and the occasional mournful call of a mopoke owl.

Gilbert shifted in his chair, glancing around at the faces of his family. His mother, Bridget, sat at the far end of the table, her once-gaunt features now filled out again after months of improved health. Her dark hair, streaked with silver, was pinned neatly at the nape of her neck, and her blue eyes—Gilbert's eyes, everyone said—sparkled with renewed vitality as she passed a bowl of potatoes to Lily.

At five years old, Lily was the baby of the family, fair-haired and delicate like their mother had been in her youth. She chattered animatedly about a blue-tongued lizard she'd discovered beneath the back steps that afternoon.

'It was as long as my arm, truly!' she insisted, stretching out her small limb for emphasis.

Beside her, thirteen-year-old Olive snorted, her freckled face alight with sisterly scepticism. 'More like as long as your finger, I'd wager.'

'Was not!' Lily protested.

'Girls.' Thomas O'Byrne's deep voice rumbled from the head of the table, though the slight upturn of his lips belied any real displeasure. At fifty, Thomas remained an imposing figure—tall and broad-shouldered, with a full beard now more salt than pepper. His weathered hands bore the marks of decades working the land, building *Ceann Mara* into one of the most respected sheep stations on the Darling.

Harry, seated across from Gilbert, caught his older brother's eye and grinned. At eighteen, Harry had inherited their father's height and build, though his features favoured their mother's side. The wooden crutch that leaned against his chair was the only visible indication of the club foot he'd been born with—a condition that defined him far less than his quick mind and quicker wit.

Gilbert took a deep breath. He'd been waiting for the right moment, and something told him it wouldn't get any easier with delay.

'I've made a decision,' he announced, his voice cutting through the family chatter.

Five pairs of eyes turned to him, and Gilbert felt a momentary urge to retreat. Instead, he straightened his shoulders.

'I'm going to enlist.'

The words hung in the air. Lily, too young to fully comprehend, continued eating her dinner. Olive's fork clattered against her plate. Harry's expression remained carefully neutral, though a muscle twitched in his jaw. Thomas O'Byrne's eyes narrowed slightly, assessing his eldest son.

It was Bridget who spoke first, her Irish lilt more pronounced with emotion.

'You'll do no such thing, Gilbert James Piner O'Byrne,' she said, her voice quiet but firm. 'This is not our war.'

'Mother—'

'You're needed here,' she continued. 'The shearing—'

'Harry can manage the books for shearing,' Gilbert countered gently. 'And Father has Jenkins and Cook to oversee the hands.'

'And who will ride the south paddocks?' Bridget demanded. 'Who will check the boundary fences after the next flood? Who will—'

'Enough, Bridget,' Thomas interjected, his tone gentle but unyielding. He turned to Gilbert. 'Gilbert has already discussed this with me. Where were you thinking of enlisting? Broken Hill?'

Gilbert nodded, grateful for his father's practical approach. 'Yes, sir. I thought I'd ride to the recruitment office—'

A scrape of chair legs against floorboards interrupted him as Bridget stood abruptly, her napkin falling forgotten to the floor.

'I'll not sit here and listen to this madness,' she declared, her voice trembling. 'You've filled his head with tales of glory, Thomas, while I've barely recovered from—' She broke off, pressing a hand to her mouth as tears welled in her eyes.

Before anyone could respond, she turned and left the room, her skirts swishing against the doorframe in her haste.

A heavy silence fell over the table.

'Should I go after her?' Olive asked, half-rising from her seat.

Thomas shook his head. 'Let her be.' He looked at Gilbert, his expression a complex mixture of pride and resignation. 'Your mother will be alright. She knows as well as I do what it means to be a man in times like these.'

Gilbert nodded, though the knot in his stomach tightened. He'd expected his mother's opposition, but the reality of her distress was harder to bear than he'd anticipated.

'The King needs every able-bodied man,' Thomas continued. 'And I've no doubt you'll do the O'Byrne name proud.'

'I wish I could go with you,' Harry said quietly.

Gilbert met his brother's gaze, recognising the complex emotions there—frustration, envy, concern.

'Someone has to stay and keep Father in line,' Gilbert replied with forced lightness. 'Besides, you're the one with the head for figures. I'd make a mess of the station accounts inside a month.'

Harry's lips quirked in acknowledgment of the familiar refrain. Since childhood, the brothers had fallen into their respective roles—Gilbert, the physical one, at home on horseback and working with the stock; Harry, the intellectual, whose disability had directed him towards books and business matters at an early age.

'Will you bring us back a German helmet?' Lily asked suddenly, her small face serious. 'Johnny Wilson's brother sent one to their family, and he brought it to school. He let me touch it, but the new tutor that the Wilsons hired said it wasn't real. Mr Haydn said it was a fireman's helmet from the city.'

'Lily!' Olive scolded.

'I'll try,' Gilbert interrupted with a gentle smile for his youngest sister. 'Though I expect I'll be back before I even reach the fighting. They say it'll all be over soon enough.'

'They've been saying that since August,' Harry pointed out. 'Yet here we are approaching the end of the year, and the papers say the fighting's only getting worse.'

Thomas shot his younger son a warning look. 'That's

enough of that talk at the dinner table.' He turned back to Gilbert. 'I'm proud of you, son. Australia needs men like you.'

The conversation gradually shifted to more mundane matters—the price of wool, the new tutor at the Wilsons' homestead school, the letter they'd received from Cousin Patrick in Sydney. Gilbert ate mechanically, his mind already racing ahead to preparations he would need to make.

It was Olive who eventually broke through his thoughts, her voice taking on a teasing lilt that immediately put Gilbert on alert.

'Matilda Ellis will be heartbroken when you tell her,' she said, eyes glinting with mischief. 'Or have you told her already?'

Gilbert felt heat creep up his neck. 'Miss Ellis will likely be too busy managing *Wambool's* east paddock to notice I'm gone,' he said, striving for nonchalance.

'Is that why you were kissing her down by the river wharf on Tuesday?' Olive asked innocently, popping a piece of potato into her mouth.

Lily gasped delightedly. 'Gilbert and Matilda sitting in a tree, K-I-S-S—'

'We weren't—I didn't—' Gilbert spluttered, then caught the triumphant look on Olive's face. 'You little fibber! You weren't anywhere near the river on Tuesday.'

Olive grinned unrepentantly. 'No, but your face just told me everything I needed to know.'

Even Thomas chuckled at that, and Harry outright laughed.

'You've been caught fair and square, Gil,' his brother said. 'Though anyone with eyes has seen how you look at her these past months.'

Gilbert groaned, running a hand through his hair. 'She's a friend. We grew up together.'

'Aye, and Bridget Piner was "just a friend" to me once,' Thomas remarked casually. 'Before she became my wife and your mother.'

This elicited another round of laughter, and Gilbert found himself smiling despite his embarrassment. The tension that had gripped the table earlier began to dissipate.

'Matilda Ellis is a fine young woman,' Thomas continued more seriously. 'Her father's raised her to know her own mind, perhaps too well for some local sensibilities. But she has a good head on her shoulders.'

'And she can outride most of the station hands,' Harry added.

'And she's pretty,' Lily chimed in. 'She let me braid her hair when she came for tea.'

Gilbert looked down at his plate, unwilling to let his family see just how true their observations were. The feelings he'd been developing for Matilda over the past year were still too new, too fragile to withstand their good-natured scrutiny.

'Have you told her you're enlisting?' Harry asked, his tone gentler now.

Gilbert shook his head. 'Not yet. She knows I've been thinking about it. I wanted to tell you all first, and I will tell her when I return from Broken Hill. I ask that you all'—he settled his gaze on Lily— 'keep my news within the family until then. Please?' He waited until they all nodded. 'I'm riding over to *Wambool* when I return to help Robert Ellis with that broken windmill. I will tell her then.'

'A windmill? How . . . convenient,' Olive drawled, earning herself another round of laughter.

As the meal concluded and the family dispersed—Olive

and Lily to their lessons, Harry to his account books, Thomas to his evening pipe on the veranda—Gilbert made his way to the kitchen, where he found his mother methodically washing the dinner dishes.

'Mother,' he began softly.

'Don't,' she said, not turning around. Her hands remained steady in the soapy water. 'I won't try to stop you, Gilbert. You're a man now, and it's your choice to make.'

Gilbert moved closer, resting a hand on her shoulder. 'I need to do this.'

Bridget finally turned to face him; her eyes red-rimmed but dry. 'I know. You're like your father that way—stubborn as the day is long, with a sense of duty big enough to swallow you whole.' She reached up to touch his cheek, her fingers damp and warm. 'Just promise me you'll come home.'

The simplicity of the request squeezed Gilbert's heart. 'I promise,' he said, knowing even as the words left his lips that it was not entirely his promise to keep.

Bridget held his gaze a moment longer, then nodded once. 'Well then,' she said, her practical nature reasserting itself, 'we'd best see about getting your things in order. You'll need proper boots for a start. And those undershirts of yours are worn thin as paper.'

Gilbert smiled, recognising the shift for what it was—acceptance wrapped in maternal concern. 'Yes, Mother.'

Later, as he sat on the edge of his bed, Gilbert's thoughts turned to Matilda. He imagined her face when he told her his news—the brave smile she would force. Tomorrow, everything would change between them. He wasn't sure how he knew this, only that the certainty of it sat in his chest like a stone.

From the small table beside his bed, he picked up a smooth

river stone—a gift from Matilda when they were children. She'd found it at the bend in the river where they often fished, its surface perfectly round and flat, unusual in its symmetry.

'A wishing stone,' she'd declared, pressing it into his nine-year-old palm. 'But you only get one wish, so make it count.'

He'd kept it all these years, never making that one wish. Now, as he turned it over in his fingers, Gilbert wondered if perhaps he'd been saving it for exactly this moment.

'Come back to me,' he whispered, imagining the words in Matilda's voice.

Outside his window, a cool night breeze stirred the leaves of the old gum tree, carrying with it the thousand scents of the Darling bush at night—eucalyptus and dust, distant rain and sunbaked earth. The familiar smells made his chest ache with a peculiar mix of longing and belonging.

How strange, Gilbert thought, to be so desperate to leave a place only to realise how deeply it resided within you. And how much stranger still to discover that a person—a girl you'd known all your life—had somehow become as essential to you as the land itself.

Tomorrow, he would ride to Broken Hill. On his return, he would tell Matilda of his plans to enlist. Then, everything would change.

But tonight, in the stillness of his childhood room, Gilbert closed his fingers around the wishing stone and allowed himself to hope that some things—the most important things—might somehow remain constant even in a world being torn apart by war.

Chapter 17

Ceann Mara - December 1915.

The billabong lay like a perfect mirror beneath the late afternoon sky, its surface occasionally disturbed by the gentle splash of a jumping fish or the delicate touch of a dragonfly. Ancient river gums stood sentinel around its edges, their gnarled roots dipping into the water, their branches reflecting on the surface. Birds called to one another across the water—the melodious warble of magpies, the harsh screech of cockatoos, the gentle cooing of bronzewing pigeons seeking evening roosts.

Gilbert had ridden straight here after returning from Broken Hill: he wouldn't wait until tomorrow when he was working with Tilly's father. He was still wearing his best shirt, now wrinkled from the journey. The enlistment papers burned in his pocket like a brand—Private Gilbert James Piner O'Byrne, 31st Battalion, Australian Imperial Force. The recruitment officer had eyed him approvingly. 'Strong lad like you will show those Germans what Australians are made of,' he'd said, stamping the papers with an air of finality.

Gilbert had nodded; a curious mixture of pride and trepidation settling in his stomach. It was done now. No turning back. He'd sent word to Matilda through one of the *Wambool* stockmen, asking her to meet him at the billabong—their place, halfway between their two properties, where the boundary line between *Ceann Mara* and *Wambool* blurred into meaninglessness. It was here they had fished as children; here they had practised skipping stones; here they had sometimes simply sat in companionable silence watching the water birds go about their business.

Now, he paced along the bank, rehearsing words in his mind, discarding them, trying again. How did a man tell a woman he loved her when he was about to leave her behind?

The soft sound of hoofbeats made him turn. Matilda approached from the east, her horse picking its way carefully down the bank. She wore a simple cotton dress, the colour of the sky, and her dark hair was loose around her shoulders in a way that made Gilbert's breath catch. This wasn't the Matilda who rode fearlessly alongside the stockmen or who haggled fiercely with wool buyers. This was his Matilda, as he'd come to think of her—softer, vulnerable in a way she allowed few people to see.

She dismounted gracefully, tethering her horse to a branch before approaching him. Gilbert noticed immediately that her eyes were rimmed with red, her face pale beneath her sun-kissed skin.

'You've done it, then,' she said without preamble, her voice steady despite the evidence of recent tears.

Gilbert nodded, unable to speak past the sudden tightness in his throat. 'How did you know?'

'When I heard you were going to Broken Hill, I knew.' When?' The single word carried tightly held emotion.

'Three weeks,' he replied. 'We report to the training camp in Sydney on Christmas Day.'

Matilda turned away from him then, moving to the edge of the billabong where she stood looking out across the water. Her back was straight, her shoulders squared, but Gilbert could see the slight tremor that ran through her.

'Tilly,' he said softly, coming to stand behind her. 'Please look at me.'

'I knew you would go,' she said, still facing the water. 'I've known since the day war was declared. I saw it in your eyes.'

'I have to,' Gilbert said, his voice steady.

'I know.' She turned to him then, and the raw emotion in her eyes nearly undid him. 'That's why I love you, Gilbert O'Byrne. You do what needs doing, no matter the cost.'

Love. The word hung between them, at once a revelation and a confirmation of something they had both known for months, perhaps years.

'Tilly,' he whispered, reaching for her.

She came into his arms with a small sound that might have been a sob, burying her face against his chest. Gilbert held her tightly, one hand cradling the back of her head, feeling the softness of her hair beneath his fingers.

'I should have told you sooner,' she murmured against his shirt. 'I shouldn't have waited until you were leaving.'

Gilbert drew back just enough to see her face. 'How long?' he asked.

A watery smile touched her lips. 'Forever, I think. But I only realised it last winter when you brought soup to our house when Father was ill. You sat with him for hours, reading the newspaper while he dozed. You thought I didn't see you from the kitchen, but I did.'

Gilbert remembered that day—Robert Ellis feverish with influenza, Matilda exhausted from caring for him. He'd done what anyone would do, or so he'd thought.

'I've loved you since the day you beat Tommy Wilson in that horse race,' he confessed. 'You were fourteen, wearing your father's old hat, and you looked so proud when you crossed that finish line.'

'That was four years ago!' Matilda exclaimed, pulling back to look at him properly. 'And Father and Cecil were cross at me that day, because they had a bet on Tommy Wilson.'

Gilbert smiled sheepishly. 'I know. I was afraid you'd laugh at me if you knew how I felt.'

'I would never,' she said seriously.

The sincerity in her voice emboldened him. He lowered his head slowly, giving her time to pull away if she wished. Instead, Matilda rose on her tiptoes, meeting him halfway.

Their first kiss was gentle and tentative—a question being asked and answered. Gilbert's hands trembled as they came to rest at her waist, and he felt Matilda smile against his lips.

'I'm not made of china, Gil,' she whispered.

Something unleashed inside him then—months of longing, the knowledge of their limited time, the heady realisation that she wanted this as much as he did. His next kiss was deeper, more urgent, and Matilda responded in kind, her arms winding around his neck, her body pressing closer to his.

They sank to the ground beside the billabong, the soft grass a bed beneath them. The setting sun cast everything in golden light, transforming the dusty Darling bush into something magical. Time seemed to slow, then stop altogether as they explored this new territory between them—each touch, each kiss, a discovery.

Later, as they lay side by side watching the first stars appear in the darkening sky, Gilbert felt a profound sense of rightness despite the uncertain future that awaited them. Matilda's head rested on his shoulder, her hand over his heart. The night birds had begun their chorus, and somewhere in the distance, a dingo called to its pack.

'I have something to tell you,' Gilbert said finally, his voice low in the gathering dusk.

Matilda propped herself up on one elbow to look at him, her expression curious. Her hair fell in a curtain around them, and Gilbert reached up to tuck a strand behind her ear.

'Before I left for Broken Hill, I spoke with Father,' he continued. 'Asked him about the parcel of land near the north bend in the river—you know, the one with the stand of old gums and that rocky outcrop?'

Matilda nodded, her eyes widening slightly. 'The place where you can see both homesteads on a clear day.'

'That's the one.' Gilbert sat up, taking both her hands in his. 'Father said he'd been waiting for me to ask. Said he'd already planned to give it to me when I turned twenty-one.'

The significance of this wasn't lost on Matilda. In this vast country where land was life itself, such a gift was the most tangible expression of a father's faith in his son's future.

'Gilbert,' she breathed, her voice scarcely audible above the sounds of the bush.

'I love you, Matilda,' he said firmly, his gaze steady on hers. 'And I will come back. We will make our life on our Darling River and build our home on that bend.' He paused, squeezing her hands gently. 'Will you marry me, Tilly? I will ask your father for your hand if you agree.'

Tears welled in Matilda's eyes, spilling down her cheeks unchecked. For one terrible moment, Gilbert thought he'd misunderstood everything, that she was trying to find a gentle way to refuse him.

'Yes,' she whispered, then louder, 'Yes, Gilbert. Yes.'

The simple word held the love that he felt for her. Gilbert pulled her into his arms again, his own eyes damp as he pressed his face into her hair.

'I'll come back to you,' he promised. 'No matter what happens over there, I'll come back.'

They sat entwined as the last light faded from the sky, the billabong now a dark mirror reflecting the emerging stars. The bush enfolded them in its ancient embrace—the scent of eucalyptus and the water, the whisper of leaves in the gentle evening breeze, the occasional plop of a creature breaking the surface of the billabong.

'We should head back,' Gilbert said eventually, though it was the last thing he wanted. 'Your father will be wondering.'

Matilda nodded reluctantly. 'Will you come to speak with him tomorrow?'

'First thing,' Gilbert promised. 'Though I doubt it'll be a surprise. I'm sure he has been waiting for me to ask.'

They rose, brushing grass from their clothes, reluctant to break the spell of the evening. As they walked towards their tethered horses, Matilda suddenly stopped, turning to face the billabong once more.

'I want to remember this,' she said quietly. 'Exactly how it looks tonight.'

Gilbert stood beside her, taking in the scene. The water was ink-dark now, scattered with reflections of stars. The silhouettes of the river gums stood like sentinels against the night sky. A chorus of frogs had begun their nightly serenade, punctuated by the distant call of a mopoke owl.

'When I'm over there,' Gilbert said, 'this is what I'll think of. This place, this moment, you.'

Matilda leaned against him, her head fitting perfectly beneath his chin. 'Promise me another thing?'

'Anything.'

'Promise you'll write to me. Every chance you get. I want to know everything—where you are, what you're seeing, what you're thinking.'

'I promise,' Gilbert said solemnly. 'Though I'm not much of a letter writer.'

'You'll learn,' Matilda said with a certainty that made him smile.

As they mounted their horses and prepared to ride in opposite directions—Gilbert to *Ceann Mara*, Matilda to *Wambool*—a curious reluctance seized him. Three weeks suddenly seemed an impossibly short time before he would leave this land, this life, this woman. Yet in another sense, those three weeks stretched before them like a lifetime—time enough to secure their future, to create more memories that would sustain them both through the coming separation.

'Goodnight, Tilly,' he said softly.

'Until tomorrow, Gil,' she replied, her smile visible even in the darkness.

As he rode home across the familiar landscape, Gilbert felt strangely at peace despite the enormity of the changes ahead. The stars above were the same stars that had guided his grandfather to this land nearly fifty years before. They would be the same stars shining over the battlefields of Europe. And they would be the same stars guiding him home again when it was all over.

The war couldn't last long; everyone said so. All year they'd been saying by Christmas, perhaps, he would soon be back here where he belonged, building a home with Matilda on the bend in the river, watching their sheep graze on the rich pastures of their combined inheritance. The future stretched before him, bright with promise despite the shadow of war.

As the homestead came into view, lamplight glowing in the windows like a beacon, Gilbert sent a silent prayer of gratitude into the night for all he had been given—and all he had found—on his beloved *Ceann Mara.*

Chapter 18

Ceann Mara - Saturday, early May.

Two months after her previous quick trip to *Ceann Mara*, Erin stood in the motorhome, packing for Cat's wedding. The bridesmaid dress hung in its garment bag, a pale blue creation that Cat had chosen with meticulous care. She had ordered Erin's dress from the Wagga branch of the bridal chain, and Erin had been astounded when the dressmaker had to take it in considerably. Beside it lay the shoes, the jewellery; all the trappings of a celebration Erin was determined to participate in. There was still no word from Jack, and she had begun logging in to Qantas to check the flight dates and times into Sydney.

Maybe he was going to surprise her and arrive without any warning. He couldn't stay away forever.

Or could he?

Jill arrived to see her off; Erin was particularly proud of the ease with which she took down the annexe and packed up the motorhome.

'Thanks for everything these past months,' Erin said as Jill hugged her. 'I don't know how I would have managed without you.'

'That's what friends are for,' Jill replied, squeezing her hand. 'How are you feeling about going home?'

'Better than last time,' Erin admitted. 'I think . . . I think I'm starting to find my feet again.'

'And Jack?' Jill's voice was careful, gentle.

Erin looked over the river. 'Sometimes I find myself not caring. Not the way I should.'

'Oh, sweetheart.' Jill wrapped her in another hug, the gentle pressure releasing tears Erin hadn't known were waiting. 'You look after yourself, you hear me? Whatever happens with Jack, you're going to be okay.'

'I know,' Erin whispered, and the strange thing was, she did know. The certainty had been growing alongside her bank balance, her manuscript, and her reconnection with family. She would be okay, with or without Jack in her life.

As she drove towards the highway carrying her home and to Cat and Logan's wedding, Erin watched the familiar landmarks of her temporary refuge recede. She was leaving stronger—not whole, but rebuilding, one day at a time.

She plotted the next chapters of her novel in her head as she drove. Perhaps some stories did have happy endings, even if they came after chapters of uncertainty and pain. Erin wasn't sure yet if hers would be one of them, but for the first time in months, she found herself curious to turn the page and find out.

The Darling River stretched beside the dusty road like a silver ribbon, its path carved through red earth and scarred granite. Erin guided her motorhome along the winding track, each familiar bend bringing her closer to home. The vast emptiness of western New South Wales spread around her, broken only by the occasional cluster of river gums and the swooping flight of galahs against the endless blue sky.

Three more weeks. Three weeks on top of the original three of Jack's contract, and there was still no word of his return. She hadn't heard from him, apart from a brief single sentence text telling her of the three-week extension, but she allowed herself to hope. And then reality hit. Knowing that he could text proved that there was something wrong. Why couldn't he tell her more?

What was happening?

But there was something right about coming home to *Ceann Mara*, even if only temporarily. The property had been in her family for four generations, its Irish name— "head of the sea", an optimistic reference to the river that was the lifeblood of their land.

The isolation that had once made her restless now soothed her. Very little mobile reception away from the homestead, no constant emails, no city noise, just the whisper of wind through the saltbush and the occasional cry of a crow. Out here, you could hear yourself think. You could heal.

When the familiar entrance to *Ceann Mara* appeared, marked by weathered gates and the old station sign, Erin hesitated and then turned the motorhome off the road leading to the homestead. Instead, she followed the rough track along the levee bank that led to the billabong, the motorhome swaying gently over the uneven ground. This had always been her sanctuary, especially during her teenage years when she and her older sisters, Róisín and Cat, would escape here to share secrets and dreams.

The late afternoon light gilded the still water as Erin parked in the familiar spot, sheltered by a stand of ancient red river gums. Her hands moved automatically through the process of setting up: extending the annexe, taking out and arranging the outdoor furniture, and positioning the portable BBQ just so. The routine was comforting, each action bringing her closer to the peace she'd been seeking.

Finally, everything was arranged to her satisfaction, and Erin sank into a camp chair, letting out a long breath. The billabong stretched before her, its surface like polished glass, reflecting the deepening sky. A pair of pelicans glided in for a landing, barely disturbing the surface of the water. This was where she and her sisters had learned to swim, had their first camping adventures, and shared their confidences about boys, their dreams, and fears.

'Welcome home,' she whispered to herself, feeling the tension of the past months ease from her shoulders. The silence wrapped around her like a familiar blanket, broken only by the gentle lapping of water against the bank and the evening chorus of magpies in the trees. She sat watching the sun sink towards the horizon, painting the billabong in shades of gold and purple.

The water rippled as a fish jumped, breaking Erin's reverie. She smiled, remembering how Cat had taught her to fish here, both of them giggling as they baited hooks with wriggling worms. Róisín, always the practical one, would bring sandwiches and lecture them about sun protection while secretly enjoying their adventures.

Here was where they'd built their makeshift raft one summer, using old drums from the shed, much to Dad's horror when he'd discovered them halfway across the billabong. Where they'd camped out under the stars, telling ghost stories until they scared themselves silly and ran back to the homestead in their pyjamas. Where Cat had told them about her first kiss, and Róisín had confessed her dreams of law school.

Dark was settling in when Erin finally stood, stretching muscles tight from driving—time to face the family. The homestead lights glowed, welcoming her through the eucalypts as she walked along the road carrying her torch.

'There you are!' Cat's voice carried across the veranda before Erin even reached the steps. Her sister enveloped her in a fierce hug. 'How are you?'

'I'm fine.'

'Where's your motorhome?'

'Down at the billabong.'

'You're not really planning to stay down there by yourself, are you?'

'Cat,' Erin sighed, recognising the worry in her sister's tone. 'I'm a big girl now.'

'After what happened to me last year—and then to Ro—'

'That was different.' Erin kept her voice firm despite the flutter in her stomach at the memory. 'I'm home now. Safe.'

'At least take the satellite phone from the office down there,' Cat insisted.

Inside, the kitchen was warm with the smell of roasting lamb and familiar voices. Mum turned from the stove, a wide smile lighting her face. 'Here's our wanderer! How was the drive, love?'

'Long,' Erin admitted, accepting another hug. 'But good to be home.'

'And Jack?' Mum's eyes were gentle. 'Have you heard from him yet?'

'No, the reception's patchy where they're staying.' Erin tried to keep her voice light. 'But I'm expecting to hear any day.'

'If you ask me—' Dad started from his position at the table, not looking up from his research papers.

'Nobody did, Dad.' Erin's tone was warm but firm. 'We've been over this.'

'All I'm saying is there's plenty of good work right here. The Murphy place is looking for a manager, and if he doesn't want to work the land, that photography studio in Bourke is always advertising.'

'Tom,' Mum warned, but Dad continued.

'Gallivanting around Australia in that caravan, and now he's gone to Africa? What kind of future is that?'

'The kind we chose,' Erin said quietly. 'The kind that makes us happy.'

A loaded silence filled the kitchen, broken only by the gentle bubbling of the saucepans on the stove. Then Dad sighed, finally looking up. His eyes were softer than his words. 'Well, you're home now anyway. Even if it is for a short while.'

'Yes,' Erin agreed, accepting the cup of tea Mum pressed into her hands. 'I am.'

'Stay for dinner,' Mum said, already pulling out an extra plate. 'I've made your favourite lamb roast.'

'And I brought the good wine,' Cat added, producing a bottle from her bag. 'To celebrate your arrival.'

The familiar rhythm of family dinner soothed Erin even more. Dad gradually softened, sharing stories about his latest finds in his ongoing family research, his eyes lighting up as he described documents he'd received from the National Library. Mum kept their plates full while subtly steering the conversation away from any contentious topics, a skill perfected over decades of managing a family of strong personalities.

'Logan's working on that old shed down by the creek,' Cat mentioned, passing the roast vegetables. 'You should see what he's found in there—shearing pictures from the 1920s.' Cat was as obsessed with the family history as Dad was.

'And perfect timing,' Dad said, enthusiasm overtaking his earlier gruffness. 'We're just getting to that era in my research.'

'Oh, Tom, let the girls eat,' Mum interrupted fondly. 'Not everyone wants a history lesson with their dinner.'

'I'd love to see them,' Erin said quickly, seeing Dad's face fall. 'Tomorrow, maybe? After I get properly settled?'

The tension eased, and conversation flowed into easier local gossip and Mum's success with the campground.

'It all looks great, Mum. I thought that when I was here when Dad came home from hospital. I just didn't get a chance to tell you.'

'It's been busy, but we've cleared the bookings from yesterday for a week.'

'So, I'll have the billabong all to myself,' Erin said.

'Until your sisters come and visit,' Cat replied with a chuckle. 'The dresses are coming tomorrow. Shea and Bridget are picking them up. Did you get yours fitted okay, Erin?'

'I did. It's hanging up in the motorhome.'

'Finally,' Mum said, collecting the dinner plates. 'I was starting to worry about those dresses.'

'They'll be perfect,' Cat assured her, but Erin caught the slight tremor of anxiety in her sister's voice.

'A week away,' Mum mused, shaking her head. 'I can hardly believe we've got a wedding here.' She flicked an apologetic glance at Erin.

'Speaking of which,' Cat turned to Erin, 'Logan's been asking about Jack. What do you think the chances are?'

'He promised.' Erin's heart squeezed. 'I'm not sure—'

Cat reached across to squeeze her hand. 'We understand. Though Logan was hoping to ask him to take some photos.'

'He'd love that,' Erin said softly. 'He always says Australian weddings are his favourite to shoot. All that golden light and open space.' She looked away.

Dad cleared his throat. 'Well, young Thomas from the photography studio in Bourke does a fine job. Local lad, proper business . . . '

'Dad,' Cat warned, but her eyes were twinkling. 'We've already booked him. Though nobody captures light quite like Jack does.'

The praise for Jack, especially from Cat, sent tears to Erin's eyes, and she quickly blinked them away.

'Well,' Mum interrupted diplomatically. 'At least we'll have all of our girls here for the wedding. That's what matters.'

The quiet peace of the billabong called to Erin. 'I should head back,' she said, standing. 'It's been a long drive. I'm going to have an early night.'

'You could stay here tonight,' Mum tried one last time. 'I put clean sheets on your bed.'

'Thanks, Mum, but I need to get the campsite properly set up. I need to get my lights sorted out, too.' Erin hugged her mother, breathing in the familiar scent of rosewater and baking that always clung to her. 'What time are you expecting Shea and Bridget tomorrow?'

'Around ten,' Cat reached out and touched her arm as Erin walked past her chair. 'And Erin? I'm really happy you're home with us. It wouldn't be right without you here.'

The walk back to the billabong was peaceful, her torchlight catching the eyes of curious kangaroos in the paddocks. The stars were beginning to appear, brilliant points of light in the darkening sky. By the time she reached her campsite, the Milky Way stretched overhead like a river of diamonds.

Erin sat in her outdoor chair and tilted her head back, gasping at the glory of the night sky. Out here, away from city lights, the stars seemed close enough to touch. She picked out the constellations Jack had taught her during their travels: the Southern Cross, Orion's Belt, the Pleiades. Somewhere on the other side of the world, under different stars, he was probably setting up his cameras, checking his settings, and preparing for another day of shooting.

'You should see this sky, Jack,' she couldn't help whispering to the night. 'Almost as beautiful as the night you taught me how to photograph stars.' She smiled at the memory, his hands steady on hers as he showed her how to adjust the settings, his voice soft in her ear, explaining about exposure times and light sensitivity.

No matter what happened, she had beautiful memories, and she would never stop loving him. Erin pressed her fingers to her lips, then raised them to the starlit sky. 'Goodnight, my love. Be safe.'

The billabong waters lapped softly at the bank, a gentle lullaby in the darkness. A cool breeze carried the scent of eucalyptus and water, and somewhere in the distance, a dingo called to its mate. She was home, surrounded by the familiar sounds and scents of the country she loved, even if part of her heart was in Africa. Next week, she'd stand beside her sister as she married the man she loved, and somehow, she would get through it.

Chapter 19

Ceann Mara - Sunday.

Erin frowned and slumped back in her chair, frustration tightening her shoulders. She'd tried everything she knew—read the instructions twice, checked all the connections Jack had shown her, even attempted that thing with the voltage meter that never made sense to her. The single LED light cast a weak glow, barely enough to read by, let alone give her enough light at night.

'Where are you when I need you, Jack?' she muttered, picking up the instruction manual for the fourth time. He'd always made this look so easy, explaining about positive and negative connections while his capable hands worked the wiring. She had one small light working, but the main switch for the outside lights remained stubbornly dead.

She'd have to swallow her pride and ask Dad or Logan to come down and look at it. The thought made her wince; Dad would just use it as another reason why she shouldn't be camping out here alone, and Logan would give her that kind, patient look that made her feel about twelve years old.

The distant rumble of a diesel engine broke through Erin's thoughts, and her heart began to race.

Jack?

Disappointed, she watched with surprise as a battered white HiAce van turned into the campsite fifty metres from hers. Mum had said the campground was closed. So much for her peaceful solitude. Hopefully, they were just here for the night.

The van circled slowly before parking, as though the driver was deliberately taking in the layout of the site. Something about that careful assessment made Erin uneasy, though she couldn't say why.

Sighing, she picked up the Anderson plug again, squinting at the connections in the fading light. Jack's voice echoed in her memory: 'It's all about the contact points, love. Make sure they're clean and tight.' But no matter how she adjusted them, nothing worked.

Five minutes later, she was so focused on the plug that the shadow falling across her table made her jump, her heart leaping into her throat as Cat's experience from last year flashed through her mind.

A man stood there—tall, broad-shouldered, and thankfully keeping his distance. His van had been moved closer to her motorhome; close-up, it looked even more weathered, as though it had seen every dirt road between here and Darwin. But there was something incongruous about him—his hands, she noticed, were too well-kept for someone who lived rough in that old van. And his boots, though dusty, were expensive.

'Sorry,' he said, holding up his hands with an easy smile that crinkled the corners of his eyes. 'Didn't mean to startle you. Thought I should be sociable, seeing as we're the only two campers out here. Miles McKenzie.'

His voice was warm, with that laid-back drawl that seemed practiced rather than natural. His eyes moved continuously— scanning her campsite, glancing towards the homestead, taking in the details..

'Having trouble with that?' He nodded at the plug in her hands, which she was gripping like a weapon.

'My camp lights won't work.' Erin hesitated, then added, 'I'm Erin O'Byrne. I've tried everything—checked the connections, tested the power source, but nothing.'

At the mention of her name, his expression changed subtly—a flicker of something like recognition, quickly masked. Had he tensed slightly? Or was she imagining things?

'O'Byrne,' he said, making it a statement rather than a question. 'I saw the sign at the entrance. A relative?'

Erin nodded, suddenly conscious of being alone with this stranger. 'Yes. I didn't think there were any bookings this week.'

'I booked months ago,' Miles explained smoothly. 'Been traveling the Outback, visiting historic properties.' He gestured to her electrical problem. 'I've got a bit of experience with electrical stuff. Happy to take a look, if you'd like? These Anderson plugs can be tricky beasts.'

Erin studied him for a moment. His clothes were dusty but clean—worn jeans, a checked shirt with the sleeves rolled up, sturdy boots. Something made her hesitate. The way he carried himself and spoke seemed false, like someone playing a role. As though he was trying to make a good impression.

'Just the Anderson plug,' she said finally. 'It's giving me grief.'

'May I?' He waited for her nod before stepping closer, taking the plug and examining it with competent hands. 'Ah, here's your problem. The positive connection's loose, and there's a bit of corrosion on the terminals.'

She watched as he worked, noting how he kept his movements deliberate and calm, always staying where she could see him. His hands moved efficiently, but occasionally his eyes would dart away.

After a few minutes, he plugged it back into her motorhome.

'Try it now.'

Erin flicked the switch, and warm light flooded her annexe. 'Thank you,' she smiled, then her spine stiffened as he took a half-step closer.

'No worries.' He must have noticed her tension because he immediately stepped back, that easy smile returning. 'Well, I'll leave you to it. Just wanted to say g'day, let you know you're not alone out here. Though'—he glanced towards the homestead lights visible through the trees— 'reckon you already knew that seeing as you're related to them.'

'Yes,' she explained, relaxing slightly. 'I know that.'

'Lucky you.' His smile widened, but it didn't quite reach his eyes. 'Beautiful property. A lot of history in these old station homesteads.' There was something leading in the way he said it, as though fishing for information. 'Been in the family long?'

'Few generations,' Erin replied vaguely, not wanting to share too much with a stranger.

Miles nodded, apparently satisfied with even this limited information. 'I've been visiting all the historic properties along the Darling. Fascinating stories these places have.' He started walking backward towards his van. 'If you need any more help with the electrics, just give me a shout. I promise I know which end of a screwdriver is which.'

Erin found herself returning his smile despite her unease. 'Thanks. I might take you up on that.'

She watched him walk away, his long stride eating up the distance between their camps. As he reached his van, he paused to look back towards the track.

There was something intriguing about him, she had to admit. But she had enough complications in her life without adding mysterious strangers to the mix. She'd have to mention him to Mum tomorrow.

Still, as she settled into her chair with a cup of coffee, enjoying her now-working lights, she couldn't help but wonder what had brought Miles McKenzie to a billabong in western New South Wales.

Chapter 20

Ceann Mara - Wednesday.

The next few days passed in a blur of activity. Róisín arrived on Wednesday with Seth, their four-wheel drive loaded with more luggage than seemed physically possible. Erin's heart lifted at the sight of her sister.

'You look great, Ro,' Erin said as they hugged.

'I wish I could say the same about you.' Róisín hugged her close. 'Be happy for Cat, love. Still now word?'

Erin shook her head.

Upstairs, Cat's bedroom had been transformed into a makeshift bridal parlour, with dresses hanging from the picture rail and makeup scattered across every surface. Róisín and Shea were already in their bridesmaid dresses—soft blue silk that caught the afternoon light—while Cat stood before the mirror in her wedding gown, looking like something from a fairy tale.

'Oh, Erin,' she breathed as her sister entered. 'What do you think?'

For a moment, Erin couldn't speak. Cat was radiant, the ivory lace perfectly complementing her skin, her happiness so evident it seemed to illuminate her from within. Erin felt a pang—not of jealousy, precisely, but of recognition. Once, she had felt that same certainty, that same joy in her own love.

'You're beautiful,' she said finally, meaning it completely.

Cat squeezed her hand. 'Your turn. Mum's been fretting that we'd need last-minute alterations.'

As Erin slipped into her bridesmaid dress, the familiar chaos of sisters getting ready washed over her. Róisín debated hairstyles with Shea, while Bridget, still in her jeans, offered commentary from her perch on the window seat. Their mother flitted between them all, armed with pins and a determined expression.

'Oh!' Laura pressed a hand to her heart as Erin emerged in the blue silk, her eyes suddenly swimming with tears. 'My girls. All my beautiful girls.'

'Mum,' Erin protested, flustered by the raw emotion in her mother's face. 'Don't cry.'

'Happy tears,' Laura insisted, dabbing at her eyes. 'I'm allowed happy tears.'

For a moment, they were all quiet. Soon, Cat would be a wife. Their tight circle of five sisters would expand to include Logan officially, though he'd been part of their lives for years. Time was passing, lives changing, and Erin felt both the joy and melancholy of it. It made her realise how her marriage had lessened her closeness to her sisters.

'Right,' Cat said briskly, breaking the spell. 'If we don't get these dresses off, we'll have tear stains everywhere. Bridget, your turn!'

As they changed back into ordinary clothes, Erin remembered to ask about the billabong. 'Mum, I thought you said no bookings for the week? A van came in on the weekend. Has he been up to see you? He's parked beside the motorhome.'

Laura looked up from pinning the hem of Bridget's dress. 'What? Oh dear, that must be the booking from a few months back I couldn't contact. With everything happening with your father, I completely forgot. He paid in advance and asked for a site at the billabong. I sent him a map so he could see where the site was. I'd totally forgotten.'

'His name's Mackenzie.'

'Yes, that's the one. I wasn't able to contact him, and he didn't answer my emails. Still, with the wedding—' Laura fretted. 'Perhaps we should explain the situation and ask him to leave.

'It's not a problem, Mum,' Cat said. 'One camper's not going to ruin the wedding.'

'Maybe you should move closer to the house for the weekend, Erin,' her mother suggested hopefully. 'There's plenty of room.'

Erin shook her head, not meeting her mother's eyes. The thought of being surrounded by family—witnessing their love and concern up close—was overwhelming right now. The motorhome down by the billabong offered space to breathe, to process, to be alone with her thoughts.

As they walked downstairs a while later, Bridget walked beside Erin and made her smile. 'Help me convince Cat that releasing those doves at the ceremony is the worst idea in wedding history. The crows will come swooping in and there'll be carnage. Mum's about to cave, and we need reinforcements.'

As they rejoined the wedding chaos in the kitchen, Erin felt a lot lighter.

Chapter 21

Wambool - April 1916.

The afternoon sun slanted through the windows of *Wambool's* front room, casting golden rectangles across the polished floorboards. Matilda sat in her father's leather armchair, her fingers tracing the edge of the envelope that had arrived with the morning's post. Gilbert's handwriting had improved since his first letters from training camp—less rushed, more deliberate, as though each word carried greater weight now that he was in France.

She opened the envelope carefully, savouring the moment of connection despite the thousands of miles between them. A small pressed flower fell into her lap—a tiny violet, its colour faded but still recognisable. Matilda picked it up with tender fingers, then unfolded the pages within.

My dearest Matilda,

The censor will likely black out any mention of our exact location, so I won't waste ink trying to tell you precisely where I am. Suffice it to say we are some miles behind the front lines tonight, though we can still hear the distant rumble of artillery that never truly ceases.

It has been a long journey. I've seen more of the world in these past months than I ever imagined possible, though I'd trade all these sights in an instant for a glimpse of our billabong at sunset. I guess that will make you smile. I always remember the look on your face when I said I had seen Bourke! This place is a lot further away than the back of Bourke, as Dad calls anything remote.

The AIF nearly doubled in size with all the new recruits arriving. I've been assigned to the 5th Division now with several mates from the original training group. You'd like them; I think—especially Davies, a sheep farmer from Victoria who tells tales about his property that almost (but not quite) rival the splendour of Ceann Mara *and* Wambool.

We sailed, sailing across the Mediterranean. I wish I had your gift for words to describe the blue of that sea, Tilly. It's nothing like our Darling. The water is clear as glass and so deeply blue it almost hurts your eyes to look at it too long. Schools of fish followed our ship some days, flashing silver beneath the surface.

Everything here is so green and ordered—fields laid out in perfect rectangles, villages with stone houses hundreds of years old, roads lined with trees planted in straight lines. Even the wildness here feels somehow tamed and ancient, not vast and untameable like our bush.

The people have welcomed us warmly, though communication is a challenge. I've picked up a few words of French, mostly to do with ordering food or beer! The children follow us through the villages, asking for sweets and pennies. They've seen too much already, these little ones, with their fathers and brothers away fighting and their homes so close to the front.

Our training continues here, more intense now that we're so close to the real fighting. The officers speak of a big push coming soon, though, of course, they don't share the details with the likes of us. We just wait. The mood among the men is determined. We're ready to do our part, to prove that Australians can hold their own alongside the British troops who've been bearing the brunt of it for so long now.

Matilda paused in her reading, one hand drifting unconsciously to rest on her stomach. Almost five months along now, yet she was small, and the swell of her body was easy to disguise beneath her loose dresses. She had told no one yet—not her father, not even Gilbert. The secret weighed on her, yet she couldn't bring herself to burden Gilbert with this knowledge, not when he faced dangers she could scarcely imagine.

She turned back to the letter, hungry for more of his words, more connection to the man who had no idea he was to be a father.

I think often of our last days together, of the promises we made by the billabong. In my pack, I carry the small sketch you made of the river bend where we'll build our home. On nights when sleep won't come, I unfold it carefully and imagine every detail of the house we'll raise there—wide verandas to catch the evening breeze, large windows to welcome the morning light, rooms filled with books and laughter and perhaps, someday, I hope, the patter of small feet.

The violet I've enclosed comes from a meadow where we camped for two nights during our march inland. I thought you might like a small piece of this foreign world, though it's a poor substitute for the proper letters I wish I could send. So much I want to tell you must wait until I can speak freely, without worrying about the censor's black ink.

I must close now. We move again tomorrow, ever closer to where we're truly needed. Please don't worry too much. I am surrounded by good men, well-trained and determined. We look after each other. And I have the strongest motivation of all to stay safe—a future waiting for me on the banks of the Darling.

All my love, now and always, Gilbert

P.S. I dream of you every night, Tilly. In my dreams, you're always standing by the billabong, your hair loose in the wind, watching the sunset. Are you well? Your father? Is Cecil still working at the AIF office in Sydney? Tell me everything about home in your next letter. The smallest details are precious to me here—the birds you've seen, the state of the wool, whether old Jenkins is still complaining about his rheumatism. I want to hold our world in my mind, perfect and unchanged, until I return to it.

***

Matilda carefully refolded the letter, pressing it to her heart for a moment before rising to place it in the cedar box where she kept all his correspondence. The cheerful tone didn't entirely mask the undercurrents she could sense—the weariness, the tension of what remained unsaid. Gilbert had always been better at showing his feelings than describing them. Yet, even now, she could read between his carefully chosen words.

She moved to the window, gazing out in the direction of *Ceann Mara*, though the O'Byrne homestead was too distant to be seen from here. Beyond both properties lay the billabong, where they had pledged themselves to each other. Matilda rested one hand on her abdomen, feeling a newfound resolve.

'Your father will come home to us,' she whispered to the life growing within her. 'I promise you that.'

##

Wambool - early May 1916.

The morning sickness always came at noon, regular as clockwork. Matilda Ellis leaned against the stable wall, one hand braced against the rough timber, the other pressed against her mouth. She glanced around the yard to ensure no one had witnessed her moment of weakness. The station hands were all out with her father in the south paddock, and Mrs Cleary, their housekeeper, was preoccupied with the weekly washing.

When the sickness passed, Matilda straightened her shoulders and picked up the bridle she'd dropped, continuing her task as though nothing had happened. The subtle changes in her body were becoming more difficult to conceal—the fullness in her breasts, the slight thickening of her waist, the constant exhaustion that dogged her steps no matter how early she retired.

She hadn't told Gilbert. Not yet. Each time she put pen to paper, the words refused to come. How did one share such news across oceans and continents? How could she burden him with this knowledge when he already carried the weight of war on his shoulders?

It would be different if we were married, she thought, hanging the bridle on its peg with careful precision. A ring on her finger would have made everything simpler. The child would still have come earlier than convention dictated, but people would have looked the other way. The wife of a soldier at war deserved compassion, not judgement.

But she was not Gilbert's wife—only his promised bride, a distinction that made all the difference in the eyes of society. Though her father had been unexpectedly understanding, she knew others would not be so kind. Already, she felt Mrs Cleary's speculative gaze following her, noting the looser fit of her clothes, the pallor that no amount of summer sun seemed to cure.

Matilda left the stables, crossing the yard to the house, her steps measured and unhurried despite the turmoil within. She had always prided herself on her practicality, her resilience— qualities essential for survival on the land. Now, those same qualities would see her through this challenge as they had seen her through others. In her bedroom, she carefully closed the door before moving to the small writing desk by the window. Gilbert's last letter lay open beside a blank sheet of paper and her pen. He wrote faithfully, though his letters took weeks to arrive—descriptions of France, careful accounts of his daily routine that she knew were heavily censored, always ending with declarations of love and plans for their future. Their house by the billabong. Their life together when the war ended.

Matilda sat down, smoothing her hands over the blank paper. She had put off this task too long already. Something within her sensed that time was growing short, that she could no longer afford the luxury of hesitation.

The child deserved acknowledgment by its father, even from afar. And Gilbert deserved to know that a part of him would live on here, by the Darling River, regardless of what happened in the trenches of France.

She dipped her pen in the inkwell and began to write, her hand steady despite the weight of the words:

My dearest Gilbert,

Your last letter brought such joy—to know you are safe, for now at least, and thinking of home. The billabong is as beautiful as ever, though it misses your presence as keenly as I do. The river gums are heavy with blossom this season, and the black swans have returned to nest along the bank where we used to fish.

Cecil is at the AIF office and working in communications. He is most upset that his asthma prevented him from going overseas. Father is well and asks after you regularly and sends his regards. He has been a great comfort these past months, especially since . . .

Matilda paused, the pen hovering over the paper. Once written, these words could not be taken back. Yet the time for hesitation had passed. She continued:

I have news that I've been keeping to myself, Gil, but can no longer contain. In September, God willing, there will be two of us awaiting your return. The doctor in Wilcannia has confirmed what I've suspected these past months. Our child grows strong within me, already showing the O'Byrne stubbornness, I think, for the sickness that plagues most women only lasted briefly.

Father knows, though I have told no one else yet. He held me as I cried—not from shame or regret, never that—but from the weight of loving someone so far away during such a time. He has been kindness itself, and assures me that our child will be welcomed as an Ellis until you return to make me an O'Byrne in name as well as heart.

I know this news comes as a surprise, perhaps even a shock. If I could have spared you this added worry, I would have. But our child deserves to be acknowledged by its father, even across the distance that separates us. And you deserve to know that a part of you remains here, growing stronger each day, connecting you to this land you love so dearly.

Do not fear for us. We are well provided for and surrounded by those who will support us. Your mother visits often, though she does not yet know. I wait for the right moment to tell her, for I know the news will bring both joy and added worry for you.

Come home to us, Gil. Our child will need its father. I will need my husband. The billabong awaits your return, as do I, with a love that grows only stronger with passing days.

Forever yours, Matilda

She read over the letter twice, then carefully folded it and slipped it into an envelope. After addressing it to Private Gilbert O'Byrne, with his service number and battalion details she knew by heart, Matilda sat for a long moment, the sealed letter between her fingers.

Let it reach him, she prayed silently. *Let it find him well and bring him comfort, not an added burden.*

A knock at her door startled her from her reverie.

'Matilda? Are you unwell?' Her father's voice, tinged with concern.

She quickly tucked the letter into her desk drawer before opening the door. Robert Ellis stood in the hallway; his weathered face creased with worry as he studied his daughter.

'I'm perfectly fine, Father,' she assured him, lifting her chin slightly. 'Just catching up on correspondence.'

Robert nodded, though his gaze remained troubled. 'Cooper mentioned you seemed a bit peaked in the stables earlier.'

So, someone had noticed after all. Matilda felt a flash of irritation at the station hand's observation, quickly suppressed. 'A momentary spell. Nothing to concern yourself with.'

'You're working too hard,' her father said firmly. 'You need to consider—'

'I will not be treated as an invalid,' Matilda interrupted, her voice low but resolute. 'This child is a blessing, not an illness.'

Robert sighed, reaching out to touch her cheek gently. 'Of course it is. But you are precious too, daughter. To me, and the young man waiting for you in France. I am sad that your mother is no longer with us to share the joy of you with child.'

Matilda felt tears threatening and fought them back with

practiced determination. She had done enough crying in the privacy of her room. Outside those four walls, she would remain the Matilda everyone expected—capable, composed, undaunted by circumstance.

'I've written to Gilbert,' she said, changing the subject. 'About the baby. The letter will go with tomorrow's post.'

Her father's expression softened. 'Good. He should know.'

'And if he—' Matilda couldn't finish the thought aloud, though it haunted her nights: *If he doesn't come home. If our child never knows their father.*

'Then his child will know of him through us,' James completed the thought for her, his voice gentle but firm. 'Through the stories we tell, the legacy he left on this land, the love that created new life even in the shadow of war.'

Matilda nodded, grateful for her father's steady presence, his unwavering support when he could have reacted so differently to her situation.

'Now,' Robert continued, his tone deliberately lightening, 'Mrs Cleary has prepared a cold lunch. You'll join me on the veranda, and then you'll rest for an hour before we ride out to check the east paddock fencing.'

Matilda opened her mouth to protest the prescribed rest, then closed it again at her father's raised eyebrow. Choosing her battles wisely had always been her strength. The hour's rest would be a concession to keep the peace, nothing more.

'As you wish, Father,' she said with the ghost of a smile. 'Though I'll remind you that pregnant women have been working this land since the first settlers arrived. I'm hardly the first to carry a child while working the land.'

'No,' Robert agreed, offering his arm with old-fashioned

courtesy. 'But you are the only daughter I have, and the only mother my grandchild will know. Indulge an old man's caution.'

Matilda took his arm, allowing him this small victory. As they walked towards the veranda, her thoughts returned to the letter in her desk drawer, and to Gilbert, so far away across the sea. She imagined him receiving her news—the surprise, the joy, the renewed determination to survive that knowledge would bring.

The child within her was their promise to each other, a piece of their shared future already taking shape. She placed her free hand briefly on her stomach, still flat enough to conceal beneath her loose blouse.

Be safe, Gil, she thought, her silent plea extending across oceans. *Come home to us.*

Later that afternoon, as promised, Matilda rode out with her father to check the east paddock fencing. The rhythm of the horse beneath her, the familiar landscape stretching to the horizon, the vast Australian sky overhead—all served to settle her spirit, to reaffirm her connection to this land that had shaped generations of both the Ellis and O'Byrne families.

She would face whatever came with the same resilience that had allowed her ancestors to survive in this harsh but beautiful country. She would raise her child with stories of its father's courage, of the love that had blossomed by the billabong, of the heritage that ran as deep as the Darling River itself.

And when the war ended—as it must, eventually—she would either welcome Gilbert home to meet his child, or she would carry on without him, keeping his memory alive in the child who would be his legacy.

Either way, Matilda Ellis would endure, her back straight,

her gaze steady, her heart faithful to the man she loved and the child they had created together.

Chapter 22

France - June 1916.

The French soil beneath Gilbert's boots felt strange, nothing like the sun-baked earth of home. The rain had fallen steadily since their arrival in Marseille, and they moved north by train and foot.

The constant rain had turned the ground into thick mud that sucked at every step. Their column trudged wearily from the transport ships, carrying kits heavy with equipment that already seemed inadequate against the unfamiliar coolness of a European summer. When his battalion arrived in the Armentières sector for "nursery" trench familiarisation, the weather had warmed, with intermittent rain and close, humid conditions as they settled into the line.

'Bit different from the Darling, hey?' The voice came from beside him, belonging to a lanky soldier with a wisp of a red beard and tired eyes that still managed to crinkle with humour. 'Jimmy McPherson. Sheep station near Deniliquin.'

Gilbert shifted his pack and extended a hand. 'Gilbert O'Byrne. Wool near the Darling.'

'Thought I recognised the type,' Jimmy grinned. 'You can always spot a river boy. They stand taller than us plains fellas.'

Gilbert found himself smiling, the first genuine one since leaving Australian shores. 'That's what gave me away?'

'That, and you've been looking at this mud like it's personally offended you.' Jimmy gestured ahead where an officer was attempting to organise the troops. 'Come on, I'm bunking with some decent blokes. Better than getting stuck with city boys who don't know a ewe from a wether.'

The "decent blokes" turned out to be three more Australians and a New Zealander—a group who had already seen action at Gallipoli. They made room for Gilbert in their tent with minimal fuss, accepting Jimmy's introduction with nods and the offer of tins of bully beef.

'Cooper,' said a square-jawed man with eyes that looked as though he had seen too much. 'That's Williams, Ferguson, and the Kiwi's Taylor.'

'Don't mind Cooper,' Ferguson said, passing Gilbert a mug of something that smelled strongly alcoholic. 'He's forgotten how to talk to new people. Gets you like that after Gallipoli.'

Gilbert took the mug, nearly choking on the first sip. 'What the bloody hell is this?'

'French farmer's moonshine,' Williams explained. 'Tastes like sheep dip, but works a charm against the cold.'

As darkness fell, Gilbert found himself sitting outside the tent with these men who were strangers yet somehow familiar. The distant thunder of artillery occasionally punctuated their conversation, but they spoke as if it were merely a summer storm rolling in the background.

'You'll get used to it,' Taylor told him, noticing Gilbert's flinch at a particularly loud barrage. 'After a while, it just breaks the silence. It's that silence you need to worry about.'

Gilbert nodded, uncertain how anyone could become accustomed to the sounds of war. He thought about the station, where the loudest noise was the shearing shed at full capacity or the occasional thunderstorm rolling across the plains. What would Matilda make of this constant loud hammering of death?

Matilda. Her face appeared in his mind, as clear as if she stood beside him. He touched the pocket where her photograph lay protected, alongside the letter she'd pressed into his hand at the station platform.

Read it when you need to remember why you're fighting, she'd whispered.

He hadn't opened it yet. Somehow, admitting he needed that comfort felt like acknowledging his fear, and fear was a luxury he couldn't afford just yet.

'Got someone waiting at home?' Cooper asked his first direct question to Gilbert.

'Yes,' Gilbert answered simply.

Cooper nodded, understanding in his gaze. 'Best thing and worst thing, that is. Gives you something to fight for, but also something to lose.'

The others murmured agreement, and Gilbert realised each of these men must carry similar photographs, similar letters, similar fears.

'First time I saw a man die,' Ferguson said abruptly, 'I forgot about home for three days. Couldn't remember my wife's face, my kids' names, nothing. Brain just . . . shut it away.' He took a long drag from his cigarette. 'Then it all came flooding back, and I cried like a baby. No shame in it if it happens to you.'

'What Ferguson's trying to say,' Williams added, 'is that we all go through it. Homesickness hits harder than any Fritz bullet.'

As they talked, Gilbert began to understand. These men had created a piece of Australia here in this muddy corner of France – their accents, their humour, their shared understanding of a land so different from this one. They were his anchor in this strange new world.

Later, alone on his bedroll, Gilbert finally took out Matilda's letter. The paper was worn already from being carried across oceans; her handwriting as familiar as his own. As he read her words—full of love and worry and pride in him—he could almost smell the eucalyptus and the red dust of home.

I've planted a gum tree by the billabong, she wrote. *Every day it grows taller will be another day closer to your return.* Gilbert folded the letter carefully and placed it back in his pocket next to his heart. Tomorrow would bring more of the same— training, marching, and eventually fighting. But tonight, wrapped in Matilda's words and surrounded by the snores of men who understood the burden of distance, he allowed himself to remember the red earth and blue skies of home.

It would be there waiting for him, he told himself.

The morning brought inspection, their new commanding officer striding down the line of weary Australians with a clipboard in hand. Gilbert stood at attention, body stiff from the unfamiliar ground he'd slept on.

'Name?' the officer barked, reaching Gilbert.

'Private Gilbert O'Byrne, sir.'

'O'Byrne?' The officer frowned, consulting his papers. 'Got you down as Gilbert James Piner here.'

Gilbert's stomach dropped. 'There must be some mistake, sir. It's O'Byrne. Gilbert James Piner O'Byrne from the Darling River.'

'No mistake. Says Gilbert James Piner plain as day.' The officer made a notation. 'Clerical error somewhere along the line. Happens more than you'd think with you colonial boys and your strange names.'

'But sir—'

'Take it up with the quartermaster if you must. Next!'

As the officer moved on, Jimmy leaned over slightly. 'Tough luck, mate. Same thing happened to Ferguson. He's really MacDonald, but the paperwork got botched at Melbourne.'

Gilbert stood frozen, a strange sense of loss washing over him. The O'Byrne name had been on Australian soil for three generations, carried with pride from Ireland before that. His great-grandfather had carved it into the main beam of the homestead; his father stamped it on every wool bale they shipped. Now, with the stroke of some anonymous clerk's pen, that connection had been severed.

Later, queuing for rations with his new companions, Gilbert found himself studying the identity disc hanging around his neck. Sure enough, he hadn't noticed the small writing said PINER, G. Not O'Byrne. Not the name Matilda would be writing to. Not the name that would appear in casualty lists should the worst happen.

'Don't take it too hard,' Cooper said, appearing beside him with his tin plate. 'Out here, your name means less than the man standing next to you when bullets start flying. As long as your family has the right unit, you'll get your letters. Have a word to the runner next time he brings the weekly batch out.'

'It was my mother's maiden name. It's just—' Gilbert struggled to explain. 'O'Byrne means something back home. It's tied to the land, to our history.'

Ferguson nodded in understanding. 'War has a way of stripping everything down. You're just meat and bone here, no matter what fancy name you carried before.' He shovelled a spoonful of unidentifiable stew into his mouth. 'Besides, your land won't forget who you are, no matter what they call you on paper.'

Gilbert touched the pocket where Matilda's letter rested. At least she knew him by his true name. At least the river gums and the billabong waters would remember an O'Byrne, not a Piner, should he never return.

'Think of it this way,' Jimmy added with a wink. 'Makes for a good story when you get back home. How the army stole your name but couldn't take your spirit.'

Gilbert managed a smile, though the loss felt strangely profound. Another piece of home, another connection, fading with each mile that separated him from Australian soil. But as he looked around at the men who had welcomed him—men who understood the value of names and land and belonging—he realised Ferguson was right. What mattered here was not what was written on paper, but what he carried in his heart.

Tonight, he decided, he would write to Matilda and tell her about becoming Gilbert James Piner. She would laugh about it in her next letter, he was sure. And somehow, that thought made the burden lighter.

Chapter 23

Ceann Mara - Wednesday night.

Twilight was settling over the billabong when Erin returned to her motorhome, the water's surface turning from blue to silvery-grey as the light faded. Her neighbour was sitting outside his van, a small fire crackling in a portable fire pit, his face illuminated by the dancing flames. He looked up as she approached, offering a friendly nod.

'Hey there,' he called. 'How was the family reunion?'

'Chaotic,' Erin replied with a tired smile. 'In the best way.'

'That's families for you. Blessing and curse all rolled into one.'

Erin hesitated, then decided to address the situation directly. 'Actually, I spoke with my mum about your booking. She'd tried to contact you to cancel it. With everything happening with Dad's heart attack and now the wedding . . . '

'Wedding?' Miles raised his eyebrows.

'My sister Cat is getting married on this weekend. Here, at *Ceann Mara.*'

'Ah.' Understanding dawned on his face. 'Hence all the comings and goings up at the homestead. So, I have to leave?' He didn't sound impressed.

'They'll be using the camp kitchen and grounds for the reception. Mum feels terrible about the mix-up with your booking.'

Miles set down his mug, his expression thoughtful. 'I booked this site ages ago as soon as—' he hesitated and broke off..

'Look, if you keep cooking here, and just use the amenities block as necessary, it will be fine.'

'That's great. Please assure your family that I won't go there unless absolutely necessary.'

'The wedding is on Saturday,' Erin added with a smile.

'Saturday.' He nodded, his eyes crinkling at the corners. 'I'll make myself scarce for the big day.'

'We don't mean to make you feel unwelcome,' Erin said quickly. 'It's just—'

'A family affair. I understand completely.' Miles gestured to the fire. 'I've just boiled the billy. Fancy a coffee?'

Erin glanced back at her motorhome, lonely in the fading light. The thought of sitting by herself held no appeal. 'I'd love one, thanks.'

Miles busied himself with mugs and the ancient metal billy, his movements practiced and efficient. 'How do you take it?'

'Black, thank you.'

His smile was enigmatic in the firelight.

They sat in companionable silence for a while, watching as the first stars began to appear in the deepening blue above. The familiar night sounds of the outback settled around them—frogs starting their evening chorus, the occasional splash from the billabong as fish rose to feed, the distant call of a mopoke.

'Lights still okay?' Miles asked eventually.

Erin nodded. 'They've been working perfectly since you fixed them. Thanks again for that.'

'Happy to help.' He stirred the fire with a stick, sending sparks spiralling upward. 'Why are you camped down here if that's your family?'

The question caught Erin off guard. 'I'm in my motorhome.

It's my home.'

'Of course.' Miles nodded. 'And you've chosen to camp down here, away from your family.'

Erin stared into her coffee, unsure how to respond. There was no judgement in his tone, just quiet observation.

'Sometimes family can be a bit much,' she said finally. 'Especially when they worry about you.'

'And are they? Worried?'

'Wouldn't yours be? If you were camping alone by a billabong?' She raised her eyebrows. 'Beside a stranger.'

Miles laughed softly. 'Fair point.' He looked up at the stars, now brilliant against the dark sky. 'My family . . . well, let's just say we're not exactly the close-knit type. Not like yours here at *Ceann Mara* seem to be.'

'You know how to pronounce the station name?'

'It's on the sign at the entrance,' he pointed out. 'Plus, places like this, family names tend to be local landmarks. *Ceann Mara*. Head of the sea. Irish?'

'Yes.' She was surprised at his knowledge. 'My great-great-great grandfather came from Ireland. Built this place from nothing.' Erin felt a surge of pride despite herself. 'The O'Byrnes have been here ever since.'

'Deep roots.' Miles nodded appreciatively. 'That's something rare these days.'

'What about you?' Erin found herself curious. 'Where are your roots?'

A shadow passed over his face, there and gone so quickly she might have imagined it. 'Scattered to the wind, I'm afraid. I'm more of a rolling stone.'

'Like Jack—' Erin said without thinking.

Miles looked at her curiously. 'Jack?'

Erin bit her lip, regretting the slip. She stood abruptly. 'I'm off to bed now. More wedding preparations tomorrow.'

'Of course.' Miles stood as well, making no comment on her sudden change of mood. 'Thanks for letting me know about the wedding. I'll keep well out of the way.'

'You don't have to hide completely,' Erin found herself saying. 'Just . . . maybe avoid the amenities during the ceremony and reception. If you can.'

'I'll be out.' His smile was warm in the firelight. 'Goodnight, Erin. Sleep well.'

As she walked back to her motorhome, Erin was struck by how easy it had been to talk with Miles—a stranger who somehow didn't feel like one. There was something comforting in his quiet presence, something that reminded her of the calm she felt with Jack.

She paused at her door, looking back at the solitary figure by the fire. Miles had returned to his seat, his attention seemingly focused on the flames, but something in his posture made her wonder if he was watching her. A slight shiver ran through her, not entirely unpleasant, as she stepped inside and closed the door behind her.

##

The next two days passed quickly as family and visitors arrived for the wedding. The campground near the house gradually filled with familiar faces and excited chatter. Erin watched from the small fold-out chair beside her motorhome as cars kicked up dust along the dirt road, each bringing more guests to celebrate the upcoming ceremony: O'Byrne cousins, Cat's Sydney friends, Scarlett, Jilly and Gavin, and Logan's sister from Queensland.

By Friday, the campground was buzzing with activity. Visitors occupied every available space—the lucky early arrivals had secured cabins, while others brought caravans and pitched tents beneath the river gums.

The night before the wedding brought an unexpected calm. The preparations were complete, the marquee stood ready for tomorrow's festivities, and after a warm family dinner filled with laughter and last-minute toasts, a gentle stillness was settling over the campground. The sisters had met at the far end of the billabong for a toast to Cat before dinner. Erin knew that they were still worried about her and forced a smile to her face.

'It's been far too long since we were all together down here.' Erin hugged Cat and Róisín in turn as Shea filled a glass for her. As they sat and chatted and reminisced, Erin felt calm descending.

The small family dinner that followed had been perfect—all the people Erin loved most gathered around the dining room table, passing dishes and sharing stories. Only Logan was missing, having joined Seth for a small celebration at their property across the river, honouring tradition by not seeing the bride on the eve of their wedding.

Since her call to the magazine, there had been nothing from Jack. She had started logging into Qantas and checking the flight dates obsessively, hoping against hope that he might be on one of them and arrive here tomorrow morning. Maybe he was going to surprise her. He couldn't stay away forever. Or could he?

Back in her motorhome, Erin carefully lifted down her dress for tomorrow. Beside it lay her shoes, all the trappings of a celebration she was determined to participate in despite the hollow feeling in her chest. She ran her fingers over the silky fabric, trying to focus on tomorrow's joy rather than her own heartache. She promised Cat she'd take it up to the house this afternoon.

As soon as she got back from the homestead, Erin refreshed her email; a habit she'd let go of over the past weeks. Nothing, nothing, and then—

Her breath caught. Jack's name appeared in bold in her inbox, the subject line simply: "*Tomorrow.*"

Erin's hands trembled as she clicked on the message. For a moment, she allowed herself to imagine what she wanted it to say: that he was on his way, that he'd realised what they had was worth fighting for, that tomorrow he'd be standing among the guests with that crooked smile she loved so much.

When she read it, the pain was duller than before, like a bruise fading to yellow.

Erin, I'm so sorry, I just can't get there. Natalie has made it clear the magazine needs me here. I'll call as soon as I can and explain. I'll be back soon. Jack

The words blurred as tears filled her eyes. Two brief lines, and nothing about them coming back together, nothing about missing her, nothing about love. Just "can't get there" and "Natalie" in the same breath. Natalie.

What isn't he telling me? The brevity of the message left too much space for her fears to fill in the blanks. The explanation about the magazine seemed hollow—surely, they could let him go? He could have insisted unless there was something more keeping him there.

Unless Natalie was more than just his assistant now.

She picked up her phone and her fingers shook as she texted him a one-word answer.

Fine.

Inside her motorhome, with the sound of the river flowing steadily outside, Erin curled up on her side in the narrow bed. Tears came silently at first, then in shuddering waves that eventually carried her into fitful sleep, her pillow damp beneath her cheek and her heart heavier than it had been in weeks.

Chapter 24

Ceann Mara - 11th May - the wedding.

'Erin, where are you?'

Erin barely noticed her mobile buzzing until she felt the vibration through her fingertips, her hand clenched around the edge of the table as she gazed out of the window towards the billabong. She'd been watching a cockatoo dip down to the water for quick sips, fluttering back to its perch to preen its feathers before diving down again. In those moments, as she watched the bird, she could almost forget Jack's email.

'Erin, are you there?'

'Oh—yes, Mum. Sorry. What's wrong?'

'What's wrong? Where are you, sweetheart? Cat's getting herself all wound up, and everyone's worried. Dad wanted to drive down in the ute, but I wouldn't let him because he's all dressed up.'

'What time is it?' she asked, glancing around, feeling disoriented. 'I thought I had another forty-five minutes before the photographer arrived.'

'Erin, that's not much time, love! Are you ready?'

A silence hung in the air before her mother asked, 'Sweetheart, have you done your hair?'

Erin touched her damp hair, still half-wet from the shower she'd had half an hour earlier. 'Yes, yes—I showered, and I've washed it.'

'Well, hurry up and get up here as soon as you can. Do you want me to send down the quad runner to pick you up?'

'No, it's okay, Mum. I'll just put the awning down in case

the wind comes up, and I'll drive up—'

'Don't worry about that; I'm sending Seth now. Be ready, sweetheart.'

Erin blinked, looking around the small space of her motorhome. It'd been ten hours since she'd read Jack's email, and the words—knowing he wouldn't be there—still hit her like a punch to the chest. The date registered on her; it was four months today since she'd seen him off at the airport. A world away.

Now, she stared at the water and fought back tears. She'd stood under the shower until the hot water had run out and then pressed a cold flannel to her eyes to try to get rid of her red-rimmed eyes.

She held back a sob and forced herself to focus. There was no time to dwell on her situation. She had a wedding to go to—even if it was the last place she wanted to be right now. Cat was glowing with happiness, and for Cat and Logan, it was wonderful. But through the night, Erin's heart had been shattering, piece by piece.

And now, here she was, about to watch Cat and Logan marry, ready to start their life together as husband and wife. She'd have to watch Seth and Róisín too.

For God's sake, she was supposed to be the one settled in her marriage, with two and a half years behind her, feeling fulfilled.

Instead, she was living alone in a motorhome on the edge of her family's billabong, without the faintest idea of what her future held.

Because if there was one thing she knew for sure, it was that she wouldn't be spending it with her husband.

Erin's feet dragged as she made her way along the levee

bank towards the homestead. The early afternoon sun caught the windows of the old homestead, making them gleam like reproachful eyes. Cars lined the driveway—sleek city vehicles mixed with dusty utes—and the sound of laughter drifted across from the camp kitchen to the manicured lawn where white chairs waited in neat rows.

Her chest tightened. The last thing she felt like doing was attending a wedding, even her beloved sister's. She hesitated at the front gate, tugging at her damp hair.

'Quick, sweetie!' Dad stood at the front door, looking uncomfortable but distinguished in a properly fitted suit. He tugged at his collar. 'They're all waiting for you upstairs. Your mother's got your dress hanging up, and she's ready to do your hair.'

'I'm sorry I'm late, Dad. I overslept.' The words caught in her throat.

He studied her face. 'Are you okay, love? You look a bit pale.'

'I'm fine.' The lie came easily. Too easily.

Taking a deep breath, Erin hurried past him and up the familiar staircase, automatically skipping the creaky third step from the top. The sound of excited voices and popping champagne corks guided her to Cat's old bedroom.

'Finally!' Four voices chorused as she entered. The room was a whirlwind of activity—dresses, makeup, and her sisters in various states of preparation.

Her mother rushed forward, champagne flute in hand. 'Drink this, then sit. We've got work to do with that hair.'

Her pale blue bridesmaid dress hung from the wardrobe door. Róisín, Shea, and Bridget were already transformed into visions of elegance.

Then Erin saw Cat. Her sister stood by the window in her wedding dress, radiant with happiness, and Erin's eyes filled with tears. Cat crossed the room and pulled her into a hug. 'Don't you dare cry,' Cat whispered, but her own eyes were suspiciously bright. 'Sit. Let Mum fix your hair.'

Erin sank into the chair, forcing a smile as she sipped her champagne. No one mentioned Jack's absence, though she felt it like a physical presence in the room. She caught Shea watching her with concern but turned away, focusing on her reflection as Cat worked magic with the curling iron.

Half an hour passed in a blur of hairspray, lipstick, and more champagne. When they finally made their way downstairs, the sun was starting to sink towards the horizon, casting a golden glow over everything.

Dad waited with an old sulky, Cat's favourite horse pawing the ground impatiently. It was only a short distance to the ceremony site, but Cat had always dreamed of arriving in the traditional way. Erin watched her sister's face light up at the sight and felt her heart crack a little more.

The ceremony area was a testament to their mother's planning. Market lights strung between the ancient river gums created a canopy of stars. White chairs faced an arch twined with native flowers, the Darling River providing a perfect backdrop. Logan waited there, looking both nervous and ecstatic.

Erin took her place with her sisters, clutching her bouquet like a shield. As Cat and Dad made their way down the aisle, Erin's gaze drifted to a chair in the third row where Jack should have been sitting. All she could hear was that one clear word echoing in her thoughts: Natalie.

##

The reception was everything a country wedding should be. Tables groaned under platters prepared by the local CWA ladies—a pig on the spit, roast meats, and vegetables from surrounding farms. Their mother, forced to be a guest rather than a helper, beamed with pride as she watched her daughter dance with her new husband.

The champagne flowed freely, perhaps too freely in Erin's case. As the sun set and the market lights took over, casting their warm glow over the celebrations, she found herself growing increasingly melancholy. The happiness surrounding her only emphasised the hollow feeling in her chest.

'Okay, spill it.' Shea cornered her by the dessert table, concern written across her features. 'What's really going on with Jack?'

The champagne had loosened Erin's tongue. 'He's with *her* right now,' she whispered, throat tight.

'Her who?' Shae frowned.

'Natalie. His assistant. I got a text last night. She made it clear the magazine needed him there. More like *she* did.'

'Erin, no.' Shea's face softened. 'Not Jack. You know he wouldn't.'

Erin shook her head; the lack of calls, the scant emails and infrequent texts told a truth that Jack wouldn't. 'You don't know what he's like anymore. I don't know what he's like anymore.'

The party wound down slowly, Cat and Logan departing in a shower of rose petals and good wishes. Erin helped with the cleanup, trying to keep busy. Shae stayed close to her, and she appreciated her care.

'I want you to stay up here in the house tonight, in your old room,' Mum insisted, with a worried glance when Erin stumbled at the back steps as she helped carry leftovers to the kitchen.

Too tired to argue, Erin followed her mother upstairs. She curled up on her old bed, wishing she could go back to being that bright-eyed seventeen-year-old with the world at her feet before she'd fallen in love with a man who'd promised to show her the world but was now showing it to someone else.

Mum sat on the side of the bed, her fingers smoothing Erin's hair. Sleep came slowly, and when it did, she dreamed of endless African plains and a man with a camera walking away from her, always just out of reach.

Chapter 25

Ceann Mara homestead - Sunday.

The morning sun streamed through gaps in the old curtains, painting stripes across Erin's childhood bed. For a moment, she lay still, trying to orient herself. Then the previous day crashed over her—Cat's wedding, Jack's absence, too much champagne.

Her head throbbed as she pushed herself up. The old bed creaked, the sound achingly familiar. A glance at her phone revealed no missed calls and no messages. Of course not. Jack would be sleeping now, on the other side of the world. With Natalie.

The thought twisted in her stomach like a physical pain, sharp enough to make her catch her breath. Over two years of marriage, and now she couldn't even picture his face without seeing him turning away from her, camera in hand, always chasing the next shot, the next . . . her mind shied away from completing that thought. Erin glanced at the bridesmaid dress in a crumpled heap on the floor as she headed for the bathroom. She would never wear blue again; it would remind her of her unhappiness last night.

Downstairs, she found her mother in the kitchen, already cooking despite having hosted a wedding the day before. The kitchen was alive with morning chaos, sunlight streaming through the French doors that opened onto the wraparound veranda. The old Aga cooker dominated one wall, while copper pots hung from the ceiling rack Mum had installed years ago. The massive wooden table in the kitchen—crafted from river red gum by Erin's great-grandfather—could seat twelve comfortably, and this morning it was cluttered with plates, coffee cups, and the detritus of a family breakfast.

'Where's Róisín and Seth?' Erin asked, sliding onto one of the bentwood chairs, trying to ignore how the room seemed to spin slightly.

'Getting packed,' Bridget said around a mouthful of pancake. 'They've got some big meeting in Canberra tomorrow.'

Mum moved between the cooker and the large wooden island bench, expertly flipping pancakes while simultaneously keeping an eye on the bacon. The kitchen smelled of coffee, maple syrup, and fresh herbs growing in terracotta pots along the windowsill.

'I'm making up platters to take down to the camp kitchen,' she said, gesturing to an array of covered plates. 'For the guests who stayed over last night. Shea, love, can you take more coffee down?'

'I'll help,' Bridget offered, already reaching for the thermos.

'Not until you've finished your breakfast,' Mum said firmly, but her eyes were twinkling.

The screen door banged, and Róisín burst in, her dark hair still damp from the shower. 'Seth's just taking our bags to the plane,' she announced, snagging a piece of bacon. 'Thanks for breakfast, Mum, but we'd better get moving.'

'Not without proper goodbyes,' Mum insisted, pulling Róisín into a hug.

Dad appeared in the doorway; his eyes were bleary.

'You okay, Dad?' Erin asked, sympathising. Her eyes probably looked like that too.

'I'm fine. Just one whiskey too many. That Seth's a bad influence.' He ruffled Erin's hair as he passed, something he hadn't done since she was a teenager. 'Almost like old times,' he said, his voice gruff with affection. 'All my girls in the kitchen.'

Erin dug deep, finding a smile from somewhere. 'How's the family history going, Dad?'

His face lit up. 'We've just about sorted Samuel. Found him and his wife, Breda and a couple of children, but then they moved to Melbourne, we think. Can't figure out why they'd leave the station, or where exactly they went—'

'Not today, Tom,' Mum interrupted, patting his shoulder with a fond smile. 'Let the girls have their breakfast in peace.'

'You should see the new puppies at the clinic,' Shea was saying, reaching across to steal a piece of bacon from Bridget's plate. 'Three kelpie crosses. The runt's absolutely stolen my heart.'

'Don't even think about it,' Laura warned, but she was smiling. 'Five dogs here is more than enough.'

'But I'm the vet nurse, Mum. It's practically my duty to rescue them.' Shea's eyes sparkled with mischief. 'Besides, you know Dad's always wanted a younger working dog. Poor old Boris is getting long in the tooth.'

'Speaking of work,' Bridget interjected, scrolling through something on her phone, 'Another commission just came in for my website design business. That's three this month.'

Tom looked up from his notebook. 'That's wonderful, love, but—'

'I know. I still need to finish school,' Bridget finished for him, rolling her eyes. 'It's just so pointless being stuck at boarding school when I'm already making more than my teachers.'

'Your education comes first,' Laura said firmly. 'Just a few more months.'

'Besides,' Shea teased, 'who else would be there to look after the younger girls? Someone needs to keep the O'Byrne reputation for mischief alive.'

'As if I have time for mischief between classes and coding,' Bridget retorted. Then she turned to Erin, her expression brightening. 'Hey, speaking of careers, when are you going to get back to yours? You were always the writer in the family. Remember all those journalism competitions you won in school?'

The kitchen went suddenly quiet. Erin's coffee cup froze halfway to her mouth, the familiar ache in her chest sharpening into something unbearable.

Dad had pulled out his notebook, despite Mum's warning, and was now very intently studying his notes. Róisín was telling Mum about her upcoming meeting, gesturing a bit too enthusiastically with her piece of bacon, trying to cover the awkward moment.

The scene was so familiar, so normal, that for a moment, Erin could almost forget about Jack. Almost. But then Seth appeared in the doorway, in his cargo pants and bomber jacket, and she remembered how Jack used to look heading out on assignment, camera bag over his shoulder, that eager light in his eyes . . .

'Ready to go, Ro?' Seth asked, accepting the coffee Mum thrust into his hands.

'Thanks for everything,' Róisín said, hugging everyone goodbye. 'The wedding was perfect, Mum.'

Erin watched her sister leave, trying to ignore the knot in her stomach. Everything was changing. Cat married, Róisín flying off to her important environmental law career, and her upcoming marriage . . .

Erin set her cup down with a sharp clink. 'I need to head back.'

'But you've hardly eaten,' Laura protested, concern etching her features.

'I'm not hungry.' The words came out harder than she'd intended. She pushed back her chair, needing to escape before anyone could see the tears threatening. 'Thanks, Mum.'

As she hurried from the kitchen, she heard Shea hiss, 'Nice one, Bridge.'

'What? What did I say?'

The screen door closed behind Erin, cutting off Bridget's confused voice. Around her, the homestead bustled with post-wedding activity, but Erin barely noticed, her mind full of all the dreams she'd set aside to follow Jack around the world. Dreams that now felt as murky as the brown waters of the billabong.

The walk back to her motorhome felt longer than usual. The morning was already warm, promising another hot autumn day. A mob of kangaroos watched her pass, then bounded away across the paddock, their movement catching the eye of a wedge-tailed eagle circling overhead.

Even though the water was still brown from the floods earlier in the year, the slight morning breeze ruffling the surface of the billabong was a pretty sight. Water birds stalked the shallows, and somewhere in the distance, a kookaburra's laugh echoed across the water.

As she came around the bend in the track, she saw smoke rising from near her camp. For a moment, panic gripped her— was it a bush fire? —but then she remembered. Miles was there.

She slowed her pace, suddenly conscious of her rumpled hair and last night's makeup probably smeared across her face. Through the trees, she could make out his white van.

'Morning, Erin.' His voice was quiet, careful. 'Hope my fire's not too close to your setup.'

Erin hesitated at the edge of her camp. 'It's fine.'

He stood slowly, like someone used to dealing with skittish animals. Something in his manner—the careful distance he kept, the way he seemed to understand her wariness—made her relax slightly. 'It's fine,' she repeated, then added, 'Excuse my appearance. It was a big night.'

'Weddings usually are.' There was no judgement in his tone, just quiet sympathy.

'A bit too much wine,' she admitted.

'Ah.' He nodded towards his fire. 'I've got fresh coffee brewing. Real coffee, not instant. You're welcome to a cup, if you'd like.'

'I'll just have a wash.' She hurried inside, dragged a brush through her hair, and swallowed two paracetamol.

The coffee was indeed good, strong and smooth. They sat in surprisingly comfortable silence, watching a pair of galahs squabble in a nearby tree. The morning air was still cool but held the promise of heat to come.

'Please tell me you're not a photographer, Miles,' she said suddenly, surprising herself.

Miles laughed, a genuine sound that seemed to startle even him. 'God, no. Can't frame a shot to save my life. Why?'

'No matter,' she murmured, but her hand tightened on her mug.

'I'm actually between jobs at the moment,' he offered, not pressing about her question. 'Doing a bit of travelling, clearing my head. Sometimes you need to step away from everything to figure out what's next.'

Erin nodded, understanding all too well. She was about to respond when the distinctive sound of a small aircraft caught her attention. Looking up, she watched the Cessna fly over. 'That's my sister, Róisín, and her partner Seth,' she explained. 'They're headed back to work.'

'Big family?'

'Five girls.' She smiled despite herself. 'Dad always jokes that he gave up trying for a boy after the fifth daughter.'

As they talked and she shared her family history, Erin found herself studying Miles' profile when he wasn't looking. There was something compelling about him, but also something she couldn't quite put her finger on. Something flickered in his eyes so quickly she might have imagined it.

But his smile was warm, his manner gentle, and when he spoke about his travels, she found herself drawn into his stories. It was nice, she realised with a pang, to have a conversation with someone who stayed still, who didn't constantly scan the horizon for the next perfect shot.

The thought of Jack hit her again, a wave of grief so strong it made her gasp softly. Miles glanced at her but didn't comment, just quietly poured her another coffee. His silence was a gift, she realised. No questions, no well-meaning advice, just the space to feel what she needed to feel.

As she stood to leave, Miles turned to rinse the coffee cups, and she caught a glimpse of something on the table—what looked like a detailed property map spread beneath a notebook. But when he turned back, his smile was so genuine, his manner so easy, that she pushed the observation aside. After all, plenty of travellers carried maps. And for the first time since Jack's email, she felt like she could breathe properly again.

Chapter 26

Ceann Mara - late Sunday afternoon.

The wind had picked up considerably since sunset, bringing with it clouds of red dust and memories of yesterday's celebrations. Erin stood back, watching as Miles worked on securing the anti-flapper to her motorhome's awning, his movements precise despite the growing darkness.

'That wind's really come up,' he commented, his voice carrying over the rustling of nearby trees. 'There were willy-willies all over the road on my way back from Tilpa this morning.'

'What were you doing down there?' Erin asked, curiosity getting the better of her. She wrapped her arms around herself against the cooling evening air.

Miles straightened up, brushing dust from his hands. 'I camped at the pub last night. Your family didn't need a stray camper during the wedding.'

'That was good of you. Besides, the noise might have disturbed you. They were a rowdy lot last night.'

'I looked at some furniture in a couple of old houses yesterday afternoon,' he explained, a hint of passion creeping into his voice. 'I collect pieces, restore them. There's something about bringing those old treasures back to life.'

Erin nodded, and they sat quietly for a while.

'How's the head this afternoon?' he asked, changing the subject with a slight smile.

'I'm fine,' Erin responded, then noticed him studying her.

'When are you heading out?' he asked.

'Heading out?'

'Yeah, where's home for you? Now that the wedding's over?'

Erin gestured to the motorhome behind them. 'This is home. I'm not sure when I'll leave yet.' The thought of being alone, away from her family, sent a shaft of fear running through her.

His eyes dropped to her left hand, and she caught the subtle movement, noting how he registered her wedding ring. 'That's home?'

'Yes, it is,' she confirmed, then turned the question back on him. 'What about you?'

'I came from the west,' he said vaguely.

'Broken Hill? Further west?'

Miles's green eyes seemed to catch the last of the day's light, and his white teeth flashed in his tanned, rugged face. Erin found herself tilting her head, wondering about this man and his small, dented van. She'd noticed the rust spots mixed with the red dust earlier that morning as she walked down to the billabong.

'I'm from the *real* west,' he said with a hint of mischief.

'What's the real west?'

'Western Australia.'

'You're a long way from home.'

He nodded, running a hand through his hair. 'Had the opportunity to come check out some of the historic homes, the abandoned places along the Darling River.' His gaze drifted to her fire and the hot plate set up nearby. 'Anyway, I won't interrupt your dinner. Better get my own started.'

'Do you have to light a fire, or have you got a gas stove too?'

'I need to collect some wood and get a fire going,' he admitted.

Erin hesitated for a moment, looking at her well-established fire. 'My fire's going; hot plate's plenty big enough. You're welcome to use it after I'm done with my chicken.'

'You sure?'

'Yeah, of course.'

An hour later, Miles had pulled up a chair beside her. His steak was cooking while Erin picked at her chicken and salad. Her appetite was non-existent. Their conversation stayed light, skimming across topics like the weather and road conditions, neither venturing into anything too personal. Yet there was something in the space between their words, in the way the firelight played across their faces, that relaxed her.

The wind continued to rise, carrying with it the comforting scent of the outback night. Erin knew she should go up to the house—Mum had wanted her to come up for dinner, concerned about her being down after the wedding. But something kept her here, watching the sparks from their shared fire dance upward into the darkening sky.

Chapter 27

France - July 1916.

Mud. That was Gilbert's overwhelming impression of the trenches—not the fighting, not the constant danger, but the all-pervading, inescapable mud. It clung to his boots and his uniform, worked its way into his rifle despite his meticulous cleaning, and even seemed to taint his food. After the scorching heat of Egypt, where they had trained, the cold, wet conditions of summer in northern France had been a shock to the system.

'Penny for 'em, Piner,' came a voice to his left.

Gilbert looked up from his mess tin to see John Davies settling beside him on the fire step, his own dinner balanced precariously on his knees.

'Just thinking about the mud,' Gilbert replied, shifting to make room. 'Reckon I'd forgotten what it felt like to be dry.'

Davies laughed, a sound that seemed unnaturally loud in the gathering twilight of the trench. 'Mate, when we get home, I'm going to fill a bloody bathtub and stay in it for a week.'

'Your missus might have something to say about that,' Gilbert said with a smile.

'She can join me,' Davies responded with a wink that set several nearby soldiers chuckling.

Gilbert returned to his meal—some unidentifiable stew with chunks of tough meat and softened vegetables, but hot at least, which was luxury enough these days. The narrow trench, reinforced with sandbags and rough timber, stretched away in both directions, following its zigzag pattern designed to limit the impact of shell blasts. Overhead, the evening sky was visible in a narrow strip, darkening now as the sun set somewhere beyond the devastated landscape.

'Mail come through for you today?' asked Cooper, a lanky Queensland cattle drover who manned the Lewis gun at the far end of their section.

Gilbert nodded. 'Sent a letter to my girl. Don't know when it'll reach her.'

'The one with the picture?' asked Wilson, the youngest of their group at barely eighteen, his face still rounded with boyhood despite the weeks in the line.

'That's the one,' Gilbert confirmed, unable to suppress a smile at the mention of Tilly. The small photograph he carried of her standing beside her horse, her expression serious as she gazed at the camera, had become something of a mascot for their section. The lads teased him mercilessly about it, but there was no malice in it, only the good-natured ribbing of men who had become closer than brothers.

'Proper beauty, she is,' Wilson said appreciatively. 'Got that look about her, though—like she'd box your ears if you stepped out of line.'

This brought another round of laughter. Gilbert shrugged, not bothering to deny it. 'She's broken in wilder colts than you lot,' he said.

'Tell us about your place again, Piner,' requested Reynolds, a former bank clerk from Sydney whose fastidious nature somehow survived even these conditions. 'The river and the sheep and all that.'

It had become something of a ritual in the quieter moments—each man sharing stories of home, keeping the memories alive, reinforcing their determination to return there.

Gilbert had told them about *Ceann Mara* countless times, yet they never seemed to tire of hearing about the vast open spaces of western New South Wales, so different from the crowded confines of their current existence.

'The Darling's probably running high now, with the winter rains,' Gilbert began, settling back against the trench wall. 'When it floods, it spreads out across the plains like an inland sea. The water brings everything to life—birds by the thousands, fish jumping, the grass growing so fast you can almost watch it happen.'

He paused, taking a sip of the lukewarm tea from his mug. 'Our homestead sits back from the river, so it stays dry even in the worst floods. My great-grandfather built it that way, clever old bugger. From the veranda, you can see for miles—sheep country mostly, the best wool in Australia if you ask my father.'

'Better than Davies' scrubby Victorian pastures, eh?' Cooper teased.

'Watch it, Queensland,' Davies retorted good-naturedly. 'Our Merinos would make your cattle look like they're wearing sackcloth.'

Gilbert continued, the familiar description flowing easily. 'The billabong near our boundary line is the best spot—cool even in summer, with river gums hanging over the water. That's where I asked Matilda to marry me, before I left for training.'

'Romantic bastard,' Wilson said admiringly.

'Not so much,' Gilbert admitted with a small smile. 'I'd been working up the courage for months. Probably would've waited even longer if the war hadn't come along.'

'War's good for that, at least,' Reynolds observed quietly. 'Makes a man know what matters.'

A companionable silence fell over the group, each lost in

their own thoughts. The distant thunder of artillery provided a constant backdrop, but Gilbert had grown accustomed to it, able to distinguish by sound alone between outgoing and incoming shells, between danger and relative safety.

Sergeant Kelly appeared at the corner of their bay, his weathered face looking more lined than usual in the fading light. 'Piner, Davies, you're on listening post tonight. Two till four.'

They nodded acknowledgment. The listening post—a shallow hole in no-man's-land beyond their wire—was a nerve-wracking assignment, requiring absolute stillness and silence as they strained to detect any movement from the German lines.

'Word is we're moving up tomorrow,' Kelly added, his voice deliberately casual. 'Brass has been in meetings all day. Something's brewing.'

The men exchanged glances. Rumours had been circulating for days about a major offensive, but this was the first semi-official confirmation they'd received.

'Any details, Sarge?' Cooper asked.

Kelly shook his head. 'Nothing solid. Just be ready.' He moved on, delivering similar news to the next group along the line.

'Well, lads,' Davies said after a moment, his customary grin replaced by a more sober expression, 'looks like we might finally earn our keep.'

'We'll be right,' Wilson said with the unshakeable confidence of youth. 'The Huns won't know what hit 'em once the Aussies get going.'

The others murmured agreement, the bravado a necessary shield against the fear they all felt but rarely acknowledged. Gilbert joined in, clapping Wilson on the shoulder, making the expected jokes about showing the Germans some real fighting men. But his thoughts had already travelled across oceans to the billabong, to Matilda, to the future he had promised her.

As darkness fully enveloped the trench, stars emerged overhead, and he searched the sky for something familiar. A flicker of excitement stirred in him when he spotted the teapot. Gilbert traced the spout with his eyes, following it to the Archer of Sagittarius — the same figure that once stood high above the Darling River in summer. But here, in this northern sky, it sat strangely low.

Tonight, for a few hours at least, he could close his eyes and be home again, walking along the riverbank with Matilda's hand in his, planning their life together in a world without war.

Chapter 28

Ceann Mara - May.

In the week after the wedding, Erin went to the house each day. She talked to Dad about the family history—he'd moved on to Gilbert O'Byrne now and couldn't source a death certificate. Dad's glasses perched at the end of his nose as he squinted at his laptop screen.

'The records during World War I are scattered,' he sighed, taking a sip from his mug of tea. 'Gilbert seems to vanish into thin air.'

Erin leaned over his shoulder, studying the genealogy website. 'Have you tried the Australian War Memorial site?'

'Three different parishes,' Dad grumbled. 'Not a trace.'

The morning sun spilled through the study window, illuminating dust motes dancing in the air. Dad's organised chaos of folders and notebooks covered every surface, sticky notes marking potential leads. It had become his pre-retirement project, piecing together the fragments of their lineage.

Mum came running into the study in a panic, not long after Erin arrived on Wednesday. 'Oh Erin, love, would you do me a favour? I forgot I had tennis club today. I've lost track of the days since the wedding. Can you take a basket of food over to Reg next door for me? It's packed, ready to go.'

She was already dressed in her tennis whites, car keys jingling in her hand, her hair pulled back in a ponytail.

Erin smiled; Mum could have passed for her older sister. 'Reg McGillvray?' she asked

'Yes, poor man. He's not well. I promised him some of that

lasagne I cooked yesterday.' Mum was already backing towards the door.

'Wait—Reg McGillvray? Doesn't he bail up any visitor with a shotgun?'

Mum paused in the doorway. 'I've already called him to let him know you're coming instead of me. He's . . . particular about visitors. Just leave the basket on the porch if he doesn't answer. And don't take Boris with you—Reg is funny about dogs since his own cattle dog went missing.'

Before Erin could respond, Mum was gone in a flash of white and hurried footsteps, leaving Dad chuckling and shaking his head.

'Your mother,' he said fondly, turning back to Gilbert O'Byrne's elusive history, 'has always adopted our needy locals. Even the ones who fire warning shots at trespassers.'

'That's not funny, Dad,' Erin said, though she smiled despite herself. 'Is it true what they say about him? That no one's been in his house since his wife died?'

Dad's expression sobered. 'Betty died about five years ago. He hasn't been the same since. Your mother's the only one he lets visit. Says he likes her lasagne.' Dad adjusted his glasses. 'He's not well, Erin. Liver, we think. Turned down treatment.'

On Friday afternoon, Erin parked in the shade of an old river gum at *Dunleavy*. She gathered the picnic basket of food and the small cooler bag from the tray. All was quiet as she walked across to the gate. Beyond the fence, several old cars and trucks lay abandoned in tall grass. The old homestead sat fifty metres from the gate, weathered and in need of repair, but still standing proud beside the river.

'What do you want?' The voice that greeted Erin was gruff

and husky, floating out from the shadows.

'Mr McGillvray?' she called. 'It's Erin O'Byrne from next door.' Adding the Hayes to her name would only confuse him. Dad had been pleased to hear that she had kept her name along with Jack's; he was proud of the O'Byrne name and the history it carried.

'What do you want?' His tone held suspicion. 'Come to look at my water again? Told you not to come back here.'

'No, that's not me. You're thinking of my sister, Róisín.' Erin kept her voice steady and friendly. 'Mum's put together a food basket for you, but she had to go up to Louth today. Can I bring it in?'

'Gate's locked,' he stated flatly.

'Could you unlock it?'

'You'll have to climb over. There's a gap in the fence next to it. You can put the food through, then climb over.'

After checking the long grass around the gate for snakes—a habit ingrained since childhood—Erin pushed the supplies through the gap before hoisting herself over.

The walk to the house seemed longer in the growing heat. She balanced the cooler bag strap on her shoulder and held the basket carefully in front of her. Despite Reg telling her to come over the gate, she was wary. The stories of his shotgun warnings to unwanted visitors weren't easily forgotten.

A door creaked closed as she approached the house, and she spotted a figure standing in the shadows of the veranda. Her heart quickened until Reg stepped into the light—thankfully without his infamous shotgun.

'Just put it there on the step,' he directed.

'It needs to go in the shade, sir,' Erin replied respectfully.

Something flickered across his weathered face at the respectful address.

'Alright, alright, bring it up here.' He watched her carefully as she approached, avoiding the rotted timber step as she lifted the basket to the veranda. The cooler bag followed.

'Mum's packed a few meals for you,' she explained. 'Including some of those pies she makes.'

Reg tilted his head, studying her. 'You're the one who used to ride well, aren't you?'

'I am.'

'Thought you were married and away travelling.'

'Word certainly gets around,' Erin said with a slight smile, noting his interest in having a conversation.

'Where've you been?'

'You name it, we've been there. Every state and caught lots of fish. Bit better than the yellow belly and carp we get in this river.'

'Nothing wrong with yellow belly,' he defended quickly. 'Not a bad feed. Keeps me going.'

He examined her for a long moment, his head cocked to one side, and he disappeared into the dark hallway with the basket, returning moments later for the cooler bag. 'Stay there,' he said, handing her the empty basket.

'I will, Mr McGillvray. But the stuff in the cooler bag needs to go in the fridge straight away.'

His laugh revealed just two yellow stumps on his bottom jaw. 'Ain't got no fridge inside. Haven't had electricity for two years.'

'Oh, right.'

'Don't worry, I've got an ice chest out in the shed,' he said. 'Now you stay there, won't you?'

He disappeared into the depths of the hall, and Erin wondered where he got the ice from.

He returned quickly. 'Come over to the shed with me. I was about to have a cup of tea. You can have one with me.'

'Thank you, that would be nice,' Erin said, following him across the parched earth. To her surprise, he talked the whole way.

'You were in the pony club, weren't you?'

'I was. You've got a good memory.'

'Very good horsewoman, you were. Ever done anything with it?'

She shook her head regretfully. 'Would you believe I haven't been on a horse for three years?'

'Well, you're wasting your talent. You know, we always used to say you'd be good enough for the Olympics, Betty and me.'

'Betty?' she questioned.

'My wife, God rest her soul. She's been gone five years now.'

'I was sorry to hear that. She was always Mrs McGillvray to me.'

'You've got good manners for a girl.' He chuckled. 'Better manners than that sister of yours who came here wanting to close off my river and take my water.'

Erin hesitated; she thought about arguing. It wasn't worth it, and it didn't matter anyway. Reg was being friendly, and that seemed more important than correcting his version of events.

They reached an old shed between the house and the river. He pushed open the door, revealing a table and two plastic chairs. 'Sit down there and I'll make you a cuppa.'

Erin's eyes widened at the sight of sheep droppings caught in the cracks in the wooden table, teaspoons resting nearby. Trying not to grimace, she picked up one of the spoons and discreetly wiped it clean on her T-shirt, guessing she'd need it when the tea arrived.

The hiss of a gas stove came from inside, and moments later, Reg emerged with a brown teapot and two cracked mugs.

'Hope you take it black because I ain't got any milk. Last milking cow went about the same time as Betty, and I never bothered anymore 'cause I never took milk in my tea.'

'That's fine,' she said. 'Listen, I know Mum put a cake in there. Would you like me to get it?'

'No, no, you stay right there. I'll go and get it. What sort of cake?'

'I think it was carrot cake.'

'Good. She knows I like them. She's a good woman, that Laura. You've got a fine mum there, even if she did raise your rude sister.'

While he was gone, Erin took the opportunity to give both mugs a thorough wipe with her handkerchief. The water might be questionable, but at least it was boiled.

Reg returned with the cake, pouring tea into both mugs and taking a large swig of his own. 'Ah, good old Bushell's tea,' he said, smacking his lips. 'Now, tell me why you're home.'

'I came home for Cat's wedding.'

'But you're still here.'

'Well, my husband's overseas on a work assignment . . . '

'What's he do? One of them stupid government jobs in another country?'

'No, he's a photographer. Takes photos of wildlife for an international magazine.'

Reg nodded slowly. 'Can't see any harm in that. When he comes back, though, what's he gonna do for a real job? Your country boy gonna come help Tom over on the station?'

'Not sure,' she said softly.

There was a long silence as they sipped their tea.

'Who's staying in that motorhome I saw over near the billabong? Been there a while now.'

'That's me. I'm staying there.'

'Why aren't you staying in the house with your parents?'

'I like space and privacy,' she said, adding with a small smile, 'Like you.'

'Fair enough.' He took another sip of tea. 'Your parents are lucky to have good kids. Except that one I said.' His face darkened momentarily before he continued, 'What are the others doing?'

Erin was surprised by his knowledge of her family as she explained about her sisters' various pursuits. His memory was sharp, remembering details she wouldn't have expected him to know.

'How's your old man since his heart attack?' he asked. 'Lucky he didn't cark it.'

'He's doing well, coming back slowly. Spending most of his time on the family history now.'

'Waste of bloody time, that is. What's the point in learning about the past?' His voice grew harsh. 'I was sad for a few weeks when Betty died, but there's no point crying over spilt milk, love. My boys don't ever come near me, and that's a blessing, the way they turned out. Gotta move on.'

The conversation continued, moving through family histories and current events, until Erin realised how much time had passed. 'I should go,' she said, rising. 'Dad'll be wanting his lunch.'

'Been nice to have a chat, love.' His voice had softened again. 'Give me a call when you've got the next box to come over. Tell Laura not to waste her time just dropping everything and running over—she's got a lot to do. But if you're still here, you bring it over and we'll have another cuppa together. Have a good old chinwag.'

Walking back to the ute, Erin felt a mixture of sadness and understanding. Sometimes loneliness wore a gruff mask and carried a shotgun, but underneath was just someone wanting connection, even if they didn't quite know how to ask for it.

Chapter 29

July 19, 1916 - Fromelles.

The world had shrunk to the width of a trench.

Gilbert leaned against the muddy wall, his shoulders pressed between Davies and Wilson as they waited in the packed front line. The air hung heavy with the scent of unwashed bodies, cordite, and fear—a smell he'd grown accustomed to these past months, though he doubted he would ever find it familiar.

Up and down the line, men checked and rechecked their equipment—adjusting ammunition pouches, tightening helmet straps, fingering bayonets with nervous hands. Few spoke. They'd been briefed on the objective that morning: capture the German lines opposite their position, a salient known as the Sugar Loaf. Support the main offensive on the Somme by preventing German reinforcements from being sent south.

Simple orders. Nearly impossible task.

Gilbert fumbled in his breast pocket, finding the letter that had arrived with the morning's delivery—the first from Matilda in nearly three weeks. He'd already read it twice, hungrily absorbing every word, memorising phrases to replay in his mind during the long, dark watches of the night. Now, in these final moments before the whistles blew, he slipped it out once more.

'Another love letter, Piner?' Wilson teased, though the young soldier's voice lacked its usual carefree lilt.

Gilbert nodded, not bothering to hide his smile as he carefully unfolded the pages. Wilson wouldn't begrudge him this small comfort—none of them would. Each man had his own talisman against fear: a photograph, a Bible, a lucky coin. For

Gilbert, it was Matilda's letters, her neat handwriting a tangible connection to a world that sometimes seemed like a distant dream.

His eyes fell immediately on the passage that had stopped his heart earlier:

I have news that I've been keeping to myself, Gil, but can no longer contain. By spring, God willing, there will be two of us awaiting your return. The doctor in Wilcannia has confirmed what I've suspected these past months. Our child grows strong within me.

A child. His child. The knowledge had blazed through him like bushfire, scouring away the accumulated grime of war, leaving behind something clean and bright and terrifying in its intensity. He was to be a father. Somewhere across oceans and continents, in the sun-baked land along the Darling River, life continued. New life grew.

'Mail up!' came the whispered alert, passed man to man down the trench.

Gilbert carefully refolded the letter, returning it to his breast pocket, directly over his heart. There was no time to write a proper reply now, but he would scrawl a hasty note when he could—a few lines expressing his joy, his love, his renewed determination to survive this day and all the days after until he could return to her.

Sergeant Kelly moved among them, his weathered face revealing nothing of his thoughts. 'Check your ammunition, lads. Five minutes.'

The knot in Gilbert's stomach tightened. Five minutes until the artillery barrage lifted. Five minutes until the whistles blew and they climbed over the top into the teeth of German machine guns.

He found himself taking mental inventory of his body, as if memorising the sensations of being alive: the damp wool of his uniform against his skin, the weight of his rifle, the tight squeeze of his boots, the pulse throbbing in his throat. These ordinary discomforts seemed suddenly precious—proof that his heart still beat, that blood still flowed through his veins, that he remained Gilbert O'Byrne of *Ceann Mara* and not merely another anonymous soldier in this vast machinery of war.

'You thinking about home, mate?' Davies asked quietly beside him.

Gilbert nodded. 'The billabong on our property. There's a spot where the river gums hang over the water, makes a kind of green cave on hot days. Coolest place for miles.'

Davies smiled, his eyes distant. 'Sounds perfect.'

'It is. And it's where I'm going to build our house when I get back. Already picked out the exact spot.' Gilbert surprised himself with the steadiness in his voice. 'Matilda's expecting. Just found out in her letter.'

Davies clapped a hand on his shoulder, his grip fierce with understanding. 'Then you'd best keep your head down today, new papa. That little one's going to need you.'

'All of us,' Gilbert said, including Wilson with a nod. 'We're all getting home.'

None of them acknowledged the fragility of such promises.

A whistle shrilled further down the line—an officer checking that his men were ready. Not the signal to advance, not yet, but a reminder that it would come soon. Gilbert found his hands moving automatically, one last check of his equipment even as his mind filled with images of home.

The red dirt track leading to *Ceann Mara's* homestead. His

mother in the kitchen garden, hands black with soil. His father's quiet pride the day they'd brought in the season's first shearing. Harry's laughter as they raced their horses across the paddocks. Olive's fierce concentration as she practised her letters. Little Lily's solemn face as she presented him with a drawing before he left.

And Matilda. Always Matilda. Standing by the billabong at sunset, her hair loose around her shoulders, her hand outstretched towards him. Matilda now, with their child growing within her, waiting for his return.

'One minute!' The alert rippled down the line, tightening every face, straightening every spine.

Gilbert took a deep breath, filling his lungs with the damp, close air of the trench. He allowed himself one final, fleeting thought of the Darling River—the play of sunlight on its surface, the scent of eucalyptus carried on the breeze, the endless blue of the Australian sky.

Then he pushed it all away, focusing only on what lay immediately ahead. The next few hours. The next few minutes. The ground he would need to cover, the moves he would need to make. Survival.

'Ten seconds!'

Men tensed all around him, a collective coiling of muscle and will. Gilbert's hand found the small river stone in his pocket—Matilda's childhood gift that he'd carried through Egypt and France, a small piece of home that had become his good luck charm.

'Fight for the man beside you,' Sergeant Kelly called out. 'Nothing else matters out there.'

The seconds stretched, elastic with tension. Gilbert became aware of his heartbeat, unnaturally loud in his ears. He thought of the child he would not see for months yet. A son with his eyes, perhaps. Or a daughter with Matilda's determination.

The whistles blew.

'Over the top, lads! For Australia!'

Gilbert moved on instinct, scrambling up the rough-hewn steps to the parapet, Davies at his side, Wilson just behind. The roar of the final artillery barrage filled the world, shells screaming overhead to crash into the German lines. Smoke and dust clogged the air, giving the battlefield an otherworldly quality, as if they were charging not across French soil but into some biblical underworld.

His boots hit the ground of no-man's-land, and he was running, crouched low, rifle at the ready. All around him, Australian soldiers poured from the trenches, a tide of khaki surging forward towards the German wire.

The first machine guns opened up, their staccato chatter cutting through the thunder of the artillery. Men fell, but the line pressed on. Gilbert fixed his eyes on the objective, refusing to look at the bodies already beginning to litter the churned earth. Cooper. Mcpherson. On the ground. One foot in front of the other. Keep moving. Stay with your section.

A shell exploded nearby, showering him with dirt and debris. He stumbled but kept his feet, Davies steadying him with a quick hand on his arm. They pressed on, the German trenches growing closer with each lurching step.

Through the smoke and chaos, Gilbert caught glimpses of the enemy lines—concrete emplacements, coils of barbed wire, the muzzle flashes of machine guns. So many machine guns. Far more than intelligence had suggested. The Germans had been waiting, ready for them.

Men were falling all around now, dropped by machine gun fire or caught in the sudden eruption of shells. The Australian line began to thin, gaps appearing where entire sections were cut down in seconds.

'Keep moving!' an officer shouted, his voice barely audible above the din. 'Push through to the wire!'

Gilbert pressed on; his world narrowed to the few yards of ground directly ahead. The weight of his pack dug into his shoulders. Sweat ran into his eyes despite the relative cool of the evening. His lungs burned with each breath, the air thick with gun smoke and dust.

A bullet snapped past his ear, so close he felt the air move. Another tore through the sleeve of his tunic without touching flesh. The machine guns were finding their range.

In that moment, as death flew all around him, Gilbert felt a strange clarity. This might be it. This muddy field in France, so far from the sunbaked plains of the Darling, might be where his life ended. The thought brought not fear but a fierce regret—for the child he might never know, for the life with Matilda he might never live, for the house by the billabong he might never build.

'Wire ahead!' someone shouted. 'Wire cutters forward!'

Gilbert dropped to one knee behind a slight rise in the ground, providing covering fire as the designated men moved forward with their cutters. The German machine guns intensified, concentrating on the vulnerable soldiers exposed at the wire.

'Piner!' Sergeant Kelly materialised beside him, his face blackened with dirt and gunpowder. 'Take Wilson and three others. Work your way left to that shell hole, then push through where Johnson's cleared a path in the wire. The rest of us will draw their fire.'

Gilbert nodded, quickly signalling to Wilson and the others. This was it—the moment when abstract orders became immediate action, when the fate of his life balanced on decisions made in seconds.

As he prepared to move, time seemed to slow, extending a single heartbeat into an eternity. In that stretched moment, Gilbert allowed himself one final thought of home. Not of the place, but of the feeling—of belonging, of purpose, of love. Of Matilda waiting by the billabong, her hand protectively cradling their unborn child.

'I'm coming back to you,' he whispered, a promise carried away by the wind and gunfire.

Then he was up and running, leading his small group towards the shell hole, towards the gap in the wire, towards whatever fate awaited on the other side.

Behind him, the sun was low over the battlefield, painting the smoke-filled sky in shades of red and gold—not unlike the sunsets over the Darling River, though Gilbert had no time to notice the similarity. His world had contracted to the next few seconds, the next few steps, survival focused to a single, burning point.

Chapter 30

Ceann Mara - Saturday.

Erin sat underneath the annexe in the shade of a spreading river gum at the side of the billabong. Miles had headed out before light as she lay sleepless in her motorhome. She was a little bit concerned that an interaction between them last night had been a bit—it was hard to think of a word—maybe, off, and he'd decided to move on.

There had been nothing from Jack, and she'd focused on coping mechanisms these past few days. Life was back to normal at the station; she was the only visitor left now, although when she'd said that last night, Mum shook her head.

'Never a visitor, love.'

She'd been reading about meditation and how to stop all the thoughts running around in her head. The website had been full of flowery language about "finding your inner peace" and "connecting with your higher self"—the sort of stuff that would have her sisters in stitches if they knew she was even considering it.

'Honestly,' she muttered, scrolling through the instructions, 'these city people would pay good money to sit in a paddock and breathe.' She'd grown up learning that the best way to clear your head was to get on a horse and ride until your troubles couldn't keep up. Or help Dad with the mustering. Or join Mum in the garden. Anything but sit still and "observe your thoughts like passing clouds".

But three sleepless nights in a row had made her desperate enough to try anything, even this hippy-dippy nonsense. What would old Reg say if she could see her now, cross-legged on her camp chair, trying to "cultivate mindful awareness"? He'd probably tell her to go help with the shearing if she needed something to take her mind off things.

Still, here she was, following the instructions on her phone: "Sit comfortably with your spine straight. Close your eyes. Focus on your breath moving in and out of your body. When thoughts arise, acknowledge them without judgement and let them float away like clouds in the sky."

'Float away like clouds,' Erin snorted. 'Right.' Her thoughts weren't floating anywhere—they were stomping around her head like a mob of kangaroos. Every time she tried to focus on her breath, Jack's voice would pop into her mind, or she'd remember something she needed to buy in town, or wonder if she should visit Reg next door.

The website said to count breaths: in for four counts, hold for seven, out for eight. She tried it, but by the third breath, she was already thinking about Jack and Natalie sharing a tent in Africa. The more she tried to push the thoughts away, the more insistent they became. This was exactly why country folk didn't go in for this sort of thing—too much real work to be done to sit around contemplating their navels.

'Too busy,' she murmured to herself. 'No time for sitting around breathing.' But that wasn't true anymore, was it? She had nothing but time out here by the billabong. Time to think, time to worry, time to imagine Jack and Natalie . . . no. She squared her shoulders and tried again. Spine straight. Eyes closed. One more time.

To her surprise, after five minutes of trying and failing, she finally managed to clear her mind, focusing on her fingertips as the website had suggested. For a brief moment, she felt it—a strange sense of quiet, like the stillness just before dawn when the world hadn't quite woken up yet. It was almost peaceful, almost . . .

Then a loud rustle in the long grass broke her concentration. The black snake moved with fluid grace through the dried grass, its scales catching the afternoon light. At least two metres long, it carved a silent path through the tussocks, leaving a subtle trail in its wake. Erin watched, fascinated, as its muscular body propelled it forward in perfect S-curves. These red-bellied blacks were common along the billabong, more interested in the frogs and small lizards than in humans.

The snake paused at the water's edge, its forked tongue testing the air before gliding into the billabong without so much as a ripple. In the brown flood water, its body became a dark ribbon, undulating gracefully as it swam. Erin wasn't bothered by snakes. She'd seen many of them in her childhood, and probably more by good luck than care, she and her sisters had never been bitten. They'd seen a couple of dogs die over the years—dogs that hadn't been trained properly and didn't know when to leave snakes alone. Dad was very firm about getting kelpies, the only breed that could be properly trained not to attack snakes. She tracked its progress across to the far bank, where it disappeared into the thick grass beneath the river gums.

The encounter reminded her of the past few nights when Miles had sat by her campfire. He'd told her about his close call with a brown snake up north, and she'd found herself sharing stories about growing up here, about the childhood adventures she and her sisters had survived more by luck than good judgement.

Last night, Miles had fallen silent, and when she'd looked

up, she'd found him watching her with an intensity that made her uncomfortable. She'd had a couple of wines by then—something she'd been doing too much lately. After the wedding, when she'd had three or four champagnes, the hangover the next morning hadn't been pleasant. She'd driven up to Louth the day before yesterday to get out on her own—she hadn't told Mum because she would've wanted to come too—and called into the general store. Mrs Higgins wasn't there, and Erin didn't recognise the youngish woman behind the counter. Mandy was embroidered onto her shirt, but Erin didn't get into a conversation as she bought some groceries and a couple of bottles of white wine. Her hand had hovered over a bottle of whiskey, but she'd told herself no, that was getting too serious. In the end, though, she'd bought it anyway. If Miles came over for a drink, she could offer him something stronger than wine.

She'd asked him last night, after her second glass of wine, where he was heading next. He'd been vague earlier, shrugging off questions about where he'd come from and where he was going.

'I can tell you some good places to camp,' she said.

'I'll miss our chats when I leave,' he said, pushing himself to his feet. His hand ran up her arm, and then he stood behind her, massaging the back of her neck.

Erin froze when he spoke. 'If you ever need any comfort, Erin, all you have to do is ask.'

She knew immediately what he meant, and stiffened beneath his warm fingers, although a small, hurt part of her whispered, *Why not? Jack's over there with perfect Natalie.*

But she knew she couldn't.

'I'm fine, thank you.' She stood and spoke quickly. 'I'm

going to bed.' Out of habit, she'd locked the door, then wondered if Miles heard the click and thought she was trying to tell him something.

##

Erin walked up to the house when she gave up on the meditation. Now that all the family had departed, it was just Mum and Dad in the homestead; life had settled back into a normal routine. While Logan was away, Dad was taking a break from station work for a few days and focusing on the family history research.

The smell of Mum's quiche wafted out—caramelised onion and bacon, if she wasn't mistaken; her stomach growled.

'There you are, love.' Laura was pulling the quiche from the oven, the golden pastry perfectly browned. 'Your timing's spot on. Thanks for dropping off that food to Reg yesterday. How was he?'

Erin smiled. 'The usual, but he did give me a cuppa, and we had a good yarn. He certainly doesn't look well.'

Tom looked up from his papers spread across one end of the kitchen table. 'Good to see you, sweetheart.' He started gathering up his notes—more family history research, by the looks of it.

'Leave those out, Dad,' Erin said, trying to sound normal. 'I'd love to hear what you've found.'

Her parents exchanged a quick glance that she pretended not to notice. They were being careful with her, she realised. As though she might break.

'Well,' Tom said, settling back with his papers, 'I've discovered a little bit more about Gilbert.'

Laura set the quiche on the wooden board in the middle of the table. 'That can wait until we've eaten, Tom.'

But Erin was grateful for the distraction. 'No, go on, Dad.'

Her father's face lit up the way it always did when he talked about family history. He shuffled through his papers, but before he could answer, Laura cut in.

'When do you think Jack will be home?' The question hung in the air as Erin pushed a piece of quiche around her plate. 'Not sure now . . .' She swallowed hard. 'The contract's been extended. Could be even longer if they like his work.' She tried to keep her voice steady. 'He's already talking about new magazines being interested.'

Laura's fork stilled and she frowned.

'He says it could set us up for life.' The words tasted bitter in her mouth. 'He and Natalie are apparently getting some incredible shots.'

'Natalie?' Tom's voice sharpened.

'His assistant.' Erin's fingers tightened on her fork. 'The magazine assigned her to help him.'

'When I was in hospital,' Tom said, 'Cat discovered a whole lot about Samuel, the other brother who first came over. We're still following that path too.'

Erin forced herself to take another bite of quiche, grateful for her father's attempt to change the subject. 'That's great, Dad. I'm happy to keep helping you until Cat comes home. Then I'd better get back and see if I've still got a job.'

Her parents exchanged a glance, but didn't speak.

They finished the meal in relative quiet, the silence broken only by Tom's occasional comments about shipping records and parish registers. Erin managed a few more bites of the quiche, though it tasted like cardboard in her mouth. When Laura started clearing the plates, Erin stood.

'I should go,' she said softly. 'Thanks for lunch, Mum.'

She caught the worried glance her parents exchanged again, saw her mother's lips purse with concern, but she couldn't bear to stay any longer. Half of what she'd told them had been made up on the spot, but she couldn't bear to have them asking more questions.

Instead of taking the usual track back to her camp, she chose the longer route that wound past the old shearing sheds. The walk would do her good, give her time to settle her thoughts.

When she finally rounded the bend to her campsite, she stopped short. The patch of grass where Miles had parked was slightly flattened, the ashes of his last campfire a grey smudge against the earth. She hadn't noticed this morning that everything else had gone: his table, chair, and the large gas lamp he'd used to cook by. She stood there for a long moment, surprised by the tangle of emotions the empty site stirred up.

Relief? Yes, there was some of that. But there was something else too—a hollow feeling that might have been disappointment, or maybe just another reminder of how easily people could disappear from your life.

'Right,' she said aloud to the empty campsite. 'Time for that walk.'

She turned away from her motorhome and headed towards the far end of the billabong. The afternoon stretched ahead of her, empty and quiet, but at least out here she didn't have to pretend everything was fine.

Mum's quiche sat heavily in Erin's stomach as she walked the perimeter of the airstrip. The packed earth runway held the heat, and she found herself remembering all the times she'd watched planes take off and land here—Royal Flying Doctor Service visits, mustering helicopters, and the family Cessna.

At the far edge of the billabong, she found a spot under an ancient river gum. The water stretched out before her; its surface ruffled by the afternoon breeze. Close to shore, a spoonbill waded through the shallows, sweeping its distinctive bill back and forth through the water. In the distance, a flock of pink-eared ducks scattered across the sky, heading towards the Menindee Lakes.

Pelicans soared overhead, riding the thermals with barely a wing movement, while sacred kingfishers darted low over the water, their brilliant blue plumage flashing in the sun. A group of red-necked avocets picked their way along the muddy edges, their slender upturned bills perfect for sifting through the silt.

Erin ran her fingers through the short grass beside her, enjoying its softness. The floodwaters had receded weeks ago, leaving behind lush growth. Her hand encountered something hard beneath the grass—not a root or a branch, but something deliberately placed.

Frowning, she brushed away the dirt and pulled up tufts of grass. A small stone emerged, roughly rectangular and clearly worked by human hands. As she cleared more grass away, she could make out an inscription, the letters weathered but still legible:

G.P.O. 1895-1916.

Loved lost and in my heart forever.

Matilda

Her breath caught. G.P.O? The Gilbert Dad was looking for; it was coincidental after he had just spoken about Gilbert.

Her fingers traced the letters, worn smooth by time and weather. A century of floods and droughts had passed over this stone, but grief still echoed across the years. The weathered inscription stirred something deep in Erin. A love so strong that someone had carved it in stone, yet the beloved's name was missing. She thought that she and Jack had shared a love that deep, but she'd been wrong.

She ran her fingers over the date again—1916. Was it a memorial to Gilbert? Had Matilda lost her love in the trenches of World War I? Had she sat here by the billabong, just as Erin was sitting now, feeling like her world had ended?

At least Matilda had known for certain. The telegram would have come, bringing its devastating news in cold, official words. But Erin was trapped in uncertainty, reading between the lines of emails, trying to decipher what wasn't being said. *Natalie says I can't come home. Natalie, Natalie, Natalie.*

She looked out over the water. A pied cormorant dove beneath the surface, emerging several metres away with a silver fish flashing in its beak. Life went on, didn't it? Even after loss, even after heartbreak. The birds still fished, the sun still set, and the world kept turning.

Pulling her phone from her pocket, she snapped a photo of the stone. Dad would want to know about this—it was another piece of their family history puzzle. She'd show him in the morning. Maybe researching Matilda's story would give her something to focus on besides her own troubles.

Chapter 31

Lobamba - Mid-May.

The evening air hung heavy with moisture as Jack leaned against the balcony railing of his hotel room, staring at his phone. He'd managed to get brief access to the service, and there was a reply from Erin, sent over a week ago.

One word.

Fine.

He couldn't bear to think about how much she would think he'd let her down, not getting to the wedding. And then there was no bloody service to reply to her, or phone service to call.

Frustration and helplessness clawed at him as the mountain landscape of Eswatini spread out before him, mist clinging to the valleys as twilight deepened. Under different circumstances, he would have been captivated by the view, already planning how to capture it through his lens. Instead, his thoughts remained stubbornly fixed on a sheep station half a world away and the woman who was confused and hurting. He couldn't blame Erin; one of the hardest things he'd ever done was emailing to say he wouldn't be at Cat and Logan's wedding.

'Brooding again?'

Jack turned to find Natalie stepping onto the balcony, two glasses of wine in hand. He shook his head: she had no idea of privacy, and often came into his room without knocking. She offered one glass to him, the ruby liquid catching the last of the day's light. Her blonde hair was loose around her shoulders, still damp from a recent shower, and she'd changed from her practical field clothes into a loose sundress that highlighted her tanned shoulders.

'Not brooding,' he said, accepting the wine. 'Just pissed off at the lack of internet.' He wasn't going to tell her about the email from Erin. He was going to figure out what to do himself.

Natalie leaned against the railing beside him, close enough that he could smell her perfume—something expensive and floral that seemed incongruous with their dusty surroundings. 'About the outback princess?'

Jack frowned. 'Don't call her that.'

'Sorry,' Natalie said, not sounding particularly apologetic. She took a sip of her wine. 'But you have to admit, there's something almost medieval about your situation. The photographer falling for the daughter of the manor, pledging to bridge two worlds . . .' She waved her free hand dramatically.

'It's a sheep station, not a manor,' Jack said dryly. 'And Erin's hardly a princess.'

'No? The way you describe her, wandering around her father's vast lands, communing with nature, rescuing injured animals—'

'You make it sound romantic. It's hard work, what the O'Byrnes do. Their family settled there in the nineteenth century.' Jack turned back to the view, deliberately putting a few more inches between them. 'Anyway, what brought you looking for me? Did we get clearance for tomorrow's village shoot?'

Natalie sighed, setting her glass down on the small table between the balcony chairs. 'Always business with you lately, Jack. Yes, we got clearance. The local chief is expecting us at nine.' She moved to stand in front of him, forcing him to meet her gaze. 'But that's not why I came.'

Something in her tone made Jack instantly wary. Natalie was brilliant at her job—her eye for composition enhanced his own photography. But there had been an undercurrent since they'd arrived; a subtle tension that he'd been careful not to encourage.

'We need to talk about your work on this assignment,' she said, her voice softening. 'You're distracted, Jack. The shots you've been getting are technically perfect, but they're missing that spark that Lars saw in your Kimberley photographs.'

'I wasn't aware of that.'

'It's more than that.' Natalie moved closer, placing a hand on his arm. 'I'm worried about you. These emails from your wife—' She nodded towards his phone. 'You're not happy.'

Jack pulled away, uncomfortable with her touch and the direction of the conversation. 'Erin and I are fine. We're just adjusting to the distance. And I miss her.'

'Are you sure you're fine? Because from where I'm standing, it looks like she's already moving on.'

'You don't know what you're talking about,' Jack said sharply. 'And it's not really any of your business. My personal life is just that. Personal.'

Natalie's expression was a mixture of concern and something else—something he deliberately chose not to identify. 'Don't I? No phone calls. Classic signs of someone creating distance.'

Jack felt a flare of anger, not least because her words touched on fears he'd been trying to ignore. 'There's no bloody service. How can she call?'

'I understand what you're going through,' Natalie ignored his protest, moving closer again. 'When Carl and I broke up after that Amazon assignment, it was because the distance showed us what we'd been denying for months—that we wanted different lives.'

'Erin and I aren't breaking up,' Jack said firmly.

Natalie smiled sadly. 'Maybe not. But Jack, be honest with yourself. How will this work in the long term? Your career is taking off. After this spread is published, you'll be in high demand internationally. Are you really going to give that up for life in a motorhome in a country town?'

The question hit a nerve. It was the same question he'd been asking himself during sleepless nights in various hotel rooms across Eswatini. He loved Erin—of that he had no doubt. However, loving someone and building a life with them were entirely different challenges.

'I don't know,' he admitted quietly. 'I'll figure it out.'

'Life's too short for "figuring it out",' Natalie said, reaching up to touch his face gently. 'We should grab happiness when it's right in front of us.'

There was no mistaking her meaning now. Jack stared at her, momentarily speechless as her fingers traced his jawline.

'Natalie—'

'Don't tell me you haven't thought about it,' she whispered, stepping closer until there was barely space between them. 'All those late nights reviewing shots, the conversations that go on for hours . . . there's always been something between us, Jack. You know it as well as I do.'

Before he could respond, she leaned forward and pressed her lips to his. For a heartbeat, shock kept him frozen in place. It had been weeks since he'd been touched, months of tension and loneliness building within him. For one dangerous moment, he felt himself responding.

Then Erin's face flashed in his mind—not smiling as he usually thought of her, but with the vulnerable expression she'd worn when they'd said goodbye at the airport, trying so hard to be brave about their separation.

Jack pulled back firmly, placing his hands on Natalie's shoulders to create distance between them.

'I can't,' he said quietly.

Natalie's expression hardened slightly. 'Can't? Or won't?'

'Both.' Jack stepped back, putting the balcony chair between them. 'I'm flattered, Natalie. And I'd be lying if I said I wasn't tempted. But I love Erin. I'm committed to her.'

'Committed,' Natalie repeated, her tone suddenly brittle. 'Such an old-fashioned concept.'

'Call it what you want. I made a promise.'

She studied him for a long moment, her professional composure reasserting itself. 'And what about your career, Jack? Your promise to yourself? You've worked hard to get where you are now. Will you go back to working in a pub, slipping out when you can to take photographs? You have a rare talent, and it would be criminal not to take advantage of what *Terra Lens* can offer you.'

'I can have both,' he said, with more confidence than he felt.

Natalie picked up her wine glass, draining it in one long swallow. 'Can you? Because from where I'm standing, you'll have to choose. And soon.' She set the empty glass down with deliberate care. 'You should know that Lars is considering you for the Southeast Asia series next year. Six months, covering Vietnam, Cambodia, Laos—it would make your career.'

Jack felt a surge of excitement at the mention of such a prestigious assignment, immediately followed by a wave of guilt. Another six months away from Erin after they'd already spent so much time apart.

'Of course,' Natalie continued, 'I have considerable influence with Lars. As assistant editor, my recommendations carry weight.'

The implication hung in the air between them.

'Are you threatening me?' Jack asked quietly.

Natalie laughed, though there was little humour in the sound. 'Threatening? No. Just stating facts. Lars trusts my judgement about which photographers work well with the editorial team.' She smoothed her dress, a gesture that somehow emphasised the curves beneath. 'It's a close-knit industry, Jack. Relationships matter.'

Jack felt a cold anger replacing his earlier confusion. 'So that's it? Sleep with you or watch my career suffer?'

'Don't be crude,' Natalie snapped. 'I'm simply pointing out that personal and professional choices often intersect. You should think carefully about what—and who—you really want.'

She turned to leave, pausing at the balcony door. 'We have an early start tomorrow. I suggest you get some sleep and reconsider your priorities.' With that, she stepped back into the hotel, letting the door close firmly behind her.

Jack remained on the balcony, his untouched wine forgotten, his thoughts in chaos. The practical part of him recognised the threat to his career for what it was. Natalie could make things difficult for him at *Terra Lens*. The Southeast Asia assignment would almost certainly go to someone else. Future opportunities might mysteriously dry up.

Yet beneath that professional concern lay something more fundamental—clarity about what truly mattered to him. He picked up his phone again, scrolling to the last photo he'd taken of Erin before leaving Australia. She was standing by the billabong at sunset, her profile outlined against the golden light, unaware of the camera. There was a serenity in her expression that had captured his heart from the beginning.

Making a sudden decision, Jack pulled out his phone and then realised there was no point sending a text. It wouldn't go. He'd lost count of the texts that had red "not sent" symbols against them.

For nearly an hour, he paced his room, his thoughts churning. Natalie's words about his career echoed in his mind. The Southeast Asia series would indeed be career-defining—the kind of prestigious assignment photographers waited years to land. Six months documenting some of the most visually compelling locations in the world, with *Terra Lens'* considerable resources behind him.

All that stood between him and professional advancement was Natalie's recommendation. Or lack thereof.

He thought of the sacrifices he'd already made—the years of thankless freelance work, living out of a backpack, passing up a stable job managing his father's hotel to chase his dreams. He was so close to breaking through to the level he'd always aspired to reach.

Then he thought of Erin, of the life they might build together. Would she understand if he explained the situation? That sometimes, in competitive fields, compromises had to be made? That it didn't have to mean anything beyond securing his future—their future?

Jack caught his reflection in the hotel mirror, barely recognising the conflict in his own eyes. This wasn't who he was. Or was it? Perhaps he had never truly been tested before.

With a deep breath, he made his decision.

Ten minutes later, Jack stood outside Natalie's door, his heart pounding uncomfortably in his chest. He raised his hand and knocked firmly, three sharp raps against the wooden door. As he waited for her to answer, he still wasn't entirely sure what he would say—or what he would do.

Chapter 32

Ceann Mara - Monday.

After Dad had been down to the billabong with Erin to see the stone she'd discovered, he closeted himself in the study for a couple of days; it had almost transformed into a makeshift war room. Erin had agreed to help him sort through some of the files that had been emailed in response to his request. Tom had printed out pages and pages of various documents.

'I won't be much help, but I can sort and staple.' It was good to focus her mind on something different, and Erin had enjoyed the morning so far.

'Another pair of hands is a great help, love.'

Maps of Europe, yellowed newspaper clippings, and photocopies of military documents covered every surface. Tom stood at the centre of it all, glasses perched on the end of his nose as he pored over a ledger dating back to 1914.

'He was still here in March 1915,' Tom said, tapping a faded entry. 'Gilbert P. O'Byrne. Twenty sheep were lost in the February floods, replaced with purchase from Wambool Station in March.'

Erin looked up from the stack of correspondence she'd been methodically sorting by date. 'So, Gilbert was definitely managing the property before he enlisted.'

'Managing it brilliantly, by all accounts,' Tom replied, a hint of pride in his voice. 'The ledgers show increasing wool yields each season from 1912 to 1915.

'Was Gilbert your grandfather?' Erin was confused.

'No, his brother Harry was my dad's father. Your great-grandfather.'

Erin shook her head as the late afternoon sun slanted through the windows, catching dust motes disturbed by their research efforts. 'I have no idea how you keep all this in your head. How many generations have been on *Ceann Mara* now?'

Her father looked up with a smile. 'Catching the family history bug, love?'

'Well, it is interesting,' Erin conceded.

Tom turned to the big document drawer beneath the family photo that had been taken at Broken Hill a few years back. He pulled out a laminated A3 sheet and found a clear space on the table.

'There you go. The easiest way is to see the family tree drawn up.' His calloused finger pointed to the top of the tree. 'Our line comes from Thomas, who was born in 1828. He built *Ceann Mara.*'

'And his brother Samuel had the paddle steamers. I knew that much.' Erin nodded.

'Then Thomas's son, James—actually, James was his brother Sean's son, but that's another story—took over, and his son, another Thomas, was Gilbert and Harry's father. Then there was my dad, William, and now I'm the third Thomas O'Byrne of *Ceann Mara.*'

The pride in her father's voice almost brought tears to Erin's eyes. 'I can see why you and Cat are so interested. It really brings the family to life, doesn't it?'

'It does. Now that you know the lineage, take a look at the photos on the wall alongside our family photo. We've got most of the generation, including one with Gilbert and Harry, and their two sisters taken in 1911, when Lily, the younger one, was a baby.'

Erin spent a few minutes looking at the photos before returning to sorting the documents. She paused and held up a copy of a handwritten note. 'This might be something, Dad. It's addressed to Gilbert, postmarked December 1915.'

Tom joined her at the table as she carefully extracted the fragile paper from within. The handwriting was delicate but assured, the ink faded to a soft sepia.

'My dearest Gilbert,' Erin read aloud, 'Thank you for the lovely afternoon by the river. Father would be most displeased to know I shirked my duties to spend time in such pleasant company, but some secrets are worth keeping—' She paused, scanning ahead. 'It's signed "Your M".'

'M for Matilda,' Tom murmured. 'That must be from Matilda Ellis.'

The discovery of the stone with Matilda's name carved into it had reignited Tom's enthusiasm to search for information about Gilbert. The connection between the neighbouring families had been mentioned in family lore, but details had been scarce, the relationship between Gilbert and Matilda reduced to whispers and speculation over the decades.

'She was careful not to be too explicit,' Erin observed, still reading. 'But listen to this: 'I find myself counting the days between our meetings with a schoolgirl's eagerness that would mortify me if anyone knew. When you spoke of your dreams for *Ceann Mara*, I could almost see myself within them, though I know such thoughts are premature and perhaps foolish.'

Tom smiled, reaching for the letter. 'Not premature, just ill-timed. With the war happening—'

The sound of the screen door slamming announced Laura's arrival before she appeared in the doorway, carrying a tray.

'You two missed afternoon tea,' she said, placing the tray on the one clear corner of the desk. 'Any progress?'

'We've found a letter from Matilda to Gilbert,' Erin said, accepting a mug of tea gratefully. 'They were clearly more than just neighbours.'

Laura smiled, leaning against the doorframe. 'A romance next door. Do you think that's *Dunleavy*? Reg McGillvray's place?'

Tom nodded. 'Yes, it is. *Dunleavy* was formerly known as *Wambool*. I found the record of the change in the nineteen fifties.'

'I hope Gilbert came home safely from the war,' Laura said.

'We're not sure yet, love. More research to do,' Tom said as he and Erin looked at each other. The stone and absence of Gilbert from family records after 1916 indicated perhaps there wasn't going to be a happy ending.

'Here's another,' Erin said, carefully opening a different envelope. 'August, 1915. The handwriting's different—more masculine.'

'Gilbert's?' Laura asked, moving to look over her shoulder.

'No, it's to Gilbert and signed Robert Ellis. That would be Matilda's father, perhaps?' Erin scanned the contents. 'Listen to this: I understand your dilemma, Gilbert. The call to serve is strong, especially with recruitment posters plastered across town and those damned white feathers being handed out. But you're doing essential work here. The country needs its wool and its wheat as much as it needs its soldiers. Think carefully before you make your decision.'

'So, he was considering enlisting as early as August 1915,' Tom said thoughtfully.

'What changed his mind?' Laura wondered.

Erin continued sorting through the correspondence, arranging letters chronologically on the table. 'There's a gap here—nothing for September.'

Tom returned to the ledger, turning pages carefully. 'The station records continue normally after that, though. Sheep counts, wool shipments, equipment purchases.' He paused, squinting at an entry. 'Wait. October 18th, 1915. "Meeting with R. Ellis re: boundary dispute resolved amicably." That's unusual enough to be noted specifically.'

'A boundary dispute with the Ellis family? That seems at odds with Gilbert's relationship with Matilda. Maybe that's why there's a gap in the personal correspondence,' Erin suggested. 'There might have been some sort of falling out between the families.'

'It's all supposition and your coffee's getting cold,' Laura said.

'Sorry,' Tom said, absently reaching for one of the cups on the tray. With his other hand, he held up a manila folder. 'The local newspaper archives from Broken Hill Library from 1914 and 1915. The librarian allowed me to photocopy the relevant pages.'

Once his coffee cup was empty, he spread several sheets on the table in front of Erin. 'There is a report here from early December 1915 regarding a recruitment drive held at the town hall in Broken Hill. Lists of local men who enlisted that day.'

Her finger traced down the column of names. 'Here he is! —G. Piner O'Byrne of *Ceann Mara* Station.'

'G. Piner?' Mum asked, looking over her shoulder.

'Gilbert Piner,' Tom explained. 'Piner was his mother's

family name. He sometimes used both.'

'The article mentions that several local properties would now be managed by family members as the young men headed off to training camp,' Erin continued. '*Ceann Mara* is specifically mentioned as being "left in the capable hands of Harry O'Byrne Jr, younger brother of the enlistee".'

'That would be my grandfather,' Tom said. 'He was a year younger than Gilbert's nineteen.'

Erin had been sifting through another pile of correspondence as they spoke. 'Here's something,' she said suddenly. 'A letter written by Matilda dated February 20th, 1916. A couple of months after Gilbert left. But there's no salutation, so I'm not sure who it's written to.'

The room fell silent as she carefully smoothed out the photocopy. 'I write this with a hand that trembles and a heart that breaks. I miss Gilbert so much.' Erin paused, looking up. 'The next part is smudged—tear stains, maybe?'

'Read what you can,' Tom urged gently.

'I pray for his safety with every breath. What am I to do now with the future we planned in those golden afternoons by the river? What am I to do with the love that grows within me, in more ways than one? Perhaps it is a blessing that he went without knowing. Perhaps some burdens are best carried alone…' Erin's voice faltered.

'She was pregnant,' Laura whispered, the realisation settling over the room like a physical presence.

'I could not ask him to forsake his duty,' Erin continued reading. 'My choice has been made. But know that whatever happens, whatever becomes of us, my heart remains his, as surely as the river flows past our lands. Forever Gilbert's.'

Silence filled the study. Outside, a kookaburra laughed, the sound jarring against the gravity of Matilda's sorrow.

'So, Gilbert went to war not knowing he'd fathered a child,' Tom said quietly.

'And Matilda was left to face the consequences alone,' Erin added. 'I wonder why she wrote that? Was it to someone in her family? Or just a letter to herself? Or a diary entry?'

'Perhaps she didn't tell anyone that Gilbert was the father, and she wanted there to be a record of it somewhere. But it's all speculation.' Tom reached for the letter, examining it carefully. 'This changes our understanding completely. We've been searching for what happened to Gilbert, and now there's another branch of the story we never knew existed.'

'What happened to the child?' Laura asked. 'If Matilda was pregnant in late 1915, the baby would have been born in 1916.'

'And that baby would be . . .' Tom calculated quickly, 'my father's half-sibling.'

As he spoke, the sun dipped below the horizon, and Tom reached for the light switch before he carefully placed Matilda's letter on the table, his expression thoughtful. 'We'll find them both,' he said quietly. 'Gilbert and his child. Wherever they ended up, we'll find them.'

Chapter 33

Battle of Fromelles - July 1916.

The world had narrowed to the width of a shell hole.

Gilbert O'Byrne lay half-submerged in muddy water, the metallic taste of blood filling his mouth. Above him, the evening sky flashed with artillery fire, illuminating the churned earth of no-man's-land in brief, hellish tableaux. The noise was overwhelming—the thunder of shells, the rattle of machine guns, the screams of wounded men—yet somehow distant now, as though heard through layers of wool.

He tried to move, to push himself up from the fetid water, but his body refused to obey. The pain that had initially seared through his chest with each breath was fading to a cold numbness that spread outward from his core. Gilbert knew what that meant. He had seen it too many times in the past hours not to recognise it in himself.

'Piner! Gilbert!'

The voice came from somewhere to his right. With tremendous effort, Gilbert turned his head. John Davies was crawling towards him, his face blackened with dirt and gunpowder, a dark stain spreading across his left shoulder.

'Christ, mate,' Davies said as he reached the shell hole, sliding down beside Gilbert. 'Been looking for you since the retreat was called. Half the company's gone.'

Gilbert tried to speak, but a wet cough wracked his body instead, bringing a fresh wave of copper-tasting warmth to his mouth.

Davies' expression changed as he saw the extent of

Gilbert's wounds. His experienced farmer's eyes took in the shrapnel tears across Gilbert's torso, the unnatural angle of his right leg, the spreading crimson that darkened his sodden uniform.

'Stretcher bearers will be coming through soon,' Davies said, his voice deliberately steady. 'We'll get you back to the aid station.'

They both knew it was a lie. The sun was setting. No stretcher parties would venture this far into no-man's-land in darkness, not with German machine guns still sweeping the field at regular intervals.

'Letter,' Gilbert managed, his voice a ragged whisper. 'Inside pocket. And stone.'

Davies understood immediately. With gentle hands, he reached into Gilbert's breast pocket, extracting the water-stained envelope addressed to him from Matilda Ellis, *Wambool* Station, New South Wales, Australia. The paper was soaked through with blood and mud, but the address remained legible. Wrapped between the pages was a smooth stone.

'I'll make sure she gets these,' Davies promised, tucking the letter securely into his pocket. 'You've my word.'

Gilbert nodded, the simple movement requiring all his remaining strength. The numbness had reached his fingertips now, a strange mercy dulling the pain but bringing with it an inexorable coldness.

'Tell her,' he whispered, 'about the sunset. Tell her I remembered.'

'I will, mate,' Davies assured him, though confusion flickered in his eyes. 'What else? What do you want me to tell her?'

Gilbert's mind drifted, the immediate horror of the battlefield momentarily receding. He saw the billabong instead, painted gold by the setting sun. Matilda stood at its edge, her hair loose around her shoulders, her face turned towards him with that smile that had always been just for him.

'The baby,' he murmured, his voice fading. 'Didn't know . . . till today. Her letter came . . . this morning. So, she knows I knew.'

Davies leaned closer, struggling to hear over the continuing barrage. 'She's having a baby? Your baby?'

Gilbert managed the barest nod, a ghost of a smile touching his lips despite everything. A child. His child. The knowledge had sustained him through the nightmare of the day's fighting, a talisman of hope clutched tight as he led his men across the killing ground towards the German wire.

A shell burst nearby, showering them with dirt and debris. Davies ducked instinctively, shielding Gilbert's body with his own. When he looked back down, Gilbert's eyes had taken on a distant quality, focused on something beyond the hellscape surrounding them.

'Not supposed to be this way,' Gilbert said, his voice surprisingly clear for a moment. 'Was going to build her a house . . . on the river bend. She would've loved it, John. Verandas all around, to catch the breeze.'

'Sounds like a proper place,' Davies said, his voice thick. 'A man couldn't ask for better.'

'The river runs high in winter,' Gilbert continued, lost in the vision. 'Floods the plains sometimes. Like an inland sea, my grandfather used to say. You should see it . . . the birds come from everywhere. Thousands of them.'

'I'd like that,' Davies said gently. 'Sounds like God's own

country.'

Gilbert's breathing had grown shallow, each inhale a visible struggle. The darkness at the edges of his vision was encroaching steadily inward, but he fought against it, clinging to consciousness with the same stubborn determination that had defined his short life.

'Davies,' he whispered, 'you'll find her? Promise me. Tell her . . . tell her I was thinking of her. At the end.'

Davies gripped Gilbert's hand, his calloused palm against the younger man's increasingly cold fingers. 'I swear it, Gilbert. On my life. I'll find her and tell her everything.'

A strange peace settled over Gilbert's features. The distant thunder of artillery continued, but it no longer seemed to touch him. In his mind, he was already far away, standing by the billabong with Matilda's hand in his.

'She'll need help,' he murmured. 'My father . . . will do right by her. Tell her . . . to go to *Ceann Mara*.'

'I will,' Davies promised again. 'What's the name of your property again? So I can find it?'

'*Ceann Mara*,' Gilbert repeated, the Irish name rolling off his tongue with practiced ease. 'On the Darling River . . . near Wilcannia. Tell her . . . I kept my promise. I came back to her . . . every night in my dreams.'

His voice faded to nothing on the last word. For several minutes, Davies remained beside him, one hand on Gilbert's chest, feeling the increasingly sporadic rise and fall beneath his palm. Around them, the battle continued its senseless rhythm—flares illuminating the sky, machine guns chattering, men crying out for mothers who couldn't hear them.

Gilbert's last conscious thought was not of the war, nor of

the mud that was slowly claiming his body. It was of Matilda standing by the billabong, one hand resting protectively on her stomach, the future they would never share contained within that simple gesture. In his mind, he reached for her across the impossible distance, across oceans and continents, across the boundary between life and what lay beyond.

'I'm sorry, Tilly,' he thought as darkness finally enveloped him. 'I tried to come home to you.'

The stars emerged above the battlefield, indifferent to the suffering below. The same stars that shone over the Darling River, over *Ceann Mara* and *Wambool*, over the billabong where two young people had pledged themselves to each other in what now seemed another lifetime entirely.

Private Gilbert James Piner O'Byrne, service number 2741, 5th Division, Australian Imperial Force, died at 9:17 PM on July 19, 1916, in a shell hole near Fromelles, France, thousands of miles from the land and the woman he loved. He was twenty years old.

In the growing darkness, Davies remained by his side, keeping vigil until he was certain his friend was gone. Only then did he carefully remove Gilbert's identity discs, one to stay with the body, one to be returned to headquarters. With fingers numbed by cold and grief, he transferred Gilbert's few personal possessions to his own pockets—his identity disc, a worn photograph, a smooth river stone, and the final letter from home that had arrived that morning with its life-changing news.

'I'll find her, mate,' Davies whispered, closing Gilbert's vacant eyes with a gentle pass of his hand. 'I promise you that.'

A flare burst overhead, bathing the scene in harsh white light. Davies ducked instinctively, then used the momentary illumination to orient himself towards the Australian lines. With a final glance at his fallen friend, he began the treacherous journey back across no-man's-land, Gilbert's final messages tucked safely against his heart.

Behind him, the darkness reclaimed Gilbert O'Byrne, the mud of France beginning its slow work of embracing a son of Australia who would never again see the sunsets over the Darling River.

Chapter 34

Ceann Mara - Monday afternoon.

Making her way home along the track from the homestead to the billabong, Erin's steps slowed as she caught sight of Miles' white van.

He was back.

Her heart lifted before she could stop it, and guilt followed immediately as she thought of Jack.

Miles sat in his camp chair and raised his enamel coffee cup in greeting. The rich aroma of real coffee drifted across the space between them. Hard to believe he had a proper coffee maker in that small van of his.

He disappeared inside and emerged with a second cup. 'Perfect timing.'

Erin hesitated, then nodded; maybe some company wouldn't be bad. 'Thanks.'

'Been for a walk?' he asked, pouring the coffee with a smile

'Just needed to clear my head.' She settled into the spare chair, careful to keep some distance between them. 'I thought you'd moved on.'

'Went for a long drive for a couple of days.' He handed her the coffee. 'Been looking at a couple of old homesteads up near Bourke. I'm a bit of a history buff—I love exploring these old properties, imagining the stories they could tell.'

Something about the way he said it made her think of the memorial stone, but she kept quiet. Instead, she sipped her coffee, watching the afternoon light play on the billabong's surface.

'I'm surprised you came back. Find anything interesting?' she asked, more to fill the silence than out of real curiosity.

'A few promising sites.' His eyes had that intense look again, the one that made her uncomfortable. 'These old properties, they're full of secrets, aren't they?'

Erin shifted in her chair, suddenly aware of how close they were sitting, how isolated it was down here by the billabong.

##

The sunset painted the billabong in shades of amber and rose, the water like liquid gold where it caught the light. Erin felt foolish now about her earlier hesitation as she carried the whiskey and two glasses to where Miles sat by the water's edge.

'Peace offering,' she said, holding up the bottle. 'I'm sorry if I was a bit rude the other night.'

He smiled, and in the waning evening light, his face was shadowed. 'No need to apologise. You were upfront with me. We all have our secrets.'

They sat in comfortable silence as the sun disappeared beneath the horizon. A gentle breeze stirred the river gums, carrying the sweet scent of wattle blossom. A family of kangaroos emerged from the scrub, the joey testing its balance as it hopped towards the water. On the far bank, an echidna waddled through the tussocks, oblivious to their presence.

'This is good whiskey,' Miles said, swirling the amber liquid in his glass. His voice was quieter than usual, thoughtful. 'Reminds me of the one Lisa and I shared on our wedding night.'

'Lisa?'

'My wife.' He gave a bitter laugh. 'Soon to be ex-wife, once the courts finish with us.'

The pain in his voice was raw. Erin leaned forward. 'I'm sorry.'

'Should have seen it coming, I suppose. All she cared about was her career, her next promotion.' He took another sip of whiskey. 'I wanted kids, you know? A family. A home.' His voice caught. 'She said children would hold her back.'

Tears pricked at Erin's eyes; she was moved by the longing in his voice.

'Sometimes I think I wasted ten years of my life trying to make her happy,' he said softly. 'Trying to be enough.'

The words hit too close to home. Erin blinked hard, remembering how many times she'd wondered if she was enough for Jack, if she'd ever be as interesting as his photography subjects, as helpful as Natalie . . .

'Sorry,' Miles said, noticing her tears. 'Didn't mean to dump all that on you.'

'No, it's . . . ' She wiped her eyes quickly. 'It's fine. Sometimes it helps to talk.'

A sacred kingfisher swooped low over the water, its wings catching the last rays of sun like blue fire. The evening was settling around them, soft and intimate as a whisper.

The night settled deeper around them, stars beginning to prick through the darkening sky. Miles refilled their glasses; his movements deliberate in the gathering dusk.

'I've been all over the countryside looking at old properties,' he said, leaning back in his chair. 'You wouldn't believe some of the pieces I've found. Colonial cedar wardrobes just rotting away in abandoned homesteads, Victorian hall stands being used as firewood.' He shook his head. 'Criminal, really.'

'You restore furniture?' Erin asked, curious despite herself.

'It's my passion.' His voice warmed with enthusiasm.

'There's one piece I'm searching for—a cedar wardrobe from the colonial period. Distinctive brass fittings, carved medallion on the front panel. They only made a handful of them in the 1850s. I've seen photos, but never the real thing.' He sighed. 'Worth a small fortune to the right collector.'

Erin's stomach tightened. She'd been in Reg's cluttered house many times as a child and remembered the mountains of furniture buried under years of collecting. There had been a cedar wardrobe in one of the boys' rooms, hadn't there? Something grand and old that Betty used to polish every Sunday before she passed, Mum said.

She'd turn in her grave if she could see the state of *Dunleavy* now.

'Anyway,' Miles continued, 'I keep hoping I'll stumble across one in these old properties. People don't always know what they've got.'

Erin thought of the antiques in their homestead, pieces that Thomas and Cat had brought with them from Ireland. The furniture that had witnessed generations of O'Byrne history. She took another sip of whiskey, keeping her face neutral. 'Mum asked me to check on old Reg McGillvray next door,' she said, changing the subject. 'I went over a few days ago, and I'm going over tomorrow too.'

'That property up the road with the other historic homestead on it?'

'Yes, that's the one, but it's gone to rack and ruin.'

Miles' eyes lit up. 'Maybe he has some colonial furniture he'd like to get rid of?'

'He has a lot of everything, but he won't get rid of it. Reg is a hoarder.' She smiled, remembering. 'I went to school with his boys. They were wild ones, ended up in all sorts of trouble, but Reg was always kind to me. Used to give me boiled lollies when I'd ride over on my pony.'

'Sounds like a character.' Miles' voice was casual, but something in his expression made her think of that watchful dingo again.

'He is.' Erin stood, suddenly needing space. 'I should probably turn in. Early start tomorrow if I'm going to visit him.'

'I could come with you,' Miles offered. 'Help carry things. Meet a local identity.'

'No,' she said, too quickly. 'I mean, Reg is funny about strangers. Better if I go alone.'

In the darkness, she couldn't quite read Miles' expression, but she felt his eyes on her as she gathered the glasses and bottle. The whiskey had left her head slightly fuzzy, and she was grateful for the cool night air clearing her thoughts.

As she walked back to her van, Miles called after her softly. 'Thanks for sharing the whiskey, Erin. And for listening. It's been a long time since I've talked to anyone about Lisa.'

She turned, silhouetted against the starlit sky. 'Sometimes it helps to talk to a stranger.'

'Are we still strangers?' His voice held a note she couldn't quite interpret.

'Goodnight, Miles.' She didn't answer his question, just continued to her van, that uneasy feeling creeping back despite the whiskey's warmth in her blood.

Inside, she checked the time on her phone. It was late, but she was restless. Jack wouldn't leave her thoughts tonight. The time difference meant he'd probably just be waking up now, maybe heading out for another day of shooting with Natalie. She pushed that thought away, not wanting it to spoil the peaceful feeling the evening had brought.

Erin opened her laptop and composed an email to Jack. An honest email from her heart. She'd send it from the house tomorrow when she had service.

Dear Jack,

I know this contract could set us up for life, and I understand why you had to take it, though some days that's harder than others. I miss you. I miss us. I miss the way we used to share everything, even the tough times.

Cat's wedding was beautiful. I wanted to share it with you—all the moments I knew you'd want to capture. The morning light on the river during the ceremony, the way Dad's eyes glistened when he walked her down the aisle, the golden sunset during their first dance. But most of all, I wanted to share the way it felt, watching my sister begin her married life while ours feels like it's hanging by a thread.

I'm being honest here, Jack. When you write about Natalie, about how well you work together, how she understands the technical side of things—it hurts. I know she's probably a great assistant, and I know the magazine assigned her to help you, but I need you to understand how it feels for me.

I found something out here by the billabong—a memorial stone. A woman named Matilda left it for someone she loved and lost. It made me think about what really matters. Whatever's happening between us, whatever this distance is, I want to fight for us. But I need you to fight too.

Please don't just tell me about the shots you're getting or what Natalie thinks about the locations. Tell me about you. Tell me what you're feeling. Tell me if you're as scared as I am about where we're heading.

I love you, Jack. Not just the good parts, not just the easy days. All of it. Even now, even scared and angry and confused, I love you. Please email me back, or ring me if you can. I'm confused.

Come home when you can. We need to talk—really talk.
Your Erin

She read it over three times before moving her cursor to the save button.

Calm filled her, and her thoughts moved to poor old Reg and his lonely life. Tomorrow she'd head over early, before the heat of the day set in. She'd take him the meals Mum would have ready, maybe stay for another cuppa and listen to some more stories about the old days.

As she got ready for bed, she could hear Miles moving around his camp, the soft clink of him washing up their glasses, the crackle of his fire being banked for the night. It was nice having company, she thought, then immediately felt guilty. But it didn't have to mean anything. Just two lonely people sharing a sunset and some whiskey.

Still, as she drifted off to sleep, her dreams were a confused jumble of Jack's face and Miles' intense gaze across the firelight.

Chapter 35

Ngwempisi Wilderness Area - Monday.

Jack woke before dawn, his mind clearer than it had been in weeks. Last night's decision still felt right in the cold light of morning. He'd gone to Natalie's door just after dinner, but Natalie hadn't answered, despite the light visible beneath her door and the soft sounds of movement inside. He'd been determined to have an honest conversation about his growing discomfort with the situation—the excessive luxury, the constant connectivity issues, her subtle but unmistakable flirtations.

After three increasingly insistent knocks, he'd returned to his room, unsettled but somehow relieved. The conversation was necessary, but would have been difficult.

That night, staring at the unfamiliar ceiling with its lazily spinning fan, Jack had reached a decision. He would find his own way to contact Erin, regardless of what Natalie claimed about local communications. And he would complete this assignment professionally, keeping his interactions with Natalie strictly business from now on. The way she'd looked at him over drinks, her casual touches that lingered too long—none of it would sway him.

He dressed quickly, grabbing his wallet and passport. The lodge was quiet in the pre-dawn hours, most guests still sleeping off their safari excursions or evening drinks. Jack made his way down the carpeted hallway towards reception in the lodge, hoping to find Banele, the night clerk, who was always helpful when he was on reception.

'Morning, Mr Hayes,' Banele greeted him, looking

surprised to see anyone at this hour. 'You're up early.'

'Need to sort something out,' Jack explained. 'I was wondering if there's any way to get an internet connection reliable enough to book a flight. My family situation has changed, and I need to head home for a while.'

A small lie, but necessary. Jack had no intention of abandoning the assignment, but he needed to contact Erin, to hear her voice, to reassure himself that she was okay.

Banele frowned. 'The hotel internet is still down, unfortunately. There's a café in town that has Wi-Fi, but I'm not sure if it's open early. I can arrange a car if—'

A movement outside caught Jack's eye. Through the large sliding glass door that led to the hotel's garden, a familiar figure stood beneath a jacaranda tree, her back to the building. Natalie. And in her hand, unmistakable even at this distance, was a satellite phone.

Jack froze, his conversation with Banele fading to background noise. The satellite phone Natalie had claimed never materialised. The one she'd assured him *Terra Lens* was 'still trying to sort out'. The connection to the outside world she'd told him repeatedly didn't exist here.

As he watched, she laughed at something the person on the other end said, her body language relaxed and animated. This wasn't a business call or a brief check-in. This was a casual conversation, the kind people had when connectivity wasn't an issue at all.

A slow, burning anger began to build in Jack's chest. For weeks, he'd been unable to reach Erin, to tell her he'd arrived safely, to hear about Tom's health, to share the wonders he was experiencing. For weeks, he'd trusted Natalie's explanations about poor infrastructure and remote locations. And all that time, she'd had the means to connect sitting in her pocket.

'Mr Hayes?' Banele's concerned voice finally broke through. 'Are you alright?'

'Fine,' Jack managed, his eyes still fixed on Natalie. 'Just thinking.'

'About the internet café? It's not far—'

'Actually, Banele,' Jack said, his voice low and controlled despite the anger coursing through him, 'I need to make a phone call. An urgent one. To my wife in Australia.'

Banele looked apologetic. 'As I mentioned, our lines are still—'

'I know.' Jack turned to face him fully. 'But it seems my colleague has a satellite phone that might work. If you'll excuse me.'

He moved towards the sliding door with purposeful strides, his mind racing. Why would Natalie deliberately keep him from contacting Erin? What possible advantage could she gain from isolating him? The questions tumbled through his mind, each more disturbing than the last.

As he stepped into the garden, the humid morning air heavy with the scent of tropical flowers, Natalie's back was still to him. She was laughing again, the sound almost musical in the quiet garden.

'No, I told you, it's going perfectly,' she was saying. 'Jack has no idea. By the time this assignment is over—'

'No idea about what, Natalie?' Jack's voice cut through the morning stillness.

She whirled around, the satellite phone still pressed to her ear, her eyes widening with shock and something else—calculation, maybe even fear. For a moment, they simply stared at each other, the truth hanging between them like a physical thing.

'Lars, I'll call you back,' she said quietly before ending the call, her composure returning as she slipped the phone into her pocket. 'Jack. You're up early.' Her voice was steady, but her eyes darted briefly to the hotel entrance, measuring the distance.

'Apparently not early enough,' he replied, his voice cold with a fury he barely recognised in himself. 'We need to talk about that satellite phone you claimed didn't exist.'

'There's been a misunderstanding—'

'No,' Jack cut her off. 'No more lies. What was that about me having "no idea"? What exactly is going "perfectly" according to plan? What bloody plan?'

Natalie assessed him for a moment, then her shoulders relaxed slightly as she seemed to make a decision. 'Fine. The contract you signed.'

'What about it?'

'Did you even read the fine print, Jack?' There was a hint of condescension in her tone now. '*Terra Lens* doesn't just get publishing rights to the images you take on assignment. They get *all* rights. In perpetuity. Including any similar photographs you take in the future. We own you.'

Jack felt his stomach drop. 'That's not what Lars told me.'

'Lars tells photographers what they want to hear. It's how we get the best talent for the lowest price.' She shrugged. 'You were especially easy—so eager for your big break, so naively grateful. Most photographers at least hire a lawyer.'

'And the phone?' Jack gestured to her pocket. 'The "communication problems"?'

A flicker of something crossed her face before disappearing. 'Lars thought it would be better if you . . . focused.

No distractions from home.'

'My father-in-law had a heart attack,' Jack said, his voice deadly quiet. 'And *you* kept me from calling my wife.'

'It was nothing personal.' Natalie's tone was clinical. 'This is business, Jack. We needed you completely immersed in the project, not distracted by domestic dramas. Your wife would have managed—'

'Her name is Erin,' Jack snapped. 'And this assignment was supposed to set us up financially, not separate us.'

A slight smile curved Natalie's lips. 'Well, about that . . . Lars and I had a little wager going,' she said, a casual cruelty entering her voice. 'He thought you'd break within the first month—demand contact with your precious wife, maybe even quit the assignment. I told him you'd be more . . . malleable. I know men very well. That the isolation, the distance, the right kind of attention would make you forget all about your little outback woman.'

Jack felt a cold dread settling in his stomach. 'You deliberately kept me from contacting my wife.'

'Of course we did.' Natalie smoothed her dress with deliberate care. 'Distractions are bad for creativity. It's company policy with our premium assignments—total immersion. Most photographers don't bring so much . . . baggage with them.'

'My wife isn't baggage,' Jack said through clenched teeth. 'And you had no right—'

'We had every right,' she interrupted smoothly. 'It's in the contract you signed. Section 12, paragraph 4— "Photographer agrees to maintain focus on assignment objectives, limiting external communications as determined necessary by editorial staff." You really should read the fine print, Jack.'

The realisation hit him like a physical blow—how carefully they'd isolated him, how deliberately they'd controlled his communications. And how bloody naïve he'd been.

The implication hung in the air between them. Jack felt sick as he realised the additional layer to her manipulation—the lingering gazes, the casual touches, the deliberate isolation from Erin. It hadn't just been about controlling his work; she'd been trying to control him entirely.

'I want to see the contract again,' he said flatly. 'And then I'm calling my wife.'

'No time. We leave for the reserve in two hours,' Natalie reminded him, her tone professional once more. 'There's a schedule to maintain.'

'The schedule can wait. This can't.' Jack held out his hand. 'The phone, Natalie. Now.'

She hesitated, then something in his expression made her relent. She pulled the satellite phone from her pocket and placed it in his palm, her fingertips brushing his wrist in one last attempt at manipulation.

'Just remember, Jack,' she said softly, 'no matter what you decide about the rest of the assignment, those photos you've already taken? They're ours now. All of them.'

Jack closed his fingers around the phone, his mind racing. He'd been played for a fool, but this wasn't over. Not by a long shot.

'We'll see about that,' he said quietly before turning and walking back towards the hotel, the satellite phone—his lifeline to Erin—clutched tightly in his hand.

Chapter 36

Ceann Mara - Tuesday.

The sun was already hot as Erin stepped out of her van carrying her laptop. She'd walk up to the house and see if Mum had anything ready to take over to Reg, and send the email to Jack. She'd slept fitfully, waking several times with that nagging guilt about Reg's furniture. Miles had seemed so passionate about restoration—surely it wouldn't hurt to ask Reg if he wanted to sell any pieces? The extra money would be more useful than a homestead full of old furniture.

She walked towards Miles' van, rehearsing what she'd say, but stopped short when the door swung open. Miles emerged wearing nothing but a pair of navy boxer shorts, his bare chest catching the morning light. He stretched, all lean muscle and tattooed chest, clearly unaware of her presence.

'Oh!' Erin spun around quickly, her face burning. 'Sorry!'

'Erin?' She heard rustling behind her; presumably him grabbing some clothes. 'Give me a sec.'

She stared fixedly at the billabong, watching a pelican make a graceful landing on the water. Her heart was racing, and she wasn't sure if it was from embarrassment or . . . something else. Jack's face flashed in her mind, and the guilt intensified.

'Decent now,' Miles called, amusement clear in his voice. 'Though nothing you wouldn't see at the beach.'

She turned cautiously. He'd pulled on a pair of cargo shorts but remained shirtless. 'I just . . . I was thinking about what you said last night. About the furniture.'

'Oh?' He started setting up his camp stove for coffee, his

movements deliberate.

'I could ask Reg if he's interested in selling anything. He's got quite a collection, though most of it's probably not worth much.'

Miles' hands stilled on the coffee pot. 'That's thoughtful of you.' He looked up, meeting her eyes. 'But I wouldn't want to impose.'

'It's no imposition. He might appreciate someone who values old pieces.' She was babbling now, uncomfortable with his steady gaze. 'Anyway, I should go. I've got meals to deliver.'

'Sure you don't want company?'

'No!' The word came out too forcefully. 'I mean, like I said, Reg is funny about strangers. Better if I go alone first, sound him out.'

Miles nodded, but something shifted in his expression. 'Another time then.'

As Erin walked away, she could feel his eyes on her back. That uneasy feeling from last night returned, warring with her guilt about possibly misjudging him. After all, he'd been nothing but kind, sharing his pain about his failed marriage.

Still, she was glad she'd said no to him coming to Reg's with her.

##

When Erin picked up one of the work utes from the shed, her eyes were drawn to the back corner, where Cat had pointed out where Dad had come off his motorbike and had his heart attack. The memory of that day still sent shivers through the family, but they had so much to be grateful for. Dad was almost back to his old self now, and more importantly, he was happy. Mum was fully involved in everything again—the CWA, tennis club, and all her other committees. Next week, she and Dad were flying to Broken Hill for his specialist appointment. The last time they'd driven down, sharing the driving between them, and now he'd got the all-clear to fly his plane again, which had pleased him no end.

She drove the ute around to the front door of the homestead. The old Toyota had seen better days, its once-white paint now dusty and scratched from years of faithful service on the property. She carefully placed the basket of food Mum had left on the kitchen table onto the passenger seat, checking to make sure nothing would spill.

The screen door creaked as Erin closed the ute door.

Dad stepped out onto the veranda; his reading glasses perched on the bridge of his nose. Despite looking better than he had in weeks, there was still a fragility about him that made Erin's heart clench. The heart attack had scared them all, even if he tried to play it down.

'Morning, love,' he called, making his way down the veranda steps with deliberate care. 'Heading over to old Reg's again?'

'Yeah, thought I'd better get there before it gets too hot.' She closed the ute door, the familiar squeak making her smile. Some things never change. 'Making any progress?'

Dad's face lit up, the way it always did when someone asked about his historical projects. 'The National Library sent through some fascinating files. There's this journal from 1889 that mentions the original homestead. Cat's going to be beside herself when she sees it.'

'She'll probably cut her honeymoon short just to come read it if you told her,' Erin laughed.

'You know your sister. History's in her blood.'

'Poor Mum. At least she's got one normal daughter.' Erin grinned.

Dad's eyes crinkled with amusement. 'Normal's overrated. Besides, it gives us an interest, keeps the mind sharp.' He tapped his temple meaningfully.

Erin leaned against the ute, studying her father. 'How are you really feeling, Dad? We haven't had a proper chat since I've been home.'

Something flickered across his face—fear maybe, or uncertainty. 'Still getting my head around it, to be honest. Never thought I'd have a heart attack. But the doctors reckon it was the physical result of the bike falling on me that triggered it.' He attempted a smile. 'Few years left in this old fella yet.'

'I've noticed you're letting Logan handle more of the heavy work, though.'

'He's good value, Seth too.' Dad paused, and Erin could feel the unspoken comparison hanging in the air. Her Jack, for all his good qualities, wasn't cut out for farm life. He never had been.

'That fellow camping down by the billabong. Is he still there?'

Heat crept up Erin's neck. 'We've just been talking this morning. He's interested in old furniture. He goes around to different homesteads, looking for specific pieces, and takes them back to his place to restore them.'

'Won't fit much in that old HiAce van I saw.'

'True.' Erin frowned. 'I didn't think of that.'

Dad's eyebrows drew together. 'Anyway, be careful next door. Reg isn't the man he used to be, not since the boys—' He trailed off, but they both knew what he meant. The McGillvray boys' arrest had broken something in their father.

'I remember being terrified of Reg when I was younger,' Erin said, trying to lighten the mood. 'Remember when you used to send me over on the bike with phone messages for him?'

'Yes, his phone was cut off because he didn't pay his bill. At least he wasn't shooting at people back then.' Dad shook his head. 'He's convinced himself now that the house is full of treasures. Reality is, most of the good stuff's long gone. It's full of junk.'

'Miles thought there might be some colonial pieces worth restoring.'

'Last time I was there, the place was more cobwebs than furniture. He's a hoarder.' Dad studied her face. 'Reg thinks he has a lot of valuable stuff in that house, when there's nothing of any value there.'

'Are you sure? I thought there was some old colonial furniture in there.'

'Not the last time I was there. Knowing Reg, he probably used it for firewood.'

'Okay, I'll tell Miles it's a waste of time.'

'You be careful with this Miles character too. You've always been too trusting, love.'

'Dad—'

'I mean it. A man turns up out of nowhere, camping on our land, suddenly interested in old furniture?' He held up his hands at her expression. 'Just saying, that's all.'

'He's a nice guy,' Erin insisted. 'Just passionate about restoration work. He's helped me out a couple of times too.' She could tell Dad was concerned, so she wouldn't mention the wine or the whiskey.

'Well, if he's looking for furniture to restore, he can come look at ours.' Dad's chin lifted stubbornly. 'Not that I'm selling any of it, mind.'

Erin couldn't help but laugh. 'I've already worked that out, thanks, Dad.'

A magpie warbled from the old gum tree, reminding Erin of the time. 'I better get going if I want to catch Reg before he starts his afternoon patrol.'

'Erin?' Dad waited until she looked at him. 'I know you think I'm being an old worrywart, but . . . just be careful, okay? With Reg, with Miles, with everything. We nearly lost Ro this year. Don't fancy going through that again.'

The vulnerability in his voice made her throat tight. Crossing the space between them, she hugged him gently, feeling the slight tremor in his frame that hadn't been there before the heart attack.

'Love you, Dad,' she whispered.

'Love you too, chicken.' The childhood nickname made her smile. 'Now go on, before Reg starts taking pot shots at shadows.'

Erin climbed into the ute, the familiar smell of leather, dust, and farm dogs making her feel at home. As she drove away, she caught sight of her father in the rear-view mirror, still standing in the yard, watching her go. Some things about coming home never changed: the way Dad worried, the way Mum fed everyone, the way the past and present seemed to blur together as though she'd never left.

##

That afternoon, when Erin returned from her visit to *Dunleavy,* she went back to the billabong for a while. Miles wasn't there, and she busied herself making a dessert for dinner at the homestead.

The familiar silhouette of the beautiful homestead stood against the darkening sky, warm light spilling from its windows. Mum's gardens were full of colour; she'd obviously worked hard to get them done for the wedding. A surge of contentment made Erin smile. All she needed now was an email from Jack to say he was coming home to her.

She walked up to the homestead carrying the dish of apple crumble she'd made for dessert. Inside, the house hummed with activity. Mum moved about the kitchen, laying out plates, while Dad set the dining table. The aroma of roast lamb and rosemary filled the air.

'Perfect timing,' her mother called when she spotted Erin. 'Dinner's almost ready.'

Erin placed the dessert on the counter and gave her mother a quick kiss on the cheek. 'Smells great, Mum.'

'How was your visit to Reg, love?' her father asked, pausing to hug her.

Before Erin could answer, the back door swung open, and Logan strode in with Cat following close behind. The newlyweds had just returned from their honeymoon, and happiness spilled from them.

'The lovebirds return,' Tom said with a grin. 'How was the coast?'

'Brilliant,' Logan replied, his hand finding Cat's. 'Though coming back to this dry heat is a shock to the system.'

Cat smiled, tucking a strand of hair behind her ear. The wedding band glinted on her finger, still new enough to catch her own attention occasionally.

'You two look disgustingly content,' Erin teased, though

her smile was genuine.

'Married life agrees with us,' Cat replied with a laugh, turning to hug Erin. 'How are you?' she asked softly.

'I'm good.' It was getting easier to smile.

Laura pulled a bottle of wine from the fridge. 'We should have a proper welcome-home toast.' Amid the greetings and hugs, they all somehow managed to get dinner on the table, glasses filled, and everyone seated.

As Logan and Cat shared stories about the coast, Erin found herself thinking about her visit to *Dunleavy*.

'How was Reg today?' her mother asked, as if reading her thoughts. 'I've been meaning to check on him again, but the tennis club has been so busy with the charity tournament coming up that I haven't had a chance. Thanks for taking the meals over to him.'

Erin pushed her baked potatoes around her plate. Her appetite was still low. 'Not good, Mum. It's really sad. His place is—' she hesitated, searching for a kind way to describe what the place was like. 'It's a hovel, honestly. There are piles of newspapers dating back years, and dirty dishes everywhere. He seems confused sometimes, too. He called me Betty a few times.'

Her father's brow furrowed. 'Poor old fellow.'

'I know,' Erin said quietly. 'He corrected himself, but it was heartbreaking. And he looks terrible—thin, and his skin has this yellow tinge. I don't think he's taking any medication.'

Laura sighed. 'I've tried to get him to see Dr Matthews, but he refuses. He told me doctors killed Betty with their treatments.'

'Maybe we should call social services,' Erin suggested.

'He'd never forgive us,' Tom said. 'He's got his pride.'

The conversation stalled as Laura brought out the apple crumble and ice cream. As they ate the dessert she'd cooked in the motorhome oven, Erin found herself thinking about Reg.

'I might go back and visit him again tomorrow,' she said. 'Take the leftover crumble over.'

Her mother gave her an approving smile. 'That's kind of you, love. Just . . . be careful. Reg can be unpredictable.'

Chapter 37

Dunleavy - Wednesday afternoon.

Erin knocked on Reg's door, a container of homemade soup balanced in one hand. The afternoon sun cast eerie shadows across the overgrown yard. He hadn't bailed her up at the gate this time.

When Reg finally opened the door, Erin was struck by how much worse he looked. His eyes were yellower than before, his skin drawn tight across his cheekbones.

'Hello, Mr McGillvray. I've brought you some soup today.'

Reg stared at her for a long moment. 'Betty?'

'No, it's Erin. Laura's daughter.'

Recognition flickered across his face. 'Course it is. Come in then, if you're coming.'

Erin hesitated, surprised by the invitation after his previous insistence that no one had entered his house. She stepped carefully inside, the smell of neglect immediately apparent—unwashed dishes, musty furniture, the stale air of a house that hadn't been cleaned in years.

'Kitchen's this way,' Reg muttered, leading her through a dark, narrow hallway lined with dusty photographs.

The kitchen was cluttered with dirty cups and plates. Reg swept some newspapers off a chair. 'Sit if you want.'

Erin moved a saucepan full of nails along the counter and placed the soup container beside it. 'Would you like me to heat this up for you? Do you have a gas stove?'

'The boys took the microwave,' Reg said suddenly, his

gaze drifting to the window. 'Took it when they cleaned out the shed. Said they needed it more than me.'

'Your sons?' Erin asked gently.

'Left their things here, you know,' Reg continued as if she hadn't spoken. 'All those years, storing their junk in my sheds. Then they come and take what they want.' His hands trembled slightly as he adjusted his worn cardigan. 'Left the good stuff though. They don't know value when they see it.'

'What kind of things did they leave?' Erin asked, cautiously curious.

Reg's eyes narrowed. 'Why're you asking about that? You working with them now?'

'No, I'm just—'

'Betty always said they'd be back for their things. Said a father shouldn't throw away what belongs to his sons.' His voice took on a rambling quality. 'Those boxes in the north shed. Been there for ten years. Told 'em it was taking up space I needed, but they said to keep it safe.' He made a dismissive gesture. 'Now Danny's gone and Michael doesn't even call.'

Erin tried to redirect the conversation. 'The soup is chicken and vegetable. My grandmother's recipe.'

'I saw that fellow poking around, you know,' Reg said abruptly. 'Coming onto my property, looking in my sheds.' His voice rose. 'Always people wanting what's mine!'

'What fellow, Mr McGillvray?' Erin asked.

'That man. I ran him off.' Reg's breathing quickened. 'He was looking at the sheds. How'd he know about that? Did Michael send him? It's my property!'

Erin set a gentle hand on the table near him, not quite touching. 'No one's trying to take your things, Mr McGillvray.'

'The deed says it's mine! Everything on this land is mine now!' His face flushed with agitation. 'I told Betty I'd keep it safe, but they keep coming back. They keep trying to find it!'

'Find what?' Erin asked before she could stop herself.

Reg slammed his palm against the table, making Erin jump. 'I won't tell them and I won't tell you! It's mine now. Mine to keep!'

His breathing had become laboured, his yellowed face contorted with emotion. Erin stood slowly, recognising that the situation was deteriorating.

'I should go and let you rest, Mr McGillvray. I'll come back tomorrow, shall I?'

'They left it here,' he mumbled, suddenly deflating. 'All those years ago. Said it would be safer with me than with them.' His eyes, momentarily clear, fixed on Erin. 'Sometimes it's better not to know things, girl. You remember that.'

'Me?' Erin asked, confused.

But Reg had already turned away, his attention on something outside the window. 'You should go now. It'll be dark soon.'

##

The late-afternoon sun cast a golden light across the billabong as Erin pulled up to her caravan. She sat motionless behind the wheel for several minutes, her hands still trembling slightly. The visit to Reg had left her unsettled.

When she finally stepped out of her car, she noticed Miles sitting on the small step outside his van, a book open on his lap. He looked up at her approach, his expression immediately shifting to concern.

'You okay? You look like you've seen a ghost.'

Erin sat heavily in the other chair. 'I just came from Reg

McGillvray's place.'

'The old bloke next door?'

She nodded, running a hand through her hair. 'He invited me in this time. His place is—' she trailed off, searching for the right words. 'It's bad, Miles. He's not well. Physically or mentally.'

Miles closed his book. 'What happened?'

'His conversation was all over the place. One minute he was talking about his sons taking things from the shed, the next he was ranting about people trying to steal from him.' She wrapped her arms around herself despite the warm evening. 'He mentioned a stranger—said he caught him looking around the property.'

'Someone he didn't let onto the place?' Miles frowned.

'Yes. Reg got agitated talking about his sons and something they had left in one of his sheds. He kept saying, "they keep trying to find it" and that it's his now.' She shook her head. 'When I asked what he meant, he nearly exploded.'

Miles leaned forward. 'That's bizarre.'

'He's confused. Liver failure can affect the brain.' Erin sighed.

'Think there's anything to it?'

'No. I think he's got dementia. He shouldn't be living there alone.' She absently twisted a strand of hair around her finger. 'I won't be able to stop worrying about him. He's all alone in that house, getting more confused by the day.'

'Will you go back?' Miles asked.

Erin nodded. 'Someone needs to check on him. Mum does when she can, but she's really busy for the next couple of weeks.'

'Next time you go, I'll come with you,' Miles said firmly.

'It sounds dangerous.'

She looked up, surprised by the offer. 'You don't have to do that.'

'I know.' His eyes met hers. 'But I want to. Nobody should face that kind of situation alone—not you, and not him either.'

The sun dipped lower towards the horizon, casting long shadows across the billabong. In the distance, a kookaburra laughed, the sound echoing across the water.

'Thank you,' Erin said quietly.

Chapter 38

Mbabane - Wednesday.

It had taken Jack two days to reach Mbabane. Natalie had been one step ahead of him. The satellite phone was locked, and when he'd tried to find her to get the password, there had been no sign of her. In disgust, he threw the phone on the floor in front of her room and strode down the corridor.

The realisation of how dependent he'd become on both Natalie and the magazine stung worse than the sunburn spreading across his neck.

'You're on your own,' she said, her voice cold with finality before walking away when he told her he was leaving. With no other options, Jack packed his belongings into his weathered backpack, leaving behind the camera equipment that belonged to the magazine.

His visit to the local internet café had not been a success— 'Lines down,' they'd told him with apologetic shrugs. Three hours of trying to find a working connection had yielded nothing but frustration and increasing desperation. He needed to contact the magazine and find out what the hell was going on before his career imploded alongside whatever remained of his marriage.

In his wallet: a useless credit card, fifteen American dollars, and not a single *lilangeni*—the local currency. He hadn't bothered to exchange money; Natalie had taken care of all that. Another oversight in a growing list of dependencies he'd failed to recognise until now.

'Malkerns,' Banele told him when he'd asked about the nearest place with reliable communications. 'Thirty kilometres north. But often it is like us here with interruptions, so best to go to Mbabane. They have a good hotel, international phones.'

Jack positioned himself on the outskirts of town, thumb extended towards the road leading him to Mbabane.

Monday had yielded nothing but dust from passing trucks and curious stares from locals. His water bottle was half-empty when a battered pickup truck finally slowed beside him. The driver, an elderly man with deep creases around his eyes, spoke limited English.

'Mbabane?' Jack asked hopefully.

The man nodded. 'Halfway. Malkerns. I go to pineapple farm.'

Jack climbed into the truck, grateful for even partial progress. The metal seat burned through his jeans as they bumped along the uneven road, passing through landscapes of rolling hills dotted with homesteads and grazing cattle. Women walked along the roadside, balancing impossible loads on their heads; children waved excitedly at the passing vehicle, and Jack felt utterly, hopelessly out of place.

It was dark before they reached the pineapple farm. Jack thanked the driver and found himself standing beside stacks of freshly harvested fruit. A worker offered him a slice, the sweet juice temporarily distracting him from the twenty kilometres that still separated him from Mbabane.

'You stay night,' the farmer said.

'Thank you.' He spent the night lying on some hessian bags in a shed, listening to the torrential rain on the roof all night.

The next morning, the farmer, whom he now knew as Chuk, pointed to the road and shook his head. 'Too wet.'

Jack's next ride came mid-afternoon on Wednesday—a minibus packed with schoolchildren returning from a field trip.

Their teacher, a woman named Sibongile, spoke excellent English and refused his attempt to offer payment.

'You are a visitor to our country,' she said simply. 'It would be poor hospitality to leave you stranded.'

The children peppered him with questions—was he a movie star? Did he know Taylor Swift? Was America really like in the films? Their curiosity and laughter eased some of the tension that had knotted itself between his shoulders.

The minibus dropped him at a crossroads five kilometres outside Mbabane. The sun was beginning to dip towards the horizon. Jack started walking, his backpack growing heavier with each step, his mouth dry despite rationing his remaining water.

A man on a motorbike gave him his final ride, the wind cooling Jack's sunburned face as they weaved through increasing traffic. Buildings began to appear more frequently, taller and more modern than those in Lobamba. Street lights flickered on as they entered the city proper.

'Mountain Inn,' the motorcyclist suggested when Jack asked about a hotel with international phone service. 'Best place.'

Now Jack stood in the dusty street of Mbabane, trying to figure out what to do.

The Mountain Inn stood on a hill overlooking the city, its façade promising comforts Jack had taken for granted just days ago. He stumbled into the lobby, dishevelled and dusty, drawing curious glances from the staff.

'I need a room,' he said, placing his credit card on the counter and hoping it would work. 'And a phone that can make calls to Australia.'

The receptionist processed his card—the transaction approved to Jack's immense relief—and handed him a room key. 'International calls can be made from your room or the business centre, sir.'

Chapter 39

Mbabane - Wednesday 9.00 p.m. Eswatini time.

Jack dropped his backpack to the floor and fell onto the bed, knowing he had time to sleep. With the eight-hour time difference, it was about five a.m. on Thursday at home. He was tempted to ring Erin now, but common sense prevailed. It had been four months; he could wait another three hours. He set the alarm for midnight and fell into a deep sleep.

A soon as the alarm woke him, he reached for the phone beside his bed. His fingers trembled slightly as he called Erin's mobile, but it went straight to voicemail.

'Erin, it's me, finally. Call me back as soon as you can. I'm on the way home.'

He scrolled through his phone and found his mate Trevor's number, calculating the time difference and hoping someone would be in his law office by now.

The international dial tone hummed in his ear, each ring stretching into eternity. When the call connected and the familiar voice answered, Jack closed his eyes, a wave of relief washing over him so intensely that for a moment, he couldn't speak.

'Hello? Trevor McIntyre speaking. Who is this?' the voice repeated.

'It's Jack Hayes, Trevor,' Jack breathed out a sigh of relief. 'I'm in Eswatini. In Africa. There's been a situation, and I need help. I've been very foolish.'

As he began explaining the circumstances of the past few days, Jack gazed out of the window at the lights of Mbabane twinkling in the darkness. He'd made it—barely, humbled, and with a new appreciation for self-reliance—but he'd made it.

'Let me get this straight,' Trevor said after Jack finished recounting his ordeal. 'The assistant from *Terra Lens* deliberately blocked your communication, lied, and essentially abandoned you in the wilderness with no money and no way to get back?'

'That about sums it up,' Jack admitted, rubbing his temple where a headache was forming. 'It's complicated. Let's say we had a professional disagreement.'

'That's beyond professional disagreement, Jack. That's potentially criminal negligence on the magazine's part. One more question, do you have the SD cards from your camera?'

'No, Natalie collected them every day and gave me another one.'

'Okay, I'll make a note of that, too.'

Jack sighed. 'I can't think about all that at the moment. Right now, I just need to get home. I've managed to get to Mbabane and secure a hotel room for tonight on my credit card, but I can't book a flight without more funds. The card's nearly maxed out. I've tried to call Erin but had no luck.'

'I understand. Let me make some calls and see what I can arrange. Text me her number, and I'll try from here too. I'll get back to you as soon as I can.'

'Thanks, mate. I'll owe you big time.'

After texting Erin and *Ceann Mara's* numbers to Trevor, Jack tried her number again, cursing when it went straight to voicemail. The isolation was maddening, especially now that he had access to a phone.

##

Mbabane - Thursday 6.30 a.m. Eswatini time.

Hours later, as the sky lightened over Mbabane, Jack's mobile rang. He lunged for it, nearly knocking over the bedside lamp. He'd tried Erin every twenty minutes for the past two hours, and his frustration was growing. 'Erin?'

'No, it's Trevor. Good news, Jack. I've managed to sort money out for you. And I've booked you on a flight back to Sydney via Johannesburg and Perth at six o'clock tonight, your time. You'll pick up your flight to Sydney in Perth about four on Friday afternoon. It's tight, but you should be home within twenty-four hours.'

Jack sank onto the edge of the bed, so tired, he was confused by all the flights and times Trevor had reeled off, but relief flooded through him. 'Trevor, I can't thank you enough. When do I leave here?'

'I've arranged for a car service to pick you up later this morning to take you to King Mswati III International Airport to connect with your flight to Johannesburg. You've still got your passport, I hope?'

'Yes, I do.'

'Text me the number, and I'll be able to confirm your flights, and then I'll text you the details. As soon as you text me your account details, the funds should be in your account within the hour—it should be enough to cover your hotel stay and transport costs. I'll also email you all the booking details and references.' Trevor paused. 'Jack, I also took the liberty of contacting the magazine's legal department.'

Jack tensed. 'What did they say?'

'They're concerned about the situation, to put it mildly.

Especially after I mentioned the possibility of a lawsuit for endangerment and abandonment of a contractor in a foreign country. They're very interested in hearing your side of the story when you return.'

A grim smile crossed Jack's face. 'I bet they are.'

'More importantly,' Trevor continued, 'I tried reaching Erin for you.'

Jack sat up straighter. 'Did you get through?'

'No, unfortunately. Her mobile went to voicemail, and no one answered at the homestead. I left messages at both.'

Jack's stomach tightened with worry. 'That's not like them. Someone's usually around.'

'It could be nothing—poor reception, they're out working the property, any number of innocent explanations,' Trevor reasoned. 'But given your situation and your urgency in contacting Erin, I also put in a call to the police station nearest to *Ceann Mara*.'

'And?'

'They said they'd send someone out to check if no one can contact the family by tomorrow. The sergeant knows the O'Byrnes and said it wasn't unusual for them to be unreachable occasionally, given the remote location of the station.'

Jack nodded, though Trevor couldn't see him. The local police were familiar with the rhythms of outback life. What seemed alarming to city dwellers was often just normal isolation for rural properties.

'Thank you, Trevor. For everything.'

'Get some rest. Your car will be there at noon. sharp. And Jack?'

'Yes?'

'Next time you go to Africa, perhaps consider a different

magazine.'

Despite everything, Jack laughed. 'Believe me, I've learned my lesson. I doubt there will be a next time.'

After ending the call, Jack lay back on the bed, feeling as though an immense weight had been lifted from his shoulders. In less than twenty-four hours, he would be heading for *Ceann Mara*, free from the contract that had become a trap, and with Trevor's legal support behind him. He only hoped that would be enough.

One more time, he reached for the phone and dialled Erin's number. The familiar international tone sounded, followed by the unanswered ringing that had become the soundtrack to his anxiety.

'Come on, Erin,' he murmured, tapping his fingers nervously against the notebook. 'Pick up.'

But like every other attempt, the call eventually went to voicemail. Jack closed his eyes, fighting down the rising panic. Soon, he would be on his way. That would have to be enough.

Jack stood up abruptly and tried Erin's number one more time. Voicemail again.

'Erin, it's Jack. Please call me as soon as you get this. It's urgent.' He paused, wondering how much to say over an unsecured line. 'Call my mobile. I'll be on a plane in about six hours. I need to know you're okay, love.'

He hung up, staring at the phone, his frustration building into genuine worry. Something wasn't right. He could feel it.

'I'm coming home,' he whispered to the empty room, as if the words could somehow reach across the ocean to Erin.

Chapter 40

January 1919 - Wilcannia

The paddle steamer *Murray Belle* rounded the bend in the Darling River, its rhythmic churning echoing across the water. Steam billowed from its stack against the clear blue sky as it made its slow approach to the Wilcannia wharf. Matilda Ellis stood motionless among the small crowd that had gathered, her hands clasped tightly before her to stop their trembling.

The war was over. The armistice had been signed two months ago, the news reaching even this remote corner of New South Wales via telegram. Churches had rung their bells, people had poured into the streets with flags and impromptu bands, celebrations erupting throughout the district. Peace had come at last.

But peace brought its own anxieties. Now began the long wait for Australia's sons to return home—those who had survived and were able to make the journey. Each steamer that navigated the Darling brought the possibility of returning soldiers, or at least news of them.

Matilda scanned the deck as the vessel drew closer, searching for a familiar figure among the passengers lining the rails. Her heart leapt at the sight of uniforms—one, two, three men in Australian khaki—but even at this distance, she knew none of them was Gilbert. Wrong height, wrong build, wrong way of standing.

Still, she waited as the steamer docked and passengers disembarked. Perhaps there would be news, a letter, word of some kind.

'Miss Ellis.'

Matilda turned to find Doctor Williams beside her, his medical bag in hand as he prepared to board for his monthly circuit of the river stations.

'Any luck today?' he asked gently.

She shook her head, summoning a smile that didn't reach her eyes. 'Not today.'

The doctor's gaze was kind but concerned. He had been the one to confirm her pregnancy, the one who had delivered little James in the early hours of a September morning in 1916. One of the few who knew the child's true parentage, bound by professional confidentiality.

'You cannot keep doing this, Miss Ellis. Every steamer, every mail coach—it's wearing you down.'

'I'm perfectly well,' Matilda replied, the familiar response automatic by now.

Doctor Williams sighed. 'The war has been over for weeks now. If Private O'Byrne was in a position to send word—'

'Some men are only now being released from prisoner-of-war camps,' Matilda interrupted, her voice low but intense. 'Others are recovering in hospitals. Communications are still disrupted across Europe. There are countless reasons why there's been no word. My brother keeps us informed.'

'Will Cecil be home soon?'

Matilda shook her head. 'He has done well in Sydney, has been promoted and chosen to stay there.'

The doctor nodded. They both knew Matilda was clinging to increasingly remote possibilities, but he would not be the one to extinguish that final flicker of hope.

'How is the boy?' he asked instead.

At the mention of her son, Matilda's expression softened. 'Growing every day, and following Father around, chattering non-stop.' A genuine smile briefly illuminated her features. 'He has his father's eyes.'

'Give your father my regards,' the doctor said. 'And Mrs Cleary as well. That woman is worth her weight in gold, keeping your secret all this time.'

Matilda nodded in agreement. 'I should get back,' she said, glancing at the sun's position. 'Father will be returning from the south paddock soon, and James will be waking from his nap.'

'Of course.' Doctor Williams tipped his hat. 'Take care, Miss Ellis. And perhaps . . . consider permitting yourself to rest. From the waiting, I mean.'

Matilda offered no response to this gentle suggestion. With a polite nod, she turned and walked towards where she'd tethered her horse at the edge of town. Another day, another steamer, another disappointment. Yet she would be back the next time a vessel was due, and the time after that. She could do nothing less, not while even the faintest possibility remained.

The sun was setting as Matilda approached *Wambool Station*, painting the landscape in shades of orange and gold. In the distance, she could see her father on the veranda, young James balanced on his hip as they watched for her return.

At the sight of her horse, James began to bounce excitedly in his grandfather's arms, his chubby hands reaching out. Robert Ellis set the boy down, and he ran towards her, coming to a stop at the top of the veranda steps.

'Mama!' he called. 'Did you see the boat?'

Matilda dismounted quickly, leaving her horse ground-tied as she hurried to scoop up her son. His solid weight in her arms, his warm breath against her neck as he chattered about his day—these sensations anchored her, pulling her back from the edge of despair that threatened after each futile visit to the wharf, each painful conversation at *Ceann Mara*.

At three years old, he was growing more like his father every day—the same determined set to his jaw, the same thoughtful blue eyes that seemed to take in everything around him. She'd chosen his name because it had been Gilbert's middle name, a perpetual memory of the man who would never know his son.

'Has he been good?' she asked her father, pressing a kiss to James's dark curls.

'An absolute terror,' Robert replied with a fond smile. 'Tried to climb into the water trough twice. Has your determination, that one.'

And his father's courage, Matilda thought, though she kept the observation to herself.

Together, they went inside as darkness fell across the station. Tomorrow would bring its own challenges—another day of waiting, of working, of wondering. But for now, Matilda had this—her son holding her hand, her father's steadfast presence, the familiar comfort of home.

It would have to be enough.

As she settled James for the night, singing softly as his eyelids grew heavy, Matilda allowed herself to imagine an alternate reality—one where Gilbert had returned from war, where they lived in the house by the billabong he had promised to build, where their son grew up knowing his father's laugh, his father's stories, his father's love.

The fantasy was both comfort and torment, a dream she

could not quite relinquish despite increasingly accepting the probability that it would never come to pass.

'Sleep well, my brave boy,' she whispered as James drifted into slumber. 'Your father would be so proud of you.'

Outside, the Australian night enfolded *Wambool* Station in darkness lit only by stars—the same stars that shone over distant France, over battlefields now silent, over graves both marked and unmarked where a generation of young men lay in eternal rest.

Matilda stood at the window for a long time, gazing up at those impassive stars, searching for answers in their ancient light. None came, only the soft breathing of her sleeping child and the whisper of the night breeze through the river gums—sounds of life continuing, of time passing, of a world slowly healing from wounds too deep to name.

Tomorrow, she would be strong again. Tomorrow, she would continue the work of living. Tomorrow, perhaps, she would begin to accept what her heart already knew.

But tonight, she allowed herself one more evening of hope, fragile as it was. One more night of waiting for a miracle that grew more distant with each passing day.

Chapter 41

Ceann Mara - Thursday night.

The fire crackled between them, casting a warm glow across the billabong. Erin and Miles sat in camp chairs near the water, close enough that their elbows occasionally brushed. A half-empty bottle of shiraz stood on the small folding table alongside the remains of the meal they'd shared—a simple but delicious pasta Miles had insisted on cooking.

'I still can't believe you managed a decent carbonara on that tiny camp stove,' Erin said, taking another sip of her wine.

Miles smiled, the firelight catching in his eyes. 'You'd be surprised what you can make with minimal equipment. I once made a three-course meal on a single burner when I was—'

The crunch of tyres on gravel interrupted him. Headlights swept across the clearing as a vehicle approached, momentarily blinding them. Erin shaded her eyes, recognising Logan's ute as it came to a stop.

'Evening,' Logan called as he stepped out, his voice carrying an edge that immediately put Erin on alert. He walked towards the fire, his gaze moving from the wine bottle to the two chairs positioned close together, then to Miles. 'Didn't realise you had company.'

'Logan, hi,' Erin said, straightening in her chair. She tried to ignore the guilt that shot through her. She and Miles must look very cosy. 'We were just having dinner. Do you want to join us for a drink? There's more wine.'

Logan remained standing, hands in his pockets. 'No, thanks. Just came to let you know, Cat and I are heading into town tomorrow if you need anything.' His eyes never left Miles. 'Don't think we've been introduced.'

Miles extended his hand. 'Miles McKenzie. I'm staying over there.' He gestured to his van.

Logan shook his hand with visible reluctance. 'Logan Wainwright. Erin's brother-in-law.'

'Ah, the groom?' Miles raised an eyebrow.

Logan nodded, and an uncomfortable silence settled over them. He made no move to sit, instead rocking back on his heels, his expression unreadable in the flickering light.

'Settled back in okay?' Erin asked, attempting to ease the tension.

'Fine,' Logan replied tersely, then turned to Miles. 'What brings you to *Ceann Mara*? Not many tourists choose to stay out here.'

'I'm between jobs,' Miles said evenly.

'What line of work are you in, Miles?'

'Bit of this, bit of that. Mostly restoration work recently.'

'Restoration? Like furniture?'

Miles nodded. 'Among other things.'

Logan's jaw tightened.

'Logan, was there anything else you needed?' Erin said as annoyance filled her.

Logan finally broke his stare-down with Miles to look at Erin. 'Just looking out for you, that's all.' He stepped backward. 'I should head back. Cat's waiting for me at the river.'

'I'll walk you to the track,' Erin said, setting down her wine glass.

When they reached the ute, out of earshot from the fire, Erin turned to Logan. 'What was that about?'

'What's he doing here, Erin?' Logan asked quietly. 'You

barely know him. Is there something going on between you?'

'No!' she snapped. 'He's just a guy taking some time off. And frankly, it's none of your business.'

'It becomes my business when strangers start showing up.' His voice was low but intense. 'Have you asked him how he found out about this place? The billabong isn't exactly in tourist guides.'

'Logan, stop,' Erin hissed. 'You're being ridiculous.'

He opened his car door. 'Just be careful, okay? Something doesn't feel right.'

After Logan drove away, Erin stood for a moment, collecting herself before returning to the fire. Miles was feeding another log into the flames, his face contemplative.

'I'm sorry about that,' she said, reclaiming her seat. 'Logan can be a bit . . . protective. He was a policeman, and I guess that can still taint his perspective.'

'No matter,' Miles replied with a shrug. 'I'm used to being treated like that where I came from.'

Erin studied him across the fire. 'Where did you come from?'

Something flickered across Miles's face—a hardness she hadn't seen before. For a brief moment, his easy-going demeanour slipped, revealing something colder underneath.

'A place where people make judgements based on appearances,' he said finally, his voice carrying an edge that made Erin's skin prickle. 'Where who your family is matters more than who you are.'

Erin shifted in her seat, suddenly aware of how isolated they were. The question about the furniture transport that had been on the tip of her tongue—how he'd managed to move such large pieces by himself in just a small van—died unasked.

The silence stretched between them until Miles seemed to notice her discomfort. His expression softened, the familiar smile returning.

'About tomorrow,' he said, changing the subject. 'What time should we head over to Reg's?'

Erin hesitated. 'Actually, after thinking, it might be better if I went alone. He gets agitated with new people, and—'

'Erin,' Miles cut in gently but firmly. 'After what you told me about his condition, I don't think going alone is a good idea. What if he becomes more than just verbally agitated?'

She fidgeted with her wine glass. 'Maybe I should try to get my mum to come instead.'

'Your mum needs you to do it, remember?' Miles leaned forward. 'I promise I'll hang back if he seems uncomfortable. But at least let me drive you there. I'll wait outside if necessary.'

Erin looked at him, caught between her growing unease and his seemingly genuine concern. The hardness she'd glimpsed was gone, replaced by the Miles she'd come to know over the weeks.

'I'll think about it,' she said finally. 'Let me see what tomorrow brings.'

Miles nodded, apparently satisfied with that answer. As the fire died down to embers, Erin found herself watching him more carefully, wondering what other sides of Miles McKenzie she had yet to see.

The tension of Logan's visit eased as Erin stoked the campfire, watching the sparks rise into the darkening sky. Miles sat across from her, his face illuminated by the dancing flames, the usual intensity softened by the shadows.

The firelight played across his features as he gazed into the flames, reminding Erin of how little she actually knew about him. The mysteries surrounding his past and his interest in the area nagged at her.

'Can I ask you something?' she ventured, deciding to face her curiosity directly.

Miles looked up, his expression open. 'Of course.'

'How do you manage to transport furniture in your van? It doesn't look big enough for some of the pieces you've described working on.'

If the question surprised him, he didn't show it. Instead, he laughed lightly.

'It's a bit of a magic trick,' he admitted. 'The back is fitted with a custom rack system I designed myself. Breaks down entirely flat against the walls when not in use, but when deployed, it can secure pieces at multiple angles.' He set his mug down, using his hands to illustrate. 'I can stack smaller pieces efficiently, and for larger ones, I have these specialised straps and padding systems.' Miles leaned forward, warming to his subject. 'Additionally, I've made modifications to the interior. Removed the standard bulkhead and reinforced the floor. You'd be surprised what you can fit in there with the right configuration. For the really massive pieces, I have a collapsible trailer that stows underneath.'

His explanation was detailed, enthusiastic, and entirely plausible. Erin felt slightly foolish for her suspicions.

'That's actually quite clever,' she said.

'Necessity breeds invention,' Miles replied with a shrug. 'When you work independently, you have to get creative with your resources.'

As the night lengthened, Miles shared stories of furniture

restoration jobs gone wrong, clients with unreasonable expectations, and beautiful pieces rescued from obscurity. His passion seemed genuine, and his knowledge extensive. Erin found herself relaxing, the camaraderie of the campfire dissolving her earlier fears.

'Would you like to come with me when I take his meals over tomorrow?'

'If that's okay, I'd love to look around his place.' Miles smiled.

'You'll get a shock. It's nothing like *Ceann Mara*.'

When they finally said goodnight, Erin fell asleep to the gentle sounds of the billabong, her suspicions laid to rest.

Chapter 42

Ceann Mara – Friday.

Even though it was early, the morning sun was already warm as Erin stepped out of her caravan, keys in hand and a mental list of tasks for the day forming in her mind. She stopped short when she spotted Miles leaning against his van, clearly waiting for her.

'Morning,' he called, pushing himself upright. 'Thought I'd catch you before you headed out.'

Erin forced a smile. 'You're up early.'

'Early riser,' he replied with an easy grin that didn't quite dispel the unease she felt from the previous night. 'Thought I'd see if you needed help with anything today.'

'Just some errands,' she said vaguely. 'I'm going to pick up the food basket for Reg.'

Something flickered in Miles's eyes. 'Perfect timing. When you collect the meals from your mum, I might come up and meet them now that the wedding's over and things are back to normal.'

Erin hesitated, feeling cornered. There was nothing wrong with his request—it was perfectly reasonable for someone staying at the property to want to meet the owners. But something about his eagerness made her uncomfortable. She felt as though he was ingratiating himself and, for the first time, considered moving up to the house.

'I'd love to see some of your old furniture,' he added, his tone casual but his eyes intent. 'You mentioned your family had some antiques.'

What could she say? A refusal would seem rude and suspicious, especially given his apparent interest in restoration work. Reluctantly, she nodded.

'Sure, I'm heading up there now.'

The drive to the homestead was filled with Miles's questions about the property and its history. Erin answered automatically, her mind preoccupied with how quickly she seemed to be losing control of the situation.

At the house, her mother greeted them warmly, showing none of Logan's suspicion. Miles was all charm, complimenting the homestead and asking thoughtful questions about its age and restoration. Tom, Erin's father, appeared from his study, drawn by the unfamiliar voice.

'Dad, this is Miles McKenzie. He's staying down at the billabong.'

Tom shook Miles's hand firmly. 'Good to meet you, Miles. Erin mentioned she had a neighbour for company.'

'Your daughter's been very kind,' Miles said. 'This is a beautiful property. I understand it's been in the family for generations?'

That was all it took to get her father talking about the homestead's history while Laura packed the food for Reg. Miles listened with apparent fascination as Tom showed him through to the dining room, gesturing to the cedar sideboard and the mahogany table that had belonged to his grandmother.

'This craftsmanship is exceptional,' Miles said, running his hand along the sideboard's edge. 'You don't see joinery like this anymore.'

'It was made by a German cabinetmaker in Sydney, around 1890,' Tom explained, clearly pleased by Miles's interest.

Erin stood in the doorway, watching the exchange with

growing discomfort. Miles fit too well into their world, asking all the right questions and making all the appropriate observations. Perhaps Logan's suspicions were rubbing off on her, but something felt calculated about his interest.

When they returned to the kitchen, Laura and Erin were discussing Reg's deteriorating condition.

'He couldn't remember which day it was when I visited,' Laura was saying. 'And the house . . . ' She shook her head sadly.

'It's good of Miles to go to Reg's with you,' Tom said, clapping Miles on the shoulder. 'Sounds as though he should be going into care.'

Erin shot her father a look, but the damage was done. Miles's role in the visit to Reg had been cemented.

'Actually,' Laura said, wiping her hands on a tea towel, 'I'm sorry, Erin, but I have to take the little ute to Louth this morning. Your father's driving the Land Cruiser to Bourke for a service.'

Erin felt a flutter of unease. With Cat and Logan in Broken Hill for the day, that left her alone on the property with Miles. 'Will you be back tonight?'

'Late,' Laura said, checking her watch. 'I've got errands to run after Louth. I probably won't be back until after dinner.'

'And Dad?'

'He'll be late home. The service centre can't fit him in until lunchtime. You'll have to take one of the quad runners.'

Before Erin could respond, Miles stepped forward. 'I'll take Erin in my van. It's no trouble at all.'

Laura beamed at him. 'That's very kind of you, Miles.'

Erin knew she couldn't get out of it now. The visit to Reg had transformed from a simple delivery of food into an excursion with Miles that her parents actively supported. Any objection would seem unreasonable.

'That's . . . great,' she managed, taking the basket from her mother. 'We should probably get going soon.'

Chapter 43

Dunleavy - Friday morning.

Miles chatted easily with her parents as they walked to his van, promising to stop by again soon, offering to look at an antique clock that Tom mentioned was having problems. Erin sat silently as they drove away, the basket of food on her lap.

'Your parents are nice people,' Miles said as they turned onto the dirt road that led to Reg's property. 'Your father knows his antiques.'

'He's a history buff,' Erin replied, watching the familiar landscape roll by. 'Always has been.'

'And your mother—she reminds me of my own. Always looking after everyone.'

Erin glanced at him, searching for any sign of insincerity, but his profile revealed nothing but calm interest.

'You never really told me about your family,' she ventured.

Miles's hands tightened slightly on the steering wheel. 'Not much to tell. Ordinary people, ordinary lives.'

The conversation lapsed into silence as they approached Reg's property. Miles slowed the van as they neared the gate.

'Should I park here and wait?' he asked.

Erin hesitated, then shook her head. 'We might as well both go in. He's expecting food, but—'

Her words died in her throat as a figure emerged from behind the river gum at the gate, shotgun raised and pointed directly at the van.

'Get off my property!' Reg shouted, his thin frame trembling with rage or fear or both. The barrel of the shotgun gleamed in the sunlight.

Miles stopped the van immediately, raising his hands slightly from the steering wheel. 'That's not good,' he said softly, his voice remarkably calm for someone staring down the barrel of a gun.

'It's me, Reg,' Erin called through the open window. 'Laura's daughter. Remember? I've brought your food.'

Reg's bloodshot eyes moved from Erin to Miles, suspicion etched into every line of his yellowed face. 'Who's he? I don't know him. I told you not to bring strangers here!'

'This is just my friend,' Erin said, her heart pounding. 'He's helping me today. We've brought lasagne from Mum.'

The gun wavered slightly, but Reg didn't lower it. 'Everyone wants something,' he muttered. 'Everyone's looking. But they won't find it. I promised Betty.'

Miles slowly reached for the door handle. 'Let me talk to him.'

'No!' Erin grabbed his arm. 'He's confused. He might shoot.'

'I know what I'm doing,' Miles replied, his eyes fixed on Reg. There was that hardness again in his expression, but also a confidence that made Erin hesitate.

'Trust me,' he said, and before she could stop him, he was opening the door, one hand raised in a gesture of peace.

'Mr McGillvray,' he called, his voice steady. 'I know you don't want strangers on your property. I respect that. I'm just here to help Erin bring you some food, that's all.'

Reg stared at him; the gun still raised, but his finger had moved slightly away from the trigger. 'What's your name?' he demanded.

'Miles McKenzie.'

Something flickered across Reg's face—recognition, confusion, Erin couldn't tell. But slowly, the barrel of the shotgun lowered.

Miles glanced back at Erin, giving her a small nod. She slipped out of the van, clutching the food basket, her legs unsteady beneath her.

'Can we come in, Reg?' she asked gently. 'Just to drop off the food?'

Reg looked between them, indecision warring on his face. Then, with a sigh that seemed to deflate his entire body, he stepped back from the gate.

The passenger door of the van slammed, and Erin stiffened, worrying that Reg would shoot. She turned to see where Miles was, and Erin was surprised to see him pull the keys from the ignition and lock the driver's side. It was such a deliberate gesture—at odds with the casual, easy-going manner he normally projected.

'Do you really need to lock it out here?' she asked, balancing the picnic basket on her hip.

Miles pocketed the keys, his eyes scanning the property. 'I don't want Reg taking my van.'

Something about his answer struck Erin as strange. Reg was many things—reclusive, possibly ill, certainly eccentric— but he wasn't a car thief. Before she could dwell on it further, the sound of a shotgun being cocked captured her full attention.

'I thought I told you to piss off!' Reg shouted, his thin frame emerging from behind a shed, the shotgun levelled at them.

'It's me, Reg,' Erin called, her heart racing. 'I've brought your food.'

Miles glanced back at Erin, giving her a small nod. She slipped forward, clutching the food basket, her legs unsteady beneath her. Reg stood on the other side of the gate, the shotgun under one arm.

'Maybe put the gun away,' Erin said softly.

Reg's shoulders slumped. 'Come on then,' he said. 'But just for a minute. You know I don't like visitors.'

As they followed Reg towards the house, Erin noticed Miles studying the property intently, his eyes lingering on the outbuildings and sheds scattered across the yard. His demeanour had shifted subtly—the easy-going charm replaced by something determined.

Inside, the house was exactly as Erin remembered from her previous visit—cluttered, dusty, the accumulated detritus of a life in stasis since Betty's death. She placed the basket on the kitchen counter, carefully moving aside some newspapers to make space.

'Mum made you fresh lasagne,' she said, trying to sound cheerful. 'And there's apple crumble for dessert.'

Reg merely grunted, his attention now on Miles, who was moving through the front room with purpose, examining framed photos on the wall.

'These your sons?' Miles asked, pointing to a faded picture of two young men standing beside a much younger Reg.

Reg's face clouded. 'What's it to you?'

'Just making conversation.' Miles's tone was casual, but his eyes were sharp. 'Which rooms were theirs growing up?'

Erin frowned. It was a specific and odd, question, and one that seemed to upset Reg.

'What's it to you?' he spat out. 'You can piss off now.'

Erin put her hand on Reg's arm to calm him down as she

glared at Miles. His skin was thin and dry beneath her fingers.

'Why do you want to know that?' she asked Miles.

His eyes flicked to her, cold and dismissive. 'None of your business.'

'What?'

The abrupt change in his tone sent a chill down Erin's spine. This wasn't the charming, helpful Miles who had befriended her at the billabong. This was someone else entirely.

Miles moved towards the main door and, with a deliberate motion that made Erin's heart skip a beat, turned the lock.

'What are you doing?' she asked, unable to keep the alarm from her voice.

'Making sure we're not interrupted,' Miles replied, his attention already moving to the hallway. 'Mr. McGillvray, I need to see your son's rooms. Where are they?' He pointed at Erin. 'You come too, so I can keep an eye on you.'

'What the hell are you doing?' Erin took a step towards him, but stopped suddenly when he raised one hand, his fingers curled in a fist.

'Shut up.' The look on Miles' face frightened her.

Reg stiffened, his face contorting with sudden anger. 'You get out of my house! Nobody goes in there. Nobody!'

'The north shed too,' Miles repeated, his voice harder now. 'Where your boys stored their bikes. Tell me which one that is.'

Erin stepped back, confusion and fear mingling as she watched the scene unfold. Miles was no longer pretending to be a casual visitor. Whatever he wanted from Reg, it had nothing to do with helping her.

'I think we should go,' she said, moving towards the door.

Miles turned to her, his expression chilling. 'We're not

going anywhere until I get what I came for.'

Reg began to ramble, his words spilling out in an agitated stream. 'They left it here, said I had to keep it safe. Not my fault what they did. I told Betty it would bring trouble. I told her!'

Erin reached for her phone, her fingers trembling as she tried to dial, but the familiar 'No Service' indicator mocked her from the screen. Of course—Reg's property was in a dead zone. She'd forgotten that from her previous visits.

Miles noticed her attempt and smiled thinly. 'No reception out here. I've checked the place out a few times.'

Erin stared at him, realisation dawning. 'You didn't just happen to camp at our billabong, did you? You came here specifically. For whatever's in that shed.'

'Smart girl,' Miles said, his attention returning to Reg. 'Now, let's try again. The key to the north shed. Where is it?'

Reg was shaking now, whether from fear, anger, or both, Erin couldn't tell. 'I won't tell you. I promised the boys. I promised Betty.'

Miles sighed, reaching into his jacket and producing something that glinted in the dim light of the kitchen—a knife. 'I'm running out of patience, old man.'

Erin gasped, backing against the counter. 'Miles, stop it! This is insane!'

'My name isn't Miles,' he said without looking at her. 'And you really should have taken your brother's advice about strangers, Erin. You are rather naïve.'

The casual mention of Logan sent another wave of fear through her.

How long had this man, whoever he was, been watching them? Planning this?

Reg's eyes darted to a drawer in the kitchen, a reflexive

motion that didn't escape Miles' notice. He moved swiftly, yanking the drawer open to reveal a jumble of keys, old receipts, and miscellaneous household items.

'Which one?' he demanded, holding the knife closer to Reg.

'Reg, come and sit down,' Erin said, her mind racing for a way out of this situation. The door was locked, Miles—or whatever his name was—had the keys to the van, and they were too far from any neighbours for shouting to be effective.

Miles grabbed Erin and put the knife against her throat. 'Which one?'

Reg's face crumpled, tears forming in his bloodshot eyes. 'The brass one,' he whispered. 'With the notch.'

Miles let go of Erin and rifled through the drawer, eventually holding up a tarnished brass key with a distinctive notch in its shaft. He smiled, pocketing it.

'Good. Now, both of you are going to stay right here while I check out the shed.' He gestured with the knife. 'Move to that corner. Sit down.'

Erin helped Reg to the corner of the kitchen, where they both sank to the floor. Miles took a roll of duct tape from his jacket pocket—he'd come prepared, she realised with mounting horror—and quickly bound their hands.

'I'd tape your mouths too, but there's no need. No one around to hear you anyway,' he said with a cold smile. 'Don't try anything stupid.'

As he moved towards the door, Erin found her voice. 'What is it? What are you looking for?'

Miles paused, seeming to consider whether to answer. 'Let's just say your friend Reg's sons were involved in some interesting businesses back in the day. They left something very valuable here for safekeeping. Something that people have been looking for, for a very long time.'

'And then what?' Erin asked, her voice shaking. 'After you find it? What happens to us?'

His expression told her everything she needed to know.

'You should have stayed at the homestead, Erin,' he said quietly. 'You really should have.'

With that, he was gone, the sound of his boots on the porch fading as he made his way towards the north shed.

Beside her, Reg's breathing had become shallow and rapid.

'Reg,' she whispered urgently. 'Reg, we need to get out of here. Is there another way out of the house?'

Reg's eyes were unfocused, his confusion worse than she'd ever seen it. 'Betty?' he murmured. 'What's he want?'

Despair filled Erin. Reg was no help in this state, and with her hands bound, her options were severely limited. Whatever Miles, or whoever he was, was looking for in that shed, she had no doubt he'd do anything to get it—including ensuring there were no witnesses left behind.

She twisted her wrists against the duct tape, ignoring the burning pain as it scraped her skin. Somewhere in the distance, she heard the sound of a door opening, followed by the crash of items being thrown aside.

Chapter 44

Dunleavy - Friday night.

The kitchen door banged open. Erin's head snapped up to see Miles, filthy and furious, framed in the doorway. His clothes were covered in dust and cobwebs, his face streaked with grime, and his eyes blazed with a volatile rage that made her shrink back against the wall.

'Nothing,' he spat, kicking an empty bucket across the floor. 'Absolutely nothing! How many bloody wardrobes are there in this dump?'

Erin had spent the past two hours working desperately at the duct tape binding her wrists, rubbing it against a jagged edge of the skirting board she'd found behind her. She'd managed to fray it, but not break through, and now her wrists were raw and bleeding beneath the adhesive.

Miles stalked across the kitchen, grabbed a glass from the sink, and filled it with water. He drank deeply, water spilling down his chin, then slammed the glass down so hard it cracked.

'Two hours in that filthy shed,' he muttered, more to himself than to her. 'Must have gone through every box, every cupboard. Nothing!'

Erin swallowed hard, her mouth painfully dry. She hadn't had anything to drink since that morning, yet her bladder was painfully full.

'I need a drink,' she said, her voice cracked and thin. 'And I need to use the bathroom.'

Miles turned to her, as if only just remembering she was there. A slow, cruel smile spread across his face.

'You thought you had problems before with your missing Jack, sweetheart,' he sneered. 'Now you can help me. I might even let you go if you find what I'm looking for.'

He crossed to where Reg sat slumped beside her. The old man had drifted in and out of consciousness, occasionally mumbling Betty's name or calling for his sons. Miles kicked Reg's foot.

'Useless old bastard,' he muttered, then reached down and grabbed Erin's arm, yanking her to her feet. 'Your turn to help.'

He dragged her down the hallway, his fingers digging painfully into her arm. Erin had never been in this part of the house before, and her eyes widened as she saw the extent of Reg's hoarding. The narrow corridor was lined with stacks of newspapers that reached almost to the ceiling. Boxes filled with mysterious contents were piled against the walls. Clothes, books, broken furniture—all of it layered with dust and cobwebs.

As they passed one particularly precarious pile of rubbish, there was a rustling sound, and Erin caught sight of a scaled tail disappearing beneath the detritus. Miles jumped back, his grip momentarily loosening on her arm.

'Bloody hell,' he gasped, eyes fixed on where the snake had vanished. 'We could be here for days.' He turned to her, his expression calculating. 'You are going to help me,' he said, producing the knife from his pocket again. 'No funny business. If you run, I'll kill the old bloke. Understand?'

Erin nodded, her eyes wide with fear. 'Okay.'

Miles cut the duct tape from her wrists; the knife blade uncomfortably close to her skin. When the binding fell away, the pain of blood rushing back to her hands was almost overwhelming.

'What are we looking for?' she asked, flexing her fingers

to restore circulation.

'In here? A bag in a wardrobe,' Miles said, his eyes scanning the cluttered passage.

'What sort of bag?' she asked.

'Probably a big black garbage bag.'

Erin's mind was racing, trying to formulate some plan, but the immediate needs of her body were becoming urgent. 'I need to use the bathroom,' she said again.

Miles snorted. 'Good luck with that. You'll need to find one in this mess.'

They pushed further into the house, opening doors to rooms so filled with accumulated junk that they could barely see the floor. Eventually, they found what had once been a bathroom. An ancient lavatory with a rusty chain stood against one wall, its bowl stained a dark, unsettling brown. The rest of the space was filled with stacked magazines, empty medicine bottles, and what looked like every towel Reg had ever owned.

'Here you go,' Miles said with a mocking bow. 'Your luxury facilities.'

Erin hesitated at the doorway. 'Can I have some privacy?'

Miles laughed. 'Not a chance. Door stays open, and I stay right here.'

The humiliation burned through her as she picked her way to the toilet, keenly aware of Miles watching her every move. She had no choice—her bladder was painfully full, and she couldn't think straight with the discomfort.

Mortified beyond words, she used the filthy toilet while Miles leaned against the doorframe, knife casually displayed in his hand, his eyes never leaving her. The chain, when pulled, produced an alarming gurgle but somehow managed to flush.

As she adjusted her clothing with shaking hands, her mind was working furiously. She couldn't escape—not with Reg's life at stake. She had no doubt Miles would follow through with his threat. The house was too remote for screaming to be effective, and without phone reception, she couldn't call for help.

Her only option was to play along while looking for an opportunity. If she could find whatever it was Miles was searching for, perhaps she could use it as leverage.

'What's so important about this bag?' she asked as they moved back into the hallway.

Miles gave her a calculating look. 'My future,' he said finally. 'Courtesy of Michael McGillvray.'

'Reg's son?'

'Among others.' Miles pushed open another door, revealing what might once have been a bedroom, though it was now so filled with boxes that the bed was barely visible.

Erin stepped carefully into the room, her eyes darting around for anything that might help her—a weapon, a hidden exit, anything. But there was only junk, dust, and the oppressive knowledge that her life now depended on finding something that might not even be there anymore.

'There's going to be a lot of wardrobes in this old homestead. I think there are twelve bedrooms.' Her voice shook, and she cleared her throat.

'Start looking,' Miles ordered, gesturing with the knife. 'The sooner we find it, the sooner I get away from this dump and this situation ends.'

The unspoken threat in his words sent a chill down her spine. Erin knew with terrible certainty that "ending" this situation might not mean freedom for her or Reg—unless she could find a way out that she couldn't see yet.

Chapter 45

Sydney International Airport - Friday 8.00 p.m.

Sydney International Airport bustled with travellers as Jack Hayes finally cleared customs and border control, his body aching from the fourteen-hour flight from Johannesburg. Despite his exhaustion, adrenaline coursed through him as he pulled out his phone and switched it on, watching impatiently as it connected to the Australian network.

The moment the signal bars appeared, he dialled Erin's number. Straight to voicemail. Again. The knot in his stomach tightened. It wasn't like her; she always had her phone on.

Pulling his carry-on behind him, Jack made his way to a quieter corner of the arrivals hall and tried the homestead landline. He'd been unable to sleep on the flight, his mind racing with worst-case scenarios, each hour in the air feeling like an eternity as he remained disconnected from any news about Erin.

The phone rang once, twice, three times . . . and then, it clicked as someone lifted the receiver.

'O'Byrne residence.' Tom's familiar voice came through the line.

'Tom, it's Jack. I've just landed in Sydney.' The words tumbled out in a rush; his voice hoarse from the dry air of the airplane.

'Jack? You're back?' His tone was cold.

'Yes. Do you know where Erin is? I've been trying to call her since yesterday.'

Jack's voice must have shown his distress because Tom's tone changed. 'She's here. In the motorhome down at the billabong.'

'I need to tell her I'm home. My lawyer arranged flights. I'm about to board the Broken Hill flight. I need to talk to her; can you ask her to ring me?'

'Lawyer? Are you alright?'

'I'm fine. It's a long story.'

'I'll drive down and bring her back to the house. The service is more reliable here. Works intermittently at the campsites.'

'Thank you. If I don't answer her call, tell her I'll have boarded. I'll call from Broken Hill.'

As he hurried to the boarding gate, Jack's instincts were telling him that something was wrong.

Chapter 46

Ceann Mara - Friday 8.15 p.m.

Tom set down the phone, concern etched across his weathered face. Laura appeared in the kitchen doorway, wiping her hands on a tea towel.

'That was Jack?' she asked, noting her husband's expression. 'It didn't sound good.'

'No, something's obviously happened. He said he's okay; I need to get Erin up here. He's been in touch with his lawyer.'

'I'll put the kettle on,' Laura said, already moving towards the stove. 'You go and get Erin.'

Tom grabbed his keys and headed out to his ute. The night was clear, the stars brilliant above the property as he drove the familiar track down to the billabong. His headlights swept across the campsite, illuminating Erin's motorhome, which stood dark and silent.

He was relieved to see that the white van belonging to that fellow Miles was gone. There had been something about him that had set Tom's teeth on edge, despite his charming manner. Too smooth by half.

Tom pulled up alongside the motorhome and cut the engine. The silence of the outback night wrapped around him as he approached the door.

'Erin,' he called, knocking firmly. 'It's Dad. Wake up, sweetie.'

No response. He knocked again, this time louder. 'Erin? Jack called. He wants you to call back.'

The continued silence sent the first tendril of concern

snaking through Tom. He tried the door, only to find it locked.

'Erin!' His knocking had become pounding, loud enough to wake the dead. After his fourth attempt, genuine fear began to take hold. Was she in there ill? Had she fallen and hurt herself? Was she just soundly asleep after a few drinks?

He raced back to his ute and sped back to the shed, grabbing a toolbox and a crowbar. The thought of breaking into Erin's motorhome made him wince, but concern for his daughter overrode everything else.

Back at the billabong, he worked quickly, hating the sound of metal giving way as he forced the door. 'Erin? It's Dad. I'm sorry about the door.'

The interior of the motorhome was dark and empty. No sign of Erin, no note explaining her absence. Her bed was made; nothing appeared disturbed. It was as if she'd simply walked out and not returned.

Fear now a solid weight in his chest, Tom drove back to the homestead much faster than was safe on the rutted track. Laura was waiting on the veranda, a mug of tea in her hands. Her face fell when she saw he was alone.

'She's not there,' Tom said, his voice tight. 'The motorhome is empty. No sign of her. I broke in.'

'Could she be out walking?' Laura suggested, though her tone lacked conviction. 'Or visiting someone?'

'At this hour? Without leaving a note?' Tom shook his head. 'Her phone's not answering either.'

'She could have had an accident,' Laura whispered, her hand at her throat.

Tom pulled out his mobile phone. 'I'm going to get Logan over here. We'll search the property for her.'

'I'll call Logan. You call Jack and let him know what's

happening.'

As Laura went inside to make the call to Logan, Tom faced the grim task he'd been dreading. He had to call Jack back.

He dialled Jack's number, each ring tightening the knot in his stomach.

'Tom?' Jack's voice was immediately alert, hopeful. 'Is she there? Can I talk to her?'

'Jack, I—' Tom's voice caught. 'She's not at the motorhome. We can't find her.'

There was a moment of stunned silence, then: 'What do you mean, you can't find her? Where the hell is she?'

'We don't know. The door was locked, everything looked normal inside, but she wasn't there. Her phone goes straight to voicemail.'

A string of explosive curses erupted from the other end of the line, Jack's voice rising with each word.

'Jack, calm down, we're getting Logan over. We're going to search the property thoroughly,' Tom tried to reassure him, though his own worry was mounting by the second.

Laura appeared beside him, gently taking the phone. 'Jack, it's Laura. Listen to me, love.'

Jack's voice was raw with fear and anger at himself. 'Laura, what's happening? Where is she?'

'We're going to find her,' Laura said firmly. 'But there's something you should know. Erin's been . . . she hasn't been herself lately. She's been spending a lot of time alone at the billabong. She seemed withdrawn, depressed even.'

'Depressed?' Jack's voice cracked. 'Because of me? Because I haven't been able to contact her?'

'I don't know, love. She hasn't really opened up to us.'

Jack's rage exploded through the phone; a torrent of abuse directed at himself.

'This is all my fault. I should never have gone on this bloody assignment. The damn magazine and their bloody contract!'

When Jack finally ran out of breath, Laura spoke again, her eyes meeting Tom's with shared concern. 'We're going to find her, Jack. I promise you.'

'I'll be there as soon as I can. I'll hire a car at Broken Hill,' Jack said, his voice now under control, but determined. 'Please keep me in the loop.'

After ending the call, Tom and Laura stood in grim silence until the sound of Logan's truck rumbling up the driveway broke the spell.

Logan burst through the door; his face tight with worry. Cat was behind him. 'Any word?'

Tom shook his head. 'Nothing.'

'What's going on, Dad?' Cat's face was white.

'That Miles bloke,' Logan said immediately. 'I told you there was something off about him. Has his van gone?'

'Yes,' Tom confirmed. 'No sign of it down at the billabong.'

Laura's hand flew to her mouth. 'No. It couldn't be him— he seemed like a nice man when we met him this morning; he was up here.'

'That doesn't mean anything,' Logan said grimly. 'I never trusted him. He was looking around the place—'

Tom grabbed a torch from the kitchen drawer. 'Right now, we need to focus on finding Erin. Logan, you take the east side of the billabong. I'll take the west. Laura, can you bring the phone in case Erin comes back or calls?'

As they headed out into the darkness, torch beams cutting through the night, Tom tried to quell the rising fear. His daughter was out there somewhere. She had to be all right. She had to be.

The darkness at the billabong was absolute, broken only by the sweeping beams of their torches as they called Erin's name. The moon, a thin white sliver, offered little illumination as Tom, Laura, Logan, and Cat spread out along the water's edge. They continued searching, calling Erin's name into the darkness, checking every place she might have fallen or become trapped. Cat examined the area around Erin's usual swimming spot, while Tom methodically worked his way through the stand of eucalyptus trees where she often sat to read.

'Nothing,' Cat reported, rejoining the group after half an hour. 'No sign of her.'

The tension was palpable, each of them imagining scenarios worse than the last. Tom's jaw was set in a hard line, his movements becoming increasingly frantic as each minute passed without a trace of his daughter.

'Erin!' Tom's voice echoed across the still water, swallowed by the vastness of the outback night. 'Erin, can you hear us?'

Each of them moved carefully through the undergrowth, the beam of their torches catching occasional reflections in the eyes of nocturnal creatures. Tom's light swept across a fallen log, then froze as it illuminated the sinuous form of a brown snake slithering into the shadows.

'Watch for snakes,' he called out, his voice tight with worry. 'Eastern browns are active at night.'

Tom and Laura moved to search the river along the other side of the airstrip, where Erin often walked. They called until they were hoarse.

Chapter 47

Broken Hill Airport - Friday 11.00 p.m.

'What do you mean you don't have anything available?' Jack's voice rose, drawing glances from other weary travellers at the rental car counter. 'I need a car now.'

The young woman behind the counter tapped at her keyboard with infuriating slowness. 'I'm sorry, sir. It's peak tourist season, and with the—'

'I don't care about the season,' Jack cut in, pushing his credit card across the counter. 'Check again. There must be something.'

His body ached from the fourteen-hour flight, but adrenaline kept him upright, fuelled by the growing certainty that Erin was in danger. Every minute spent in this fluorescent-lit purgatory was a minute too long.

The woman sighed and tapped a few more keys. 'We do have one vehicle available, but it's in our premium category. A BMW 5 Series. It's considerably more expensive than—'

'I'll take it,' Jack said immediately. 'Just get me the paperwork.'

'I'll need to run your credit card first.'

Jack nodded impatiently, drumming his fingers on the counter as the transaction processed. Now, at least, money wasn't an obstacle.

'Approved,' the clerk said, sounding slightly surprised. She slid a tablet across the counter. 'If you could just fill out these forms . . .'

Jack scrawled his signature across the digital forms, barely reading the terms. 'Keys,' he said, hand outstretched.

Ten minutes later—ten minutes that felt like hours—Jack strode through the parking garage, clicking the key fob until the headlights flashed in response. The sleek black BMW gleamed under the fluorescent lights; a machine built for speed.

Jack flung his carry-on and camera bag into the passenger seat with no thought for the expensive lenses inside. Equipment that he would normally handle with reverent care was now just baggage, obstacles to be cleared before he could drive.

The GPS came to life as he started the engine, the polite voice asking for a destination. Jack punched in *Ceann Mara*, noting the estimated arrival time with a grimace. Even pushing the speed limit, he was looking at a long drive. He pulled out his phone, dialling Tom's number, but it went straight to voicemail. No service—they must be at Reg's place already.

As the BMW surged forward, Jack gripped the steering wheel so tightly his knuckles whitened. 'Hold on, Erin,' he whispered to the empty car. 'I'm coming.'

Chapter 48

Dunleavy - Friday 11.00 p.m.

The stench was the worst part. It clung to everything—decades of neglect, rodent droppings, food left to rot, and the musty odour of papers yellowing with age. Erin's clothing was filthy, streaked with dust and cobwebs, her hands blackened from digging through piles of forgotten possessions. Her stomach had long since stopped growling, now a hollow ache that matched the throbbing in her temples.

The night had passed as Miles forced her to sift through the unimaginable accumulation in what had once been the bedrooms of Reg's sons. The first room had been bad enough—a bed buried beneath boxes of old magazines, fishing equipment tangled with clothes that had disintegrated with age, and photographs curled with damp.

The second room was worse. A window had broken years ago, allowing in rain and wildlife. Possums had nested in one corner, leaving droppings and the skeletal remains of their meals. Mould bloomed across the ceiling in patterns like abstract art. The smell made Erin gag repeatedly as Miles pushed her to dig deeper into piles that shifted treacherously beneath her hands.

With each passing hour, with each wardrobe opened and each drawer emptied, Miles's rage intensified. He kicked at the debris, sending clouds of dust billowing through the stale air, cursing with increasing venom.

'If I've wasted all that time getting here and leave empty-handed, you'll all pay for it,' he snarled, his face contorted with fury. 'I'll burn this place down and your bloody parents' place too before I go.'

The threat sent ice through Erin's veins. Her parents, Cat and Logan, the homestead—all suddenly at risk because of whatever was hidden in this hovel. Whatever Miles was looking for, the stakes were much higher than she'd initially understood.

'Can I please go and check on Reg?' she asked, trying to keep her voice steady despite her exhaustion and fear. 'We need to eat too if we are going to keep searching. I'll make us a cup of tea.'

Miles stared at her, suspicion warring with practicality in his eyes. Finally, he nodded, gesturing with the knife towards the door. 'Fine. Make it quick.'

The kitchen was a welcome relief from the suffocating bedrooms, though it had its own smell from unwashed dishes and rotting food. Reg remained on the floor where they'd left him, but his eyes were open now, tracking their movement as they entered.

Erin crouched beside him, her heart aching at his vulnerability. 'Are you alright, Reg? Let's sit you up. I'm going to make a cup of tea.'

For the first time that night, Reg seemed lucid, his gaze clear as it met hers. Erin held her breath, terrified of what he might say. If he mentioned his rifle or tried to alert her to some means of escape, Miles would surely silence him permanently.

But Reg merely nodded, his cracked lips parting in a grateful smile as she helped him to sit up against the kitchen cabinet. 'Tea would be good,' he said, his voice a rough whisper.

Miles watched them from the doorway, knife still in hand, as Erin filled the kettle and placed it on the stove. She found three mismatched mugs in the sink, rinsing them as best she could under the tepid tap water. In a moment of clarity, Erin remembered the basket of food she'd brought from her mother. 'The food my mum sent over—we could eat that.'

Miles considered this, then nodded. 'Where is it?'

'I left it on the counter,' Erin said, gesturing towards the basket still sitting where she'd placed it when they first arrived.

The basket was a welcome sight amid the squalor of the kitchen—Laura's familiar wicker container covered with a checkered cloth. Inside was the promised lasagne, along with a container of apple crumble and a loaf of homemade bread.

Erin set about serving the food, finding plates in the cupboard that were less filthy than others. She wiped them as best she could with a dishcloth that had seen better days. The kettle whistled, and she made tea.

Reg gestured vaguely towards the cupboard under the sink. 'Might be some long-life milk in there.'

The cupboard yielded a carton of milk out of date by about four years. When Erin opened it, the sour smell made her gag.

'I'll have mine black,' she said, setting the kettle down.

'I can't wait for it to cool. I need a cuppa, now. I'll have the milk.' Reg reached for the carton. 'It's fine,' he insisted, pouring a generous amount into his tea. Erin winced as she saw lumps of sour milk floating on the surface of his mug, but Reg seemed unbothered, stirring it casually as if this were perfectly normal.

The three of them ate in silence—Erin and Reg perched on rickety chairs at the table, Miles standing with his back to the wall, eyes constantly moving between them and the door. Mum's lasagne was cold, but the couple of spoonfuls she forced down helped restore some of her flagging energy.

When they'd finished eating, Miles gestured with the knife.

'Back on the floor, both of you.'

He found a roll of packing tape in a drawer and secured them again, this time binding their ankles as well as their wrists. Erin winced as the tape pulled at her skin, already raw from the earlier binding.

'Any grog in this place, old man?' Miles asked, scanning the cluttered kitchen.

Reg seemed more lucid after he'd eaten. He hesitated, then nodded towards a cabinet beneath the sink. 'Behind the cleaning stuff.'

Miles rummaged through the cabinet and emerged with a dusty bottle of whiskey; its seal unbroken. He tore it open and poured a generous measure into one of the used mugs, knocking it back in one swallow before pouring another.

'I'm going to get some sleep,' he announced, checking that their bindings were secure. 'We start again at first light.'

He grabbed the bottle and shuffled a pile of newspapers into a makeshift pillow, positioning himself in front of the door. Within minutes, his breathing had deepened into a rumbling snore, one arm flung across his face, the other still clutching the knife even in sleep.

Erin's eyes moved restlessly around the kitchen, cataloguing the depressing evidence of Reg's decline. Mounds of newspapers, dating back decades, were stacked against the walls, their headlines chronicling events long forgotten. Dirty dishes filled the sink and spilled onto every available surface. Cobwebs hung from the ceiling like macabre decorations, dust thick enough to write in coating every surface.

The smell was a complex tapestry of neglect—mildew from damp that had never been addressed, rotting food, unwashed linens, and the sharp tang of rodent urine. Beneath it all was the stale, sour scent of a house that hadn't known fresh air in years, windows sealed shut by grime and disuse.

On the floor beside her, she could hear Reg's laboured breathing. He seemed more alert than he had been all day, his eyes darting around the room, occasionally settling on Miles with undisguised hatred.

Finally, he turned to her, his gaze meaningful as he nodded towards the pantry and mouthed, 'Another gun.'

Erin's heart leapt. If she could somehow reach it . . .

But the tape around her wrists and ankles was too tight, too secure. She strained against it, feeling the adhesive rip at her skin, but it wouldn't give. Miles had been thorough this time, wrapping the tape in multiple layers, learning from her earlier attempt to free herself.

Across the room, Miles snored on, the whiskey bottle half-empty beside him. Occasionally, he would stir, his fingers tightening reflexively around the knife before settling back into his alcohol-induced slumber.

Erin closed her eyes, exhaustion threatening to overwhelm her. She needed to think, to find a way out of this nightmare before dawn broke and the search resumed. Miles's fury would only grow with each passing hour that the mysterious bag remained unfound.

She thought of her family, unaware of her danger. Of Jack, somewhere in Africa. Of the homestead, standing peaceful under the stars while Miles plotted to burn it to the ground.

There had to be a way out. There had to be.

Chapter 49

Ceann Mara - Saturday 3.00 a.m.

It was almost three a.m. by the time Tom and Laura met up with Cat and Logan back at the campground.

'No sign of her anywhere,' Logan said. 'It's time we called the police.' He walked across to the other campsite where Miles had camped. 'Nothing here.'

Laura's torch swept across the campsite once more, lingering on the damaged door of the motorhome. Something nagged at the edge of her consciousness—a detail overlooked in the rush of worry.

'Tom,' she called suddenly. 'Was my picnic basket in the motorhome?'

Tom frowned, momentarily confused by the question. 'I didn't notice it. Why?'

'The basket I sent with Erin this morning—for Reg.' Laura's eyes widened with realisation. 'Tom, she could still be over at Reg's. Maybe he's sick and she's staying there with him?'

Hope flickered across Tom's face. 'Of course—the food run. With everything that's happened, I completely forgot.'

They hurried back to the motorhome, searching the small space more thoroughly this time. Logan checked the annexe while Cat examined the storage compartments outside.

'No basket,' Logan confirmed, emerging from the annexe.

'She was going over with Miles in his van,' Laura said, pieces falling into place.

'Perhaps he's still around and helping her,' Cat suggested.

'Reg might have taken a turn for the worse.'

'She would have come back to call for help if he was ill. There's no phone service over there,' Logan reminded them, his expression darkening. 'Never has been. That's why Reg never bothered getting a mobile.'

Tom's mind raced through the possibilities. If Erin was at Reg's, why hadn't she come back or sent word with Miles? It wasn't like her to stay away without letting them know.

Unless she couldn't leave.

The thought settled like a stone in his stomach.

'Logan,' Tom said, decision made. 'You and Laura go up to the house and call the police. Cat and I will go over to Reg's place. If we're not back soon, follow us.'

Logan nodded, his hand falling to rest on the rifle he'd brought along—a precaution against snakes, he'd said, but Tom now suspected there was more to it. 'You take care over there. We won't be far behind you.'

Tom clasped his son-in-law's shoulder briefly, grateful for his steady presence. 'Let's hope it doesn't come to that.'

As Tom and Cat climbed into the ute, Laura pressed a small first aid kit into her husband's hands. 'Just in case,' she said, her voice barely above a whisper. 'Bring her home, Tom.'

The headlights carved a path through the darkness as they drove away from the billabong, following the rutted track that would eventually connect with the road to Reg McGillvray's property. Beside him, Cat checked her phone periodically, hoping for a signal that never appeared.

'What do you think happened?' she asked finally, breaking the tense silence.

Tom's hands tightened on the steering wheel. 'I don't

know. But I don't like that this Miles character disappeared at the same time as Erin.'

'Logan never trusted him,' Cat said, gazing out at the passing landscape, ghostly in the moonlight. 'Said there was something wrong about the way he watched the place.'

Tom said nothing but pressed his foot harder on the accelerator, sending the ute bouncing over the uneven ground. If Erin was at Reg's, they'd find her. If she wasn't—if Miles had somehow harmed her—

He couldn't finish the thought. Wouldn't allow himself to imagine the worst. Not yet.

Chapter 50

Dunleavy - Saturday 4.00 a.m.

The night pressed close around Tom's ute as he and Cat approached Reg McGillvray's property, headlights cutting through the darkness before Tom switched them off for the final approach. The ramshackle homestead loomed ahead, a darker shadow against the star-filled sky.

'No lights,' Cat whispered, scanning the property. 'Not looking hopeful.'

Tom cut the engine; the sudden silence was heavy around them. In the distance, a lone dog barked aggressively, the sound carrying across the open landscape.

They moved cautiously towards the house, torches pointed at the ground to avoid announcing their presence too obviously. The yard was littered with abandoned farm equipment, weeds growing high around rusted metal.

As they passed one of the sheds, Tom's torch beam caught something that made him stop suddenly.

'Sshh. Look,' he whispered, gesturing with the light. 'That's Miles's van.'

The white van was parked behind the shed, partially hidden from view from the main road. Its presence confirmed their suspicions—Miles must have brought Erin here, and for some reason, they hadn't returned.

Cat drew closer to her father, her voice barely audible. 'Something's wrong, Dad. If they were just helping Reg if he was ill, Erin would have called us.'

Tom nodded grimly, his hand moving to the rifle he'd

brought along. 'We need to check the house. Carefully.'

***

Inside the darkened kitchen, Miles jerked awake at the sound of a car engine. He'd fallen into a whiskey-induced slumber, but his instincts—honed by years of living on the wrong side of the law—had alerted him to the potential danger.

He moved silently to the window, peering through a gap in the grimy curtains. In the moonlight, he could make out two figures moving towards the house, one carrying what looked like a rifle.

'Shut up,' he hissed, turning back to where Erin and Reg sat bound on the floor.

Erin had been drifting in and out of a fitful doze, but she was instantly alert at the change in Miles's demeanour. Hope surged through her—someone had come looking for her.

Miles activated the flashlight on his phone, the harsh beam illuminating the kitchen just enough for Erin and Reg to see him clearly. His face was twisted with fury and fear as he moved towards them, knife in hand. He crouched before them, bringing the blade close to Erin's throat. With his free hand, he made a slashing motion across his own neck, the message unmistakable.

Erin nodded, her heart hammering in her chest. If she made a sound, if she tried to alert her rescuers, Miles would kill her—and likely Reg too. The old man seemed to understand as well, closing his eyes in resignation.

Miles extinguished the light and moved silently towards the door, knife at the ready. Outside, footsteps crunched on the gravel, drawing steadily closer to the house.

Chapter 51

Dunleavy - Saturday 4.30 a.m.

Miles moved to the small annexe at the kitchen door and pressed himself against the wall, knife clutched in his white-knuckled grip as the footsteps outside grew louder. As he stepped around the corner, Erin could see the silhouette of his head as he peered cautiously through the grimy window, but she was out of his sight.

'Two of them.' His voice was deathly quiet. 'One's got a rifle.'

Erin's heart leapt—her father had come for her. Or Logan. Either way, help was mere metres away, yet Miles stood between them with a knife and murderous intent.

In the dim moonlight filtering through the window, Erin looked desperately around the kitchen. Her bound hands had gone numb hours ago, but she'd been working at the tape whenever Miles wasn't watching. The duct tape had stretched slightly, not enough to slip her hands free, but enough to give her a fraction more movement.

Her gaze fell on the bottom drawer where Miles had found the keys earlier. It stood slightly ajar, the contents just visible. Among them, she could make out the glint of something metallic—perhaps scissors or a knife.

Miles peered around the doorway. 'If you make a sound,' he whispered fiercely, 'I'll kill them before they even get through the door. Understand?'

Erin nodded, her eyes wide with what she hoped looked like fear rather than determination. When he went back into the annexe, she shifted slightly, her bound feet pushing against the floor to move her incrementally closer to the drawer.

Outside, a voice called softly, 'Erin? Are you in there?'

It was her father. Miles tensed, and she saw a shadow as he raised the knife as if he might somehow stab through the door at the sound. His attention was fully on the approaching threat now, and Reg and Erin were out of his sight again.

With her heart pounding so loudly that she was sure Miles would hear it, Erin continued her subtle movements towards the drawer. Beside her, Reg began to cough—a deep, rattling sound that seemed to go on and on, drawing Miles's annoyed glance.

'Shut him up!' Miles hissed from the annexe.

Erin leaned towards Reg, ostensibly to quiet him, but used the movement to push herself another few centimetres towards the drawer. 'It's okay, Reg,' she whispered soothingly. 'Try to breathe.'

Reg's coughing subsided into laboured breathing, but he held Miles's attention for those crucial seconds. Now, with her back to the counter, Erin was close enough to reach behind her. Her fingers, numb and clumsy, fumbled blindly for the drawer handle.

A torch beam swept across the front yard and lit the kitchen window above the sink. 'They're coming to the door,' she heard him mutter. 'I'll take them as they enter.'

Erin's fingers closed around the drawer handle. With agonising slowness, she pulled it open wider, praying the hinges wouldn't squeak. Her hand delved inside, feeling past old takeaway menus, rubber bands, and what felt like a tangle of string.

Then her fingers touched cold metal—the serrated edge of a steak knife.

A knock sounded at the door, firm and authoritative. 'Reg? It's Tom O'Byrne. Are you in there?'

Miles stepped into the kitchen, positioning the knife for a strike. 'Shut up,' he mouthed at Erin and Reg, drawing his finger across his throat once more.

Erin's fingers closed around the knife handle. With a silent prayer, she began sawing awkwardly at the tape binding her wrists, the blade catching and slipping on the adhesive.

'Reg? Erin?' Tom called again, his voice more insistent. 'If you're in there, please answer.'

The knob rattled as someone tried the door. Miles stepped back into the annexe and tensed, preparing to strike. Erin sawed faster, feeling the tape beginning to give.

'It's locked.' Cat's voice came from outside. 'Should we force it?'

'Wait,' Tom replied. 'Let me check around the front first.'

Footsteps moved away from the door. Miles stayed there, clearly torn between following the movement and staying positioned for an ambush. 'They're splitting up,' he muttered, frustration evident in his voice.

The tape around Erin's wrists finally parted. The sudden freedom sent pins and needles shooting through her hands, but she had no time to relish the sensation. As Miles edged towards the kitchen window to track Tom's movements, Erin leaned forward and cut the bindings around her ankles.

'My rifle. Pantry,' Reg whispered into her ear, so softly she barely caught it. 'Behind the flour.'

Erin nodded imperceptibly, her eyes on Miles as he peered through the back window. The pantry was on the other side of the kitchen—she'd need to cross directly behind Miles to reach it.

A noise at the back door drew Miles's attention. 'Not a sound,' he whispered harshly, moving back into the annexe.

It was now or never. Three steps, that was all she needed. Erin stood and took the first, then froze as a floorboard creaked beneath her weight.

Miles whirled around; his face filled with rage as he saw her standing. 'You little—'

He lunged, but Erin was already moving, desperation lending her speed. She threw herself towards the pantry, yanking open the door and falling inside as Miles's knife slashed through the air where she had been standing a second earlier.

Frantically, she pushed aside cans and boxes, searching for flour. Her hand connected with a large plastic container, and behind it, the unmistakable cold metal of a rifle barrel.

Miles reached the pantry door just as Erin's fingers closed around the gun. She swung around, bringing the rifle up between them. Miles stopped short, his knife still raised.

'Get back,' Erin said, her voice steadier than she'd expected. 'It's loaded.'

Miles assessed the situation, his eyes darting from the rifle to Erin's face. 'You won't shoot me,' he said, taking a step forward. 'You don't have it in you.'

'Don't test me,' Erin replied, chambering a round with a decisive click. 'I've been shooting since I was ten.'

The standoff lasted only seconds before Miles made his decision. He feinted left, then lunged right, trying to get around the rifle barrel. Erin swung with the weapon, catching him hard across the temple with the stock.

Miles staggered, momentarily stunned. Erin pushed past him, rifle trained on his chest as she backed towards Reg.

'Drop the knife,' she ordered.

Miles glared at her, blood trickling from his temple, but he didn't comply. His gaze shifted slightly, focusing on something behind her. Erin didn't fall for the trick, keeping her eyes and the rifle trained on him.

Then she smelled it—smoke.

Glancing over her shoulder, she saw flames licking up the wall behind Reg. During the struggle, a kerosene lamp had been knocked over, setting fire to the piles of newspapers that filled the kitchen. The dry, brittle papers caught quickly, flames spreading with frightening speed.

'Reg!' Erin cried, moving towards him while trying to keep Miles covered.

Outside, voices shouted in alarm as the glow of the fire became visible through the windows.

'Fire! There's a fire inside!' Cat's voice carried clearly.

The back door shuddered as something heavy slammed against it. Miles, seeing his opportunity in the chaos, ran out towards the front of the house. Erin swung the rifle towards him but hesitated to shoot. That moment of hesitation was enough— Miles disappeared through the door into the night.

The back door gave way with a crack of splintering wood as Tom burst in, rifle in hand. His eyes widened as he took in the scene—the spreading fire, Erin with Reg's rifle, and Reg still bound on the floor.

'Erin! Thank God!' He rushed to her side while Cat moved to help Reg.

'Miles went to the front,' Erin said, coughing as smoke began to fill the room. 'He's had us tied up all night. He's looking for something—a bag of something.'

'Let's get out first, explanations later,' Tom said, helping Cat lift Reg to his feet. 'This place is going up fast.'

They stumbled out into the night air, Reg leaning heavily on Tom and Cat as the fire spread through the house behind them. In the distance, a vehicle engine roared to life—Miles making his escape in his van.

'Should we go after him?' Cat asked, looking towards the sound.

Tom shook his head. 'Erin and Reg need medical attention. We'll call the police from the homestead.'

Chapter 52

Dunleavy - Saturday 4.45 a.m.

Laura and Logan met Jack when he arrived at *Ceann Mara* and told him that they thought Erin might be over at Reg McGillvray's place. Logan jumped in the front, and Laura climbed into the back. Five minutes later, the black BMW skidded to a halt in a cloud of red dust, the engine still running as Jack threw open the door and stumbled out. The scene before him was chaos—flames licking at the homestead, smoke billowing into the night sky, and a small group of people huddled near the yard gate.

But Jack saw only one person.

Erin stood there, covered in soot, her clothes torn and dirty. Her eyes, reflecting the orange glow of the fire, widened at the sight of him. For a heartbeat, neither moved, as if the world had frozen in place.

'Jack,' she whispered, her voice barely audible over the crackling fire. 'Oh, my God, Jack.'

Her legs buckled beneath her, and he was already running to her, closing the distance between them in desperate strides. He caught her before she fell, his arms wrapping around her with the fierce emotion he'd been holding in during the long drive from Broken Hill.

'I've got you,' Jack murmured, his voice breaking as he pulled her against his chest. 'I'm here, sweetheart. I've got you. I'm never going to leave you again.'

Erin's fingers clutched at his shirt, her body trembling against his. She smelled of smoke and fear, but she was alive—

gloriously, miraculously alive.

'How did you know?' she asked, looking up at him with disbelief. 'How did you find me?'

'I called *Ceann Mara* as soon as I landed in Sydney. Your dad couldn't find you.' Jack brushed a strand of hair from her face, his eyes scanning every inch of her for injuries. His thumb gently wiped a smudge of ash from her cheek. 'Are you hurt? Did he—'

'I'm okay,' she said, wincing slightly as she shifted in his arms. 'Just some bruises. Miles wanted information about something hidden there. He made me search with him.'

Jack's jaw tightened; Logan and Laura had filled him in on the way over.

'We'll have to go back to *Ceann Mara* to call the police again and tell them what's happened. No service here,' Tom said.

Behind them, Cat and Logan were supporting Reg, the older man limping badly. The fire had spread to the entire east wing of the homestead now, the flames shooting to the sky.

Jack cupped Erin's face in his hands, his eyes searching hers. 'When I got that call from your dad . . .' His voice caught. 'I thought I might lose you before I ever had the chance to tell you the truth.'

'What truth?' Erin asked, her hands holding his wrists. The doubt in her voice broke his heart.

'That I've been a fool. That I should never have gone to Africa.' Jack pressed his forehead against hers. 'The only thing I worry about is the thought of not having you in my life.'

Tears cut clean tracks through the soot on Erin's face. 'In the end, I knew you'd come home to me,' she whispered, her voice gaining strength despite her exhaustion. 'I struggled, but I knew you would.'

Jack pulled her close again, his heart hammering against his ribs. He could feel hers doing the same, their rhythms finding each other despite everything that had tried to tear them apart.

'We need to get you to a doctor,' he said, reluctantly loosening his embrace to look at her properly.

The sound of an engine starting made them both turn. Headlights swept across the yard as Tom's ute pulled away, Reg visible in the passenger seat, with Cat in the middle and Logan behind the wheel.

'We should go too,' Erin said, but she made no move to step out of Jack's arms. 'To see if Reg is alright. And to make sure Miles, or whoever he is, isn't at home.'

Jack nodded, but he couldn't bring himself to let her go just yet. Instead, he brushed his lips against her forehead, a promise in the gesture.

'We will. But first, I need you to know something.' He waited until her eyes met his again. 'Whatever happens next, even with that lowlife still out there and with whatever he was after gone up in flames, we face it together. No more secrets, no more running. Just us, getting through this together. Okay?'

Erin's smile was tired and strained. 'Together,' she agreed quietly, her hand finding his and holding tight.

Behind them, the old homestead groaned as another section of roof collapsed in a shower of sparks. As Jack led Erin towards the BMW where Laura and Tom waited, he held her close to him. Even with the danger still present and the chaos surrounding them, Jack could feel the tension finally leaving her body. Guilt sat heavily on him. None of this would have happened if he'd been home with Erin.

Chapter 53

Ceann Mara – Saturday 7.30 a.m.

The call they were hoping to get came not long after sunrise. Tom answered, his face transforming from weary concern to cautious relief as he listened to the voice on the other end.

'They got him,' he announced as he hung up, looking around at the family gathered in the kitchen. 'Police intercepted him about fifty kilometres outside of Bourke. He's in custody.'

A collective exhale seemed to pass through the kitchen. Erin, still wrapped in Jack's arms where she'd been since they returned to the homestead, closed her eyes briefly.

'Did they say anything else?' Logan asked, hands curled around his coffee mug.

Tom nodded. 'They ran his prints. Turns out his real name is Marcus Sheridan. He's got a record going back years—break and enter, fraud, assault. He did time in Casuarina Prison in Perth about five years ago.'

'Perth?' Laura looked up from the frying pan where she was cooking breakfast. 'Isn't that where—'

'Where Reg's oldest boy ended up,' Tom confirmed. 'According to the police, Marcus—Miles—shared a cell with Michael McGillvray for eight months. The theory is that Michael told him about some hidden proceeds from their drug operation. Money and drugs stashed at the homestead.'

'The black garbage bag he was looking for in the wardrobe,' Erin murmured, her voice hoarse from smoke and exhaustion. Despite not having slept all night, she had refused to let Jack out of her sight. Even for her shower, Jack had waited just outside the shower screen, talking to her through it while Laura brought clean clothes for her to change into.

'Looks that way,' Tom said, running a hand through his hair. 'The irony is, if there was anything there, it's ashes now. The whole place burned to the ground.'

The smell of bacon filled the kitchen as Laura expertly flipped the rashers in the pan. 'Breakfast's nearly ready. Cat, would you set the table, love?'

It was such a normal request amid the extraordinary circumstances that it almost made Erin laugh. Her mother's response to any crisis had always been food, as if properly fed people could better face whatever challenges came their way.

As Cat moved around the table, placing plates and cutlery, Jack gently extricated himself from Erin's grip. 'I need to wash up,' he said softly, pressing a kiss to her forehead. 'I'll be right back.'

Erin nodded reluctantly, watching him disappear down the hallway. The separation, even momentary, left her feeling nervous.

Logan crossed the kitchen to stand beside her, his expression uncharacteristically gentle. 'You did good, sis,' he said quietly. 'Getting yourself and Reg out like that? Not everyone would have kept their head in that situation.'

'I didn't feel brave,' Erin admitted. 'I was terrified the entire time.'

'That's what makes it brave,' Logan replied simply. 'Being scared and doing it anyway.'

When Jack returned, Logan intercepted him near the doorway.

'Good to have you back, mate,' he said, extending his hand. 'Things weren't right around here without you.'

Jack shook Logan's hand, surprise evident on his face. Their relationship had always been cordial but distant, Logan's protective nature towards Erin creating a subtle barrier between them.

'Thanks,' Jack said. 'I should never have left.'

'Don't beat yourself up,' Logan advised. 'From what you've said, you didn't have much choice in the matter.'

Jack's expression darkened. 'I had a choice in taking the assignment. And in trusting Natalie.'

Laura began serving breakfast—eggs, bacon, toast, and her homemade tomato relish. The family settled around the table, the familiar ritual providing a semblance of normalcy amid the chaos of the past twenty-four hours.

For several minutes, there was only the sound of cutlery against plates as everyone ate. Erin, despite her exhaustion, found herself ravenous. Next to her, Jack picked at his food, clearly still troubled.

'What exactly happened with *Terra Lens*?' Tom asked finally, breaking the silence. 'If you don't mind talking about it.'

Jack set down his fork with a sigh and explained how Natalie had tried to claim his work as the magazine's property, even the photographs outside the specific assignment parameters.

'When I refused to sign over all the rights, she terminated the contract on the spot,' Jack said bitterly. 'She took the satellite phone, withdrew my credentials, and left me stranded in the Ngwempisi Wilderness Area. If not for Trevor arranging funds and flights, I'd still be there.'

'That's outrageous,' Tom said, clearly appalled. 'Surely

that's grounds for legal action.'

Jack nodded. 'Trevor's on it. He's a good mate and has a very good reputation in criminal law; he's already started proceedings against the magazine. But the whole experience has left me questioning everything.'

'What about your work?' Laura asked. 'Your photographs?'

'All in limbo,' Jack replied. 'They're claiming ownership of everything I shot while in Africa, regardless of whether it was part of the assignment or not. Trevor says we have a strong case, but it could take months to resolve.'

'So that's why you couldn't contact me?' Erin asked softly.

Jack squeezed her hand. 'Without the satellite phone, I had no way to make calls or email you. I finally made it to Mbabane and got hold of Trevor, but by then . . .' He trailed off, the worry of those days still evident in his eyes. 'I'm thinking of giving up photography altogether.' Jack stared into his coffee. 'After this—I just don't know if I can trust myself or the industry anymore.'

'No, you're not,' Erin said firmly. Everyone turned to look at her. 'It wasn't your fault, Jack. *Terra Lens* used you. That doesn't mean you should abandon your talent or your passion.'

'Erin's right,' Laura added. 'You can't let the Natalies of the world win by giving up what you love.'

Jack looked unconvinced, but he reached for Erin's hand under the table, squeezing it gently.

'You know,' Tom said, clearly changing the subject to lighten the mood, 'while you were away, Erin made quite the historical discovery.'

Jack turned to her, eyebrows raised. 'You did?'

Tom launched into the story of the stone Erin had found at the billabong, his enthusiasm building as he described the faint carving of Matilda's name.

'We think it might be connected to Gilbert O'Byrne,' Cat chimed in, her excitement evident. 'The ancestor who disappeared after World War I.'

'Cat's been researching his war records,' Tom explained. 'And now with the stone Erin found—'

Cat took over. 'It's the first connection between the two families: *Wambool Station,* now called *Dunleavy,* and *Ceann Mara.* It's like pieces of a puzzle finally coming together.'

Despite her exhaustion, Erin found herself smiling at her father's and Cat's enthusiasm. Solving the mystery of Gilbert O'Byrne had been a priority for some months, and the stone's discovery had breathed new life into their research.

'Sounds like I've missed quite a bit of action,' Jack said, a hint of his old smile returning.

'You're here now,' Erin said softly. 'That's what matters.'

Outside, the sun had fully risen, bathing the homestead in golden light. The crisis of the night had passed, leaving them all battered but intact. Miles—or Marcus—was in custody. Reg was receiving medical care. The immediate danger had ended.

Yet as Erin looked around at her family's faces, she couldn't shake the feeling that they'd only uncovered the first layer of a much deeper mystery—one that somehow connected a missing World War I soldier, a century-old romance, and a burned-down homestead.

For now, though, Jack was home. They were safe.

Chapter 54

Ceann Mara - August.

Two months after the fire at *Dunleavy* and Jack's return, the billabong lay peaceful under the morning sun. He stood at its edge, watching dragonflies dance across the water's surface.

He set his camera on a nearby stump and ran a hand through his hair, still damp from his dawn swim. The physical labour of helping on the station had been therapeutic—a way to channel the restless energy that came with rebuilding not just a house, but a marriage.

The sound of footsteps made him turn. Erin approached, carrying two mugs of coffee. She wore one of his old flannel shirts over her jeans, the sleeves rolled up to her elbows. Her hair was longer now, pulled back in a loose ponytail.

'Thought you might need this,' she said, offering him a mug. 'You were gone when I woke up.'

'Thanks.' Jack accepted the coffee, careful not to let their fingers touch. These small courtesies had become their rhythm—polite, caring, but with an invisible boundary neither quite knew how to cross. 'I couldn't sleep. Thought I'd come down and sit by the water.'

Erin nodded, sipping her coffee as she studied the marked-out floor plan. 'Dad says the shearing crew will be here next week.'

'That's good,' Jack said, searching for something else to add. Conversation had never been difficult between them before. Now, every exchange felt weighted with unspoken words.

They stood in silence for a moment, watching a pair of

black swans glide across the billabong.

'I've been thinking,' Jack said finally. 'About what you said last week—about taking things one day at a time.'

'And?' Erin's voice was carefully neutral.

'And you were right.' He turned to face her fully. 'I keep wanting to fix everything at once. To make grand gestures that somehow erase what happened.'

'Jack—'

'Please, let me finish.' He set his mug down, needing both hands free as he searched for the right words. 'When I was in Africa, I had this . . . revelation that I was making a terrible mistake. That I should never have left you. But it wasn't a sudden thing, Erin. It was gradual. I'd see something beautiful and think how you would describe it. I'd take a photograph and know it wasn't complete until you'd seen it.'

He picked up a smooth stone from the water's edge, turning it over in his palm. 'Then when I couldn't reach you, when I realised how Natalie had manipulated everything—I panicked. All I could think was getting back to you.'

Erin's expression softened slightly. 'I understand that part.'

'But what I didn't understand—what I'm still trying to understand—is how much damage I did by leaving in the first place.' His voice caught, and he had to look away. 'Watching you walk around the homestead like a visitor in your own family, seeing how careful everyone is with you . . . knowing that's because of choices I made—'

'It wasn't just you, Jack.' Erin stepped closer, though still maintaining that careful distance. 'I made choices too.'

'But I broke something between us,' he admitted, the truth he'd been avoiding for weeks finally emerging. 'I broke your trust. And I don't know if I can fix that with just words or promises.'

Erin was quiet for a long moment, her gaze on the distant hills. 'You know what hurt the most?' she finally asked. 'It wasn't the distance or even the silence. It was realising how easily you seemed to adapt to a life without me in it.'

The words hit Jack like a physical blow. 'God, Erin, no—'

'I know now that's not what happened,' she continued. 'But when those emails started coming—so brief, so impersonal—I thought I was watching you gradually forget me.'

'I never forgot you,' Jack said fiercely. 'Not for a single day.'

'I believe that now.' She met his eyes. 'But trust isn't just about believing someone's words. It's about feeling safe with them again.'

Jack nodded, understanding settling heavily in his chest. 'And you don't feel safe with me yet.'

'I want to,' she whispered, and the vulnerability in her voice made his heart ache. 'I'm trying.'

'What can I do?' he asked simply. 'Tell me, and I'll do it.'

Erin considered this; her expression thoughtful. 'Stop trying to fix everything at once,' she said finally. 'Stop tiptoeing around me like I'm going to break. And maybe . . . just be here. Here, not planning the next trip, or a house or the next project. Just be present with me, with this place, with what we're building.'

'I can do that,' Jack promised, meaning it completely.

As if to demonstrate, he settled on the grass beside the billabong, patting the space next to him. After a moment's hesitation, Erin joined him, close but not touching.

'Tell me about your book,' he said. 'The one you've been

working on while I was gone. Cat mentioned you'd made real progress.'

Surprise flickered across Erin's face. 'You want to hear about my writing?'

'I always want to hear about your writing,' Jack said honestly. 'I'm sorry if I haven't shown that enough.'

She studied him for a moment, as if assessing his sincerity, then began speaking hesitantly about her historical novel. As she described the characters and the research she'd done, her voice grew stronger, more animated. Jack listened intently, asking questions, watching how her hands moved when she explained the narrative structure.

When she finished, a small smile touched her lips—the first genuine smile he'd seen directed at him in weeks. 'You really were listening.'

'I always listen to you, Erin. I just don't always show it well.' Jack hesitated, then added, 'Would you let me read some of it? When you're ready?'

'You hate historical fiction,' she pointed out.

'I don't hate it. I just usually prefer photographs to capture history.' He smiled ruefully. 'But it's important to you, which makes it important to me.'

Erin nodded slowly. 'I'll think about it.'

They sat in silence for a while, this one more comfortable than the last. The morning warmed around them, kookaburras laughing in the river gums.

'I should head up to the house,' Erin said eventually. 'I promised Dad I'd help him sort through those old journals he found in one of the sheds that survived the fire at *Dunleavy*.'

Jack nodded, making no move to follow. 'I'll be here.'

The simple statement hung between them, carrying more

emotion than any elaborate promise could have. Erin held his gaze for a moment longer before turning towards the homestead path.

Jack remained by the billabong, thinking about what she'd said. Being present. Actually here. It sounded simple, yet he knew it would require a fundamental shift in how he approached their relationship—fewer grand gestures, more consistent presence.

He pulled out the small notebook he'd started keeping since his return, a practice suggested by Seth of all people. 'Sometimes,' Seth had told him, 'you need to slow down enough to capture what's really important, not just what looks good through a lens.'

Jack opened to a fresh page and began writing:

Today I learned that Erin's novel has a dual timeline—one in the present, one in 1750.

Things to remember: Ask about her progress regularly. Offer to read sections without pushing.

Small steps. Being here. Actually present.

He closed the notebook, a sense of purpose settling over him. The road back to Erin would be long—longer than he'd initially hoped—but for the first time, he could see it clearly. Not a quick fix or a dramatic reunion, but a patient rebuilding, one day at a time.

***

'Damn it!'

Jack looked up from the photograph he was editing to see Erin standing in the doorway of his makeshift studio in the homestead's sunroom. Her expression was a mixture of frustration and sheepish embarrassment.

'What's wrong?' he asked, saving his work before giving her his full attention—a small change he'd been consciously practicing.

'The motorhome's battery is dead,' she explained. 'It won't start.'

'Want me to take a look?'

Erin nodded, relieved. 'Would you? I know you're busy with your portfolio—'

'It can wait,' Jack said, already standing.

They walked together to where the motorhome was parked near the old equipment shed. Jack had been helping Logan reorganise the shed, making space for the motorhome during the construction of their new home. The familiar vehicle looked forlorn in its temporary shelter, dust covering its once-shiny exterior.

'When was the last time you started it?' Jack asked, opening the hood.

'About two weeks ago,' Erin admitted. 'I've been so caught up in the book, I forgot to buy a new battery. It's been playing up for a few weeks. I didn't start it much after Cat's wedding.'

Jack nodded, inspecting the battery connections. 'These are corroded. That's part of the problem.' He glanced at her. 'Hand me that wire brush?'

As they worked together to clean the terminals, Jack found himself noticing how comfortable it felt—this simple act of solving a practical problem side by side. It reminded him of their early days on the road, when every mechanical issue had been a team effort.

'Remember that time near Broome when the alternator died?' he asked.

Erin smiled, the memory clearly a good one. 'And we had

to wait three days for the part to arrive? We camped right on that deserted beach.'

'Best fish I ever caught,' Jack recalled. 'Though you claimed I cheated because that local fisherman showed me the exact spot.'

'You did cheat,' she insisted, but her eyes were bright with amusement.

Jack finished cleaning the terminals and reconnected the cables. 'Try it now.'

Erin climbed into the driver's seat and turned the key. The engine sputtered, then caught, rumbling to life.

'You did it!' she called through the open window.

'We did it,' Jack corrected, closing the hood. 'But we should probably drive it more regularly, or we could install a trickle charger.'

Erin nodded, then hesitated, her fingers tapping the steering wheel. 'I was thinking of heading into Broken Hill to the library.'

'Sounds good,' Jack said, stepping back to give her space to pull out.

'I thought maybe you could come with me,' she added quickly. 'If you're not too busy. The light would be good for landscape shots on the drive back.'

Jack stared at her, momentarily speechless. This was the first time since his return that she'd directly invited him to accompany her anywhere—a small thing, perhaps, but significant.

'I'd like that,' he said simply, careful not to overreact and scare her off. 'Let me grab my camera.'

An hour later, they were on the road to Broken Hill, the familiar landscape of western New South Wales unfolding around them. Erin drove while Jack sat in the passenger seat, observing how the afternoon light played across the red earth and sparse vegetation.

'I forgot how much I missed this,' Erin said after they'd been driving in comfortable silence for some time.

'The drive?' Jack asked.

'Being on the move,' she clarified. 'Just going somewhere, anywhere, with no particular schedule. We were good at that, weren't we?'

The past tense made Jack's heart clench, but he kept his voice steady. 'The best. No one could find a free camp spot like you.'

She smiled at the memory. 'And no one could charm a grumpy station owner into letting us stay on their property like you.'

'Team effort,' Jack said, echoing his words from earlier.

They lapsed into silence again, but it felt different now—reflective rather than strained. The road stretched before them, a ribbon of possibility.

'I've been thinking,' Jack said carefully, 'about what you said last month. About being present.'

Erin glanced at him before returning her attention to the road. 'And?'

'I think I'm starting to understand what you meant.' He looked out at the passing landscape. 'For too long, I was always chasing the next thing—the next location, the next shot, the next opportunity. Even when we were on the road together, I was never fully there.'

'You were there more than you think,' Erin said softly. 'You noticed things no one else would see. That's what makes your photography special.'

'But I didn't notice what was most important,' Jack admitted. 'I didn't see how my leaving would affect you. How it would make you feel . . . dispensable.'

Erin's hands tightened on the steering wheel. 'I never said that.'

'You didn't have to.' Jack turned to face her profile. 'I saw it in how you retreated into yourself after I came back. How careful you became around me, as if preparing for me to disappear again.'

A tear slipped down Erin's cheek, but she made no move to wipe it away. 'I hate feeling this way,' she whispered. 'I hate being afraid to trust you completely again.'

'I know.' Jack resisted the urge to reach for her, respecting the boundary she still needed. 'And I hate that I made you feel that way. But Erin, I swear to you, I will spend every day showing you—not telling you, showing you that you can trust me again.'

They drove in silence for several more kilometres, the only sound the hum of the engine and the occasional call of a bird outside. Finally, Erin spoke, her voice steadier.

'I found something yesterday when I was looking through our old travel journals.' She gestured towards her bag on the floor. 'There's a manila folder in there. Can you get it?'

Jack retrieved the folder, opening it to find a stack of photographs—not his professional work, but the personal shots they'd taken during their travels. On top was a picture of Erin standing beside the motorhome at Uluru, sunrise painting the massive rock formation in shades of pink and gold behind her.

'Turn it over,' Erin instructed.

Jack flipped the photograph to find his own handwriting on

the back: Erin at dawn, Uluru. The moment I knew I wanted to marry her. October 2021.

The memory rushed back with startling clarity—Erin waking early to watch the sunrise with him, her hair tousled from sleep, her eyes wide with wonder as the first rays touched the ancient monolith. How he'd looked at her and suddenly seen his future with perfect clarity.

'I remember this,' he said, his voice rough with emotion. 'You were wearing my jacket because you'd forgotten yours. You said the rock looked like it was blushing.'

Erin nodded, a smile touching her lips despite the tears still shimmering in her eyes. 'You proposed three weeks later in Darwin.'

'Best decision I ever made,' Jack said without hesitation.

'Mine too,' Erin replied softly.

They reached the outskirts of Broken Hill, the stark beauty of the outback giving way to the resilient charm of the mining town. Erin navigated the streets with familiar ease, parking near the library.

Before they got out, she turned to him, her expression serious. 'I'm not there yet, Jack. I want to be, but I'm not.'

'I know,' he said, understanding she was talking about fully trusting him again. 'We have time.'

'But I'm trying,' she continued. 'And I think . . . I think we're heading in the right direction.'

It wasn't a declaration of complete forgiveness or restored trust. It was something more valuable—an honest acknowledgment of where they were and the hope of where they might go.

'That's all I ask,' Jack said.

As they walked towards the library, Jack deliberately kept

a respectful distance, not reaching for her hand as he once would have done without thinking. But halfway there, Erin closed the gap between them, her fingers finding his and holding tight.

A small step. Perhaps the most important one yet.

Chapter 55

Ceann Mara - April 1919.

The country had changed in subtle ways since the war's end. Matilda noticed it as she rode across the familiar landscape towards *Ceann Mara*—a heaviness that hung in the air, a quietness that seemed to extend beyond the natural stillness of the bush. Australia had sent its sons to fight in distant lands, and too many had never returned. Those who did came back altered, shadows of their former selves moving like strangers through the lives they had once known.

The track to *Ceann Mara* was familiar beneath her horse's hooves. Matilda had made this journey countless times since childhood, but never so frequently as in the past two years. Every few weeks, she rode over, ostensibly to exchange preserves or books or news of stock movements with Bridget O'Byrne. In reality, her visits served a hidden purpose—to glean any information the O'Byrne family might have received about Gilbert.

Ceann Mara came into view as she crested the low rise above the river. The homestead looked much as it always had— solid, enduring, a testament to the O'Byrne family's determination to carve a life from this harsh but beautiful land. Smoke rose from the kitchen chimney, curling lazily into the autumn sky. A group of working dogs lounged in the shade of the veranda, rising with mild interest as Matilda approached.

She dismounted carefully and tethered her horse to the hitching post. The front door opened before she could knock, and Olive O'Byrne stood framed in the doorway, her youthful face set in a frown.

'Matilda,' she said, her smile warm despite the shadows beneath her eyes. 'We weren't expecting you today.' At sixteen, Olive had grown into a serious young woman, stepping up to manage the household as her mother's health declined.

'I was in town for supplies,' Matilda explained, the familiar excuse coming easily. 'Thought I'd stop by on my way home.'

Olive took her arm as they walked towards the house. 'Mother's having a good day. She's in the parlour with some of Gilbert's old things.' Her voice dropped. 'The news of the armistice has given her new hope. She's convinced he'll be home soon.'

In the parlour, Bridget sat surrounded by items from Gilbert's childhood—a wooden horse he'd carved under his father's guidance, school primers with his name inscribed in a boy's careful hand, a cricket bat worn smooth from use. She turned as they entered, her face brightening at the sight of Matilda.

'Matilda, dear girl,' Bridget greeted her with a wan smile. 'Come see what I've found. Gilbert's things for when he returns. He'll want these keepsakes, don't you think?'

'I'm sure he will,' Matilda agreed, taking the seat beside Bridget. She reached for the older woman's hand, finding it thin and cool to the touch. 'How are you today, Mrs O'Byrne?'

'Better now that this dreadful war is over. The waiting has been the hardest part, but that's done with now. It's just a matter of time until our boy comes home.' Bridget picked up a small daguerreotype of Gilbert as a child, gazing at it fondly. 'Thomas is convinced he'll be on the first ship. I've told Cook to be prepared for a feast at any moment.'

Matilda exchanged a glance with Olive, who gave a small shake of her head. The family had received no official notification of Gilbert's status.

Guilt filled her as Olive spoke quietly to her, while Bridget's attention turned to the wooden toy in her lap. 'We've had another letter from the Red Cross. They're still searching hospitals in France and England. So many of our boys were lost in the confusion. They say it may take years to account for everyone.'

Matilda nodded, knowing there was nothing she could say to ease this particular pain. The O'Byrne family existed in a state of suspended grief—unable to mourn properly without confirmation, yet increasingly aware of what the silence likely meant. The war had been over for months. Most of the surviving soldiers had returned. Gilbert's continued absence spoke volumes.

Unlike Matilda, they did not know Private Davies' account of what had happened. She had kept that information to herself, unable to destroy their hope when she had no official confirmation to offer. She alone carried the certainty of Gilbert's fate, a burden she bore in silence out of mercy for this family who might have been hers.

'Father is convinced he's in a hospital somewhere, suffering from shell shock or amnesia,' Olive continued. 'And Harry has written to every Australian office in London.'

Bridget picked up the toy, her fingers stroking it. 'Gilbert will come home to us soon.' She stared at Matilda and then smiled. 'And how is your little charge at *Wambool*? That poor orphaned child you've taken in. James, isn't it?'

'Yes, James,' Matilda replied, the name catching slightly in her throat. 'He's well. Growing bigger every day.'

'Such a blessing, children,' Bridget said softly. 'Even in the darkest times, they remind us that life continues.' She leaned forward, patting Matilda's hand. 'You'll make a wonderful mother someday, when Gilbert comes home.'

Matilda forced a smile, the irony of the statement twisting like a knife. 'Perhaps.'

Thomas O'Byrne entered the room, his tall frame filling the doorway. He'd aged a decade in the past two years, his once-dark beard now more grey than black, his shoulders slightly stooped as though permanently burdened.

'Matilda,' he greeted her warmly. 'Good to see you. Any news from town?'

She shook her head. 'The *Catherine Anne* came into Wilcannia yesterday. Six returned soldiers aboard, but no one from our district.'

Thomas nodded, his expression carefully neutral. Unlike his wife, he harboured fewer illusions about their son's fate after so much silence. Still, he would not be the one to extinguish Bridget's flickering hope.

'It will take time,' he said, his deep voice steady. 'The army must organise transport for thousands of men. Gilbert may well be waiting his turn in England or France.'

'Of course,' Matilda agreed, the words hollow in her mouth.

The visit continued as it always did—tea served in Bridget's best china, conversation carefully steered away from painful topics, small local news exchanged. Beneath the civility ran currents of unspoken grief, of questions that could not be asked, of truths that could not yet be faced.

As Matilda prepared to leave, Thomas walked with her to

where her horse was tethered.

'Bring the child next time you visit. It would do Bridget good to have a little one about the house.'

Matilda's heart clenched at the invitation. How simple it would be to bring James, to let him toddle around the homestead that should have been part of his heritage. To see Bridget's face light up at the presence of her grandson, even if she didn't know the relationship.

But the risk was too great. James was beginning to resemble Gilbert more with each passing day—the same blue eyes, the same determined set to his jaw, the same cowlick in his dark hair that refused to lie flat. Someone might notice, might comment, might put together pieces of a puzzle Matilda wasn't yet ready to share.

'Thank you,' she said carefully. 'But I think it best he stays with Mrs Cleary. He's at a difficult age—everything goes into his mouth, and he has no sense of valuable versus common objects.'

Thomas nodded, accepting the excuse without question. 'Another time, perhaps.'

'Yes,' Matilda agreed. 'Another time.'

As she rode away from *Ceann Mara*, Matilda allowed herself a moment of weakness, tears blurring her vision as she thought of the family so close yet so separate from her son. One day, she promised herself. One day, when hope had faded and grief had had its time, she would bridge that gap. She would bring James to meet his father's family, would tell them of Gilbert's final hours as related by Private Davies, and would give them the comfort of knowing his bloodline continued.

But not yet. Not while Bridget arranged Gilbert's childhood treasures in anticipation of a return that would never come. Not while Thomas maintained his stoic façade for his wife's sake. Not while the wounds were still too raw, the hope still too fragile.

Instead of returning directly to *Wambool*, Matilda turned her horse towards the billabong. The track was overgrown now, less frequently used since Gilbert's departure, but her mount picked its way confidently along the familiar path.

The billabong looked as it always had—timeless, serene, indifferent to the human dramas that unfolded along its banks. Matilda dismounted and, kneeling, she began searching among the smooth stones that lined the billabong, running her fingers over their water-polished surfaces. Finally, she found what she was looking for—a flat, oval stone, perfectly balanced in her palm. It reminded her of the wishing stone she'd given Gilbert all those years ago, the one Private Davies had returned to her along with Gilbert's other possessions.

Matilda slipped the stone into her pocket and made her way slowly home.

##

Two weeks later, Matilda returned to the billabong at dawn, the first pink light of day just beginning to touch the eastern sky. This time, she was not alone. Her father walked beside her, carrying a small bundle wrapped in oilcloth.

'Are you certain this is what you want?' he asked as they reached the water's edge.

Matilda nodded, her expression resolute. 'This was our place. It seems right.'

Robert studied his daughter's face for a moment, then unwrapped the bundle, revealing a small stone plaque. He had carved it himself in his workshop over the past week, working late into the night after the station hands had retired. The inscription was simple:

G. P. O. 1895–1916.

Loved lost and in my heart forever.

Matilda

Nothing that would immediately identify it as a memorial to Gilbert James Piner O'Byrne. Just enough for Matilda to know, to have a private place to come when the weight of absence grew too heavy to bear alone.

Together, they dug a small hollow at the base of the largest river gum, its ancient roots spreading outward towards the billabong. Robert lined the hollow with smaller stones, then carefully set the plaque in place, securing it with a mixture of earth and river clay that would harden over time.

When the memorial was complete, they stood back, a respectful silence falling between them. The Australian bush was waking around them—kookaburras calling their raucous greeting to the day, the gentle rustling of wallabies moving through the undergrowth, the first stirrings of a breeze among the river gums.

'He was a good man,' Robert said finally. 'I would have been proud to call him son.'

Matilda's eyes filled with tears. 'Thank you for this, Father. And for understanding.'

Robert placed an arm around his daughter's shoulders. 'Will you tell his family? About James, I mean?'

Matilda shook her head. 'Not yet. They're still hoping he'll come home. It would be cruel to tell them now, only for them to lose him all over again.' She paused. 'One day, when they're ready to accept that he's gone, I'll tell them about their grandson.'

'And what about James? When will you tell him about his father?'

Matilda gazed at the small memorial, now already looking as though it belonged among the roots of the ancient tree. 'When he's old enough to understand, I want him to know who his father was, to be proud of him.' She looked up at her father. 'Will you help me keep this place a secret until then? I don't want anyone else to know.'

'You have my word,' her father promised. 'Until you decide otherwise.'

As they walked back towards their horses, a curious sense of peace settled over her. The grief was still there, would always be there, but having this small marker, this tangible connection to Gilbert, eased something within her. The billabong would keep their secret, just as it had witnessed their love. And one day, she would bring their son here to understand the legacy of the father he would never know.

Chapter 56

May 1919 - Ceann Mara.

The first signs of autumn had begun to touch the river gums, a subtle shift in colour heralding the changing season. Matilda rode slowly towards *Ceann Mara*, her thoughts as heavy as the leaden sky overhead. It had been almost a month since her last visit—James had fallen ill with a fever, requiring all her attention until he recovered. Now, with her son safely in Mrs Cleary's care, she had finally found time to make the familiar journey across country.

As she approached the homestead, Matilda was struck by its altered appearance. The gardens, once Bridget's pride, showed signs of neglect. The veranda that had always welcomed visitors with polished floorboards and comfortable chairs looked in need of repair, a loose shutter banging gently in the breeze.

Olive met her at the door, her young face drawn with exhaustion.

'Matilda. We weren't expecting you.'

'I should have sent word,' Matilda apologised, suddenly conscious of her unannounced arrival. 'Is this a bad time?'

Olive shook her head, stepping back to allow Matilda inside. 'Mother's having one of her difficult days, but she'll be glad of the company. She asks after you often.'

The interior of the house felt changed as well—darker, quieter, as though the building itself had absorbed the family's prolonged grief. Matilda followed Olive to the parlour where Bridget sat by the window, a shawl around her shoulders despite the mild day.

The change in Gilbert's mother shocked Matilda, though she was careful not to let it show on her face. In just a month, Bridget seemed to have aged years. Her once-dark hair hung in thin grey strands, her cheeks hollowed, her eyes—Gilbert's eyes—sunken and over-bright in her pale face.

'Matilda,' Bridget greeted her, her voice a thread of its former self. 'Have you brought news? Has there been word?'

The familiar question caught in Matilda's throat. Once, she would have offered reassurances, keeping alive the fiction that Gilbert might yet return. Today, looking at the ravages grief had carved into this once-vibrant woman, the kind lies felt cruel.

'No news, Mrs O'Byrne,' she said gently, taking a seat beside Bridget. 'I've come to see how you're keeping.'

Bridget's gaze drifted to the window, to the paddocks beyond where her eldest son had once worked. 'He isn't coming back, is he?'

The simple question, asked with such resignation, broke something in Matilda's heart. 'I don't believe so,' she answered softly, taking Bridget's frail hand in her own. 'I think we must accept that Gilbert gave his life for his country.'

Tears welled in Bridget's eyes but did not fall. 'I've known it for some time, I think. A mother feels these things.' She turned back to Matilda, her gaze suddenly intense. 'He loved you, you know. From the time you were children. He would watch for you whenever you came to visit.'

'I loved him too,' Matilda whispered, the admission both painful and freeing. 'We were to be married when he returned.'

Bridget nodded, as though this confirmed something she had long suspected. 'He would have built you that house he was always planning. By the billabong.' A faint smile touched her lips. 'Thomas had already set aside the land for him.'

Matilda felt her composure threatening to crack. She had come today intending to tell Bridget about James—to give this grieving mother the comfort of knowing her son lived on in his child. Looking at Bridget's fragile state, however, she hesitated. Would such news bring joy, or would it only compound the pain of all the years lost, all the moments Gilbert would never share with his son?

'Mrs O'Byrne,' she began carefully, 'there's something I should tell you. Something about Gilbert and me—'

Before she could continue, Bridget was seized by a violent coughing fit, her thin body shaking with the force of it. A handkerchief pressed to her lips came away stained with crimson, and Matilda felt a cold dread settle in her stomach.

Thomas appeared in the doorway, alerted by the sound. Without a word, he crossed to his wife, lifting her slight form in his arms with practised care.

'I'm sorry, Matilda,' he said over his shoulder as he carried Bridget towards their bedroom. 'She tires easily these days. Perhaps you could come back next week?'

'Of course,' Matilda replied, rising quickly. 'Please, is there anything I can do?'

'Olive will see you out,' Thomas said, his focus entirely on his wife as he disappeared down the hallway.

Olive reappeared moments later, her eyes red-rimmed but her voice steady. 'I'm sorry about that. The doctor says it's consumption. She's been declining since winter.'

Guilt washed over Matilda. She should have visited sooner, should have noticed Bridget's deteriorating health on previous visits. 'Why didn't you send word? Father and I could have helped.'

'Mother didn't want anyone to know,' Olive explained, walking Matilda to the door. 'She kept saying she needed to stay strong until Gilbert returned.' She paused, her composure faltering slightly. 'I think today is the first time I've heard her acknowledge that he won't.'

Matilda impulsively embraced the younger woman. 'If you need anything—anything at all—send someone to *Wambool* immediately. Day or night.'

Olive nodded, returning the embrace briefly before pulling away. 'Thank you. I should get back to Mother now.'

As Matilda rode home, the grey sky finally released its burden, rain falling in gentle sheets across the parched landscape. She welcomed it, letting the drops mingle with the tears she had held back at *Ceann Mara*. Her chance to tell Bridget about James had slipped away, perhaps permanently. The knowledge sat like a stone in her chest—another loss among so many.

Chapter 57

Ceann Mara - June 1919.

A week later, the message arrived at *Wambool* by way of a station hand from *Ceann Mara*. Robert Ellis received it in the yard, reading the brief note with a grim expression before calling for Matilda.

'Bridget O'Byrne passed during the night,' he told her, his voice gentle. 'The funeral is tomorrow at midday.'

Matilda nodded, accepting the news with outward calm, though her heart ached for the woman who should have been her mother-in-law, for the O'Byrne family facing yet another loss, for young James who would never know his grandmother.

'I'll have Mrs Cleary prepare something to bring to the family,' she said, practicalities providing a shield against overwhelming emotion. 'Will you come with me?'

'Of course,' her father assured her, resting a weathered hand on her shoulder. 'We stand with our neighbours in times of sorrow.'

The funeral was held the next day in the small cemetery on *Ceann Mara* land, where generations of O'Byrnes rested beneath the Australian sky. A modest gathering of neighbours and friends stood solemnly as Bridget was laid to rest, Thomas a statue of contained grief beside the grave, Harry supporting a weeping Lily, Olive standing straight-backed and dry-eyed throughout the service.

Matilda remained slightly apart, acutely aware of her ambiguous position—not quite family, yet more than a neighbour or friend. The secret knowledge of James, now almost three years old and securely at home with Mrs Cleary, weighed heavily upon her. Bridget had died, never knowing she had a grandson and that Gilbert's line continued.

As the mourners dispersed after the service, Thomas approached her, his face deeply lined with exhaustion and sorrow.

'She spoke of you at the end,' he said quietly. 'Asked me to give you this.'

He pressed something into Matilda's palm—a small silver brooch, Celtic knotwork surrounding a polished river stone.

'It was Gilbert's first gift to his mother, when he was just a boy,' Thomas explained. 'He found the stone by the billabong and asked me to help him set it. Bridget wanted you to have it.'

Matilda closed her fingers around the brooch, emotion threatening to overwhelm her carefully maintained composure. 'Thank you,' she managed. 'She was a wonderful woman.'

Thomas nodded, his gaze drifting towards the fresh grave. 'She never stopped believing he might come home. Perhaps it's a blessing she's gone to find him instead.'

Something in his tone—a blend of resignation and terrible certainty—told Matilda that Thomas had accepted his son's death. He had simply been waiting for Bridget to find her own peace with it.

'Mr O'Byrne,' she began, the words of revelation forming on her lips. Now, with Bridget gone, perhaps it was time to tell him about James. To give this family some comfort in their darkest hour.

But looking at Thomas's lined face, at the slump of his shoulders beneath the weight of fresh grief, Matilda hesitated. This was not the moment to add more emotion to an already overwhelming day. James was thriving, safe, and loved. The truth of his parentage had waited this long; it could wait a little longer.

'If there's anything at all we can do,' she said instead, 'please don't hesitate to ask.'

Thomas thanked her with a nod before turning back to his remaining children. Matilda watched them for a moment—this family that should have been hers, that was still her son's by right of blood if not by acknowledgment. One day, she promised herself. One day soon, she would bridge the gap between them.

As she and her father rode back to *Wambool*, the late afternoon sun broke through the clouds, casting shadows across the familiar landscape. Ahead lay home, and James, and the future they would make together even without Gilbert. Behind remained *Ceann Mara*, and memories, and connections not yet fully revealed.

The river stone brooch pressed against Matilda's palm, cool and smooth like the wishing stone Gilbert had carried into war. A piece of the land they both had loved, a token of what might have been, a promise of what still could be.

It would have to be enough.

Chapter 58

Ceann Mara - May 1934.

The late autumn sunlight reflected on the billabong as Matilda and James made their way along the familiar track. At nineteen, James had grown into a young man of serious demeanour and quiet strength, his resemblance to Gilbert now unmistakable to anyone who had known him.

'Where exactly are we going, Mother?' James asked, ducking beneath a low-hanging branch. 'We passed the best fishing spots half a mile back.'

'Just a little further,' Matilda replied, her heart quickening as they approached the bend in the track that would bring the old river gum into view. 'There's something I want to show you.'

James followed without further question, his innate patience one of the many qualities that reminded Matilda daily of Gilbert. He had grown up surrounded by the love of the Ellis family, accepted without question as Matilda's son, his lack of a father rarely mentioned in the polite society of rural Australia, where the war had left so many children fatherless.

The billabong appeared before them, its surface peaceful in the late afternoon light. The same black swans that had been there for as long as Matilda could remember glided across the water, their elegant necks curved in perfect symmetry.

'It's beautiful,' James observed, stopping beside her. 'But we've been here before. Many times.'

'Yes,' Matilda agreed, 'but today is different.'

She led him to the ancient river gum, its massive trunk gnarled with age, its roots still embracing the small stone plaque she and her father had placed there sixteen years earlier. Time and weather had softened its edges, moss growing around its borders, making it look almost as though it had grown there naturally.

Matilda knelt beside it, brushing away fallen leaves to reveal the simple inscription. James crouched beside her, his expression curious.

'G.P.O.,' he read aloud. '1895-1916. Loved lost and in my heart forever. Matilda.'

He looked up at his mother, a question in his eyes.

Matilda took a deep breath. 'Those are your father's initials,' she said quietly. 'Gilbert James Piner O'Byrne.'

'You've always told me my father died in the war, but not that he was one of the O'Byrnes.' James stared at her, then back at the stone. 'From *Ceann Mara*?'

Matilda nodded. 'We were to be married when he returned from the war.' She paused, gathering strength. 'He died at the Battle of Fromelles in July 1916, two months before you were born.'

James was silent for a long moment, his hand hovering over the stone as though afraid to touch it. 'Why didn't you tell me before?' he asked finally, his voice steady despite the emotion she could see in his eyes.

'At first, you were too young to understand. Then . . .' She sighed. 'The O'Byrne family had no confirmation of his death. His body was never recovered, and he didn't return from the war. It seemed cruel to intrude on their grief with my own claims. I knew he hadn't survived, but his mother always held out hope.'

'So, they don't know about me? That I'm his son?'

Matilda shook her head. 'Bridget—his mother—died still believing he might come home. Thomas passed away three years later. Harry runs *Ceann Mara* now with his wife and children.'

'My uncle?' James asked softly.

'Yes. And Olive and Lily are your aunts. Lily married a man from Melbourne and rarely returns, but Olive still lives at *Ceann Mara*. She never married.'

James sat back on his heels, absorbing this information. 'All these years, I've been riding past the home of my father's family, never knowing?'

Matilda shook her head, regret shadowing her features. 'I had planned to tell your grandmother. I went to *Ceann Mara* with that very intention one morning, but Bridget was already ill with consumption by then. She was so frail, clinging to hope that Gilbert might still return.' She paused, gathering herself. 'I decided it would be cruel to tell her about you only to have her die before she could truly know you. I always thought there would be more time, but she passed away just a few weeks later.'

'And afterwards? Why not tell Thomas or Harry?'

'The moment never seemed right,' Matilda admitted. 'Thomas was consumed by his own grief, and then he too was gone within a few years. As more time passed, it became harder to explain why I'd kept you secret for so long.' She touched James's face gently. 'I sometimes wonder if I made the right choice.'

James covered her hand with his own. 'You did what you thought was best to protect everyone. There's no fault in that.'

'I'm sorry,' Matilda said, reaching for his hand. 'Perhaps I should have told you sooner, but I wanted to protect you—and them. The war left so many wounds.'

'Tell me about my father,' James requested, his gaze returning to the small memorial. 'What was he like?'

Matilda smiled, memories flooding back with surprising clarity. 'He was kind, and strong, and stubborn as the day is long when he believed in something. He loved this land with a fierceness that was part of his very being. He could ride anything with four legs, and he knew every bend in the Darling River like the back of his hand.' She paused, looking out across the billabong. 'He had your eyes—the same blue as the summer sky. And when he laughed, it was like something unlocked inside everyone who heard it.'

'Did he love you?' James asked quietly.

'Yes,' Matilda answered without hesitation. 'And he would have loved you with all his heart, James. Never doubt that.'

James nodded, emotion making his voice rough. 'I wish I could have known him.'

'You do know him,' Matilda said gently. 'He's in you—in your patience, your quiet strength, your love of the land. Every day, I see him in you.'

They sat in silence for a time, the Australian bush around them filled with the sounds of approaching evening—the chorus of frogs beginning their nightly serenade, the rustle of nocturnal creatures emerging, the soft sigh of the breeze through the river gums.

'What happens now?' James asked eventually. 'Should I go to *Ceann Mara*? Tell them who I am?'

Matilda considered the question. 'That's for you to decide. You're a man now, James, with the right to know your father's family. If you wish to go to them, I won't stand in your way.'

James looked at the stone plaque again, then at the billabong, taking in the place that had been so special to his parents. 'I think . . . I think he would want me to know them,' he said slowly. 'But I need time to consider how best to approach this.'

'Of course,' Matilda agreed. 'There's no hurry. They've been our neighbours for many years; they'll be there when you're ready.'

As the last light faded from the sky, they rose together, James offering his hand to help his mother to her feet. Before they turned to leave, he knelt once more beside the memorial, placing his palm flat against the stone.

'I'll make you proud, Father,' he promised softly. 'I'm an O'Byrne too.'

Matilda watched her son, tears blurring her vision. In that moment, with the fading light catching his profile, the resemblance to Gilbert was so acute it took her breath away. The boy she had raised alone was becoming a man, and though Gilbert had never known him, his legacy lived on in their son.

As they walked back towards their horses, James slipped his arm around his mother's shoulders, a gesture of both protection and understanding. 'Thank you for bringing me here today,' he said. 'For telling me the truth.'

Matilda leaned into his strength, grateful beyond words for this young man who bridged her past and her future. 'It was time,' she said simply.

Behind them, the billabong reflected the first stars of evening, the same stars that had witnessed young love, solemn promises, private grief, and now, finally, the beginning of understanding. The land endured, as it always had, holding the stories of those who had loved it, generation after generation, in its ancient embrace.

Chapter 59

Canberra - September.

The Australian War Memorial in Canberra hummed with quiet activity. School groups moved through the exhibits with respectful attention, elderly visitors studied displays with reverent attention, and in a corner of the research centre, Cat O'Byrne hunched over a computer terminal, frustration evident in the set of her shoulders.

'Nothing,' she muttered, pushing back from the screen as Tom approached with two cups of coffee. 'I've searched every database. Gilbert James Piner O'Byrne simply doesn't exist in the military records.'

Tom set one cup beside her and settled into the adjacent chair. 'That can't be right. We have his enlistment notice from the local paper.'

'I know.' Cat took a grateful sip of coffee. 'I've tried every variation of his name. Gilbert O'Byrne. G.P. O'Byrne. G. Piner O'Byrne. Nothing matches our Gilbert with the right age and location.'

Tom and Cat had come to Canberra specifically for this research, leaving the station in Logan's capable hands for a few days. Tom flew the station's Cessna, and Cat was seeing more and more of her father as he was in the past, as his confidence in his physical capabilities returned. Tom's discovery of another letter from Matilda had only deepened the mystery surrounding Gilbert, and the local resources had proven insufficient for their search.

'What about the Ellis family at *Wambool*? Matilda's

brother, Cecil?' Tom suggested. 'We know from his letters that he and Gilbert were friends. Maybe there's something in his service record.'

Cat nodded and turned back to the computer. 'Good idea. Cecil Ellis, *Wambool Station.*'

A few keystrokes later, a record appeared on the screen. 'Here we go. A Cecil Ellis, enlisted March 1916, three months after Gilbert. Worked in the AIF in Sydney.'

Tom leaned closer, studying the information. 'Is there any mention of Gilbert in his file?'

Cat clicked through several scanned documents. 'Nothing obvious.' She paused, scrolling more slowly. 'Wait. There's a personal effects inventory here. Items retained by him included "one letter from a Gilbert Pin . . . damaged by water, deemed unreadable".'

'Could be his middle name,' Tom said. 'That's something at least.'

A young archivist who had been helping them periodically throughout the morning approached their table. 'Any luck?' she asked.

'None,' Tom replied. 'It's as if my grandfather vanished into thin air after enlisting.'

The archivist—Amanda, according to her name badge—frowned thoughtfully. 'Sometimes, clerical errors can cause records to be filed under unexpected names. Let me try something.'

She slid into the chair Cat vacated, her fingers moving quickly over the keyboard. 'I'm searching for enlistees from your region with physical characteristics matching your description, regardless of name.'

After adjusting several search parameters, she pointed to the screen. 'Here—Gilbert James Piner. No O'Byrne. Just Piner. Age 19, height 5' 11", blue eyes, fair hair. Occupation: station manager. Previous address: Louth district, NSW.'

Goosebumps ran up Cat's arms as she stared at the screen.

'Oh my God, that's our Gilbert,' Tom said, excitement building. 'That has to be him. Someone must have made a clerical error during enlistment, recording his middle name as his surname.'

As they pored over Gilbert James Piner's service record, the pieces began falling into place. His training in Liverpool, NSW, in early 1916. His deployment to Egypt late in February. His transfer to France with the 5th Division AIF in 1916.

Amanda ran her finger down the screen. 'From other records of the AIF, I would say he completed his training in Egypt. With the Fifth Division being one of the last to leave Egypt for France, he would have arrived in France in mid-1916. War records indicate that upon arrival, soldiers received additional training tailored to trench warfare.'

Tears filled Cat's eyes. 'Oh, Amanda. Thank you. Not only have you found him, but you make it seem so real to us, too.' She glanced at Dad; tears filled his eyes too. He lifted a shaking hand and pointed to the bottom of the entry.

And then, the document that made Cat's breath catch.

'Cat.' His voice broke. 'Look at this.'

The casualty report was dated July 20, 1916.

'Killed in action, 19/20 July 1916, Fromelles, France,' Tom read, his voice barely audible. 'His body was not recovered.'

He reached over and gripped Cat's hand. Amanda slipped away quietly as they bowed their heads and paid respects to

Gilbert James Piner O'Byrne.

Chapter 60

Ceann Mara - October.

Tom and Laura stood on the veranda of *Ceann Mara* as a dust cloud approached along the driveway. Tom shaded his eyes. Beside him, Laura squeezed his hand reassuringly.

'Nervous?' she asked quietly.

'A bit,' he admitted. 'How do you introduce yourself to a family you never knew existed?'

The car pulled up in front of the house. A woman in her seventies emerged, her silver-streaked dark hair cut in a practical bob. She hesitated before approaching the steps.

'Margaret Ellis?' Tom called, moving down to meet her.

She nodded, a tentative smile forming. 'And you must be Tom O'Byrne.'

Introductions were made as they moved inside. Margaret carried a large leather portfolio and a cardboard box, which she placed on the coffee table.

'Your message found me through that genealogy website,' she said once they were settled with tea. 'I never expected anyone would be searching for Ellis family connections to *Wambool Station*. Being unmarried and keeping my maiden name throughout my nursing career made me easy to find, I suppose.'

She smiled softly. 'My brother Ross still manages our cattle property in Queensland with his sons, but I chose a different path. I must admit, your message came as quite a shock. My father James never spoke much about his early life on the property.'

'James was Gilbert's son,' Tom said, still processing the connection. 'Which would make you—'

'Gilbert's granddaughter,' Margaret finished. 'Dad married my mother, Rebecca, in 1946, after he returned from serving in World War II. I was born in 1950, and my brother Ross came along two years later.'

'Why did your father sell *Wambool*?' Laura asked gently.

Margaret smiled, a hint of sadness in her eyes. 'He never felt quite at home there after the war. When the opportunity came to purchase a cattle property in Queensland, he took it. The McGillvrays bought *Wambool* in 1952 and renamed it *Dunleavy*. Dad said it was time for a fresh start.'

'Did he know about Gilbert?' Cat asked. 'About his father?'

Margaret nodded. 'Grandmother Matilda told him the truth when he was nineteen or so. She'd raised him alone until then, never married. The family story goes that she had "loved once and completely," and saw no need to marry again. She was devoted to James. He had the letters that his father wrote from the trenches.'

She opened the portfolio and removed a sepia photograph. It showed a young woman in a high-necked blouse standing beside a river gum tree, her face serious, but her eyes alight with happiness.

'Matilda Ellis, 1915,' Margaret said. 'This was taken shortly before Gilbert left for war.'

She retrieved another photograph, this one showing a young boy sitting on a horse. 'My father James, around 1921. He was five years old here.'

The resemblance was unmistakable. The same determined

chin, the same set of shoulders that Tom recognised from the few photographs they had of Gilbert.

'He has the O'Byrne look,' Tom said. 'Even without the name, the blood shows through.'

Margaret reached for the cardboard box. 'There's something else I thought you should see.' She removed a bundle wrapped in tissue paper and unwrapped it to reveal a small wooden box. Inside, nestled on faded velvet, lay a circle of green fabric.

'His identity disc,' Cat said, leaning forward.

Margaret turned the fabric over, revealing an inscription on the rim. 'It says: G. J. PINER 2741 31 BN AIF R.C.'

'His enlistment number, his battalion and his religion,' Tom whispered. 'But how did Matilda get it?'

'There's a letter with it,' Margaret said, carefully extracting a folded paper from beneath the box's velvet lining and handing it to Cat. 'From someone named John Davies, dated November 1918.'

Cat read aloud, her voice trembling: 'Dear Miss Ellis, You don't know me, but I served with Gilbert in the 31st. He spoke of you often, and I promised him that should the worst happen, I would write to you personally. Gilbert was killed during the attack at Fromelles on the night of July 19th, 1916. We went over the top together, but only I returned. Gilbert gave me his possessions for safekeeping—his identity disc, a river stone, your letter, and a small photograph I believe to be of you. He asked that I return them to you. He wanted you to know that he had received your letter about the child, and that his last thoughts were of you both. He said to tell you he remembered the sunset and to go to *Ceann Mara*. Gilbert was a good man and a true friend. Yours respectfully, Corporal John Davies, 31st Battalion

AIF.'

Silence fell over the room.

'So, Matilda did know what happened. And Gilbert knew about the baby,' Laura said softly, her voice catching. 'He knew about his son before he died.'

Margaret carefully returned the fabric disc to the box. 'Dad kept this all his life. Grandmother Matilda would take it out each Anzac Day and hold it while listening to the dawn service on the radio. When she died in 1957, she left it to him. He passed it to me before he died in 1986.'

Tom walked to the window, composing himself. When he turned, his eyes were bright with unshed tears.

'Thank you for bringing this to us. For sharing this piece of Gilbert with us.'

'He belongs to both our families,' Margaret replied. 'It seems right that we both know his story.'

Chapter 61

Ceann Mara - December.

Three months later, a letter arrived from the Australian War Graves Commission. Cat found it in the mailbox, recognising the official letterhead immediately. She waited until the family had gathered for dinner three days before Christmas before mentioning it.

The whole family was home, and the long dining table at *Ceann Mara* was filled to capacity. Laura had outdone herself with a pre-Christmas feast—a golden roast chicken, vegetables from her garden, and fresh-baked bread that had filled the homestead with an enticing aroma. The table gleamed with the good silverware and the festive red and green placemats Laura brought out each December.

Erin looked around at her family as Dad topped up the wine glasses. Laura's gaze moved lovingly around the table, a contentment on her face that Erin hadn't seen for months. The anxiety that had lined her features during Dad's heart attack and recovery had finally eased, replaced by the warm glow of having all her daughters home.

Cat and Logan sat close together, their shoulders touching, still with that newlywed energy despite the months that had passed since their wedding. Logan whispered something in Cat's ear that made her laugh softly. Across from them, Róisín and Seth exchanged one of those private glances that spoke volumes without words.

Jack's hand found hers under the table, his thumb tracing small circles on her palm. The gesture had become his habit in recent months, a silent reassurance that he was there, present, committed, and staying. She squeezed back as her gaze settled on Shea.

Shea sat quietly, absently pushing food around her plate, her expression pensive. Something had been troubling her the past few days—a distraction in her usually bouncy demeanour. Erin had tried to draw her out during a walk by the billabong the previous day, but Shea had skilfully redirected the conversation, talking about her excitement at being accepted into a new pre-university course for veterinary training.

In contrast, Bridget practically vibrated with excitement at the far end of the table, her final year of school behind her and university ahead. Her future beckoned with possibilities, and she couldn't stop talking about her plans to study computer science in Melbourne, her voice rising with enthusiasm each time she described the program she'd been accepted into.

'Before we finish dinner,' Cat said, placing her fork down carefully, 'there's something we should share.' She glanced at Tom, who nodded. 'A letter arrived this week from the War Graves Commission.'

The conversation around the table halted. Tom unfolded the official-looking document, his fingers slightly unsteady as he smoothed it flat.

'They found him,' he announced, his voice thick with emotion. 'The DNA tests were positive. Gilbert's remains were among those recovered from the mass grave at Pheasant Wood. He now has a proper grave at Pheasant Wood Military Cemetery in Fromelles.'

A collective silence fell over the table as Laura reached for Tom's hand, her eyes shining with unshed tears.

'After all these years,' she said softly.

Róisín leaned forward. 'What happens now?'

'We'll go there,' Cat continued decisively. 'For the anniversary of the battle next July. All of us, if possible.' She looked around the table, including everyone in the invitation. 'What do you all think?'

'I'd like that,' Erin said, glancing at Jack, who nodded in agreement.

'A proper family pilgrimage,' Laura murmured. 'Gilbert would be honoured.'

'And Matilda too,' Seth added unexpectedly. Everyone turned to look at him, and he shrugged, a slight flush colouring his cheeks. 'Sorry, I've been helping Róisín sort through some of the family documents. It seems right that both families should be there.'

'I'll call Margaret Ellis and tell her what we know now,' Tom replied. 'Perhaps her family would like to join us at the cemetery. To pay their respects too.'

'Margaret Ellis?' Bridget asked. 'She was Gilbert's granddaughter?'

'Yes,' Cat agreed. 'Her father was James, Gilbert's son.'

'Both properties,' Tom said, his expression solemn yet peaceful. 'After all this time, we can finally bring him home— in our hearts, at least.'

Logan raised his glass. 'To Gilbert and Matilda,' he said. 'And to family—those we've found, and those we've rediscovered.'

'To family,' they echoed, glasses clinking around the table.

As they resumed eating, the conversation shifting to plans for the France trip, Erin noticed Shea staring into her untouched wine glass, a shadow crossing her face. Shea looked up, caught

Erin watching her, and attempted a smile that didn't quite reach her eyes.

Erin made a mental note to check on her sister properly after dinner. Whatever was troubling Shea, she shouldn't have to face it alone. That was what family was for, after all—standing together through the discoveries, the celebrations, and the struggles.

The O'Byrnes had generations of practice at that.

Chapter 62

Ceann Mara - late December.

The sunset painted the billabong in shades of amber and rose, the water reflecting the clouds like a perfect mirror. Jack helped Erin from the Land Cruiser, his hand lingering in hers as they made their way to where their motorhome had once stood.

'It feels strange to see the site vacant,' she said.

'Do you miss being on the road?' he asked, watching her face for signs of regret.

Erin considered the question as they walked to the edge of the water. Five months had passed since Miles's capture and Jack's return, and since the night of fire and revelation. Five months of rebuilding trust between them.

'I miss parts of it,' she admitted. 'The freedom, the simplicity. But not the loneliness.'

Jack nodded, understanding in his eyes. 'I got the final word from Trevor today,' he said as they settled on the wooden bench Tom had built years ago. 'The case against *Terra Lens* is settled.'

'And?' Erin prompted when he hesitated.

'I get full rights to all my Africa photographs, and damages for breach of contract.' A small, satisfied smile crossed his face. 'And a public apology.'

'That's wonderful!' Erin squeezed his hand. 'Have you decided what you'll do with the photographs?'

Jack nodded. 'I'm selling a series to *National Geographic* magazine. Not the wildlife shots *Terra Lens* wanted, but the human portraits—the human stories they weren't interested in.'

Pride shone in Erin's eyes. 'I always said those were your best work.'

They sat in comfortable silence, watching three pelicans glide across the water. The past months had been a time for decisions, of long conversations late into the night, of redrawing the boundaries of their life together.

'Dad's planning the trip to France,' Erin said eventually. 'For next July, on the anniversary of Fromelles. He asked if we wanted to join them.'

Jack considered this. Once, the thought of being tied to her family's plans would have made him restless. Now, after nearly losing everything, the invitation felt like a gift.

'I'd like that,' he said. 'It feels right to be part of it.'

Erin turned to face him fully. 'Does that mean you've decided? About staying?'

It was the question that had hung between them, unresolved until now.

Jack took both her hands in his. 'I've been thinking about what you said—about putting down roots without giving up adventure.'

He gestured towards the land that stretched around them, golden in the evening light.

'What if we built something here, on your family's land? Not right at the homestead, but maybe—' He pointed towards the bend in the river where Gilbert had planned to build for Matilda. 'There. We could design something together—studio space for my photography, a writing room with a view of the billabong for you.'

Erin's eyes widened. 'You'd want that? To settle here?'

'Not just here,' Jack clarified, his thumb tracing circles on her palm. 'This would be home base. A place to return to between assignments, between adventures. *National Geographic* wants me to do a series on traditional craftspeople around the world. They've agreed you can come too. How would you feel about that?' He gripped her hand tightly, his eyes full of hope.

'Travel together, but with a home to come back to,' Erin whispered, the concept one she hadn't given much thought to.

Jack nodded. 'Having a place that's ours doesn't mean staying still forever. It means having somewhere that belongs to us, somewhere that holds our history while we're making new memories.'

'Like this land held Gilbert and Matilda's story all these years. And all of the other family stories that Dad and Cat have discovered,' Erin said thoughtfully.

'Exactly.' Jack reached into his pocket and withdrew a small, smooth river stone. 'I found this today, down by the bend. It reminded me of the stone Gilbert sent to Matilda.'

He placed it in Erin's palm, closing her fingers around it.

'What do you reckon? Will we build our story here?'

Erin looked from the stone to Jack's face, seeing an exciting future unfold. A home to come back to. Adventures together. The freedom to go, knowing they could always return.

'Yes,' she said simply.

As the sun dipped towards the horizon, casting long shadows across the billabong, the man she loved pulled her close.

This land around them had witnessed almost two centuries of O'Byrne history—love and loss, departures and homecomings, births and deaths, stories buried and uncovered.

Erin was sure that Dad and Cat would discover more stories.

'I love you, Erin O'Byrne-Hayes,' Jack whispered against her hair. 'To infinity.'

Erin smiled against his chest, the familiar phrase healing the last cracks in her heart. 'To infinity,' she echoed, 'and home again.'

In the gentle light, a kookaburra's laugh rang out across the billabong—not mocking, but celebrating.

Welcoming them home.

Book 4

Daughters of The Darling

In the aftermath of a personal decision, Shea O'Byrne has retreated to Melbourne, abandoning her career as a vet nurse to counsel women through pregnancy loss—a pain she understands all too well. When her father's genealogical research uncovers a long-buried scandal involving the family's forgotten ancestor, Samuel O'Byrne, Shea reluctantly agrees to help investigate.

Her search leads her to Professor Eliza Westfield and her compelling brother, Heath, a cardiologist whose gentle persistence begins to crack the walls around Shea's heart. But as Tom delves deeper into the life sof Clara O'Byrne—Samuel's rebellious daughter, whose story eerily mirrors Shea's—past and present collide in unexpected ways.

When Shea's former lover follows her to *Ceann Mara,*

bringing with him the painful secret she's kept from everyone, she must finally confront the choices that have shaped her life. A sudden storm at the billabong forces Shea to decide whether some secrets are worth keeping—and if the O'Byrne family legacy of resilience and love lives on in her.

Spanning two centuries of family history, heartbreak, and healing, *Beneath Still Waters* continues the sweeping saga of the O'Byrne family, where every discovery on the banks of the Darling River reveals that our most personal struggles often echo through generations.

Shea's story, *Beneath Still Waters,* the next book in the Daughters of the Darling series, will be published in November 2025.

It is available in print for pre-order at Annie's store. **https://annieseatonstore.ecwid.com/Beneath-Still-Waters-Pre-order-November-p739746836**

eBook pre-order: **https://books2read.com/u/3nxG9o**

Acknowledgements

The Darling River is one of the most beautiful areas in outback New South Wales. In the spring of 2023, Ian and I travelled the Darling River Run from Brewarrina to Menindee in our caravan, exploring this beautiful landscape.

We stayed at *Trilby Station*, where the inspiration for this story was born. *Ceann Mara* is based on this contemporary station, which has a rich history from the nineteenth century. *Dunleavy* is a fictional version of *Dunlop Station* upriver.

Thank you to *Trilby Station* owners Liz and Gary Murray for allowing me to use information from the historical museum at the campground on *Trilby Station*. We stopped at various sites from Brewarrina to Menindee on the Darling River Run and discovered the beauty of the river. We sat by the water at sunrise and sunset and absorbed the aromas, the beauty of the trees, and the sound of the birds. It is truly a magical place, and if you get the opportunity to travel out there, make sure to do so. There are many beautiful landscapes in Australia, and the Darling River Run is right up there with them.

By the Billabong is the third book in the Daughters of the Darling series, and I'm looking forward to researching more of the series when we travel out to the Darling River Run again this autumn.

Many people supported me in writing this book, and I would like to acknowledge them here.

To the many friends I have made in the writing world over the past fourteen years who constantly support me on my journey, I often say I have found my 'tribe,' and I value the daily contact with like-minded people all over the world. Again, a special mention and thank you go to my dear friend, critique partner, and editor, author Susanne Bellamy, and to my wonderful proofreaders, Roby Aiken and Rhonda Forrest.

To my loyal readers, who eagerly await the release of the next book, I invite you to attend my library talks and stay in touch via email and social media to share your enjoyment of my stories. Without readers, there would be no need for stories!

It would be impossible to write without support in your personal life:

To Ian, the love of my life and my research partner, as we travel this magnificent country seeking stories each winter. I could not do this without you. My driver, my chef, my bringer of wine, my fisherman, and my husband of almost fifty years.

To our children and their partners and our grandchildren: thank you for your love and support.

Again, my love and appreciation go to my wonderful aunt, Maureen Smith. Aunty Maureen can no longer read due to failing eyesight, but she always tells me how proud my parents would be.

And to you, the reader: thank you for choosing this book. I hope that you enjoy it and talk about it; word of mouth is the best thing for an author.

Maybe you will want to visit this wonderful part of Australia. I hope you enjoy Erin and Matilda's stories. Shea's story will be released in November 2025.

Please sign up for my fortnightly newsletter to hear about my research and my new books. You can find it here: http://www.annieseaton.net

I would love to hear from you.

Drop me a line at annie@annieseation.net

Reviews on Goodreads are always welcome and much appreciated!

eBook links:

https://www.annieseaton.net/books.html

Print Store:

All books are available in print at Annie's store and on Amazon in paperback.

https://annieseatonstore.ecwid.com/

Awards

2023: Winner - Long contemporary novel category, RUBY award for Larapinta.

2023: Finalist - Australian Romance Readers Awards for Kakadu Dawn, the sixth and final book in the Porter Sisters series.

2018 and 2020: Finalist - for the NZ KORU Award.

2017: Winner - Best Established Author of the Year 20'7 AUSROM

2017: Winner - Author of the Year 20'4 AUSROM Best Established Author, Ausrom Readers' Choice.

2016, 2017, 2018, 2019: Longlisted - Sisters in Crime Davitt Awards

2016: Finalist - Book of the Year, Long Romance, RWA Ruby Awards for Kakadu Sunset

2015: Winner - Best Established Author of the Year AUSROM

www.ingramcontent.com/pod-product-compliance
Lightning Source LLC
Chambersburg PA
CBHW062005190726
48283CB00001BA/236